A. JAYNE

Lilies in Winter

Theives in Law Series

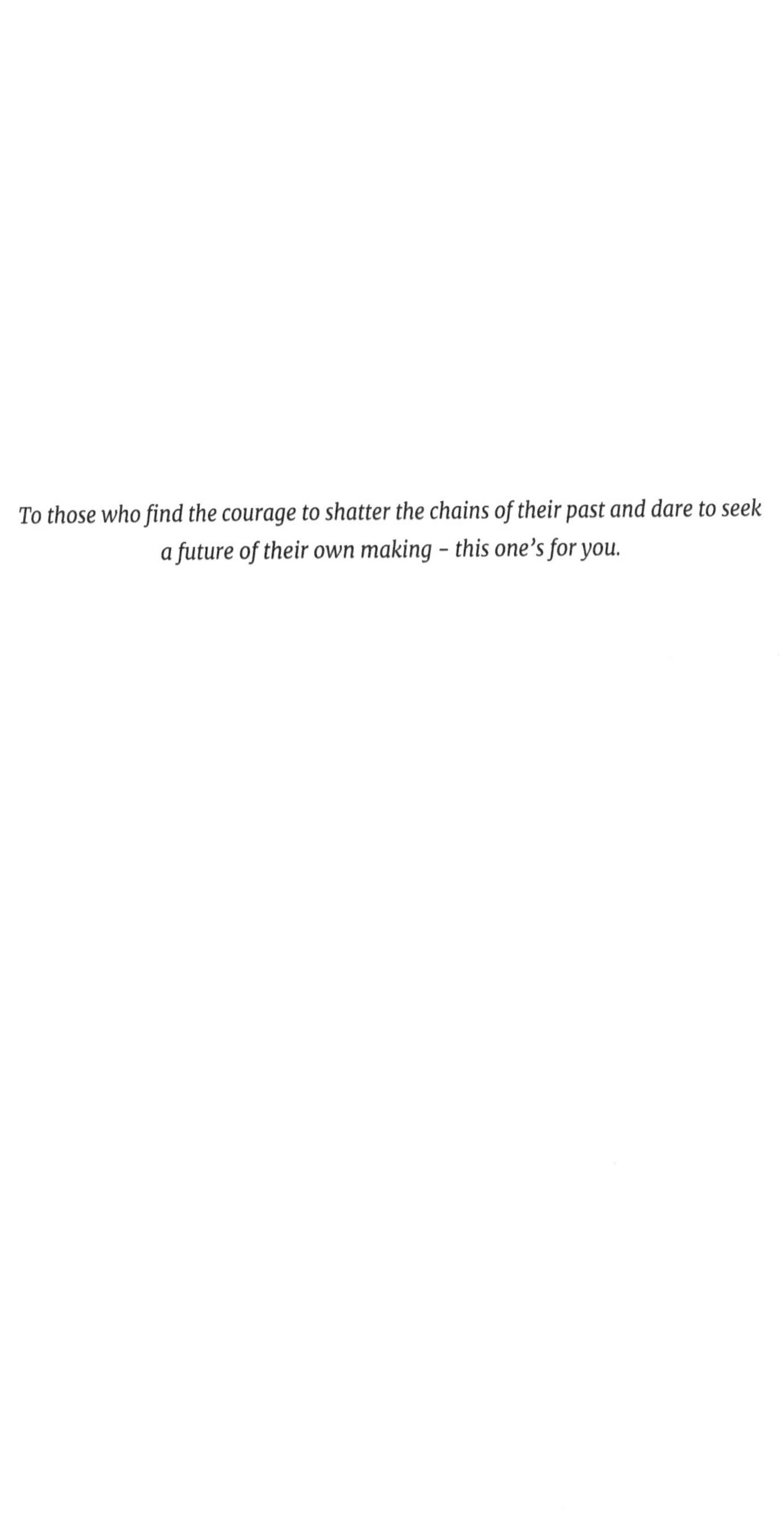

To those who find the courage to shatter the chains of their past and dare to seek a future of their own making – this one's for you.

"I choose love over fear, always. I'd rather burn in the fire after touching something true than not feel anything."

—Victoria Erickson

Content Warning

This novel contains mature themes intended for adult readers.
Reader discretion is advised for:

Content Elements

- Domestic Violence & Abuse
- Graphic Violence & Physical Trauma
- Explicit Sexual Content
- Substance Use/Abuse
- Death & Mortality
- Strong Language
- Organized Crime
- Psychological Trauma & PTSD

Reader Note: While these themes are handled with purpose, they are portrayed realistically and may be distressing for some readers. Please prioritize your mental well-being.

This warning provides general guidance but may not cover all sensitive content.

Support Resources

- **Domestic Violence:** National Hotline 1-800-799-SAFE (7233) | thehotline.org
- **Crisis Support:** Call 988 or Text HOME to 741741

- **Substance Abuse:** SAMHSA Helpline 1-800-662-4357
- **Sexual Assault:** RAINN Hotline 1-800-656-HOPE (4673) | rainn.org
- **PTSD Resources:** ptsd.va.gov | ptsdusa.org

All hot lines are confidential, free, and available 24/7. International readers: befrienders.org

Russian Terms and Phrases

__Note__: While Russian words are translated within the text, this condensed reference is provided for readers who wish to review pronunciations or explore the language further.

KEY CHARACTER NAMES (Pronunciation)

- **Zaven Lazarev** (zah-VYEN lah-ZAH-rev)
- **Natasha Alexeyeva** (nah-TAH-shah ah-lek-SAY-ye-vah)
- **Viktor Mikhaylov** (VEEK-tor mee-KHAI-loff)
- **Zoya** (ZOY-ah)

TERMS OF ENDEARMENT

- **Moye serdtse** (MOY-eh SEHRD-tseh) – My heart
- **Lyubimaya** (lyoo-BEE-my-ya) – Beloved (feminine)
- **Malyshka** (mah-LISH-kah) – Little one
- **Solnyshko moyo** (SOHL-nish-kah mah-YO) – My little sun
- **Zaychik** (ZAY-chik) – Little bunny

FAMILY & FORMAL ADDRESS

- **Babushka/Dedushka** (bah-BOOSH-kah/dye-DOOSH-kah) – Grandmother/Grandfather
- **Dyadya** (DYA-dya) – Uncle
- **Devushka/Devochka** (dye-VOOSH-kah/dye-VOCH-kah) – Young woman/Little girl

CRIMINAL WORLD TERMINOLOGY

- **Vor** (vohr) - Thief/criminal boss in the Russian underworld
- **Vorovskoy zakon** (vah-rov-SKOY zah-KON) - Thieves' code
- **Nash mir** (nash meer) - Our world

COMMON EXPRESSIONS

- **Da/Net** (dah/nyet) - Yes/No
- **Ya lyublyu tebya** (ya lyub-LYU tye-BYA) - I love you
- **Eto ya** (EH-tah ya) - It's me
- **Nashla!** (nash-LA) - Found! (feminine)

CURSES & STRONG LANGUAGE

- **Blyad'** (blyad) - Expletive (similar to "fuck")
- **Mudak** (moo-DAHK) - Asshole
- **Pizdyuk** (piz-DYUK) - Little prick

Language Note

The Russian characters in this novel speak with distinctive patterns that reflect their native language. Articles (a, an, the) are often dropped, and sentence structures may seem abbreviated or rearranged. This is intentional and reflects how Russian speakers often sound when speaking English.

Example: "Is not problem" instead of "It's not a problem"

These speech patterns become more pronounced when characters are emotional, tired, or stressed, and may improve in professional or formal settings.

This is a writing design preference of the authors, it may not be for every reader. It is meant to help draw the reader into the world and story they created.

1

Lily

The taxi lurched to a stop, jolting me out of my anxious daze. I clutched my worn duffel bag closer. Outside the smudged window, St. Petersburg sprawled in a dizzying array of colors and shapes that my tired brain couldn't process.

"*Priyekhali*," the driver grunted. [We have arrived]

I blinked. "I'm sorry, what?"

He turned, gesturing impatiently. "We here. You pay now."

"Oh, right. Sorry." I fumbled with the unfamiliar rubles, the colorful bills slipping through my trembling fingers.

Stepping out onto the sidewalk, the icy air slapped my cheeks—a stark reminder of how far I was from home. The noise of horking horns and rapid-fire Russian hit me all at once.

"*Bahgazh!*" The driver's sharp call snapped me back. [Luggage] He stood by the open trunk, gesturing at my suitcase.

"Sorry," I muttered, hurrying to grab it. The golden domes of the Kazan Cathedral caught the weak sunlight, momentarily dazzling me. Beside it, a drab Soviet-era apartment block created a jarring contrast—extreme beauty and harsh reality existing side by side.

"What the hell am I doing?" The words escaped in a cloud of vapor. My heart slammed against my ribs. "This is crazy. But it's gotta be better than—" My voice cracked as schoolchildren rushed past, their Russian words sharp and foreign.

A man collided with my shoulder, the sudden contact sending electricity through my body. "*Izvinite*," he muttered, already walking away. [Excuse me/Sorry] My suitcase clattered to the ground.

The sound transformed into something darker. The metallic scrape against ice became shattering glass, and suddenly I wasn't in St. Petersburg anymore.

His face consumed my vision, contorted with that familiar rage. The whiskey glass exploded beside my head, shards catching the light like deadly stars. The slice across my cheek burned anew. My lungs seized. The taste of copper flooded my mouth—I'd bitten my tongue, just like that night. The cold in the air pulled me back, back there. For just the briefest of moments I wasn't in Russia anymore. The street wavered, buildings bleeding into shadows that looked too much like him.

"Not now, not now." I stumbled backward, my shoulders hitting rough brick. I pressed my palms against the wall, focusing on how the frozen stone bit into my skin. Real. This was real. He wasn't here.

"You're not that scared girl anymore," I whispered, but my body betrayed the lie. I made the choice to come here. I needed to pull myself out of the darkness, I made it this far. I wouldn't let him win but my hands trembled violently, and the edges of my vision had gone dark.

"Liliya!"

The voice penetrated my spiral like a blade of sunlight.

"*Bozhe moy*, is really you!" [My God]

I turned, my movements jerky, to see a blonde woman on the steps of a nearby building. The sharp click of her boots against stone cut through the last echoes of breaking glass in my mind. Real. She was real. I was in Russia. I was free.

"Natasha! Oh, thank God."

She descended the steps with effortless grace—all long limbs and fluid motion. Her golden hair caught the weak sunlight, styled in soft waves that somehow remained perfect despite the wind. The fur-trimmed collar of her cream wool coat framed her heart-shaped face.

I was painfully aware of my own appearance—my auburn hair tangled from the long flight and winter wind, my drugstore makeup long since worn away. The oversized sweater and leggings I'd chosen for comfort now felt shabby next to her runway-ready ensemble.

She caught me in a tight embrace, and I melted into the familiar comfort of her arms. The rich, spicy notes of her signature French perfume wrapped around me like a security blanket. I clung to her perhaps a moment too long, but she didn't pull away. In this foreign world, Natasha was my only anchor to safety.

"Ah, my poor *devochka*," Natasha pulled back, her perfectly manicured hands gripping my shoulders. [Little girl] Her accent wrapped thickly around each word. "You look like hell frozen over. Come, we get you inside, warm you up with proper Russian tea. No arguments."

My hands wouldn't stop trembling. I tried to hide them in my pockets, but Natasha's sharp eyes missed nothing.

"Here, you give me this," she reached for my suitcase. "You looking ready to fall over, and these streets, they are like ice rink today."

"Thanks," I said, relinquishing the handle. "By the way, why are you calling me Liliya?"

Natasha's red lips curved into a smile as we started up the steps. "Is proper Russian version of your name. You in Russia now, darling. Must start embracing it, *da*?" [Yes] She gestured dramatically. "Besides, is sounding much more mysterious, you not think so?"

I couldn't help but laugh—my first real laugh in weeks. "Only you could make me running away sound glamorous." Then, sobering, "How did you even find this place for me?"

"Ah, I know people who know people. Is very Russian way." She winked, then steadied me as I stumbled on a step. "Careful now, these stairs very dangerous. Like those fancy American high heels—beautiful but will betray you first chance. Russian boots much more reliable, like Russian friendship."

"I'll take your word for it," I managed another smile. "Though right now, I'd kill for a good ol' American burger. You have those here?"

"Pfft, American food," Natasha sniffed with playful disdain. "We fix this terrible craving soon enough. First you try real Russian food, then you forget all about silly burgers."

My grin faded as a chill crept through me. "What if he finds me here, Natasha? I don't even speak the language, I can't read anything…"

Natasha stopped abruptly, turning to face me. The playful sparkle in her eyes hardened into steel. "Listen to me now. You already braver than you think. Hardest part?" She gestured toward the street behind us. "Is done already. You left. You flew across ocean. Everything else? We figure out together."

Her red lips curved into a fierce smile. "And remember—this is Russia. Nothing happens here without proper connections. And him? He has exactly zero connections here. Russia is big country, and you?" Her smile softened. "You have me."

I nodded, blinking back tears. The certainty in her voice made it impossible not to believe her, at least a little. "Thank you, Natasha. I don't know what I'd do without you."

As we reached the third floor, Natasha produced an old-fashioned key and opened a heavy wooden door. "Home sweet home, at least for now. It's not much, but it's safe. No one knows you're here."

I stepped into the small apartment and froze, pleasantly surprised. Despite the building's worn exterior, the space inside was cozy and welcoming. A plush couch sat beneath the window that offered a view of the golden church dome. The kitchenette, though small, was clean and stocked.

"Here, you put down duffle," Natasha directed, setting my suitcase near the door. "Can unpack later. First, you must see what I do with place."

My shoulder ached as I slipped off the heavy bag, but I barely noticed as I took in all the little touches that made the apartment feel like a home rather than a hideout. "Did you…?"

She shrugged. "Just few things from my parents' old place. Mama was happy to help—she's been trying to get rid of furniture for months. And food, of course. Cannot have you living on American takeout."

Tears pricked at my eyes. "Natasha, I don't know what to say…"

"Come, sit," she commanded, gliding to the kitchen. "First rule of Russia—everything must have tea. No exceptions."

I sank into the couch, its worn cushions surprisingly comfortable. "I can't believe you went to all this trouble for me."

"What kind of best friend would I be otherwise?" She returned with two delicate teacups. "Besides, who else would I have to remind about terrible pronunciation in Russian Lit?"

"Oh god," I laughed, accepting the steaming cup. "You're never going to let me live that down, are you?"

"*Bozhe moy*, you were disaster!" Natasha grinned. [My God] "Could not even say Dostoyevsky. Made my Russian soul hurt just listening."

"I wasn't that bad!" I protested, though memories of our shared high school days made me smile. Having a Russian exchange student live with us senior year had seemed daunting at first, but Natasha had become like a sister.

"You called him Dusty-sky, *dorogaya*. Was physical pain." [Dear/sweetheart] She mimicked my accent perfectly, making me snort into my tea. "But you shared good coffee, better gossip. Let me copy English homework. I decide then—this girl, I keep."

"My mom still asks about you," I said softly. "She was so worried when you chose to stay in Chicago for college instead of going home."

"Mama Sinclair," Natasha's voice softened with genuine affection. "She send me care packages all through university. Even after I go back to Russia, still get Christmas sweater every year."

"Remember that Thanksgiving when you tried to convince my mom that vodka was a traditional Russian contribution to the meal?"

"Was worth try! And your father, he just sit there, trying not to laugh while your mother lecture about 'proper holiday spirits.'" Natasha's eyes sparkled. "But she still let me teach you to make proper *pelmeni* next day." [Russian dumplings]

"Which became a tradition," I added, warmth filling my chest. "Every Black Friday, while everyone else was shopping, we'd be in the kitchen, flour everywhere…"

Natasha's smile faltered slightly. She reached across and squeezed my hand. "I miss those days. Before..." she hesitated, then sighed. "Before you go to college and meet him." Her voice softened with concern. "Should have come to me sooner. The moment he start showing true colors."

I stared into my tea, shame burning my cheeks. "I know. I just... I was embarrassed. Didn't want you or my parents to know how stupid I'd been."

"*Net.*" Natasha gripped my hand fiercely. [No] "You not stupid. He monster who prey on kind hearts. But now you here, where I can protect you like you protect me all those years ago. Remember Bradley Stevens?"

I smiled. "The quarterback who wouldn't take no for an answer? Until I told the whole cheerleading squad he had a highly contagious skin condition?"

Natasha threw back her head and laughed. "Was brilliant! His face when girls start running away? Priceless!"

As night settled in, Natasha showed me the rest of the apartment. "Bathroom has best water pressure in building—I make sure. And here," she opened the door to the bedroom with a flourish, "is where magic happens. Or at least good sleep."

"Magic? In a single girl's bedroom in Russia?" I snorted. "The most magical thing that'll happen here is me learning to curse in Russian."

"Then I teach you best words first," Natasha winked, then leaned in conspiratorially. "Repeat after me: '*Chyort voz'mi.*'" [Damn it]

"Chort vaz-me?" I butchered.

She burst out laughing. "Close enough! You just say 'damn it' like true Russian. We make *babushka* of you yet." [Grandmother]

The bedroom was small but cozy, with a double bed dressed in what looked like hand-embroidered linens. "These were grandmother's," she said softly. "She say they bring good dreams."

We wandered back to the living room, Natasha collecting our empty teacups along the way. As she rinsed them in the sink, she called over her shoulder, "By the way, I maybe find you job. Nothing serious, just thought you might want something to keep busy."

I settled back onto the couch. "A job? Already?"

She shrugged, drying her hands on a small towel. "Is just idea. Very exclusive club called *Zolotoy Vek*. They need hostess—greeting guests, showing to tables. Your American accent would be, how you say, exotic there." [Golden Age] She rejoined me, tucking her feet underneath her. "But only if you want. No pressure."

"A club?" My stomach tightened. "I don't know..."

"Trust me. Would be perfect for you. Just hostess position—greeting guests, showing to tables. Tips alone..." She made an appreciative noise. "But we talk details tomorrow, *da*? Tonight is for settling in." [Yes]

Natasha glanced at her watch and sighed. "Time for me to go. You need rest, and I need beauty sleep." She pulled me into a tight embrace, kissing both my cheeks. "Everything will be okay now, *milaya*. You are safe here." [Dear/sweet one]

I clung to her for a moment. "Thank you, Natasha. For everything."

"Enough thanks," she said firmly. "Is what friends do. Now, lock door behind me, yes? And remember—grandmother's linens never fail to bring good dreams." With a final wink, she was gone, her heels clicking down the stairs.

The apartment felt suddenly huge and empty. I double-checked every lock, testing each one twice before I could step away from the door. The silence pressed in, broken only by the unfamiliar creaks of the old building.

In the bathroom, I found fluffy towels and toiletries I couldn't read. The shower's hot water handle squeaked when I tested it, the pipes groaning to life. At least some things were universal.

I jumped at the sound of a car door slamming outside. The sound of voices speaking rapid Russian drifted up from the street. Normal city sounds, I told myself, but still found myself peeking through the curtains. Just people heading home, or maybe to one of the clubs Natasha mentioned.

I unpacked mechanically, trying not to think about the last time I'd packed these same clothes, hands shaking as I'd shoved them into my bag in a desperate rush to leave. His voice crept into my thoughts: "You really think you could make it without me? You can barely handle being a waitress. Face it, baby, you need me. You'll always need me."

I pushed the memory away. He'd been wrong about so many things. Now I tried to imagine myself working at some fancy Russian club, greeting wealthy clients. The thought should have terrified me. Instead, I felt a tiny spark of excitement. Maybe this was exactly what I needed—something so completely different that he'd never think to look for me here.

But as I changed into my pajamas, the doubts crept back in. What was I really doing here? I could barely ask for directions, let alone work at some elite club.

"Stop it," I whispered to myself, the Russian words outside my window a constant reminder of how far I was from home. From him. I'd chosen this. I'd reached out to Natasha, and she'd answered without hesitation. I had to make this work.

Before heading to bed, I found myself drawn to the window one last time. The street below was mostly empty now, glazed with the amber glow of old streetlamps. My eyes caught movement in the shadows—three black SUVs idling by the corner, their windows tinted to mirror-black. Men in expensive suits emerged from what looked like a high-end restaurant, their movements precise despite the late hour.

The last man to climb in paused, his hand on the car door. He turned, gaze sweeping up the street, and even from this distance, I could make out his features—sharp jawline, fierce eyes, devastatingly handsome. His expression was all business, serious and searching.

I let out a breath I hadn't realized I was holding, and it fogged the cold glass before me. Without thinking, I lifted a finger and drew a wobbly half-smile in the condensation. Not quite happy, not quite sad—fitting for my first night of freedom.

The distant sound of church bells marking midnight mixed with the strange symphony of my new neighborhood—voices calling, the rumble of cars on cobblestones, music spilling from a distant club.

I crawled into bed, the unfamiliar mattress dipping beneath my weight. The sheets smelled of lavender—Natasha's grandmother's linens, promising good dreams. As I drifted off, I found myself wondering what *Zolotoy Vek* would be like. [Golden Age] Tomorrow would bring what it would, but for now, at least I was free. And maybe, just maybe, that was enough.

2

Zaven

The antique clock on my desk chimed softly. Nine o'clock. I leaned back in my leather chair, the rich scent of aged wood and expensive leather enveloping me. My fingers traced the intricate patterns carved into the arms – a family heirloom, like so much in this office. Power isn't inherited like money or titles – it's earned with every choice, carved into your bones until legacy and identity become indistinguishable.

A memory flashed – my father, sitting in this very chair, his face carved with the grief that never fully left him after mother's death. "Zaven," he'd said, his voice rough with barely concealed emotion, "one day, all of this will be yours to protect and grow. *Nash mir.* Our world." I'd nodded then, too young to understand the weight behind his words – that he was entrusting me with not just an empire, but the legacy my mother had died protecting. That his world would become my domain to master.

"*Yob tvoyu mat,*" I muttered, reaching for the Beluga Gold Line vodka in my desk drawer. [Fuck your mother] The crystal glass caught the light as I poured. One small indulgence before another predictable evening. The first sip burned perfectly – a familiar pleasure in a world that had become too familiar.

St. Petersburg spread before me – a city where tzars once ruled and revolutionaries once bled. Now it was mine. Every light, every shadow, every secret whispered in dark corners – all under my protection, my control. A city that had yielded to me, yet still held mysteries I had yet to uncover. The illuminated dome of St. Isaac's Cathedral stood out against the darkness. Nearby, modern skyscrapers pierced the night with their cold ambition. This eternal dance between past and present, much like the balance I maintained between two worlds. Both worlds had grown too predictable lately.

The faint sound of police sirens pierced the quiet. Governor Volkov's dogs, no doubt, making their usual rounds. Another predictable move in our endless chess game – one where I consistently stayed three moves ahead.

A soft knock at the door interrupted my musings. "*Da*," I called, not bothering to turn. [Yes]

"Zaven." Viktor's measured tone carried a hint of urgency that made me look up. My old friend and right-hand man stood in the doorway, his presence solid and unchanging. His face wore its usual impassive mask – one that only I had learned to read over our years together. Something was amiss.

I studied him. The scar on his left cheek, barely visible unless you knew to look for it, was a reminder of the night he'd saved my life – and sealed our brotherhood in blood. His military bearing hadn't softened over the years; if anything, it had grown sharper, like a blade well-maintained.

"*Nu*, what's got you looking like you've swallowed a lemon, Vitya?" I asked, gesturing for him to take a seat. [Well]

Viktor stepped in but remained standing, his posture rigid with military precision. "Have word from friends at port. Is... complication with Turkish shipment."

I felt a muscle twitch in my jaw but kept my expression neutral. "Dmitri?" The name tasted like ash on my tongue.

Viktor nodded once, sharp and precise. "Is looking that way. Though he tries to be clever about it. *Stary medved* gets bolder every day." [Old bear]

"Of course he has," I muttered, standing to pour another measure of vodka. I offered one to Viktor, who declined with a small shake of his head. Always the good soldier, my Vitya. "Spill it. *Ne tyani kota za khvost*. Not in mood for games tonight." [Don't pull the cat by the tail - meaning: don't drag it out]

Viktor's lips twitched at my impatience. "Shipment was intercepted. Man at customs says was random check, but…"

"But *my ne laptem shchi khlebaem*," I finished for him, the familiar phrase rolling off my tongue. [We don't sip cabbage soup with bast shoes - meaning: we're not stupid/naive] "We're not fucking idiots. Dmitri's got someone on the inside. *Blyad*!" [Damn/Fuck] I downed the vodka in one swift motion, savoring the burn even as rage coiled in my gut, then poured another. "Your intel on customs office?"

"Is solid," Viktor assured me, shifting his weight slightly – a tell I'd learned meant he had more to say. "But Dmitri plays close now. Old bear learns new tricks."

I barked out a laugh, the sound sharp and humorless. "Learning? The old bear? *On iz drugogo testa*, Vitya." [He's made of different dough - meaning: he's cut from a different cloth] I prowled the length of my office, the plush carpet muffling my steps. "He thinks he still lives in the 90s, when brute force was enough. Fucking dinosaur doesn't understand the game has changed."

"Perhaps," Viktor said carefully, "But your father would have–"

I cut him off with a sharp gesture. "Not my father, Vitya. Old ways dying." I moved with practiced confidence, master in my domain. "Evolution doesn't wait for those who cling to outdated methods."

I turned back to the window, swirling the clear liquid in my glass as I surveyed my city. The lights reflected off the crystal tumbler, casting fractured patterns across my hand. Power isn't just about who hits hardest— it's about knowing exactly where to strike. This is why Dmitri will fall. Not because he's brutal, but because he's blind.

"If Dmitri can't see that," I said aloud, "he dies with them."

I strode back across the room to my desk, each step deliberate and unhurried. Setting down my glass with a decisive clink, my fingers absently traced the edge of the polished wood as my mind mapped countermoves with practiced ease.

"Double payment to port contact. I want to know the moment Dmitri so much as sneezes in our direction. And reach out to our friend in the prosecutor's office. Time to remind the old bear he's not untouchable."

Viktor nodded, a glimmer of approval in his eyes. "And Turkish shipment?"

I allowed myself a small, cold smile. "Let him have this one. Will make him overconfident. Meanwhile, redirect resources to Georgian route. Is time we expanded there anyway." Always one step ahead – the way I'd built my empire, the way I'd continue to grow it.

"*Khorosho pridumano*," Viktor said, the ghost of a smile playing at his mouth. [Well thought out] "Anything else, Zaven?"

I straightened my cuffs, my mind already shifting to club matters. "Need check floor tonight. You handle port contact?"

Viktor nodded, understanding the division of responsibilities without further explanation. Years of working together had made words almost unnecessary between us.

As we stepped out of my office, Viktor's transformation was immediate. His posture straightened further, his expression hardening into stone. To any watching eyes, he was now every inch the dutiful second to the *Vor*. [Thief - in this context, a criminal boss] The game continued – a game I played with expertise.

"Call when port situation handled," I said, my tone taking on its public edge. I watched as Viktor headed toward the private exit, already pulling out his phone.

The moment I entered the main area of *Zolotoy Vek* alone, its atmosphere enveloped me. [Golden Age] The steady thrum of music from below vibrated through the floorboards, promising danger and pleasure in equal measure. Tonight's air carried its usual symphony – expensive perfume, finest vodka, Cuban cigars, and beneath it all, the sharp tang of power that kept my world turning.

I made my way down the spiral staircase, my hand gliding over the cool gold-plated railing. Eyes followed my descent – some hungry, some terrified, all respectful. Another night in the kingdom I'd built, brick by brick, connection by connection, drop of blood by drop of blood.

Nikolai noticed me approaching the bar. "*Dobry vecher*, Zaven," he murmured, already reaching for the top-shelf vodka. [Good evening] His movements were quick, efficient – like the good soldier he'd been before I'd recruited him. "Is quiet night so far."

I accepted the drink with a slight nod. "Quiet is never good thing, Kolya. Means storm comes."

The main floor was starting to fill, the city's elite settling into their usual places like pieces on a chess board. They nodded as I passed – politicians wearing false smiles, oligarchs dripping with new money, and scattered among them, faces I recognized from darker corners of my domain. All of them drawn to the intoxicating blend of luxury and danger that *Zolotoy Vek* promised.

The Italians were becoming a problem. I watched them from the mezzanine – four men in suits worth more than most people made in a year, laughing too loudly, drinking too much, and worst of all, making my other guests uncomfortable. But refusing their business would create... complications. In this game, everything was about balance.

A group of newcomers caught my attention – new money, obvious from their too-bright watches and eager faces. They froze when they saw me, whispers passing between them. I fixed them with a long look, enjoying the way they squirmed.

"Zaven." Marcel appeared at my elbow, silent as always. "Yelena is asking for you. Says is urgent." His French accent wrapped awkwardly around the Russian name.

Unusual. Yelena never interrupted my evening rounds unless something was wrong.

The kitchens buzzed with controlled chaos – the sound of pans, sharp commands in a mix of Russian and French, and the rich smell of beef stroganoff and fresh herbs hit me the moment I pushed through the doors. My chefs moved like a well-oiled machine. In the center of the storm stood Yelena, clipboard in hand, her dark hair pulled back severe enough to make lesser men wince.

She caught my eye immediately, something knowing in her gaze. "Private booth," she said, already moving toward our usual spot. She walked with the grace of the former ballerina she was, spine straight as steel.

A young waitress appeared silently with champagne as we sat – Yelena's way of softening what she was about to say. She took a deliberate sip, perfect red lips curved in a slight smile that made me wary.

"So," she began, setting down her glass. "You want to tell me why Natasha Alexeyeva is hiding an American girl in your building?"

I paused mid-sip, one eyebrow raising. "Which building? Last checked, own half the fucking city." The champagne turned bitter on my tongue as realization hit. Natasha. Of course. That clever, troublesome woman.

I leaned forward, fingers drumming once on the table. "Yelena, you see everything before I do these days. Should I even keep paying my security team?" A small smirk played at my lips. "Tell me everything."

Yelena's perfect nails tapped against her champagne glass. "American girl, she arrive this morning. Make way from airport to building on Nevsky – your building. Natasha waiting there for her." She paused, dark eyes studying my reaction. "Is interesting, *da*? Natasha, she never asks for favors, then suddenly needs place to hide American friend."

I swirled the champagne in my glass, mind racing through implications. "What else you know?"

"Her name is Liliya." Yelena's lips twitched. "Young, pretty. But she running from something. Or someone." She took a deliberate sip of champagne. "Natasha thinks she could be good fit for hostess position."

"And how you come by all this?"

"Pfft." Yelena's smile was sharp as a blade. "My niece, she works security at Pulkovo. And you think anything happens in your building without I know? Is like theater – I see everything from my kitchen."

I leaned back, studying her. In fifteen years, Yelena never brought useless information. "This girl, she speaks Russian?"

"*Net*." Yelena shrugged one elegant shoulder. [No] "But Natasha say she learn quick. Has..." she paused, searching for the right word, "good instincts. Knows how to read people." Her dark eyes met mine. "Could be asset, if you wanting my opinion."

"And you think she can handle our particular... atmosphere?" In the years she'd managed *Zolotoy Vek*, Yelena had developed an uncanny ability to read people. Her judgment had never failed me.

"Is hard to say without meeting," Yelena replied, tapping one nail against her glass. "But Natasha not usually one for rash recommendations. Says girl has…" she paused, waving her hand in small circles as she searched for the words, "*kak skazat… sterzhen vnutri? What you call it? Not backbone exactly…*" [how to say… inner core/rod] Her eyes lit up. "Ah! Steel in spine."

Interesting. I sat back, letting the subtle vibration of the club's music wash over me. "Steel is one thing. Our world requires particular understanding of… nuance."

"Which is why we start her as hostess only." Yelena's lips curved into a knowing smile. "Let her learn slowly. Besides, fresh face might be good for club. Things become too predictable lately, no?"

I raised an eyebrow at her perceptiveness. Trust Yelena to notice my recent restlessness.

"When she could start?" I asked, surprising myself with my interest.

"We give her few days to settle, get over jet lag. Natasha say girl needs little time to…" she gestured vaguely, "adjust to new reality. But next week, maybe we arrange proper introduction?"

The timing was too perfect to be coincidental. I fixed Yelena with a long look, but she merely lifted her glass again, the picture of innocence. "You already having everything planned out."

"Is my job to manage club's affairs, no?" Her eyes sparkled with subtle amusement. "Besides, think of it as… investment. We see if American girl has steel under that soft exterior. Could be exactly what *Zolotoy Vek* needs – fresh blood."

"Clever as always, Yelena," I conceded, finishing my champagne. Something about this situation felt different, like the first move in a new game. "I trust you handle the arrangements?"

"*Da.* Natasha brings her for dinner, show her how club operates." She rose gracefully, smoothing her already immaculate dress. "Will give her chance to see flow of things, meet staff. More natural this way."

I nodded. Better to observe this Liliya when she was at ease, experiencing

Zolotoy Vek as a guest first. "Your way is fine. Just ensure Viktor knows. He's already on edge with Dmitri's latest game."

"*Da*, will handle." Yelena paused, then added with careful neutrality, "You know, is funny thing. When Natasha first mention American girl, thought would be typical tourist type. But way she describe this one..." She let the thought trail off suggestively.

My lips curved slightly. "Trying to pique my interest, Yelena?"

"Would I dare manipulate great *Vor*?" Her innocent tone didn't match the knowing glint in her eyes. "Simply sharing observation. Now, must check on kitchen. New caviar supplier still needs... convincing about our payment terms."

As Yelena disappeared into the controlled chaos of the kitchen, I remained in the booth, considering this new development. The club's atmosphere swirled around me – leather and perfume, whispered conversations and clinking glasses, all the familiar elements of my domain. Yet something had shifted. A new piece had entered the game.

Two women who survived in a world designed to break them both saw something in this American – something worth protecting, worth cultivating. In our world, recognizing value isn't sentiment; it's instinct. And my instinct told me this unknown woman was either going to be a valuable asset... or my most intriguing challenge yet.

I checked my watch. The night was young, and the Georgian route needed attention. Dmitri's latest move required a response. Yet as I moved through my club, acknowledging nods of respect with the slightest inclination of my head, I found my thoughts returning to this mysterious Liliya. For the first time in longer than I could remember, I felt something like anticipation. What kind of woman could inspire such confidence in both Natasha and Yelena? What kind of woman fled to a foreign country and immediately found her way into my world?

The predictable chess game that had been my life had just introduced an unexpected move. And I found myself looking forward to it.

Next week would be... interesting.

3

Liliya

"Liliya! Open up! Is criminal to waste such beautiful morning!"

Natasha's voice penetrated the apartment door like a drill, yanking me from the deepest sleep I'd had in months. A moment of panic seized me—where was I?—before reality settled back in. Russia. Freedom. Safety.

"Coming!" I called, voice still rough with sleep as I wrapped myself in the unfamiliar blanket and shuffled to the door.

Natasha burst in like a force of nature, already dressed in a tailored wool coat and what looked like designer everything. She took one critical look at my tangled auburn hair and sleep-creased face before declaring, "You need real breakfast to start new life. None of those sad protein bars. Get dressed!"

* * *

"Keep up, *devochka*!" Natasha strode ahead, somehow navigating the icy sidewalks in heeled boots while I shuffled cautiously behind. [Little girl] Her golden hair caught the weak sunlight, a beacon in the gray morning. "Best bakery in neighborhood is just ahead. You must try their *vatrushka* – is heaven!" [Russian cheese pastry]

I quickened my pace, tucking a wayward strand of auburn hair back into my borrowed wool coat. St. Petersburg spread around us, a study in contrasts. Sunlight transformed grimy sidewalks into paths of diamonds, while ancient buildings wore their centuries of history like elegant ladies draped in white furs.

Everything felt different here – the air sharper, the sounds foreign yet exciting. No one knew me. The thought made me dizzy with possibility, even as old habits had me checking reflections in shop windows, scanning for familiar faces.

"Stop this." Natasha's arm linked through mine, her touch grounding. "I see wheels turning in pretty head. No more looking over shoulder, *da*? Today is for living." [Yes]

The bakery's warmth enveloped us as we entered, bringing with it the scent of butter and sugar. An elderly woman behind the counter lit up at the sight of Natasha.

"Natasha Alexandrovna!" She bustled forward, pressing kisses to Natasha's cheeks. "And who is this?"

"This is my Liliya," Natasha announced proudly. "American friend I tell you about. She needs proper breakfast, Vera. None of that sad coffee and protein bar nonsense."

I opened my mouth to protest – I liked my protein bars – but Natasha was already rapid-firing orders in Russian, gesturing expansively. The sight made me smile. She'd been like this in college too, steamrolling over any objection with pure force of personality.

"Come, we sit." Natasha guided me to a tiny table by the window. "Must fuel up. Many things to see today." She paused, studying me with those sharp blue eyes. "How you sleep? First night in new place always strange."

"Better than I have in months," I admitted, surprising myself with the truth of it. "Those linens really do bring good dreams."

Natasha smiled, pleased. "Grandmother never wrong about such things." She stirred her tea, the silver spoon clinking delicately against porcelain. "So, today I show you important places. Where to find *produkty*—grocery store, nearest *apteka* for medicines, best metro stations. Things you need for real life, not tourist nonsense." [Products/groceries] [Pharmacy]

Before I could respond, Vera arrived with a tray laden with pastries, the steam rising from them like prayers to the winter sky.

"Eat, eat," Natasha insisted, pushing a golden-crusted pastry toward me. "Vera's *vatrushka* make you forget all American food."

The first bite melted on my tongue – sweet farmer's cheese and buttery dough that put my usual breakfast bars to shame. "Okay," I admitted, "you might have a point about breakfast."

"Of course I have point. I always have point." Natasha's eyes sparkled as she sipped her tea. "And after this, I also show you coffee shop with very important feature." She leaned in with exaggerated secrecy. "Cute barista who gives extra shots of espresso to pretty girls."

I nearly choked on my pastry, giving her a look of disbelief. "You can't be serious."

"What? Is true." She shrugged innocently. "Though you Americans, so serious about flirting. Everything must be..." she lifted her chin, putting on an exaggerated proper accent, "'appropriate workplace behavior.'" She rolled her eyes. "Boring."

The familiar teasing loosened something in my chest. This was the Natasha I remembered from college – the one who'd declare our study sessions "too depressing" and drag me out for impromptu adventures.

"Some things never change," I said, shaking my head.

"Many things change," Natasha replied, her voice softening. "But not important things. Not friendship." She reached across the table, squeezing my hand. "Now, eat more. Cannot have proper adventure on empty stomach."

Outside the bakery window, I watched people hurrying past – women in fur-trimmed coats, children in bright snowsuits, elderly men walking with deliberate care on the icy sidewalk. All strangers. All living their lives without a single thought for my presence here.

The realization felt like taking off a heavy backpack I hadn't known I was carrying.

* * *

By late afternoon, my feet ached from walking, and my mind swam with information – which metro station to use, which streets to avoid at night, where to find the best coffee, which grocery store had the freshest produce. Natasha had been thorough, marking each location on a map she'd produced from her designer handbag.

"Now, best part of day," she announced, steering me toward a cozy-looking restaurant with steamed windows and the smell of rich broth wafting from its door. "Best *borscht* in city. No arguments." [Beet soup]

My stomach tightened reflexively. We'd already had those pastries for breakfast, and a mid-morning coffee with tiny jam-filled cookies that Natasha had insisted were "barely calories, just happiness."

You're getting fat. No one wants a girlfriend who can't control herself.

His voice echoed in my head, unbidden. I could almost feel his critical gaze, the way he'd watch every bite I took, until eating became a performance of tiny portions and calculated bites.

"Liliya?" Natasha's voice cut through the memory. She was watching me with too-sharp eyes. "Where you go just now?"

"Nowhere," I said quickly, forcing a smile. "Just... not used to eating so much."

Natasha's expression darkened for a moment before smoothing into determined cheerfulness. "Ah, is American diet culture nonsense. You know what *babushka* always say? 'Food is love made visible.' In Russia, we not trust people who pick at food like little birds." [Grandmother] She linked her arm through mine, pulling me toward the door. "Besides, in winter, body needs fuel. Is science."

The restaurant was warm and dim, with dark wood panels and vintage posters on the walls. Our waitress, a sturdy woman with kind eyes, greeted Natasha like an old friend.

"You see?" Natasha said after we'd ordered. "Already they like you here. Young Masha smile so big when you try speak Russian words."

I fiddled with my water glass. "Everything feels so... different here. Like I'm different. Does that make sense?"

"Of course makes sense. Is why people travel, *da*? To remember they can be new version of self." She leaned forward, her voice gentle but firm. "And Liliya? New version of you not need permission to enjoy life. To eat good food. To laugh." Her eyes sparkled. "To flirt with handsome barista."

I couldn't help but laugh, even as I felt tears prick at the corners of my eyes. "I missed you, Natasha. I missed... being me, I guess."

"Then is simple," she said, raising her glass in a toast. "We focus on finding you again. Everything else? Is just details."

The *borscht* arrived, ruby-red and steaming, topped with a dollop of sour cream. I took a careful spoonful, the rich flavors blooming on my tongue. For the first time in longer than I could remember, food tasted like possibility instead of guilt.

I was halfway through my bowl when I noticed Natasha's knowing smirk. "What?"

"Man at corner table," she murmured, stirring her soup with practiced nonchalance. "Cannot stop looking at you. Is third time he pretend to check phone just to peek this way."

Heat crept into my cheeks as I resisted the urge to look. "You're impossible," I murmured, staring intently at my soup.

"What? Is true. Though you sit like you trying to disappear." She demonstrated, hunching her shoulders forward in an exaggerated impression of my posture before straightening into her usual elegant stance. "Should sit like you own room. And stop this—" She reached across the table, her fingers gentle as she freed my auburn hair from where I'd tucked it behind my ears. The strands fell forward, framing my face. "There. Is much better. Such pretty color, like autumn sunset. Men at club will not know what hit them."

I squirmed under her attention, but didn't fix my hair back. "Just what I need—to be some Russian guy's American souvenir," I said with a dry smile. "I'm sure that would end well."

"Is not about men," Natasha said, her voice gentler now. "Is about remembering you are worth being seen." She reached across and squeezed my hand. "Before him, you walked into room like you belonged there. I just want my friend back."

Something in her words struck a chord. She wasn't pushing me toward another relationship—she was trying to help me reclaim parts of myself I'd lost. I gave her a small, genuine smile.

"So what you're saying is I should practice my hair flip?" I joked, but with less edge than before.

Natasha immediately brightened, demonstrating with her own perfect golden waves. "Exactly! Is all in wrist movement." She launched into an elaborate explanation of hair-tossing techniques, complete with demonstration.

I found myself laughing despite everything. But beneath my amusement, I felt something else stirring – not interest in men, but a faint whisper of the confidence I used to have, before he'd systematically dismantled it.

As we finished our lunch, the afternoon light had begun to soften. My hair was still loose where Natasha had arranged it, and I found myself resisting the urge to tuck it back. Small steps, but steps forward nonetheless.

"So," Natasha said, signaling for the check. "You think about club? Maybe next week, we just look. No pressure." She tilted her head. "Could be good, you know? Meet new people, learn city better. Plus," she added with a sly smile, "dress code is very glamorous."

The thought of dressing up, of being somewhere elegant and mysterious, sent an unexpected thrill through me. It was so far from my old life of sensible cardigans and careful smiles. Maybe that was exactly what I needed.

"I'll think about it," I said, surprised to find I meant it.

Outside, the winter sun was setting, painting the snow-covered streets in shades of rose and gold. As we walked back toward my apartment, I caught a glimpse of my reflection in a shop window – auburn hair falling freely around my face, cheeks flushed from the cold and good food, standing a little straighter than I had that morning.

For the first time, I could see what Natasha saw: not a woman in hiding, but someone on the verge of becoming. The thought of the club, of stepping into that glittering unknown, still frightened me. But maybe, just maybe, it was time to be a little frightened. Time to discover who Liliya could be, in this city of golden domes and second chances.

4

Liliya

"*Nyet, nyet*! This is ridiculous!" Natasha's voice cut through the frigid night air as she argued with the valet. [No, no] "I park here every week. You know my car!"

I stood a few steps away, taking in the grandeur of *Zolotoy Vek* while Natasha gestured emphatically. The building was a striking blend of old-world charm and modern opulence. Ornate stonework, dusted with snow, framed large windows that gleamed with warm light. A heated red carpet extended from the entrance, where Russia's elite waited patiently, their expensive furs and jewels glinting under the evening lamps.

My fingers nervously smoothed the midnight blue silk dress beneath my borrowed fur coat. The week leading up to tonight had been a whirlwind—Natasha teaching me basic Russian phrases over coffee, showing me how to walk on icy sidewalks in heels, and finally dragging me through what felt like every boutique in St. Petersburg.

"No more hiding in those baggy sweaters," she'd declared during our shopping expedition. "First impressions, *devochka*. Are everything."

The valet—young and clearly intimidated—finally nodded in surrender, taking Natasha's keys with a mumbled apology.

"Can you believe?" she huffed, returning to my side. "New boy. Thinks because car is not Mercedes S-Class, should not be at front entrance." She linked her arm through mine. "Come. We use private entrance anyway."

As we made our way around the corner to a discreet side door where icicles hung like crystal daggers, I tried to settle my nerves. Just dinner, I reminded myself. Just seeing the club. No pressure.

"Yelena expects us," Natasha said, punching in a code. My stomach fluttered at the mention of the manager she'd told me about all week.

"Is she really as intimidating as you say?"

"*Da*. Don't worry." Natasha squeezed my hand, her fingers warm against mine. "She sounds scary, is actually quite scary. But fair."

The heavy door opened into a dimly lit corridor. Two broad-shouldered men in dark suits stood at attention, their eyes scanning us with professional detachment. They straightened slightly at Natasha's approach.

"Sasha, Mikhail," Natasha greeted them by name, her tone teasing. "You two still standing around looking serious? Is bad for face muscles." She nodded toward me. "My American friend I tell you about."

Mikhail, the taller one, allowed himself a slight smile. "Boss says to expect you," he said, speaking quietly into his earpiece. The other man, Sasha, rolled his eyes good-naturedly at Natasha's antics before gesturing us forward.

The moment we stepped into the main hallway, warmth enveloped us. A discreet attendant appeared, helping us out of our coats with practiced efficiency. The sudden absence of the fur's weight made me feel exposed, but Natasha's confident presence steadied my nerves.

The air was thick with expensive perfume, fine cigars, and something else—anticipation, perhaps. Or power. Our heels clicked against marble floors as we followed the curved hallway, nearly drowned out by the low hum of conversation and faint strains of a jazz quartet warming up.

Every detail screamed luxury—from ornate moldings to crystal chandeliers casting warm golden light. Through archways, I caught glimpses of the main room: plush velvet booths, a gleaming bar carved from what looked like a single piece of Italian marble, mirrored columns making the space seem endless.

As we entered the main hallway, I felt a presence before I saw her. A striking woman materialized beside us, moving with the grace of a dancer.

Her dark hair was pulled back severely, emphasizing sharp cheekbones and intelligent eyes that seemed to take in everything at once.

"Natasha," she said, her voice cool and measured. Her gaze shifted to me, assessing. "And this must be Liliya."

"Yelena," Natasha greeted warmly. "This is friend I tell you about."

"Welcome to *Zolotoy Vek*," she said, her English precise and clipped. "Please, your table is ready. Best view in house."

She gestured for us to follow, leading us through the main room. I couldn't help but notice how the staff seemed to materialize out of thin air at her approach, then disappear just as quickly. Even the few early dinner guests straightened in their seats as we passed.

Our table was perfectly positioned—tucked away enough to feel private, but with a clear view of the room. As I settled into the plush velvet chair, I felt it—that peculiar sensation of being watched. Looking up, I met the most intense gaze I'd ever encountered.

From a private booth across the room, a man was staring directly at me, his expression unreadable but commanding. Even from this distance, his presence was magnetic.

"Who is that?" I asked Natasha quietly, trying not to be obvious as I gestured with my eyes.

Natasha glanced over, her expression shifting subtly. "Zaven Lazarev. He owns club." She flicked her wrist dismissively, but something in her tone didn't match the casual gesture. "Very important man. Very... complicated." Then, louder to the approaching waitress, "We start with champagne, *da?* Best way to begin proper evening."

When I looked back at the booth, he was gone, vanished as suddenly as Natasha had identified him. But the lingering sensation of his stare stayed with me, like the ghost of a touch on my skin. At least now I knew I hadn't imagined him—or the intensity of his attention.

"Your champagne, ladies," the waitress appeared silently at my elbow, making me jump slightly. As she poured, I noticed her movements were precisely choreographed—a small production in itself.

"To new beginnings," Natasha raised her glass, her red lips curving into a knowing smile. "And to you, finally seeing what real luxury looks like."

The champagne was exquisite, tiny bubbles dancing on my tongue. Around us, the club was coming to life. The jazz quartet had begun playing in earnest, their music sophisticated and low enough to allow conversation. Well-dressed couples and groups filtered in, each seeming more elegant than the last.

"So," Yelena had reappeared, sliding gracefully into the third chair at our table. "Natasha treating you well, I hope? She can be... enthusiastic tour guide."

I smiled, relaxing slightly at the casual question. "She's been amazing. I'd still be lost without her."

"You settling in okay? First week in new country can be difficult," Yelena said, accepting a glass of champagne from the waitress without acknowledging her. Her attention remained fixed on me, observant but not unfriendly.

"It's been an adjustment," I admitted, taking a sip of champagne. "Everything is so different here."

"Different good or different bad?" She tilted her head slightly.

I considered my answer. "Different interesting. The city has so much character—all these layers of history right next to modern life."

A waiter appeared with what looked like caviar and other appetizers I didn't recognize. Natasha began explaining each dish, but I found my attention drawn to the way Yelena watched me, as though my reactions to the food revealed something important.

"You have favorite place in city so far?" Yelena asked, spreading caviar on a *blini* with practiced elegance. [Russian pancake]

"The Winter Palace was breathtaking," I said. "But honestly, I loved the little bakery near my apartment even more. The owner taught me my first real Russian phrase."

Something subtle shifted in Yelena's expression—approval, perhaps? "Ah, Vera's place. Best *vatrushka* in city." She glanced at Natasha. "You did good bringing her here. Is refreshing, someone who appreciates both grand and small things."

I watched as a group entered—all expensive suits and subtle power. The staff moved around them with practiced efficiency. Yelena followed my gaze, observing without comment.

"You enjoy people-watching?" she asked casually.

"I always have," I admitted. "I used to teach kindergarten. You learn to read the room quickly when dealing with 20 five year olds."

Her lips curved slightly. "Useful skill, especially here."

Yelena glanced at her watch with a subtle frown. "You'll have to excuse me. Always something needing attention." She rose with fluid grace. "Enjoy your dinner. I find you before you leave, yes? We talk more when you've had chance to experience the food."

With that, she nodded to Natasha and glided away, leaving me with the distinct impression I'd just been thoroughly assessed without realizing exactly how or why.

As she disappeared into the crowd, I turned to Natasha. "She's intense."

"Like everyone important in Russia," Natasha grinned, raising her champagne glass. "But she likes you. I can tell."

"How can you possibly know that?"

"Because," Natasha leaned in with a conspiratorial wink, "she actually smiled. Twice! Is practically declaration of love from Yelena." She gestured toward the menu. "Now, enough serious talk. We order beluga caviar on club's account, yes? Is best in city, and since we're here..."

Her playful smile was infectious, and I found myself relaxing as we turned our attention to enjoying the evening. Work talk could wait—tonight was about experiencing this new world.

The rest of dinner passed in a blur of exquisite food and Natasha's running commentary. Each dish was a work of art—delicate portions of beef stroganoff that melted on my tongue, caviar served on mother-of-pearl spoons, desserts that looked too beautiful to eat. The jazz quartet played on, and I found myself falling into the rhythm of the place—the ebb and flow of guests, the choreographed dance of the staff, the quiet murmur of multiple languages mixing in the air.

As we prepared to leave, Yelena materialized at our table once more. "A moment, Liliya," Yelena's voice came from behind us as we prepared to leave. Natasha squeezed my hand and moved toward the coat check, leaving me alone with the manager.

Yelena studied me for a beat before speaking. "The owner has taken interest in your application. *Gospodin* Lazarev himself suggested offering you the position." [Mister/Sir] She delivered this information with a hint of curiosity in her otherwise composed expression. "You may start as soon as you are ready. Natasha will assist with training."

My heart jumped, both at the job offer and the mention of the mysterious man who'd been watching me. "The owner? You mean—"

"Think about it tonight," she cut in smoothly. "Tell me tomorrow. Is big decision, *da*?"

As Yelena moved away, that familiar sensation washed over me again— that electric awareness of being observed. I turned slowly, knowing what I would find. Across the room, standing in a doorway framed by rich wood paneling, was Zaven Lazarev. This time, when our eyes met, there was no mistaking his interest. His gaze held mine for a deliberate moment before someone passed between us, and he vanished once more.

At the coat check, Natasha was practically buzzing with excitement. "Well? What she say?"

I slipped into the borrowed fur coat, my mind still reeling from what Yelena had revealed. "She said the owner—Zaven—offered me the job."

Natasha's eyes widened slightly before she composed herself. "Zaven himself? Interesting." She linked her arm through mine as we headed toward the exit. "This calls for special celebration tomorrow, *da*? Tonight, you sleep and think about new life."

As we stepped out into the bitter night air, I looked back at *Zolotoy Vek*. Through the windows, the chandeliers sparkled like stars, promising something I couldn't quite name. Something that terrified and thrilled me in equal measure.

I had a feeling my life was about to change dramatically. The question was: was I ready for it?

5

Liliya

"I still can't believe Zaven himself requested you for the position," Natasha said as we hurried through the staff entrance of *Zolotoy Vek*. "In all my time here, he's never involved himself with hostess hiring."

My stomach was a knot of nerves as we entered the labyrinth of back corridors. After a week of intense training, tonight was my first real shift. The polished marble floors and rich wood paneling were familiar from my training sessions, but everything felt different knowing I was now officially part of this world.

"You've mentioned that about five times today," I said, trying to keep my voice steady. "Still not helping with the nerves."

"Is good thing! Means he saw something special." Natasha's eyes gleamed mischievously. "Perhaps was your auburn hair. Russian men have weakness for unusual colors."

I rolled my eyes, but couldn't help remembering that intense gaze from across the room during my dinner visit. In all my training sessions this past week, I'd caught glimpses of Zaven Lazarev—always at a distance, always watching. But we hadn't exchanged a single word.

"The only thing I care about is not screwing up tonight," I said firmly. "Now where's the locker room again?"

"This way," Natasha guided me through a door I wouldn't have noticed if she hadn't pointed it out. "Must check makeup, hair one last time before shift meeting."

The locker room was surprisingly luxurious—all dark wood and gleaming mirrors. Several other women were already there, putting final touches on their appearances. They nodded to Natasha with familiar respect.

"Girls, this is Liliya," Natasha announced. "New hostess. Be nice, *da?*"

Before I could respond to the curious glances, Yelena's voice cut through the chatter. "Ladies. Meeting in three minutes." She appeared in the doorway, immaculate as ever. Her eyes landed on me. "Liliya. Good. Come early to review protocols."

As I followed her out, Natasha gave me an encouraging wink. My heart was pounding, but I forced myself to stand straight, channeling confidence I didn't feel. The heels Natasha had insisted I wear—"Makes legs look amazing. Trust me, you thank me later"—clicked against the marble as I followed Yelena.

"Guest list is here," Yelena gestured to a sleek tablet mounted at the hostess station. "Tonight is important night. Many VIPs." She pulled up a list of names I couldn't read. "These ones in red—must have best tables, extra attention. These in blue—personal guests of owner. They have private access to VIP lounge."

I nodded, trying to memorize the layout she was showing me. The tablet switched to a map of the club, sections marked in different colors. It was more complex than I'd realized during my dinner visit.

"Remember," she continued, her voice dropping slightly, "some guests... they think money means they own place. You are face of *Zolotoy Vek*. Firm but diplomatic, yes? Any problems..." She gestured subtly to a broad-shouldered man positioned near the entrance, his dark suit doing little to hide his obvious strength.

Her eyes swept over me with clinical precision. "You look good. Elegant, not flashy. This will work well here." The compliment was delivered so matter-of-factly that it took me a moment to recognize it as praise. "Guests respond to confidence, to... presence. You have this naturally."

"Main floor is your territory tonight," she concluded. "Natasha will shadow you first hour. Questions?"

A thousand, actually, starting with why the mysterious owner who was so particular about his club had requested me personally but hadn't bothered to speak to me. But I took a breath and attempted the phrase Natasha had taught me.

"*Ya gotova*," I said carefully, trying to sound confident despite my imperfect pronunciation. [I'm ready]

Something flickered in Yelena's eyes—surprise, perhaps even a hint of approval. "Your accent needs work," she said, but there was a new warmth in her tone. "But making effort... this is good. Russian clients will appreciate this."

She nodded once, decisive. "We continue lessons during shifts." Her lips curved into the closest thing to a smile I'd seen from her. "For now, let's see how ready you truly are."

The club was starting to come alive around us. The jazz quartet was warming up, their music weaving through the space like silk. Staff moved with practiced grace, each person knowing their exact role in this elaborate performance. For the first time since crossing the Atlantic, I felt something settle inside me—some people spend their lives searching for where they belong; others run until they stumble into it by accident.

"First guests arrive in twenty minutes," Yelena checked her watch. "Remember—smile subtle, posture perfect..." She paused, her eyes flickering over my shoulder. Something in her expression shifted minutely.

"And one more thing," she added, her voice taking on an edge I hadn't heard before. "Young *Gospodin* Volkov and his friends have been... difficult lately. If they come tonight..." She left the sentence hanging meaningfully.

Before I could ask who *Gospodin* Volkov was, Natasha appeared at my side. "Ready to start your new life, *dorogaya*?"

I took a deep breath, letting the club's atmosphere wash over me. The subtle lighting caught the crystal chandeliers, casting elegant shadows across marble floors. The air was rich with anticipation. Through the main doors, I could see the first cars beginning to arrive, their sleek shapes gleaming in the evening light.

"Ready as I'll ever be," I said, squaring my shoulders.

Natasha squeezed my arm. "Remember—you belong here now. Act like it."

*　*　*

The first hour passed in a blur of faces, names, and carefully orchestrated movements. Each interaction was a delicate dance—a perfect balance of deference and dignity. Natasha stayed close, whispering occasional corrections or warnings about particular guests.

"That one," she murmured as I led an elderly couple to their regular table, "is judge's wife. Always extra champagne, never mention husband."

I was starting to understand the complex hierarchy of the club. It wasn't just about money—though there was plenty of that on display. It was about power, connections, and secrets. Every table told a story, every seating arrangement carried meaning.

The jazz quartet had shifted to something sultry and low, the singer's voice wrapping around Russian words I couldn't understand but somehow felt. The main floor was filling up, the energy building with each arrival. I was just starting to feel like I might actually survive this night when the front doors opened, letting in a blast of cold air and loud, entitled laughter.

"*Blyad*," Natasha muttered beside me. "Young wolves arrive."

A group of men entered—all expensive suits and sharp smiles. The one in front carried himself with the particular arrogance of someone who'd never heard the word 'no.' His blonde hair and sharp jawline might have been attractive if not for the cold calculation in his eyes as they swept the room. Something in that entitled stance, the way he expected the world to bend around him, sent ice through my veins. Just like Jack, right before—

My chest tightened. The room suddenly felt too warm, too small.

"Alexei Volkov," Natasha whispered, her usual playful tone gone. Then she must have noticed my shallow breathing, because her fingers found mine, squeezing gently. "Breathe, *devochku*. You are safe here. Is different world, different rules."

I tried to focus on her touch, on the present moment. These were just potential customers. Not him. Never him again.

"Governor's son," Natasha continued, her casual tone belying the way she'd shifted slightly in front of me, creating a buffer. "Be very careful with this one. But remember—here, you have power. You have me, you have security, you have whole staff watching. Nobody touches hostess without permission. Is rule."

I plastered on my most professional smile as they approached, though something about their energy still made me want to step back. Their voices were just a touch too loud, their laughter a bit too sharp. The scent of expensive cologne mixed with something stronger—vodka, probably. But Natasha was right—this wasn't my old life. Here, I wasn't alone.

"Well, well," the one Natasha had identified as Alexei looked me up and down with unconcealed interest. "What do we have here? A new face at *Zolotoy Vek*." His English was impeccable, tinged with a British accent that somehow made him more unsettling.

I fought the urge to step away from his scrutiny. "Good evening, gentlemen. Welcome to *Zolotoy Vek*. Do you have a reservation?"

"Ah, American," he said, his smile widening at the sound of my accent. "Even better. No reservation, *devotchka*. But surely you can find a table for Alexei Volkov and his friends?"

Behind him, his friends watched with predatory amusement, speaking rapid Russian. I caught what sounded like a threat.

"I'm sorry, sir, but without a reservation—"

"My friend here thinks you might not understand who we are." His smile turned cold. "Perhaps we should speak to the manager? Or better yet, the owner?"

Natasha stepped forward slightly, her shoulder almost touching mine. "Ah, gentlemen! Is lovely seeing you again." Her voice was honey over steel. "But tonight we having full booking. Perhaps we arrange nice drinks at bar while situation... sorts itself, *da*?"

Alexei's eyes narrowed, but his smile remained fixed. His gaze slid from me to Natasha and back again. "Natasha, always pleasure. But surely you not going to let this charming new addition to staff turn us away?"

The air felt charged with tension now. Around us, I noticed other guests subtly shifting their attention to our interaction. The security guard Yelena had pointed out earlier had moved closer, his stance casual but alert.

I stood my ground, even as my heart raced. This was the moment Yelena had warned me about—the fine line between customer service and maintaining the club's standards. With Jack, I'd learned to make myself small to survive. Here, I was learning that standing tall could feel like armor—that the strength I'd always hidden was exactly what this world demanded.

"I'm sorry, sir," I said, my voice steadier than I felt, "but our policy is clear. Perhaps if you'd like to make a reservation for another night—"

The sudden silence from Alexei's friends caught my attention. Their eyes focused over my shoulder, and I felt a presence behind me—solid, unmistakable. Some people fill a room when they enter; Zaven Lazarev seemed to own the air itself, bending reality around him like gravity around a star. The subtle scent of expensive cologne and the slight shift in temperature as someone tall moved into my space made the fine hairs on my neck stand up. I knew immediately who it was without turning. That distinctive awareness I'd felt all week whenever he was nearby was unmistakable at this close proximity.

"*Gospoda*," a deep voice said in Russian, the words incomprehensible to me but clearly impactful to everyone else. [Gentlemen] The voice came from just behind my right shoulder, low and controlled, with a natural authority that required no volume.

Then, to my surprise, he switched to English. His voice was smooth, rich with authority, the Russian accent wrapping around his words. "*Zolotoy Vek* values all patrons, but has particular appreciation for those who respect staff and policies. Is clear, Alexei Sergeyevich?"

The use of what I assumed was Alexei's full name had an immediate effect. The arrogance melted away, replaced by something close to fear. Even his friends had backed up slightly.

Zaven said something else in Russian, his tone firm but not unkind. Alexei nodded, and with a few murmured apologies, he and his friends made their way to the exit.

I let out a breath I didn't know I'd been holding. When I turned to thank him, he was already walking away, his broad shoulders impeccably suited as he moved through the crowd with predatory grace. All I caught was the same magnetic presence I'd felt all week, but this time, it left me feeling oddly bereft.

Natasha appeared at my elbow, a knowing smile playing on her lips. "Well handled, Liliya," she said, her eyes twinkling with something that looked suspiciously like satisfaction.

"I... why did they leave so quickly?" I asked, still trying to process what had just happened. "They seemed almost afraid."

"Of course they afraid," Natasha said, guiding me to a quiet corner of the bar. "When man like Zaven speaks, even governor's son knows to listen. Power recognizes greater power."

She lowered her voice slightly. "In Russia, some men have money, some have connections. Zaven has both, plus something else—respect. Is rare combination." She studied my face carefully. "Money buys obedience, connections buy influence, but respect? That must be earned with blood and time. Is why governor's son fears him. Money can be lost, connections can break, but respect becomes part of who you are."

As she spoke, I couldn't stop replaying his voice in my mind—deeper than I'd imagined, commanding, with that accent that somehow made ordinary words sound like orders that couldn't be disobeyed.

"Here," Natasha slid a glass of what looked like water toward me. "Is vodka," she added with a wink. "Best Russian cure for shaky legs. Though must say, his voice does same thing to many women, not just you."

Heat rushed to my cheeks. "That's not—I wasn't—"

"Is okay," she patted my hand with mock seriousness. "I see way you stand straighter when he near. Very normal reaction. Half staff same way." She grinned mischievously. "Other half too scared to breathe."

"I'm not scared," I protested, taking a larger sip of vodka than intended. The liquid burned perfectly down my throat.

"Mmm." Natasha's smile faded into something more serious. "You did good, standing up to Alexei. Not many would dare."

"Because of his father?"

She gave me a look I couldn't quite read. "Because of many things. But enough about little wolf. You survive first test, should be proud."

Test? I wanted to ask more, but the subtle shake of her head told me this wasn't the time or place. Around us, the club had returned to its normal rhythm, as if the confrontation had never happened. But I could feel something had shifted—in the way other staff members glanced at me with new respect.

"Back to work," Natasha announced brightly. "Many more guests to charm tonight, *da*?"

The rest of the evening passed in a blur of faces and voices. Despite my aching feet, I found myself enjoying the rhythm of it—the subtle dance of making people feel important, the satisfaction of solving problems before they arose. Each time I successfully guided a guest to their table or anticipated a need, I felt a small thrill of accomplishment.

Close to closing, Yelena appeared beside me. "Good work tonight," she said simply. "Tomorrow, come one hour early. More protocols to learn."

I nodded, realizing with a start that I'd actually made it through my first night. As the last guests filtered out, I caught myself glancing toward the private areas of the club, wondering if he was still here somewhere. Something about Zaven Lazarev lingered in my mind—not just his commanding presence, but the way he'd intervened at exactly the right moment. Almost as though he'd been watching me all along.

"Ready to go?" Natasha materialized with my coat. "You look like you ready to collapse, but you did well."

"Thanks," I said, slipping into the warmth of my coat. "It was actually... fun." I surprised myself with the admission.

"See? Told you." She grinned as we walked to her car. "Though next time maybe less excitement with governor's son, *da*?"

I laughed, the tension of the night finally easing. "No promises."

As we drove through the quiet streets, Natasha glanced at me. "So. That was interesting tonight."

"Which part?" I asked, though I knew exactly what she meant.

"Zaven. He never intervenes with troublemakers." She watched my face carefully. "Security handles such things. Yet tonight..." She trailed off meaningfully.

I tried to keep my expression neutral, but something must have given me away because Natasha's lips curved into a knowing smile.

"Ah, I see that look. You try to hide, but face betrays you." She tapped the steering wheel thoughtfully. "Cannot blame you. He has this effect."

"What effect?" I asked too quickly, then immediately regretted it when her smile widened.

"Effect that makes sweet friend suddenly very interested in club owner." She laughed softly. "Is okay, *dorogaya*. Your secret safe with me."

I turned to watch the city lights blur past, hoping the darkness hid my warming cheeks. "I'm just curious why he'd break his own protocol for a new hostess."

"Makes me curious too," she said, wiggling her eyebrows suggestively. "Five years I work there, and big boss never bothers with drunk idiots like Alexei." She shot me a sideways glance. "Maybe is because you fill out that dress so nicely, *da*? Men notice such things, even serious ones." She tapped her chin dramatically. "Or maybe he sees something special in you that rest of us already know is there."

I laughed despite myself. "I think you're seeing things that aren't there."

"No," Natasha's smile softened, becoming surprisingly gentle. "I see things that are there but you not ready to admit." She reached across and squeezed my hand quickly before returning it to the steering wheel. "Is okay. New life has many surprises, *da*? Is what adventure is all about."

As the lights of St. Petersburg slipped by, I found myself thinking about that moment when Zaven's voice had cut through the tension—commanding, confident, unexpected. I'd fled across an ocean to escape one man's control, only to find myself drawn to another's power. But this felt different—not a cage closing around me, but a door opening to something I hadn't known to want.

6

Zaven

The soft murmur of conversation and tinkling of crystal filled *Zolotoy Vek* as I watched her from my private office above the main floor. Three nights had passed since our encounter with Alexei, and I found myself regularly drawn to the vantage point that offered the best view of her movements. Liliya. She had proven herself remarkably competent.

She moved through the crowd with growing confidence now, her natural grace enhanced by what she'd learned from Natasha's training. The diplomatic way she handled difficult patrons, her attentive eye for detail, her subtle management of the staff working beneath her—it was impressive for someone so new. Especially someone who hadn't been raised in our world.

I took a slow sip of vodka, letting the burn ground me. Business demanded my attention, yet I kept finding myself here, watching her work.

"The report from Tbilisi arrived," Viktor said as he entered, placing a folder on my desk. His eyes followed my gaze down to the floor below. He said nothing about my current preoccupation, but the slight raise of his eyebrow spoke volumes.

"And?" I asked, forcing my attention to the matter at hand.

"Not good." Viktor's face remained impassive, but the tension in his shoulders told me all I needed to know. "Contact went dark three days ago. Police have him."

I set down my glass. "The shipment?"

"Vanished." The muscle in Viktor's jaw ticked. "Two tons of cargo doesn't just disappear without inside help."

"Too clean for Dmitri's usual work," I said, mind racing through possibilities. Below, Liliya laughed at something Natasha said, the sound carrying even over the jazz quartet. I forced my focus away from her. "Who then?"

"Could be new player. Could be someone inside." Viktor hesitated. "Timing is... concerning. First Turkish route, now Georgian. Someone moving pieces against us."

I nodded, swirling the vodka in my glass. This pattern was too deliberate to be coincidence. Someone was testing our defenses, probing for weakness. "Have Anatoly focus on dock workers first. Someone had to physically move that shipment. Find them, we find our leak."

"Already started. Also put extra eyes on Dmitri's people, just in case."

A disturbance at the entrance caught my attention, momentarily distracting me from our business concerns. Another group from Alexei's crowd, though the pup himself was wisely absent tonight. I watched as Liliya handled them with perfect poise—no trace of the nervousness she'd shown that first night.

"She learns quick," Viktor observed, following my gaze. "Adapts well."

"Yelena says she's the most competent hostess they've had," I replied, keeping my tone neutral despite the unexpected pride I felt at her success. "Already speaking basic Russian with the staff."

Viktor nodded, his expression thoughtful as he studied me rather than Liliya. After twenty years of friendship, he could read me better than most. "You've been watching her."

It wasn't a question, and I didn't bother denying it. "She interests me."

"Enough to intervene personally with Alexei Volkov." He let the observation hang between us. "Not like you to handle such trivial matters."

I shot him a look, but he met my gaze steadily. His concern was valid—I didn't typically involve myself in minor disturbances at the club. That was what security was for. Yet I'd stepped in without hesitation when Alexei had challenged her.

"Anatoly ran deeper check on American girl," Viktor said carefully. "Thought you should know what we found."

Now he had my full attention. "Tell me."

"Ex-boyfriend. Violent type." Viktor's voice held controlled disgust. "She fled America with Natasha's help. Left everything behind. No trace."

Something dark stirred in my chest. Domestic violence—it went against everything we stood for. The *vor* might be criminals, but we had codes, principles. Real men didn't raise hands to women.

"This man," I kept my voice carefully neutral, though something primal coiled hot beneath the surface. "He still looks for her?"

"No sign of pursuit yet. He filed missing person report, but American police not take seriously. Seems she covered tracks well."

"And her connection to us?" The question that mattered most.

Viktor shook his head. "Nothing. Clean. No criminal history, no connection to rivals, no hidden agenda. Just woman running from monster wearing expensive suits."

I nodded, surprised by my relief. In our world, coincidences rarely existed. Everyone had angles, hidden motives. The idea that she was simply what she appeared to be—a woman seeking refuge, starting over—was almost too straightforward to believe.

"Though," Viktor added carefully, "timing of her arrival and these shipment problems..."

I cut him off with a sharp gesture. "*Net*, of course not." Viktor conceded. "Just noting timing." [No]

Below, Liliya turned suddenly, her eyes sweeping up toward my position as if sensing my scrutiny. For a moment, our gazes locked. Even from this distance, I could see her straighten slightly, chin lifting in acknowledgment before returning to her duties. Not fear—recognition.

"You should meet with her properly," Viktor said, watching this silent exchange. "If only to satisfy your... curiosity."

I nodded slowly, surprised by my reluctance. I'd kept my distance these past days, observing from afar, learning her patterns. The thought of direct interaction stirred an unfamiliar tension—anticipation mixed with something I couldn't quite name.

"Speaking of meetings," Viktor continued, "*Smotriny* approaches. Other *vory* expect you to attend this year." [Bride-showing ceremony] [Thieves/criminal bosses (plural)]

The women's showcase. Another archaic tradition that left a bitter taste in my mouth. The old families parading their daughters before the *vor*, treating them like prized cattle.

"The families grow restless," Viktor pressed when I didn't respond. "They have daughters of good breeding. Strategic match could strengthen position, especially with routes compromised."

"Times change," I said, watching as Liliya efficiently handled a seating dispute below. Every movement was a study in grace now, but she'd maintained that hint of freshness that set her apart. Made her different from the carefully groomed Russian daughters who'd been raised for this world.

"Not all traditions deserve preservation."

Viktor studied me carefully. "Your father would say—"

"I'm not my father," I cut him off, an edge in my voice. We both knew the old *vor* had arranged a politically advantageous marriage with my mother. A loveless union that had produced the heir he needed but little else.

A commotion near the bar caught our attention. Two men—regulars, Chinese businessmen who usually kept to themselves—were arguing heatedly in Mandarin. As their voices rose, I watched Liliya approach them. My body tensed, ready to move, but something in her posture made me wait.

She spoke softly, her voice carrying just enough authority to command attention without challenging their pride. Within moments, she had them seated at separate tables, crisis averted without security's intervention.

"Impressive," Viktor murmured.

"Yes." The word felt inadequate for the unexpected pride I felt watching her. She belonged here, in this world of power and nuance. The realization was both satisfying and unsettling.

"You should know," Viktor said carefully, "Governor Volkov has been making noise about territory since his son's... incident. Testing boundaries."

I nodded, unsurprised. "Let him posture. When we find who's compromising our shipments, we'll send a clearer message."

"And the American girl?" Viktor's question carried weight. "What's your interest there?"

I didn't answer immediately, watching as Liliya moved through the crowd with unconscious grace. Something about her pulled at my attention in ways I couldn't easily dismiss. She was unlike the others—direct yet diplomatic, strong without cruelty, observant without calculation. I found myself drawn to these contradictions, to the way she navigated complex situations while maintaining something essentially her own.

My silence stretched long enough that Viktor shifted beside me, waiting. When I finally looked away from her, I merely made a low "hmm" in my throat, neither confirming nor denying my interest.

Viktor's raised eyebrow spoke volumes. He knew me well enough to recognize fascination, even when I refused to name it.

There was wisdom in distance. In our world, connections were vulnerabilities—for both parties. Besides, I had more pressing concerns than an intriguing new hostess.

Viktor nodded, though something in his expression suggested he doubted my restraint would last. Perhaps he knew me better than I knew myself.

"The Georgian route takes priority," I said, turning away from the window. "Find our leak. Make an example."

"*Da.*" Viktor moved toward the door, then paused, a rare hint of amusement crossing his face. "And when she catches you watching her again?"

I didn't pretend to misunderstand. Below, Liliya continued her duties, unaware of how closely she was being observed. Unaware of the dangerous currents surrounding her.

"Better she doesn't know," I said. "Safer."

For her. For me. For the delicate balance I'd spent years maintaining.

Viktor nodded once, accepting my decision without comment. But as he left, I found myself drawn back to the window, watching her move through my world with growing confidence. Despite my own words, I knew the truth—my distance was temporary.

Some forces couldn't be resisted indefinitely.

7

Liliya

"I still can't believe how much they tip at the club," I said, staring at the designer boutique window where dresses probably cost more than my old monthly rent. "I've never been able to shop at places like this before."

Natasha grinned, linking her arm through mine as we navigated the icy sidewalks of Nevsky Prospekt. "Is about time you enjoy fruits of your labor! Three weeks of perfect hostessing deserves reward."

She tugged me toward the entrance, nearly making me slip. "No more borrowing my clothes. Time for proper shopping."

A street vendor's sudden movement caught my eye, and I tensed briefly before my brain processed there was no threat—just a man selling hot drinks. A month ago, when I first arrived in Russia, that would have sent my heart racing for minutes. Now I recovered in seconds, a small victory I'd been collecting lately. Still, I couldn't quite shake the feeling of being watched that occasionally crept up on me at the club—a different kind of awareness that I hadn't mentioned to Natasha.

My fifth week in Russia, and each day still brought new discoveries. The *babushka* at my local bakery had started saving my favorite *syrniki*, beaming with pride when I managed to order in broken Russian. [Grandmother] [Sweet cheese pancakes] My language skills were still atrocious, but I was picking up enough to navigate the metro and handle basic interactions at the club. Just last night, I'd managed to understand when a client ordered specific vodka brands, earning an approving nod from Yelena.

"Here!" Natasha stopped abruptly, gesturing dramatically at the store-front. "Perfect place for club clothes. Need to keep up image, *da*?"

I hesitated, old habits making me calculate costs in my head. Jack had always controlled every penny I spent, deciding what I could or couldn't buy. But that wasn't my life anymore. Here I was, about to spend money I'd earned myself.

"Stop with thinking so hard. Is making my head hurt just watching," Natasha teased. "Time to dress like glamorous woman, not college student in baggy sweaters."

As we entered the boutique, warmth enveloped us, along with the subtle scent of expensive perfume—not unlike *Zolotoy Vek*. This was clearly where the club's clientele shopped, all gleaming surfaces and soft lighting that made everything look like art.

Natasha strode in like she owned the place, greeting the saleswoman in rapid-fire Russian before turning back to me. "Okay, *solnyshko*, time to find you something that makes oligarchs drop their vodka glasses." [Little sun/sunshine]

"Natasha!" I hissed, feeling heat rise to my cheeks.

"What? Is true. Already see how they look at you in club." She rifled through a rack of dresses with practiced efficiency. "Even Zaven notices, though he tries to be subtle."

My heart did an unwanted flip at his name. "He does not," I protested, though I couldn't deny that prickling sensation I got sometimes, like electricity dancing across my skin. "He hasn't even spoken to me since that night with Alexei. No proper introduction, not even a 'hello.' Maybe he just doesn't like Americans." I tried to laugh it off. "Three weeks and the owner of the club can't be bothered to meet his new hostess?"

"Ah, but he sees you," she said with that knowing smile I was learning to both love and dread. "Trust me, is not because you American. Is because he trying very hard to keep distance."

I found myself oddly curious. "Why would he do that? Keep his distance, I mean."

"Because he want you," she said matter-of-factly, pulling out a deep emerald dress that looked impossibly expensive. "Men like Zaven do not mix business with pleasure easily. Is… complicated for them." She held the dress against me. "This one perfect. Matches your eyes, makes man want to rip it off with teeth."

I felt my cheeks burn. "I'm not trying to make anyone rip anything."

She leaned in closer, lowering her voice conspiratorially. "Should see way he looks at you when you bend over hostess stand. Like starving wolf eyeing prey." She fanned herself dramatically. "Russian men, they know how to make woman feel owned. Not like American boys playing at being men."

"Oh my god," I muttered, my whole body flushing at her words. The worst part was, I could picture it—those intense eyes traveling over my body, that commanding presence… "You're terrible."

"What? Is fact! And way he fills out suit?" Her grin turned wicked. "Though Viktor… *bozhe moy*, that man! So serious, so proper. Makes me want to climb him like tree, mess up that perfect uniform." She sighed dramatically. "Six months I try everything. Nothing! Is like trying to seduce marble statue."

I couldn't help laughing, even as I felt my face grow hotter. "I cannot believe you just said that!"

"Why not? Besides," she held up another dress, this one a deep burgundy that dipped dangerously low in back, "way he watches you? Man like that doesn't just want to take you to dinner."

"Will you stop?" I hissed, though the image her words conjured—large hands gripping my hips, that accented voice rough with need—sent heat flooding through me. "I'm trying to shop, not fantasize about my boss."

"Ah! So you do fantasize?" Her triumphant grin was positively wicked. "Tell truth—you think about him late at night? When you're alone in bed?"

"I am not having this conversation in public," I muttered, but my burning cheeks gave me away.

"Is okay, *devochka*. Natural to want powerful man. Especially one who looks at you like he wants to bend you over every surface in club."

"Nat!" But my protest came out embarrassingly breathless.

"Try this one," Natasha thrust several dresses into my arms, practically shoving me toward the fitting rooms. "Need something that makes him forget all about stupid marriage mart."

"The what?" I asked, struggling not to drop the pile of silk and lace.

"*Smotriny*," she waved dismissively. "Old tradition. Powerful men choosing wives. Very boring, very traditional. Much better to make him forget all rules, *da*?"

In the fitting room, I slipped into the emerald dress, the fabric cool against my heated skin. It fit like it was made for me, hugging curves I hadn't even known I had. The woman in the mirror looked... desirable. Powerful, even. Far from the scared girl Jack had tried to break.

"Well?" Natasha called impatiently. "Stop hiding, show me!"

I stepped out, and her low whistle made me blush all over again. "Perfect! This one makes even me want to take you home."

"You're impossible," I laughed, but couldn't help admiring my reflection.

"Trust me," Natasha's eyes gleamed as she adjusted the dress's neckline to show just a bit more skin. "Wear this to club, and Zaven won't be able to keep playing his distant watching game. Even he has limits to self-control."

The thought sent an unexpected thrill through me. What would it take to make a man like that lose control?

"Buy dress," Natasha declared. "And matching lingerie. Never know when powerful man might see it."

I fidgeted with the dress's hem, voicing the doubt that had been gnawing at me. "You really think someone like him would be interested in someone like me? After everything..." I swallowed hard. "Maybe I shouldn't even be thinking about men right now. With what happened—"

"Stop." Natasha's perfectly manicured finger pressed against my lips. "You listen to me now. You are not broken thing to be fixed. Are beautiful woman who deserve everything life offers. Including hot sex with sexy men." Her eyes softened even as her grin turned wicked. "Is new life, *da*? New Liliya. Maybe she wants one man, maybe she wants entire hockey team. Is her choice now."

I couldn't help but laugh, even as I felt tears prick at my eyes. "A whole hockey team?"

"Why not? Is your life now. Your rules." She held up a lacy black set with a triumphant smile. "Starting with proper lingerie. Make you feel sexy, powerful. Rest follows."

I was actually considering it—both the dress and the implications—when my phone buzzed. I pulled it from my bag, still laughing at Natasha's latest outrageous suggestion. The screen lit up with a notification.

My smile froze.

The world tilted sideways, all the warmth and laughter of the moment shattering like glass. My hands started shaking so badly I could barely read the words, but they burned into my brain anyway:

"Did you really think you could hide from me forever, Lily-Pad"

Lily-Pad. His pet name for me. The one he'd whisper right before...

The fitting room suddenly felt like a trap, the beautiful dress a costume I'd been fool enough to think I could wear. The mirror reflected a ghost—all the color had drained from my face, leaving behind the terrified girl I thought I'd left behind.

"Liliya?" Natasha's voice seemed to come from very far away. "What's wrong? You look like—"

The phone slipped from my numb fingers, clattering against the boutique's marble floor. The sound made me flinch violently—too much like breaking glass, like the night I'd finally run.

"He found me," I whispered, my voice breaking. "Oh god, he found me."

Natasha's playful demeanor vanished instantly. She snatched up my phone, her face darkening as she read the message. "*Mudak*," she muttered, then looked up at me with new understanding in her eyes. [Asshole] "This is him? The one you run from?"

I nodded, unable to speak past the knot in my throat. The fitting room walls seemed to be closing in.

"Get changed," Natasha ordered, her voice clipped and serious in a way I'd never heard before. "We go somewhere quiet to talk."

* * *

"His name is Jack," I began, my voice barely above a whisper. We were in a secluded booth at the back of a nearby café, the rich scent of coffee mixed with something stronger—cognac, probably. "We met in college. He was... charming at first. Star quarterback, business major, came from money. Everyone said we were perfect together."

I took a shaky sip, letting the spiked coffee burn away some of the fear. "But then things started changing. Little comments about my clothes, my friends. Always said he was just looking out for me."

Natasha's hand found mine across the table, squeezing hard when my voice cracked.

"Before I knew it, I'd stopped wearing things he didn't like, stopped talking to people he didn't approve of. I was working at a bar to help pay for school, and I had a student aide position teaching kindergarten that I loved—he hated both jobs. Said it wasn't appropriate for his girlfriend to serve drinks to other men, and that I was wasting my time with 'babysitting' when I should be focusing on my studies."

"You weren't stupid," Natasha cut in fiercely, as if reading my thoughts. "Men like this, they are expert manipulators. Like spider spinning web."

"After I quit both jobs, I became completely dependent on him financially." My fingers traced the rim of my cup obsessively. "He loved that. Used it to control everything. If I disagreed with him, he'd threaten to stop helping with tuition." I paused, the next part always harder to say aloud. "The control wasn't just financial. It escalated so gradually I barely noticed."

I shifted in my seat, drawing my shoulders in slightly as the memories pressed closer. The café's warmth suddenly felt insufficient against the chill these thoughts brought back. When I spoke again, my voice had dropped to barely above a whisper.

"The first time he hit me, I told myself it was an accident. He was drunk, he didn't mean it. He cried after, promised it would never happen again."

"But it did." Natasha's words weren't a question.

I nodded, fighting back tears. "It got worse. I tried to leave once, was going to go to my parents. But he caught me. That was... that was the worst night. Ended up in hospital with broken rib and concussion. He told everyone I fell down stairs."

"I kill him," Natasha said simply, her accent thicker with anger. "When you called me that night, asking about Russia… I knew something was wrong, but not this."

"You did enough," I cut in. "You gave me somewhere to run to. If I hadn't had that…"

"So what finally made you run?" she asked softly. "What was last straw?"

I took a shaky breath. "About a month ago. He'd been drinking, was in one of his moods. Started accusing me of flirting with his friend at a party. He grabbed a glass, and I thought…" My hand went unconsciously to my throat. "I really thought that was it. That he was going to kill me."

Natasha cursed viciously in Russian. "And now this *mudak* thinks he can threaten you here? In my city?" Her eyes flashed dangerously. "No. We not let this happen."

"What can I do?" The panic was rising again. "If he found a way to contact me, he could find out where I am. He has money, connections—"

"Stop," Natasha cut me off firmly. "You think he has connections? In St. Petersburg?" She gave a harsh laugh. "Silly boy knows nothing about real power."

Something shifted in Natasha's expression—a calculating look I'd never seen before. She stared into her coffee cup, brows furrowed in thought, clearly debating something in her mind.

"What is it?" I asked, recognizing she was holding something back. "You're thinking of something."

She hesitated, shaking her head slightly. "Is nothing. Just crazy idea."

"Tell me," I insisted, leaning forward. "Please, Natasha. I can see you've thought of something." My voice cracked slightly. "I'll do practically anything to keep him from finding me. Anything."

She studied my face for a long moment, as if gauging my sincerity—or perhaps my desperation. The playful friend who'd been teasing me about lingerie was gone. In her place was someone harder, more serious.

"Liliya," she said finally, her voice careful, measured, "there might be way to ensure your safety. Is… unconventional, but in our circles, it's not unheard of.”

“What do you mean?” I wiped at my eyes, focusing through my fear, clinging to this thread of hope.

“Remember earlier? When I mention *Smotriny*?” Natasha’s playful tone about the marriage mart was gone now, replaced with something more serious. “Maybe not such boring tradition after all.”

“That thing you mentioned about powerful men choosing wives?” The concept had seemed almost laughable earlier, when I was trying on dresses and feeling confident. Now, with Jack’s threat burning in my phone, nothing seemed funny anymore.

“*Da.* Is old Russian tradition, but has new meaning in certain... exclusive circles.” She leaned closer, voice dropping. “Men who participate... they not just wealthy, Liliya. They have kind of power your ex could never dream of challenging.”

I thought about the subtle dynamics I’d witnessed at *Zolotoy Vek*—the way certain clients commanded respect with just their presence, the way even Yelena deferred to some of them. The way Zaven had made Alexei back down with just a few words.

“How would it even work?” My voice shook slightly. “I mean, I can’t just... marry a stranger.”

“Would be arrangement, with clear terms,” Natasha explained, her expression serious. “Not like American marriage. These men understand value of discretion, of loyalty. And in return...” She paused meaningfully. “Protection. Complete protection.”

The word ‘protection’ echoed in my mind. When was the last time I’d felt truly safe? Even these past three weeks, there’d been that underlying current of fear, of waiting for the other shoe to drop. And now it had.

“But who...” I swallowed hard. “What kind of men participate in this?”

“Men with influence that extends beyond money,” Natasha explained, her voice dropping lower. “Men who command respect from police, from government, from business. Men who could make someone like Jack... vanish without trace.”

“Should talk to Yelena,” Natasha continued carefully. “She knows more about these things. Has... connections."

"Yelena?" I blinked, remembering how the club manager seemed to know everything about everyone. "What does she have to do with this?"

Natasha gave me a long look. "*Zolotoy Vek* is not just club, Liliya. Is... how you say... hub for certain connections. Yelena knows how these things work."

The implications of what she was saying started to sink in. All those nights at the club took on a different meaning—the private conversations in back rooms I'd glimpsed, the deference shown to certain guests, the subtle hierarchies I'd noticed but never fully understood. *Zolotoy Vek* wasn't just an exclusive club—it was a nexus of power.

My phone buzzed again. We both froze, but it was just Yelena with next week's schedule. Still, the reminder of how easily Jack had reached me sent a fresh wave of panic through my system.

"I can't keep living like this," I whispered, more to myself than Natasha. "Jumping at every noise, checking over my shoulder..."

"Then don't," Natasha said firmly. "Let me talk to Yelena. Just talk, *da?* No commitment. But Liliya..." She waited until I met her eyes. "You deserve to feel safe. To sleep at night without fear. If this can give you that..."

"What if..." I wrapped my hands tighter around my coffee cup, seeking warmth. "What if I end up trapped again? Trading one cage for another?"

"*Net*," Natasha's response was fierce. "These men understand honor, respect tradition. Contract goes both ways. Would be protected, yes, but also respected. Free to work, to have own life." She paused, then added with hint of her usual mischief, "Besides, might even find self enjoying arrangement. Russian men know how to treat woman right, remember?"

Despite everything, I felt heat rise to my cheeks, remembering our earlier conversation about Zaven. How different would it be, I wondered, to be protected by someone who actually cared about your well-being? To be valued instead of possessed?

I shook my head sharply. "I can't believe I'm even considering this."

"Just talk to Yelena," Natasha pressed. "She explain better than me. And Liliya?" She waited until I looked up. "Remember who you are now. Not scared girl anymore. You survive. You escape. You build new life. This?"

She gestured to my phone. "Is just next challenge to overcome."

"When?" I asked finally, the word barely audible. "When should we talk to Yelena?"

"Tonight," Natasha said decisively. "You have shift anyway. We go early, speak with her before club opens." She squeezed my hand. "Remember—just talk. Just options. *Da*?"

I nodded, though my stomach was in knots. As we stepped back into the bitter cold, I hugged my borrowed coat closer. "These men you mentioned... they really have that kind of power? To make problems just... disappear?"

"Ah, your eyes say everything," Natasha said, linking her arm through mine. "Is scary, *da*? But remember—these arrangements work because these men respect tradition, follow codes of honor." She squeezed my arm reassuringly. "Think of it as... alliance. Both sides get something valuable. Protection for you, status for them."

I let out a shaky breath, watching it cloud in the freezing air. Maybe she was right. Maybe in this glittering, dangerous city, I needed more than just a fresh start. Maybe I needed whatever protection these powerful men could offer.

Though as we walked, I couldn't help wondering if the protection might end up being more dangerous than what I was running from.

8

Liliya

Jack's message haunted me as I prepared for my shift. Each movement felt weighted with new significance—applying makeup, choosing the burgundy dress, practicing Russian phrases. Tonight wasn't just another evening at *Zolotoy Vek*. Tonight I'd be meeting with Yelena to discuss something that could change everything.

Smotriny. The word Natasha had introduced just hours ago kept circling in my mind. A tradition that might offer protection, she'd said. A way to ensure Jack could never touch me again.

My phone buzzed—Natasha: "Ready for tonight, *devochka*? No more shopping trip giggles, *da*? Tonight we be serious. And remember - Yelena expects you early."

The contrast between our playful dress shopping just hours earlier and the life-altering conversation that followed made my head spin. One moment we'd been teasing about men's hungry looks, the next discussing marriage as protection. How quickly everything had shifted in a single afternoon.

As I made my way to the club, the early winter darkness seemed to mirror my thoughts—shadows upon shadows, nothing quite as it appeared. The familiar route felt different tonight, every passing car making me tense. Jack's threat remained raw, but beneath my fear ran an undercurrent of something else—an electric anticipation I couldn't quite name.

"Liliya!" Natasha appeared as I reached the staff entrance, her eyes scanning my face. "Good, you come early like I say. Yelena waits in office."

My heart jumped. "Now? Before my shift?"

"*Da.* Better to have clear head for such talk, no?" She squeezed my arm reassuringly. "Remember what I tell you at café—you are strong now."

I didn't feel strong as I followed her through the club's back corridors, each step on the marble floors echoing like a countdown. The pre-opening club had a different energy—staff moving with practiced efficiency, transforming the space from merely opulent to seductive. Tonight, everything seemed to hold hidden significance.

Natasha led me down a corridor I'd rarely visited, stopping before an imposing mahogany door. I took a deep breath, trying to calm my racing heart.

"Remember," she murmured, squeezing my hand, "is just talk. Just options." She knocked sharply, then disappeared before I could protest.

"Enter."

Yelena's voice carried that same quiet authority that commanded respect on the club floor. I pushed open the door, trying to steady my racing heart.

Her office matched her personality—elegant efficiency with subtle hints of luxury. A painting of a stormy sea dominated one wall, the waves almost alive in the dim light. Yelena sat behind a massive desk, her piercing gaze studying me as I entered.

"Sit, Liliya." She gestured to a chair. "I believe we have much to discuss."

"I understand Natasha spoke to you about *Smotriny*," she continued, reaching for a crystal decanter and pouring two measures of what I assumed was vodka. "She also told me about your situation—the man you're running from and today's message. She thought this might offer a solution."

My fingers curled around the crystal glass she offered, grateful for something to hold. "She said it could offer protection."

"Protection," Yelena repeated thoughtfully. "*Da*, that is one aspect. But before we discuss possibilities, you must understand what *Smotriny* truly means."

She stood, moving to look out her window at the glittering city below. "What do you know of the men who come to *Zolotoy Vek*?"

"They're wealthy," I started, then corrected myself. "Influential."

"Influence," Yelena turned back to me, something intense in her expression. "This is key. The men who participate in *Smotriny* have connections that extend beyond money. The kind of connections that make ordinary problems—or people—simply disappear." She paused. "A man like the one you ran from? He would be nothing to them."

The vodka burned my throat, but I welcomed the heat. "And they look for wives through this tradition?"

"Not exactly wives," Yelena's lips curved slightly. "It's more... these men bid for the right to provide protection. Women who participate are evaluated first. Those who prove suitable are presented at *Smotriny*."

I nearly choked on my vodka. "Bid? Like at an auction?"

"This surprises you?" Her eyes held mine. "Think of what you've seen here. These arrangements are about mutual benefit—protection in exchange for status, companionship, discretion. The bidding demonstrates commitment, shows how far they would go to ensure a woman's safety."

"But what happens with the money? Who gets it?" I asked, trying to understand the mechanics of this strange tradition.

Yelena nodded, as if approving of my practical question. "The money goes into a trust for the woman. She controls it—for security, independence, whatever she needs. Some use it to start businesses, others for charity foundations. It becomes a safety net that belongs only to her, regardless of how the arrangement progresses." She leaned forward slightly. "This is important distinction—the man doesn't buy the woman. He proves his commitment while ensuring her financial independence."

"But the women have no choice in who—"

"They make their choice by entering *Smotriny*," Yelena said firmly. "By participating, they choose this path, this protection."

My mind flashed to Jack, how he'd "protected" me from friends, from jobs, from any independence. "It sounds like trading one cage for another."

"Ah." Yelena's expression sharpened. "You compare this to your American ex? No. It's not the same, Liliya. He was a weak man playing at being strong. The men I speak of?" She leaned forward. "They have no need for threats or violence. Their word alone carries weight."

"Tell me," she continued, studying me, "when Zaven stopped Alexei that night, did he need to threaten? Did he need to raise his voice?"

The memory sent an unexpected shiver through me. "No, he just... everyone just knew."

"Exactly. It's a different kind of influence." She smiled slightly. "These men command respect through presence, not fear."

I took another sip of vodka, letting the burn steady me. "But still... to be bought, to belong to someone—"

"To belong," Yelena repeated thoughtfully. "Interesting word. In Russian, belonging means many things. Yes, it can mean possession. But it can also mean finding your place—where you're protected because you have value, not because you're owned."

The distinction made me pause. I thought of how Jack had "protected" me—isolating me, controlling my every move. Then I thought of how Zaven had handled Alexei, offering safety without domination.

"These arrangements," Yelena continued, "are not about breaking spirit. They're about preserving it while offering security."

She moved to a cabinet behind her desk, withdrawing what looked like a heavy photo album bound in dark leather. "Perhaps it's easier to understand with examples. Women who chose this path before you."

My breath caught as she opened it. The photos were elegant—women at charity galas, exclusive events, looking confident and composed.

"This one," Yelena pointed to a striking blonde, "came here in circumstances similar to yours. Now she runs three charitable foundations. Her husband ensures her safety while giving her freedom to build her own legacy."

I looked up from the album, suddenly curious. "How do you know so much about this? Why do you have these pictures?"

A slight smile crossed Yelena's face. "I have been what you might call a *scout* for *Smotriny* for nearly fifteen years. I identify women with potential, guide them through the process." [Talent scout] She ran her fingers along the album's edge. "Some came to me like you—seeking safety. Others sought opportunity, connections. I maintain contact with most of them."

"So the club—*Zolotoy Vek*—it's more than just a business?"

"It serves many purposes," she acknowledged. "A meeting place. A neutral ground. A place to observe potential candidates in various situations." Her eyes met mine directly. "And yes, a place where I can evaluate who might thrive in such arrangements."

"And they're all... content with their choices?" I asked, studying the faces for any sign of hidden regret.

"Content?" Yelena considered the word. "They are safe. Respected. Free to pursue interests without looking over their shoulders. Is that not a form of happiness?" She closed the album. "But understand this isn't a fairy tale. It's an arrangement with mutual benefits and clear terms. Much depends on finding the right match."

"How would it work?" I asked, forcing myself to meet her gaze. "If I did consider it?"

"First comes an observation period," Yelena explained. "You continue working here, but certain potential candidates will take notice, evaluate how you handle yourself in different situations."

A shiver ran through me, remembering the intense looks I'd sometimes felt. "And if I pass this evaluation?"

"Then preparation begins. You would learn more about expectations, proper etiquette. Natasha would help, of course. When ready, you would attend *Smotriny* for formal introduction."

"And after someone... chooses me?"

"A contract is drawn with specific terms—your safety, your freedoms, your obligations, all clearly defined." Her eyes held mine. "These aren't marriages of love, Liliya. They're partnerships of mutual benefit. Though sometimes," she smiled slightly, "things evolve."

"How long do I have to decide?"

"The next *Smotriny* is in three weeks," Yelena said. "But your decision to begin the observation period? I need to know by the end of the week."

The reality of the timeline hit me. Less than a week to decide if I wanted to enter this world completely.

"Tonight," Yelena continued, standing smoothly, "work as normal. But watch with new eyes. See how things truly operate here. Notice the difference between those who simply have money and those who command genuine respect."

She moved toward the door. "And Liliya?" She paused, her hand on the handle. "Ask yourself this: are you more afraid of entering this world, or of remaining vulnerable to the man who's hunting you?"

The question followed me as I left her office. The club was coming alive around me, but everything looked different now. Every interaction seemed to hold new meaning, every corner potentially hiding secrets I was only beginning to understand.

As I took my position at the hostess stand, I realized I wasn't just starting another shift. I was starting my observation period—whether I'd officially decided or not.

9

Zaven

Her skin burned like fire beneath my hands, auburn hair spilling across my pillow like liquid copper. Those green eyes—defiant even now—held mine as I moved over her, her breath catching with each deliberate touch. The silk sheets tangled around us as her back arched, offering herself with a surrender that felt like victory.

"Zaven," she whispered, my name on her lips a prayer and demand all at once. Her fingers traced the tattoos across my chest, learning their meaning, their history. Learning me.

I captured her wrists, pinning them above her head as I lowered my mouth to the hollow of her throat. The scent of her—vanilla and something uniquely her—filled my senses. My control, always absolute, fractured as she wrapped her legs around my waist, urging me closer.

"Please," she breathed against my ear, the sound breaking something loose in my chest. "Take me. Hard." I claimed her mouth, drinking in her soft moans as my hand slid down her body, finding her slick and desperate for me. Her hips rose to meet my touch, shameless in her need.

"Mine," I growled against her neck, marking her with teeth and tongue, claiming what belonged to me. "Say it. Tell me who you belong to." She responded with a gasp that turned to a cry of raw pleasure as I thrust inside her, her tight heat consuming me completely.

"Yours," she agreed, those green eyes never leaving mine as I fucked her with

slow, deliberate strokes. "Only yours." The world narrowed to nothing but the exquisite feel of her beneath me, the sound of her desperate moans, the feeling of being buried deep inside her as she tightened around me—

I jolted awake, sheets twisted around me, heart hammering against my ribs. The dream clung to me like her phantom scent, so vivid I could almost taste her on my lips. My cock throbbed painfully, hard and ready for a woman who wasn't there.

The third time this week. The tenth time since she'd started working at *Zolotoy Vek*. Each dream more detailed, more consuming than the last. Three weeks of watching her from a distance, maintaining control that cost me more each day.

"*Blyad*," I growled, fist clenching in the sheets. Her face drifted into my mind again—those green eyes looking up at me from the hostess stand, the way she tucked her hair behind her ear when concentrating, the curve of her ass in that black dress she wore last Friday. The memory only intensified my ache. "Get out of my fucking head."

The clock on my nightstand read 5:43 AM. Dawn was breaking, pale light filtering through the heavy curtains. In seventeen minutes, the household staff would begin their routines. Irina would bring coffee to my study precisely at six, as she had done for the past eight years.

I swung my legs over the side of the bed, forcing the lingering dream away. Cold discipline had been my companion for too long to abandon it now, regardless of how her memory haunted me. A quick shower—ice cold—would clear my mind before Viktor arrived for our morning briefing.

* * *

The solarium welcomed me with the familiar scent of pine and earth. Snow dusted the glass dome overhead, filtering the morning light to a soft glow. Here, surrounded by the controlled wilderness of Russian nature, I could think more clearly. Each tree, each stone precisely placed, the temperature carefully regulated—just like every other aspect of my life. Or it had been, until her.

The door opened silently as Viktor entered, carrying a tray with the *samovar* and cups—our morning ritual for nearly twenty years. [Traditional Russian tea urn]

"*Yob tvoyu mat*, you look like *govno*," he observed bluntly, setting down the tray near the fur-draped chairs. [Fuck your mother] [Shit] "Dreams again, *da*?"

I shot him a warning glance, but didn't deny it. He knew me too well. "Business first."

Something like concern flashed across his face, but he nodded, pouring the strong tea as I took my seat. "Georgian route compromised again. Three workers identified—all with sudden deposits in offshore accounts."

"Dmitri's people?"

"*Da*. But documents they take—more concerning. Banking records, Swiss accounts. Names that could interest certain officials."

My fingers tightened around the delicate porcelain cup. "Timing feels deliberate."

"Is deliberate," Viktor confirmed, his expression grave. "They look for weakness. In business, in personal life."

I leaned forward, studying the steam rising from my cup. "Have Anatoly dig deeper. Not just the workers. Every connection between them and Dmitri's circle. Every meeting, every phone call."

Viktor nodded, his gaze assessing. "There is more. News about Liliya."

My heart rate accelerated imperceptibly. "What news?"

"She received threatening message. From ex-boyfriend." He pulled out his phone, checking something. "Message came from Russian number."

The implication was clear—someone in my territory had helped this man, given him means to reach her. My jaw tightened. "Tell me about this ex-boyfriend."

Viktor shifted, pulling a file from his briefcase. "Hospital visits she tried to hide. Police reports that disappeared. His family has money, connections in their town." He paused, watching my reaction carefully. "Night she ran? He threw glass at her head, tried to strangle her. She escaped while he passed out drunk."

Each word stoked something dark and deadly in my chest. Now I understood the signs I'd noticed—how she tracked exits, why she flinched at sudden movements. The scar near her temple I'd glimpsed under club lights.

"So the threatening message came from her ex?" I asked, my voice carefully neutral despite the rage building beneath the surface.

"*Da.*" Viktor hesitated, then added, "There's more. Yelena met with her last night. After Natasha told her about *Smotriny.*"

The delicate porcelain cup cracked in my grip, hot tea spilling across my fingers. I barely felt the burn. "What?"

"She's entering *Smotriny*," Viktor confirmed, watching my reaction closely. "Observation period begins this week."

"Who authorized this?" My voice had dropped to a dangerous growl. The thought of her being presented, evaluated, bid on by others—it sent a wave of possessive fury through me unlike anything I'd experienced.

"Yelena made the arrangements." Viktor's tone was carefully neutral. "And others are already circling. Petrov making inquiries. Dmitri's nephew suddenly interested. Even Volkov boy thinks he has chance."

"Alexei?" The name tasted like poison. "After how she handled him at the club?"

"Is not about her," Viktor said carefully. "Is about you. They see how you watch her these weeks. Think maybe they found crack in your armor."

The realization crystallized through my anger. "They're testing me. Using her to see how far they can go."

"*Da.*" Viktor's gaze was steady. "Liliya could be weapon they use against you. Or..."

"Or weapon I use against them." The thought burned through my rage with dangerous appeal. To claim her officially, within our traditions. To have legitimate reason to eliminate any threat to her, including her American ex. To make her mine.

"I've known you twenty years," Viktor said quietly. "Never seen you lose focus like this. Over a woman, over anything."

"She's different." The admission came through clenched teeth. "The way she handles the club, difficult clients. Learns fast, adapts fast. Not like others who enter *Smotriny* looking for wealthy husband."

"Is not just about how she handles club." Viktor's knowing look carried the weight of our friendship. "I see way you watch her. Like wolf who spots first prey after long winter." He paused, something almost amused in his expression. "How long since you took woman to bed, brother? Two years? Three?"

I didn't answer. The observation hit too close to truth. The way her dress clung to her curves as she moved through the club, how her auburn hair caught the light...

"Everything relevant when a *vor* loses focus," Viktor pressed. "Better to admit you want her than pretend otherwise. Desire like this?" He shook his head. "Is dangerous to ignore."

"Which makes her more valuable target," I countered, my tone hardening. "Other *vory* see taking her as way to challenge me. To take what they think I want."

"Have decision to make," Viktor said, watching steam rise from his cup. "Let her enter *Smotriny*, watch another *vor* claim her..." His eyes met mine knowingly. "Or admit what we both see."

I moved to stand by the water feature, watching ice crystallize at the edges. The controlled wilderness of my sanctuary suddenly felt too confined for the violence building in my blood. "Situation more complicated than simple want."

"Ah." Viktor's tone carried years of understanding. "Because of business problems? Or because she makes you feel things you cannot control?"

My silence was answer enough.

"Think about implications," he pressed. "Could solve many problems. Give legitimate reason to eliminate threats—business rivals, American ex, anyone who dares touch her. Show other families you're ready to build alliances." He stood, preparing to leave. "Just remember—whatever you decide about Liliya, about *Smotriny*, the entire underground watches. Must be careful."

As the door closed behind him, I remained in the solarium. Much as I hated to admit it, my old friend was right. Three years of perfect control, of focusing solely on business. Now Liliya had shattered that control with nothing more than a defiant glance and the quiet strength in her eyes.

The morning sun caught the fresh snow on the branches, creating patterns of light and shadow. Like her—delicate beauty concealing unexpected strength. Perhaps that's what drew me most—not just her competence at the club, but that combination of vulnerability and fire.

The decision crystallized in my mind. I would not watch another man claim what was already mine in all but name. I would not let *Smotriny* become her fate—at least, not on any terms but my own.

10

Liliya

"Keep still or I stab you in eye," Natasha muttered, wielding the eyeliner pencil like a weapon. "Tonight is not night for shaky hands."

I tried not to fidget as she applied the finishing touches to my makeup. After two weeks of preparation, of Yelena's lessons and Natasha's coaching, tonight was finally here. *Smotriny.*

"You look perfect," Natasha declared, stepping back to survey her work. "Like dangerous angel. Men will not know what hit them."

The burgundy velvet gown hugged my curves before falling in a graceful sweep to the floor. The color reminded me of rich wine, of blood. Of power. During my weeks at the club, I'd learned how to wear such things, how to move in them like I belonged in this world of luxury and danger.

"You still sure about this?" Natasha asked, her usual playful tone replaced by genuine concern. "Not too late to change mind."

For a moment, I was tempted. But then Jack's message from last week flooded back, the words burning into my mind: "Did you really think you could hide from me forever, Lily-Pad?"

My fingers traced the nearly-healed scar near my temple, remembering how the glass had bit into my skin that final night. The cold tile against my back as I cowered in the kitchen corner, the sharp crack of the whiskey glass shattering next to my head. His voice echoing: "You belong to me. You're nothing without me."

But I wasn't that frightened girl anymore. A month at *Zolotoy Vek* had changed me in ways I was only beginning to understand.

"I'm ready," I said, straightening my shoulders. The Russian words came naturally now. "*Da.* I'm ready to become myself again. Maybe someone even stronger."

Natasha held up a luxurious fur coat, white as the snow outside. "Here. Genuine sable. Borrowed from friend for tonight."

As we stepped out into the swirling snow, the icy air bit at my cheeks, a sharp contrast to the warmth of the fur. The city glittered around us, a winter wonderland that held both promise and peril.

The sleek black car wound through snow-covered streets, each turn taking us further from the familiar territory of *Zolotoy Vek* into the elite outskirts of the city.

"Remember first night at club?" Natasha asked, clearly trying to distract me from my nerves. "When you think hostess stand was going to eat you alive?"

Despite my anxiety, I laughed. "You mean when I spilled that entire tray of champagne on the Georgian businessman?"

"*Net, net.* Mean when you think proper Russian greeting too difficult. Now look—you speaking Russian, walking in killer heels, making oligarchs drop jaws." She nudged me playfully. "Maybe after tonight, will have powerful husband too, *da?*"

"Natasha!" But her teasing had its intended effect, breaking some of the tension.

"What? Is true. Have seen how certain men watch you at club." Her tone turned suggestive. "Some very powerful men who might be at *Smotriny* tonight..."

I felt heat rise to my cheeks, remembering that burning gaze I'd felt so often lately. "I thought you said this wasn't about romance."

"Is not," she agreed, suddenly serious. "Is about survival. But..." her grin turned wicked again, "if survival come with handsome, powerful man who look at you like wants to devour you? Why not enjoy?"

"So these men..." I hesitated, fiddling with my clutch. "What are they really like?"

"Ah!" Natasha's eyes lit up with wicked delight. "Finally you ask right questions! Trust me, nothing like Jack who think he big man. These men?" She fanned herself dramatically. "Know how to handle woman properly."

"Handle?" The word caught in my throat, memories of Jack's rough grabbing making me tense.

"*Net, net.* Not like that." Natasha's face softened with understanding. "Is about power, but different kind. Take Viktor, for example. Six months I try everything to seduce this man. Nothing work, but..." She bit her lip, eyes gleaming. "Way he move, way he command room without word—can only imagine what he like in bed."

"You and Viktor never...?"

"Pfft. Man is like statue. Beautiful, perfect statue that make me want climb him like tree." She sighed dramatically. "But is how all these powerful men are. So controlled, so proper. Until they not proper anymore." She leaned closer, voice dropping. "Can see it in their eyes sometimes. How they want make woman lose control."

The way she emphasized those words made something low in my belly tighten. After Jack, I'd thought I never wanted a man's hands on me again. But the way Natasha described it...

The car turned onto a long, tree-lined drive, and I caught my first glimpse of the mansion through the swirling snow. My heart began to race.

"Remember," Natasha said as the car slowed, her tone turning serious. "Tonight not about being safe. Is about catching right kind of attention. Right kind of power." She squeezed my hand. "Trust instincts. They serve you well at club, *da*?"

The mansion loomed before us, its windows blazing with light. Music drifted out into the night—not the pulsing beats of *Zolotoy Vek*, but something softer, more classical. A different world entirely.

"What if..." I swallowed hard, voicing my deepest fear. "What if none of them want me? Or worse, what if the wrong one does?"

"*Net*," Natasha's voice was fierce. "You not same girl who come to Russia month ago. Way you handle club, handle difficult men—they see this." She smiled slightly. "Besides, someone already watch you like starving wolf. Maybe tonight you finally see who."

As we approached the entrance, I noticed other women arriving—all beautiful, all looking far more composed than I felt. Some were accompanied by older women who I assumed were their mothers or aunts. Others arrived alone, their chins held high with a confidence I envied.

"Invitations, please," a stern-looking man at the door requested. Natasha handed over two ornate cards I hadn't even realized she was carrying. His eyes lingered on me a moment too long—assessing, calculating.

"Welcome to *Smotriny*," he said. "Natasha Alexandrovna, you know way. Liliya…" he paused, then added more formally, "Liliya Mikhailovna." He gestured to a young woman in an elegant black uniform. "Attendant will explain process."

I felt panic flutter in my chest at the thought of separation from Natasha. For the first time since arriving in Russia, I'd have to face this world completely alone.

She must have sensed my fear because she leaned in close. "Listen to me, *devochka*. You ready for this. Better than ready." Her eyes held mine intently. "No matter what happen in there, you not alone. I be watching. And when is done…" Her grin turned mischievous. "We drink expensive champagne and you tell me everything."

Just before the attendant reached us, Natasha gave my ass a playful smack. "Now go show these men what you made of, *da*?"

The unexpected gesture startled a laugh from me, easing some of the tension in my shoulders. Trust Natasha to know exactly how to break through my nerves.

The attendant led me down a long hallway lined with ornate mirrors and gilt-framed paintings. At a small antique desk, she paused, retrieving a heavy cream envelope sealed with dark red wax.

"Your presentation number," she said quietly, her accent thick but precise. "You will be called when is time."

Inside was a single golden card bearing the number seven. The weight of it felt significant in my palm, the embossed number catching the light.

Something about it made my skin prickle—hadn't Natasha mentioned seven being lucky in Russian tradition?

The preparation room hummed with nervous energy, filled with mirrors and elegant vanities. Women in various states of readiness turned to look as I entered, their gazes assessing, calculating.

"You must be Liliya," a voice said. I turned to see a statuesque blonde approaching, her smile warm but her eyes sharp. "I'm Anya. First presentation?"

I nodded, finding my voice. "Is it that obvious?"

She laughed, the sound reminding me of crystal champagne flutes clinking at the club. "Only to those who watch carefully. Come, let me help you prepare. Better we stay together, *da*? Night like this, alliances matter."

As she led me to an empty vanity, I couldn't shake the feeling that every movement was being evaluated. Just like at the club, when I'd feel those burning eyes following me.

I heard Mikhail Rostov is here tonight," another girl nearby whispered, adjusting her diamond earrings. "His family owns half the luxury hotels in city."

"And that new one, Dmitri's nephew," someone else added. "They say he just return from London. Very handsome."

"Hush," Anya cut them off sharply. "Tonight not time for gossip. Need focus on presentation."

A chime sounded through the room. A hush fell over the women as an elegantly dressed older woman entered, her presence commanding immediate attention.

"*Damy*," she announced, her English crisp but her Russian accent unmistakable. [Ladies] "Time has come. I am *Barynya* Petrova. Tonight, you enter world few are privileged to know." [Madam/Mistress]

We clustered around her, a flutter of silk and nervous energy. I found myself between Anya and a petite redhead who looked even more terrified than I felt.

"For those new to *Smotriny*, process is simple but stakes..." *Barynya* Petrova's eyes swept the room, sharp and calculating. "...are highest you ever face."

She held up an ornate card. "Each has number. When called, you enter ballroom for presentation. Men will observe, evaluate. If multiple show interest..." her lips curved slightly, "private bidding begins."

"Remember," she continued, "while you present yourself, final choice belongs to them. These men command empires. They seek wives worthy of such power. Any who fail to maintain proper discretion will face... consequences."

The way she said "consequences" made my skin crawl, remembering similar warnings from Yelena about the club's secrets.

"Number Four," *Barynya* Petrova called.

The statuesque brunette who'd been fidgeting with her pearls rose, chin high. Through the doors, I caught strains of her introduction - "from one of Moscow's oldest families..." before they closed again.

"Number Five."

The redhead beside me stood on shaky legs. Anya squeezed her hand. "Remember, chin up, shoulders back."

The next ten minutes felt endless. Women whispered about glimpses they'd caught through the doors—how many men were assembled, which powerful families were represented.

"Number Six."

A willowy blonde stood, smoothing her midnight blue gown. She looked confident, but I noticed her hands trembling as she gripped her skirts.

More waiting. More whispers. Someone mentioned seeing Dmitri's nephew looking particularly interested. Another swore she'd caught sight of the city's most eligible *vor*, though no one had seen him at such an event in years.

My palms grew damper with each passing minute. I wiped them discreetly on my dress, remembering how I'd learned to handle my nerves at the club. One breath in, one breath out. Just like Yelena had taught me.

The chime sounded again, crystal clear and final.

"Number Seven," *Barynya* Petrova announced, her voice silencing all conversation.

Seven. My number. My heart leapt into my throat as every head turned in my direction.

"Good luck," Anya whispered as I rose on legs that felt suddenly unsteady.

Time seemed to slow as I crossed to the door, every lesson from the past weeks running through my mind. Chin up. Shoulders back. The walk we'd practiced for hours until my feet bled. The posture that conveyed confidence I didn't entirely feel.

As my hand touched the ornate door handle, I felt a strange sense of calm wash over me. Whatever waited on the other side would determine my future. There would be no going back after this moment—no return to the frightened girl who'd stepped off the plane a month ago.

I took one final breath, steadying myself. Then I pushed open the doors and stepped into whatever fate awaited me.

11

Zaven

"Number Seven," the announcement echoed through the private viewing box.

Seven. Of course she would be seven. Even fate seemed determined to test my control tonight.

I remained in the shadows of the balcony overlooking the presentation floor, Viktor's solid presence to my right, while Natasha fidgeted impatiently to my left. The viewing box—designed for those who preferred to observe without being observed—offered a perfect vantage point. From here, I could see everything without revealing my interest to the other bidders below.

"Stop with tapping foot," Viktor muttered to Natasha. "Is distracting."

"Cannot help," she whispered back, though she did still her movements. "Is nervous for friend."

I said nothing, all my attention fixed on the doors as they slowly opened. And then—there she was.

Liliya.

The sight of her stole the breath from my lungs. The woman who had haunted my dreams for weeks now stood before me in reality, even more beautiful than in my imagination. The deep burgundy of her dress caught the light like spilled wine, making her skin glow with warmth against the rich color. Her auburn hair was swept up, exposing the elegant curve of her neck in a way that made my fingers itch to trace it.

"

But it was her posture that struck me most—the straight spine, lifted chin, steady gaze. So different from the woman who had first arrived at *Zolotoy Vek*. She carried herself with a quiet confidence now, a strength that hadn't been there before. The frightened girl was gone. In her place stood a woman who knew her own worth. Some women are born into power; others are forged by fire until they become unbreakable. I recognized the heat that had tempered her—it was the same flame that had hardened me.

"*Bozhe moy*," Natasha whispered beside me, her voice filled with pride. "Look how she hold herself. Like queen already."

Viktor shifted slightly. "*Da*. She has learned well. Your teaching, Natasha?"

"Some," Natasha admitted, her voice unusually soft. "But is mostly her. Was always there, beneath fear."

I remained silent, watching as Liliya moved gracefully to the center of the floor. From our elevated position, I could see what she could not—the hungry eyes of at least a dozen men following her every move. Dmitri's nephew, Maxim, leaned forward in his seat, naked interest on his face. Across the room, Petrov's gaze tracked her with calculating intensity. Even the Volkov boy, Alexei, watched with undisguised appreciation despite their previous encounter.

My jaw clenched at their attention. None of them were worthy of her. None of them could protect her as I could. They saw an object to possess; I saw a fortress worth defending. These men were accustomed to breaking beautiful things—I wanted to watch her become invincible.

"You crush armrest, boss," Viktor noted quietly. I released my white-knuckled grip on the carved wood, not having realized how tightly I'd been holding it.

Below, *Barynya* Petrova began her introduction. "*Devushka* Sinclair comes to us from America. She is twenty-four, educated, and as you can see, quite lovely. She speaks English fluently and is rapidly mastering Russian." [Young woman/girl]

I barely heard the woman's practiced speech. My focus remained on Liliya's face, watching for any sign of fear or hesitation. Instead, I saw only determination, a quiet strength that made something in my chest tighten.

"Interesting way she study room," Viktor observed clinically. "Eyes always finding exits, security. Good instincts."

"Is from working at club," Natasha said, pride evident in her voice. "Learn fast, my Liliya."

I shot her a sharp look at the possessive "my," which she met with raised eyebrows and a knowing smirk.

"What?" she whispered, unintimidated. "Is my friend, not my—"

Viktor cut her off with a subtle hand motion as Rostov stood to ask the first question.

"*Devushka* Sinclair, what brings American girl to our little... gathering?"

I leaned forward slightly, waiting for her answer. This was the moment that would reveal whether she truly understood what she was entering—whether she was here merely for protection or if she comprehended the deeper complexities of our world.

Her voice, when she spoke, was steady and clear. "I came to Russia seeking new opportunities. I believe that here, I can build a life of substance and meaning."

A diplomatic answer. Carefully worded. But there was sincerity in her tone that caught my attention—and apparently others' as well, based on the approving murmurs below.

Beside me, Natasha shifted again, this time closer to Viktor. I noticed how he stiffened almost imperceptibly at her proximity, though his face remained impassive.

"She do well, yes?" she whispered to him, her shoulder brushing his.

"*Da*," he answered, his tone professional though his body remained rigid. "Very composed."

Then Sokolov spoke up, his voice dripping with condescension. "Pretty words. But can American girl truly understand our world? Our ways?"

I felt a surge of irritation at his tone—the same tone he'd used when questioning my decision to expand the Georgian route. Always doubting, always undermining.

But before I could dwell on my dislike for the man, Liliya's response captured my attention.

"Understanding comes from experience," she said, meeting Sokolov's gaze directly. "I've already begun to learn, to adapt. My fresh perspective could be an asset, not a liability."

The confidence in her voice, the subtle challenge in her words—it sent a surge of heat through my veins. She was not cowed by him. Not intimidated by any of them. In our world, strength without brutality is the rarest currency—and watching her spend it so effortlessly made me want to give her my empire just to see what she would build with it.

"She has fire, this one," Viktor commented quietly.

"Always did," Natasha replied, her eyes never leaving her friend. "Just needed right kindling."

I found myself speaking before I could stop the words. "And what qualities do you bring to such an... arrangement?"

Viktor shot me a surprised look. We had agreed I would remain silent, observing only. But something had compelled me to hear her answer to this particular question.

Below, Liliya paused, considering her response carefully. I could almost see her mind working, weighing her words.

"Loyalty," she said firmly. "Discretion. And resilience that I believe would serve well in any situation."

For a heartbeat, it felt as though she were speaking directly to me, though I knew she couldn't see me in the darkened viewing box. Those three qualities—exactly what I valued most. What I needed in the dangerous game I played.

When the hands began to rise around the room—far more than for any previous presentation—something dark and possessive coiled in my chest. My own hand remained at my side, though every instinct demanded I claim her immediately. Power means taking what you want; true power is restraining yourself when you want it most. For the first time in years, the *vor* and the man within me wanted the same thing—and that made her the most dangerous woman in the room.

"You not raise hand?" Natasha whispered, sounding genuinely confused.

Viktor answered before I could. "*Vor* does not bid with others," he explained quietly. "Would be... undignified."

Natasha looked between us, comprehension dawning in her eyes. "Ah," she said, a slow smile spreading across her face. "So, different approach then?" Her gaze slid to me, far too knowing for comfort.

I ignored her, watching as Liliya was led from the room. Even in departure, she maintained that quiet dignity, that strength that had first caught my attention at the club. The door closed behind her, and immediately the room below erupted in conversation—men discussing bids, forming alliances, strategizing.

"Good show down there," Viktor commented dryly. "Like wolves fighting over prime meat."

"She is not meat," Natasha snapped, surprising both of us with her vehemence. Then, seeming to remember whom she was addressing, she added more softly, "Sorry. Is just... important to me she end up with right person. Person who see her value beyond pretty face."

Her eyes met mine directly, a challenge in them that few would dare direct at me. "Person who protect her but not cage her. Who understand difference."

"Bold talk from someone who brought her to *Smotriny* in first place," Viktor observed, his tone unreadable.

Natasha turned to him, chin lifted defiantly. "Was her choice. I present option, she decide." She stepped closer to him, crowding his personal space in a way that would have earned anyone else a swift removal. "You think I not care what happen to her? That I throw friend to wolves without thought?"

Something flickered in Viktor's usually impassive expression—surprise, perhaps, at her passion. Or something else entirely.

"Did not say that," he replied, his voice softer than I'd heard it in years. "Only that choice has consequences. For everyone."

The energy between them shifted, charged with something I had no interest in examining. My thoughts remained with Liliya, with the decision I now faced.

I moved toward the door. "Enough," I said quietly. "Bid must be placed."

Natasha turned to me, hope and wariness warring in her expression. "You have decided then?"

Had I? The image of Liliya standing proud despite her fear, refusing to be intimidated by Sokolov's condescension, filled my mind. The dream that had woken me this morning flashed through my thoughts—her beneath me, whispering my name like a prayer. But dreams fade with morning light; her courage had blazed in broad daylight. I had built an empire on calculating risks, on knowing exactly what each decision would cost. Yet for her, I was willing to pay a price I couldn't yet name.

"*Da*," I said finally. "I have decided."

Viktor and Natasha exchanged a look I couldn't quite interpret before following me from the viewing box. The decision was made. Now came the more complex part—ensuring that Liliya Sinclair became mine, while keeping her safe from the very dangers that surrounded me.

Including, perhaps, myself.

12

Liliya

The side door closed behind me with a soft click, muffling the buzz of voices from the ballroom. I set my water glass down on a nearby table, my hands still trembling from the presentation. The cool wall against my back contrasted sharply with my flushed skin as I tried to steady my breathing.

"Well done, *Devushka* Sinclair," *Barynya* Petrova's crisp voice cut through my daze. "You have garnered quite bit of interest. Now comes real test."

I straightened, smoothing down my dress. "What happens now?"

"Now, my dear, you meet potential matches. One at a time, of course." She gestured for me to follow her down a long hallway. "You have fifteen minutes with each to... get acquainted."

The word "acquainted" hung in the air, loaded with implications. I swallowed hard, remembering Yelena's warnings about these men's expectations.

"This will be your meeting room for the evening," *Barynya* Petrova gestured to an ornate door at the end of the hallway. "For your safety and... comfort, observers will be present during each meeting."

A stern-faced woman in an impeccable black suit approached, accompanied by a broad-shouldered man whose very presence commanded respect.

"*Gospozha* Ivanova will be your chaperone," *Barynya* Petrova introduced. [Madam/Mrs.] "And *Gospodin* Fedorov handles security. If at any point you feel uncomfortable, simply say 'pause' and the meeting will end immediately." [Mister/Sir]

The room beyond the door took my breath away - plush velvet couches in deep crimson, a roaring fireplace that cast dancing shadows on wood-paneled walls, floor-to-ceiling windows offering a view of snow-covered gardens. The air held notes of leather and wood smoke, wealth and power wrapped in warmth.

Gospozha Ivanova took her position in a corner, discrete but watchful, while *Gospodin* Fedorov stationed himself by the door. I had barely settled onto one of the couches when the first knock came.

As he entered, the temperature in the room seemed to drop several degrees. His cologne - dark and distinctly Russian - reached me before he did. He was older than I'd expected, perhaps mid-forties, with silver threading through his dark hair at the temples. Sharp cheekbones and a strong jaw gave his face an aristocratic severity, while pale blue eyes held the kind of coldness that came from years of wielding power. A thin scar traced his left eyebrow, the only imperfection in his otherwise striking features.

"*Devushka* Liliya Mikhailovna," he said, his voice a rich baritone that filled the room. "A pleasure to meet you properly. I am Grigory Vedenin."

He moved like a predator wearing civilized skin, each gesture precise and deliberate. When he sat, it was with the casual confidence of a man who knew his own power. His pale eyes studied me with an intensity that made the air between us crackle – he was evaluating me as much as I was studying him.

"Tell me, *Devushka* Liliya Mikhailovna," he said, his eyes never leaving mine, "why American girl run to Russia seeking protection of rich men?"

I was acutely aware of *Devushka* Ivanova in the corner, of *Gospodin* Fedorov by the door. This was a test, deliberately provocative. The crystal decanter between us caught the firelight, casting amber shadows across the rich wood table. Neither of us moved to pour.

"You assume I'm seeking protection," I said, meeting his piercing gaze. Something in me bristled at his tone, at the challenge in his words.

His laugh was short and sharp, like ice cracking. "No? Then perhaps money? Status?" He leaned forward slightly, his presence seeming to grow larger. "Many beautiful young women come to *Smotriny* thinking they play game. That they can take what they want and give nothing."

The way he watched me was predatory, waiting for me to flinch. This wasn't just an interview - it was a challenge.

"If I wanted money, *Gospodin* Vedenin," I said, my voice low but firm, "there are easier ways to get it than entering your world. And if I wanted status..." I let my gaze drift meaningfully to his scar, "I wouldn't choose a world where status comes with such obvious risks."

His eyes narrowed slightly, but I caught the glimmer of interest there. The firelight caught the silver at his temples as he studied me, and I forced myself to hold his gaze.

"Interesting," he finally said, reaching for the decanter. The liquid caught the light as he poured two measures. "Most women try to charm. You show teeth." He pushed one glass toward me. "Makes me wonder what made little American girl so... fierce."

The question hung between us. I took the glass but didn't drink, remembering Natasha's warnings about accepting drinks from powerful men. He noticed, of course. A slight smile curved his lips.

"Cautious too. Good." He lifted his own glass. "But caution can become fear. Fear can become weakness. In our world, weakness..." He let the words trail off meaningfully.

I studied him as carefully as he studied me. His power was different from Jack's - calculated, controlled. In some ways, that made it more frightening. But there was something almost like respect in the way he waited for my response.

"The difference between caution and fear," I began, but a chime sounded through the room, signaling the end of our time.

He stood with that same deliberate grace, taking my hand and brushing his lips across my knuckles. His ring was cold against my skin. "Until we meet again, *Devushka* Liliya Mikhailovna," he said, something like approval glinting in his pale eyes.

As the door closed behind him, I released a breath I hadn't realized I'd been holding. My hands trembled slightly as I set down the untouched glass, the amber liquid catching the firelight. One down. But something told me the next ones wouldn't be nearly as… civilized.

I caught my reflection in the window – cheeks flushed, eyes bright with adrenaline. Vedenin had been testing me, looking for cracks in my armor. They all would. These weren't men who wanted decorative wives or silent partners. They wanted women who could hold their own in this dangerous world of theirs.

The thought steadied me. I'd spent too long being afraid, letting Jack make me small. But the woman who'd stood her ground against Vedenin's probing questions? That was who I really was. Who I could be again.

"Next suitor comes shortly," *Devushka* Ivanova said quietly. "Remember - 'pause' if needed."

I straightened my spine, smoothed my dress. No pauses. No weakness. I might be nervous, might be stepping into a world I barely understood, but I wouldn't let them see that. Not anymore.

The door opened again, and I steeled myself. The man who entered made my blood run cold. Younger than Vedenin, perhaps in his late thirties, he carried himself with the same entitled arrogance I'd seen in Jack. His dark hair was styled perfectly, features aristocratic but cruel – high cheekbones, knife-blade nose, and a mouth that smiled without warmth. But it was his eyes that sent ice through my veins: pale green, almost colorless, with that same hungry gleam Jack's had held before he'd strike.

He moved with a predatory grace that set every instinct screaming. Even his cologne triggered something primal in my brain – that specific mix of expensive fragrance and underlying threat that I'd learned to fear.

"Ah, American flower," he practically purred, his voice smooth as silk but with an undercurrent that made my skin crawl. "I am Ivan Kavelin. What pleasure to meet you at last."

I fought to keep my expression neutral, to stop my hands from shaking. This was different, I reminded myself. I wasn't that scared girl anymore. But something in the way he looked at me – like a cat watching a wounded bird – threatened to crack the careful mask I'd constructed.

He took my hand without waiting, his grip too tight, too possessive.

Instead of customary kiss on knuckles, he turned my hand over, pressing his lips to my inner wrist while his eyes locked onto mine. The gesture was intimate, invasive. His cologne was too strong, too sweet - nothing like Vedenin's old-world sophistication.

"So, *Devushka* Sinclair," Kavelin began, settling into his seat but leaning forward, encroaching on my space. "Tell me, how... flexible you are? In aspirations, of course."

The way he said 'flexible' left little doubt he wasn't talking about career goals. His eyes roved over me in a way that made me feel naked despite my gown. I forced myself to meet his gaze coolly, channeling ice rather than the fear trying to crawl up my throat.

"I'm adaptable, *Gospodin* Kavelin. But I also have clear boundaries."

He chuckled, sound devoid of any warmth. "Boundaries? Oh, *devochka*. In our world, boundaries are merely... suggestions."

His eyes narrowed as he leaned even closer. "Question is, *devochka*, how badly you want to succeed here?"

I felt a chill run down my spine. The implication in his words was clear. From the corner of my eye, I saw *Devushka* Ivanova shift slightly, her hand moving to her ear - likely a concealed communication device.

"I am willing to work hard and be loyal," I said carefully, my heart pounding. "But not here to compromise myself."

His eyes flashed dangerously. "Compromise?" He leaned in closer, voice dropping to near-whisper. "Let me be clear with you. In this world, you either player or pawn. And pawns..." He reached out, twirling a strand of my hair around his finger. "Pawns get sacrificed."

I jerked back, my breath catching. For a moment, I was back in that apartment with Jack, the threat of violence hanging in the air. But then I remembered where I was, who I was now.

"Remove your hand," I said, my voice low but firm. "Now."

A muscle ticked in his jaw, his facade of charm cracking to reveal something ugly beneath. He leaned even closer, breath hot against my cheek. "Careful, little flower. You not want make enemies here. I could be powerful friend... or dangerous enemy. Choice is yours."

Something snapped inside me. Maybe it was his arrogance, or how he reminded me of Jack, but a calm clarity washed over me. I let my gaze drift over him slowly, then simply said, "How... disappointing."

His face contorted with rage, hand shooting out to grab my arm. "*Suka*," he snarled, the Russian curse dripping with venom. [Bitch]

The chime sounded sharply, and suddenly *Gospodin* Fedorov was there, his presence looming. "Time is up, *Gospodin* Kavelin."

After he was practically escorted out, I slumped slightly in my chair, my heart thundering in my chest. My hands were shaking, but not from fear – from adrenaline, from power. For the first time in years, I'd looked into the eyes of a man like Jack and hadn't cowered. Hadn't apologized. Hadn't made myself small.

The realization hit me like a shot of vodka – burning, dangerous, exhilarating. I'd stood my ground against someone who thought he could intimidate me, and I hadn't just survived – I'd won. The girl who'd fled America would never have dared. But here, in this strange new world, I was becoming someone stronger.

"Not many stand up to Kavelin this way," *Gospozha* Ivanova said, something like approval warming her usually stern voice. "Most women, they fear his connections too much. But you..." Her lips twitched slightly before she drew her professional mask back on. "Next suitor arrive soon. You ready?"

I straightened in my chair, smoothing my dress with steady hands. That flash of boldness had awakened something in me – a taste of who I could be when I wasn't afraid. And I wanted more.

The next three came and went - a blur of expensive suits and practiced charm. None left much impression beyond their obvious wealth and power. But the next one... he was different.

The door opened again, and I found myself facing someone unlike the previous suitors. He was younger, perhaps early thirties, with a lean build and sharp, intelligent eyes behind sleek glasses. His suit was impeccably tailored but more modern than the others, and he carried himself with a quiet confidence that didn't demand attention - it commanded it naturally.

"*Devushka* Sinclair," he said, his voice carrying hint of British accent. "Mikhail Rostov. Pleasure to meet you properly."

He extended his hand for a handshake - the gesture so normal it felt almost shocking after the formal kissing of hands. His grip was firm but not dominating, professional yet personal.

As we sat, his eyes flickered briefly to *Gospozha* Ivanova and *Gospodin* Petrov before settling back on me. "Imagine this whole process must be quite... overwhelming," he said, voice carrying note of dry amusement. "Especially for someone who come to Russia seeking fresh start."

I felt my breath catch. The casualness with which he mentioned my circumstances sent a chill down my spine, but his tone held no threat - only analytical interest.

"You seem very informed, *Gospodin* Rostov," I said carefully, watching his reaction.

His lips curved slightly. "Information is currency in our world, *Devushka* Sinclair. More valuable than money, more dangerous than weapons." He leaned forward slightly, his manner almost conspiratorial. "For example, I know American man who hunt you has connections. Money. But what he not have..." his eyes gleamed with intelligence, "is understanding of true power."

My heart raced, but not entirely from fear. There was something compelling about his directness, his obvious knowledge. "And you understand true power?"

"I understand many things." He sat back, completely at ease. "Know how information flow through city like blood through veins. Know which whispers to hear, which to ignore." His eyes met mine. "Know that someone with your... unique perspective could be valuable asset."

The way he said it - not like Kavelin's threats or Vedenin's patriarchal assessment - made me lean forward despite myself. "Asset?"

"Think about it. American woman who learns our ways but keeps Western understanding? Who sees both worlds clearly?" He smiled. "Could be powerful combination."

Something in the way he watched me shifted, became more calculating.

"I see it in your eyes," he said, studying me with that sharp gaze. "You not just seeking protection. You seeking understanding. Purpose." He reached into his jacket, movements precise and measured. "Perhaps we could help each other."

He placed a sleek business card on the table between us. Unlike the gaudy gold-embossed cards I'd seen at the club, this one was simple black with silver text.

"I offer different kind of arrangement than others here tonight." His voice dropped lower. "Not just marriage, but partnership. Chance to be player in game, not just prize."

The offer was tempting - dangerously so. "And what exactly would this... partnership involve?"

"Information. Access to both worlds. Your American contacts, combined with protection of Russian power." His eyes never left mine. "Think about it. Man you run from? Would become insignificant detail in much larger picture."

The chime sounded, but he seemed unhurried as he stood. "Take card. Think about what I say. About difference between being protected..." he paused at the door, "and being powerful."

As the door closed behind Rostov, I found myself staring at the business card, my mind whirling. Power instead of just protection. A chance to be more than just someone's wife, someone's prize. His words stirred something in me - a hunger I hadn't realized I had.

I was so lost in thought, turning the card over in my hands, that I didn't hear the next knock. Didn't notice how *Gospozha* Ivanova straightened sharply, how the very air in the room seemed to change. It wasn't until I felt it - that familiar electric awareness that made my skin tingle - that I looked up.

The man in the doorway made every other suitor fade to shadows in my memory. He commanded the space without effort, his presence filling the room like smoke - dangerous and intoxicating. Tall, with the build of someone who balanced power with precision, every movement deliberate, almost predatory. His suit, a deep charcoal gray, fit him like a second skin, the fabric rippling with each step to hint at the strength beneath.

But it was his face that stole my breath – strong features carved from granite, a jaw that could cut glass, shadowed by a day's worth of stubble. And his eyes... dark, fathomless, they held secrets and power in equal measure. When they locked onto mine, I felt stripped bare, exposed to my very soul.

That electric tension I'd felt so often at the club suddenly made perfect sense. This was the source of that burning gaze that had haunted my nights.

"*Devushka* Sinclair," he said, his voice a low rumble that seemed to reverberate through my chest. "I am Zaven Lazarev. Time we meet properly, *da?*"

13

Liliya

I felt a jolt of shock, followed immediately by a flash of indignation that heated my cheeks. Zaven Lazarev - the enigmatic owner of *Zolotoy Vek*, my elusive boss who hadn't bothered to speak a single word to me in three weeks - was standing here at *Smotriny*. As a suitor. For me.

"*Gospodin* Lazarev," I managed, my jaw tightening as I fought to keep my voice steady. "Three weeks at your club, and you choose now to introduce yourself?"

A hint of surprise flickered across his face before his expression settled into something more guarded. "World is full of surprises, *Devushka* Sinclair," he said, a dangerous amusement darkening his eyes. "Especially this world."

He reached for my offered hand, and I nearly pulled it back. But his touch was warm and surprisingly gentle, sending an unwanted heat racing up my arm that contradicted my irritation. When he released it, I immediately crossed my arms.

"So the mysterious club owner finally emerges from the shadows," I said, unable to keep the edge from my voice as we sat down. "Were you just waiting for the perfect moment to bid on me like the others?"

I noticed *Gospozha* Ivanova shift uncomfortably in her corner. The air in the room felt too thick suddenly, like the pressure before a storm.

"Hope you not find process too... taxing," he said, his intense gaze never leaving my face, completely ignoring my barb. The low timbre of his voice with that accent made something flutter in my stomach, which only fueled my annoyance.

"It's certainly been... enlightening," I replied coolly, though my skin prickled under his scrutiny. "Though I admit, your presence here is beyond surprising. It's rather presumptuous."

"Is it?" His lips curved slightly, not in a smile but something more contemplative. "Tell me, *Devushka* Sinclair, what you really know about me?"

I leaned forward, anger giving me boldness. "I know you've been watching me for weeks without a single word. I know every time I felt those eyes on me at the club, it was you. I know you could have spoken to me any time, yet you chose this setting." I gestured around us. "Where I'm essentially being auctioned off."

Something sharp flashed in his eyes—not anger, but recognition. "You are... displeased."

"Displeased?" I let out a short, humorless laugh. "You think that's what this is? For weeks I've felt someone watching me, making my skin crawl one moment and burn the next. And now I find out it's my boss, who appears as a suitor before ever having a normal conversation with me."

He studied me for a long moment, his expression unreadable. "Fair criticism," he finally admitted, surprising me. "Perhaps approach was... less than ideal."

The simple acknowledgment deflated some of my anger, leaving confusion in its wake. I'd expected defensiveness, maybe even anger at being challenged—not this calm acceptance.

"Tell me," his voice dropped lower, "what you hope to gain from *Smotriny*? Beyond obvious, of course."

"Safety," I said before I could stop myself, the truth spilling out despite my irritation. "And a chance at a new life where I'm not looking over my shoulder."

Something flickered in his eyes – understanding perhaps, mixed with something possessive that made my breath catch despite myself. It was gone quickly, but it left me feeling exposed in a way that was both unsettling and oddly thrilling.

"Both admirable goals," he said, voice sliding over my skin like warm honey, making it harder to hold onto my anger. "Though perhaps better ways to handle... certain problems. Like American ex-boyfriend who thinks he can threaten what belongs in my city."

The shift in his tone was subtle but unmistakable, like the first crack of ice on a frozen lake. My heart stuttered.

"You know about that?" I asked, my anger momentarily forgotten.

"Know many things, *Devushka* Sinclair. Know he hurt you." His jaw clenched briefly, a controlled violence in the gesture that was nothing like Jack's explosive rage. "Know he still tries to control you. Know he not understand real meaning of power."

There was something in his controlled anger—so different from the violence I'd known—that sent a confusing mix of relief and wariness through me. Before I could analyze it, a bitter laugh escaped me.

"Real power being what—buying women at marriage marts?" I regretted the words immediately, expecting cold fury.

Instead, he laughed—a rich, genuine sound that vibrated through me like a physical touch, settling low in my belly.

"Ah, there she is," his eyes gleamed with what looked like genuine appreciation. "Fiery American girl who stand up to drunk oligarchs at my club. Was wondering when I see her again."

I felt my cheeks flush with something other than anger, even as confusion swirled inside me. I'd just insulted him, yet he looked... pleased?

"You saw that?"

"See everything in my club, *Devushka* Sinclair. Especially things that... interest me." The way he said "interest" made my mouth go dry.

"That doesn't answer my question," I pressed, finding strength in challenge. "About buying women."

His expression darkened, but not with anger. The look he gave me made heat bloom across my skin despite my lingering resentment.

"You think that what this is? That what I do?" He leaned closer, his presence overwhelming my senses. "Tell me, when you feel my eyes on you at club, did you feel bought, Liliya?"

The way he said my name, dropping the formality, sent conflicting waves of irritation and attraction coursing through me. And he was right—those moments when I'd felt his gaze had made me feel many things: seen, wanted, protected, nervous, sometimes even afraid. But never owned.

"No," I admitted reluctantly. "It felt... different."

"Different how?" His voice had dropped lower, and the space between us seemed to pull like gravity.

I should have felt intimidated, should have been worried about being alone with such a powerful man. Instead, I felt caught in a dizzying whirlpool of contradictory emotions—anger at his presumption, attraction to his confidence, wariness of his power, and something deeper I wasn't ready to name.

"You know exactly how," I challenged, meeting his intense gaze, refusing to give him the satisfaction. "You've been watching me long enough. The question is why wait until now to actually speak to me?"

His lips curved into a dangerous smile. "*Da.* Have watched you grow stronger each night. Watched you learn our world." His eyes trailed over me deliberately. "Watched you become... fascinating."

"Fascinating?" I raised an eyebrow, ignoring the way my pulse jumped at his open appreciation while my pride still smarted at being ignored for weeks. "Is that what you tell all your potential brides? Or am I special because I work for you?"

Something dangerous flickered in his eyes. "You think I participate in *Smotriny* often, Liliya?" The way he said my name was like a caress that made me want to both lean in and pull away. "That I make habit of bidding on women?"

"Don't you?" The question came out breathier than I intended. He was so close now I could smell his cologne, something woodsy and expensive that made my head spin.

"*Net.*" His voice dropped lower, more intimate. "Never found reason to participate. Until now."

The implications of that statement hung in the air between us. I should have been terrified by what he was suggesting, or still angry at his presumption. Instead, I felt a maddening tangle of resentment, caution, and raw attraction.

"Why now?" I asked, though part of me already knew the answer. Could feel it in the gravity pulling between us, see it in the heat of his gaze.

"Because," he reached out, brushing a strand of hair from my face with surprising gentleness, "some things worth claiming properly. Worth protecting."

His fingers lingered near my cheek, and I battled conflicting urges to slap his hand away and lean into his touch. "I don't need another man trying to own me," I said, but my body betrayed me, swaying slightly toward him even as my mind screamed caution.

The last time I'd felt this drawn to someone, it had been Jack. He'd been charming too, at first. Powerful in his own way. I'd rushed in, letting attraction cloud my judgment, and look how that had ended. The small scar near my temple seemed to throb with the memory.

"Something troubles you," Zaven said softly, his hand dropping away. Not a question - he read it in my face, my withdrawal.

"Last time I trusted my instincts about a man," I said carefully, "I ended up running across an ocean to escape him."

Understanding darkened his eyes, followed by something fiercer - possessive, protective. "He make you doubt yourself. Make you fear your own judgment." His accent grew thicker with emotion. "This why he will pay for every mark he left on you."

The promise of violence in his voice should have repulsed me. Instead, I felt a dizzying mix of fear and reassurance, attraction and warning bells. This man was infinitely more dangerous than Jack had ever been - so why did part of me feel safer with him while another part wanted to run?

"You speak of payment and protection," I said suddenly, standing to put space between us, needing to clear my head from his intoxicating presence. "Like everything's already decided. Like I don't get a choice."

From this distance, I could study him properly. Even seated, he radiated power. The tailored suit couldn't hide the fighter's build beneath - broad shoulders, strong hands that could probably snap a man's neck as easily as they'd brushed my cheek with unexpected tenderness. His face was all harsh angles softened by surprisingly full lips, dark stubble shadowing his jaw. But it was his eyes that held me - dark and ancient as a Siberian winter.

"You not feel it too?" He didn't move from his seat, but his gaze followed me like a physical touch. "This thing between us?"

"What I feel," I turned to face him fully, my confusion hardening into resolve, "is a very powerful man used to getting what he wants. How many times have you watched me from the shadows at the club, planning this moment? Making decisions about my life without ever speaking to me?"

His lips curved slightly, appreciation rather than anger at my challenge. "Many times. Watched you grow stronger each night. Watched you learn to handle powerful men." He leaned forward, elbows on his knees. "Watched you become woman worthy of more than simple protection."

"Worthy?" I couldn't keep the sharpness from my voice, moving to stand by the fireplace. The heat at my back was nothing compared to the burn of his gaze. "So this is what - your seal of approval? Your permission to enter your world?"

Something dangerous flickered in his eyes - not anger, but rather appreciation for the challenge. He wasn't used to being questioned, that much was clear. But instead of the rage such defiance would have sparked in Jack, I saw interest. Heat.

"You question everything I say," he observed, voice low and rich with something almost like respect. "Yet still feel pull between us. Still watch for me at club, even when pretend not to."

I opened my mouth to deny it, but he rose in one fluid motion, his presence suddenly filling the room. "No more pretending, Liliya. We both know truth."

The chime sounded, but neither of us moved. His eyes flickered to *Gospozha* Ivanova and *Gospodin* Fedorov, some unspoken command passing between them. Without a word, they stepped out, the door closing with a soft click that seemed to echo in the sudden silence.

My heart pounded against my ribs, a mixture of wariness, anger, and unwanted attraction coursing through me. We were alone - the powerful *vor* and the American girl who dared to challenge him. The air between us hummed with something dangerous and magnetic, and I wasn't sure if I wanted to push him away or pull him closer.

14

Zaven

There she was.

After all this time of restraining myself, forcing distance—she stood feet away from me. The firelight caught in her hair, reminding me of how it had looked spread across my pillow in my dreams. My hands clenched at my sides. I wanted to grab that hair, pull her head back, expose her throat. Her skin was flushed now—nerves, heat—a stark contrast to the cool composure she showed at the club. Those green eyes challenged me, defiant but with an underlying vulnerability that hit me like a shot of vodka. Fuck. Just like in my dreams.

I took her in—fully, finally—without the distance of the club between us. Smaller than she seemed behind the hostess stand, but curved in all the ways that had kept me awake at night. The swell of her breasts against burgundy silk, narrow waist, hips I'd imagined gripping while I took her from behind. The way she moved—deliberate, controlled—made me think about how that control would break when I had her beneath me.

Her scent hit me harder than I'd expected. Vanilla mixed with something that was just her. Better than I'd imagined during those nights at the club when I'd catch hints of it as she passed. Standing this close, it clouded my judgment, made my blood run hotter.

"Seems we have more time, if you agreeable," I said, remaining where I stood, keeping my voice casual despite the urge to cross the room and take what I'd been denied these past weeks.

She hesitated, a flash of anger in her eyes before she nodded. "I'm agreeable." Her tone carried an edge that made my blood heat.

"You're angry I never approached you at the club," I stated directly, watching her reaction. No point dancing around what we both knew.

"Three weeks at your club, and only now you decide to speak to me?" She didn't waste time with pleasantries. "Should I be flattered that the great Zaven Lazarev finally deemed me worthy of conversation?"

Her directness sent heat straight to my core. Few in my world dared such boldness. Instead of the defense she clearly expected, I moved closer, enjoying how her breath caught. "Anger suits you, Liliya. Shows fire I first noticed." I let my gaze deliberately travel her body. "Makes me wonder how that fire translates to other... situations."

She crossed her arms, defensive but still not backing away. "You haven't answered my question."

"Distance had purpose," I said, studying how light caught gold flecks in her green eyes. "Needed to understand what kind of woman survives what you survived. What kind rebuilds herself in foreign country."

Something flickered across her face—surprise that I knew so much, perhaps. Good. Let her realize nothing escaped my notice, especially not her.

"You've been investigating me," she said, statement rather than question.

"*Da.*" No point denying what we both knew. "Your history, your strengths, your weaknesses—all relevant. Especially after how you handled Alexei." I moved closer, enjoying how her pupils dilated despite her defiance. "Many women fear powerful men. You challenge them. Interesting quality."

"And you enjoy that?" She tilted her chin up. "Being challenged?"

I couldn't help smile that spread across my face. "Most people—men, women—they cower. They agree, they flatter, they lie. You..." I trailed finger along edge of nearby table, watching her track the movement. "You stand your ground. Even now, when you should be afraid."

"What makes you think I'm not afraid?" Her voice was steady despite pulse visibly racing at her throat.

"Fear makes most people run. You step closer to danger." I closed distance between us in deliberate, measured steps. "Makes me wonder what else you do differently."

Her breath caught, but she didn't retreat. Instead, something almost like curiosity flickered in her eyes. "Is that why you're here? To satisfy your curiosity about the American hostess?"

"Partly," I admitted, seeing no reason to lie. "Curious about woman who rebuilds herself from ashes. Who chooses Russia, of all places, to start again."

"And the other part?" she asked, surprising me with direct question. Most would have flinched from knowing my interest.

I studied her carefully, weighing how much truth to offer. "Other part more... complicated. You present unique solution to certain situation."

"Solution?" Her voice sharpened. "*Gospodin* Lazarev."

"Business always involves people, Liliya." I deliberately used her first name, watching color rise in her cheeks. "Question is whether arrangement benefits both parties."

"And what benefit do you imagine I could provide?" She raised an eyebrow, challenge in every line of her body.

"Many." I let word hang between us, heavy with implication. "Most immediate—having woman who challenges me openly at *Smotriny* creates interesting... opportunity."

Her eyes narrowed slightly. "What kind of opportunity?"

"One involving mutual benefit." I moved to fireplace, giving her space to process. "You seeking protection, new start. I seeking something more... rare." I let dangerous smile play across lips. "Woman strong enough to stand in my world without breaking."

"Why would you care?" she asked, voice quieter. "I'm just an employee. One of many."

"Are you?" I turned to face her fully. "Just one of many? Tell me, Liliya— how many employees occupy my thoughts at night? How many make me consider breaking rules I've followed for years?"

Her eyes widened slightly, that delicious flush spreading down her neck.

"I don't understand what you want from me."

"Think you do," I countered, moving closer again. "Same thing you want, though pride won't let you admit. Same thing makes your body lean toward mine even as mind tells you run."

"Physical attraction isn't the same as trust," she whispered, echo of pain in her voice. "And I've learned not to trust my attractions."

Something dark and violent stirred in my chest at reminder of her past. "Then trust this," I murmured, voice dropping dangerously low. "If all I wanted was beautiful woman to warm bed, would have bent you over my desk that first night, would have fucked you until you scream my name." I watched her eyes darken at my crude words, the way her breath caught. "Would not find myself thinking of all ways I want break that control, make you beg me fuck you harder. Would not find such pleasure in way you challenge me, knowing that when you finally surrender, will be because you desperate for my cock. Because you need it deep inside you as much as I need to claim you."

The chime sounded—longer this time. Bidding would begin soon.

Her sharp intake of breath, the way her hands clenched at her sides—she was fighting her body's response to my words. Good. Let her think about it during bidding, let her imagine exactly what awaited when she became mine.

"Think about what I say," I told her, moving toward door. "About difference between man who loses control and man who exercises it. Between fear and power." I paused, looking back. "Tonight, I not here to bid. I here to claim what already mine."

I turned and strode to door, every instinct screaming to turn back, to take what we both clearly wanted. But no—first I had to ensure no other man would ever think to touch her.

Viktor waited in hallway, reading tension in my stance immediately.

"Make arrangements," I said, voice hard with certainty. "By end of night, she mine. No matter cost."

Liliya's perfume still lingering in my senses, I schooled my features into their usual mask of cool indifference. The corridor opened into the grand ballroom where the other participants mingled, the air thick with cigar smoke and the murmur of hushed conversations about both business and pleasure.

Viktor fell into step beside me, amusement dancing in his eyes. "So, finally got close to Liliya. Was worth all the patience?"

"Watch yourself, old friend," I warned, though without heat. "Speaking of watching, noticed you were quite occupied with Natasha during presentations."

"Ah, now who try change subject?" But Viktor's ears reddened slightly. "Was professional interaction only."

"Professional?" I raised an eyebrow. "So when she leaned close to whisper something that made you almost smile, was discussing security protocols?"

"She had... observations about other suitors," Viktor admitted, his usual stoic expression betrayed by slight tension in jaw. "Woman notices things most miss."

"And yet you still resist," I shook my head, grateful for this lighter moment. "Perhaps you one who need head examined."

"Says man who just dismissed bodyguards to be alone with woman he barely knows," his tone turned serious. "But joking aside... you sure about this? Other *vory* already gathering. They not like being outmaneuvered."

"Let them gather." The predator in me stirred, ready for battle. "She mine. They just not know it yet."

As we entered the main hall, Viktor leaned closer. "Rostov asking questions about Liliya. Seems particularly interested in her background."

My jaw tightened. Mikhail Rostov headed intelligence operations that rivaled government agencies. His interest was never casual. "What kind of questions?"

"How she connected to you. Whether relationship existed before club." Viktor's expression remained neutral. "Also curious about timing of her arrival in Russia."

"Interesting." I processed this information, mind already calculating implications. "Have Anatoly look into Rostov's sudden interest. Find out what he's after."

"*Da.*" Viktor nodded. "Also, Kavelin making noise about large bid tonight. Says Liliya exactly his type."

Rage threatened to break through my careful control. Kavelin—known for breaking his toys. "Let him bid," I said, voice deadly quiet. "More satisfying when he loses."

"Ah, Zaven!" boomed Mikhail Volkov, his influence in the energy sector matched only by his crude appetite for young women. "Been sampling delights on offer? American girls..." he made crude gesture. "They say very... enthusiastic."

I felt a flash of violent rage at his implication about Liliya, but kept my face impassive. "Ladies all quite... accomplished," I said neutrally, though my tone carried warning.

Anton Yakov, lean and fox-faced, leaned closer. "Come now, Zaven. Must have opinion. That blonde from New York?" His eyes gleamed with predatory intent. "Heard American girls like her enjoy getting on knees for powerful men. Or maybe redhead? She look like one who beg pretty when-"

"*Gospoda*," I cut him off, voice deadly soft. [Gentlemen] The image of Liliya pressed against a wall, begging for entirely different reasons, flashed through my mind. "Man of discretion never kisses and tells."

"Ah, but is not just kissing we talk about," Volkov laughed, crude and knowing. "Tell truth—you already fuck her? The way she look at you across room..." He made another vulgar gesture. "She practically dripping for you."

The muscle in my jaw ticked. The only thing keeping Volkov's throat intact was decades of political alliance. "Change of subject, perhaps," I suggested, voice carrying edge that made even Yakov step back slightly. "Unless you prefer discuss business in more... private setting?"

The implied threat hung heavy in the air. These men might talk about fucking and ownership, but they knew real power when they felt it. And right now, that power was considering various ways to make them bleed.

Viktor smoothly interjected, "*Gospoda*, bidding starts soon. Perhaps we should prepare?"

As the group dispersed, I exchanged look with Viktor. He nodded almost imperceptibly—he'd handle damage control, ensure my barely contained rage wasn't misinterpreted as weakness.

Once we were alone, Viktor spoke low and fast. "Yakov's been making moves in shipping industry. Trying to muscle in on St. Petersburg port operations."

I frowned, forcing my mind from thoughts of Liliya to business. "How serious is threat?"

"He leverage connections in customs office. Nothing we cannot handle, but require..." Viktor paused meaningfully, "finesse."

I nodded, already formulating plans. "Reach out to friend in ministry. Time he repay favors." My voice hardened as I added, "And make sure Kavelin understand his actions tonight were noticed. His crude interest in Liliya not appreciated."

Viktor's eyes glinted with understanding. "Consider it done. Also, Dmitri's people seen near docks again..."

We spent next minutes discussing business, conversation complex dance of half-spoken truths and coded threats. But my attention kept drifting to Liliya. Even discussing territory disputes and shipment routes, I could still taste her defiance, still feel heat of her body as she pretended not to want me.

A shift in room's energy caught my attention. Time for bidding approached. Women were being led back in, and there she was—chin lifted in that defiance that made me want to pin her against wall, make her admit what we both knew she felt.

"It seems selection process about to begin," Viktor observed.

Unlike previous years where I'd participated out of obligation, this time anticipation coursed through my veins. Liliya had awakened something in me I thought long buried beneath years of control and power.

The low hum of conversation died as *Barynya* Petrova took her place. Her presence commanded attention, a skill I'd always admired.

"*Gospoda*," she began, accent crisp and formal. "Time has come for final selections. Remember—choices made tonight shape future of our world. Power requires proper match, *da*? Strength calls to strength."

I kept my expression neutral, though my eyes found Liliya again. She stood apart from others, burgundy silk catching light, making her glow. Even scared, she held herself like queen. My queen, if she'd just stop fighting what was inevitable.

"Bidding opens now," *Barynya* Petrova announced.

Viktor appeared at my elbow with tablet. Around us, men began entering amounts, some with gleaming eyes of collectors eyeing new prizes, others with calculating gaze of those seeking alliances.

I watched Yakov's obvious interest in blonde, noting it for future leverage. Volkov's gaze kept returning to petite brunette—useful information. But my focus remained on Liliya, the memory of her heated defiance, her breathy voice as she pretended not to want me, making my blood burn.

"Your bid, *Brat*?" Viktor murmured. [Brother]

The amount I entered made even Viktor's eyebrows rise slightly. "Send message," I said quietly. "Let them know price of touching what belong to me."

Through it all, I maintained my composure, offering knowing nods here, calculated smiles there. But my attention never strayed far from Liliya. I saw moment she was informed of bids, flash of surprise in her eyes, followed by that delicious defiance.

"Seem you have competition," Viktor said, returning to my side. "Kavelin make bid, despite our... warning."

Rage coiled in my gut. "Has he?" The crystal in my hand creaked dangerously. "How unfortunate for him."

Viktor's lips twitched with what might have been amusement. "Want me remind him of consequences?"

"*Net*." Though the image of Kavelin bleeding for daring to think he could touch what was mine was... tempting. "Let him waste money on pointless bid."

I watched Liliya in her private alcove, probably being told by *Barynya* Petrova about multiple interested parties. She wouldn't know final outcome—wouldn't know I'd entered sum that made even Viktor's eyebrows rise. Amount that said clearly: mine.

"*Gospoda*," *Barynya* Petrova announced, returning to dais. "Bidding is complete. Those with winning offers will now select their matches. We proceed in order of bid amount."

Barynya Petrova materialized at my side like a ghost in black silk, her silver hair gleaming in the candlelight. Though she barely reached my shoulder, her presence commanded attention—decades of orchestrating these arrangements had given her an air of undisputed authority.

"*Gospodin* Lazarev," her voice was pitched for my ears alone. "The time has come for selection. If you would follow me?"

I caught Viktor's knowing look as I turned to follow her. The bidding had gone exactly as planned—though the amount I'd paid would have most men sweating. Now came the part that would set all of St. Petersburg talking.

She led me through a hidden door behind the main stairs, into a part of the mansion few ever saw. The corridor breathed old money and older secrets, portraits of past matches watching our progress with painted eyes.

She gestured me into her private study, where flickering firelight caught the edges of gilt frames and crystal decanters. The air felt heavy with tradition and expectation. Here, in this room, generations of *vor* had made their selections, shaped alliances, built empires.

Time to break with tradition.

15

Liliya

My heart pounded in my chest as I followed the attendant down the opulent corridor. After the bidding, *Barynya* Petrova had simply said I'd been chosen - not by whom. Now, being led to a private room for "negotiations," every step felt like walking toward my fate.

The memory of my encounter with Zaven earlier made my skin flush hot. His crude words, the way he'd made it clear exactly what he wanted to do to me... I pushed the thoughts away. For all I knew, I was about to face Kavelin or one of the other powerful men who'd shown interest.

"Here, *Devushka* Sinclair," the attendant said, stopping before an ornate wooden door. "Your... partner awaits."

I placed my hand on the cool metal handle, willing it not to shake. The burgundy silk of my dress felt too tight suddenly, my skin hypersensitive beneath it. Natasha's words echoed in my mind: "Remember who you are now, not who he made you be."

Taking a deep breath that tasted of old wood and beeswax polish, I turned the handle and stepped into the unknown.

The room enveloped me in warmth, so different from the corridor's chill. A fire crackled in a marble fireplace, its light dancing across leather-bound books and crystal decanters. The air held notes of cedar and leather, but underneath lurked that familiar cologne – the one I'd caught traces of at the club, the one that had haunted my dreams.

A figure stood by the window, silhouetted against the city lights. Power radiated from his stillness, making the spacious room feel suddenly small. As the door closed behind me with a soft click that seemed to echo in my bones, he turned.

Our eyes met across the room, and heat flooded through me. Zaven Lazarev. The most dangerous man in St. Petersburg had chosen me. Part of me wanted to run, but I forced my spine straight, chin lifting slightly. I'd survived Jack's rage, rebuilt myself in this foreign city. I could survive this man's desire – even if it made me burn.

"*Devushka* Sinclair," he said, voice low and rich with that accent that had haunted me since our earlier encounter. "I trust my selection not... disappoint you?"

The way he said it – part question, part statement – reminded me of the power he held. He'd outbid everyone else, chosen me publicly.

He began to circle me slowly, like a predator assessing his prize. But I wasn't just some prize to be claimed.

"Does my opinion matter?" I asked, proud of how steady my voice sounded.

He stopped behind me, close enough that I could feel the heat radiating from his body. "Always matters, *malyshka*," he murmured, his breath warm against my ear. [Little one] "Question is – what you planning to do now that you mine?"

I stepped away from his overwhelming presence, moving toward the business-like arrangement of chairs by the fireplace. "Perhaps we should discuss the terms of this... arrangement."

His low chuckle made something hot coil in my belly. "Still trying to pretend, *malyshka*? After what pass between us earlier?"

"That was..." I swallowed hard, remembering his crude promises, how they'd made me feel. "That was before you chose me. Now we need to be practical."

"Practical?" He moved to stand before me, blocking my path to the chairs. "Like how your body responds every time I near you? How your breath catch just now?" His eyes darkened. "How you think about what I promise to do to you?"

"I'm not here to be your fucktoy," I snapped, the crude word escaping before I could stop it. My hand flew to my mouth, eyes widening at my own audacity.

His eyebrows shot up in surprised appreciation, a slow smile spreading across his face. "Such language from elegant hostess," he murmured, seeming more delighted than offended. "No need apologize. I like when you speak true thoughts, not what you think I want hear."

Heat crept up my neck, but something about his reaction made me bolder rather than embarrassed. "Then here's another truth - if you want to negotiate a real arrangement-"

"Real arrangement?" He stepped closer, making me tilt my head back to maintain eye contact. "Tell me then, what kind of arrangement you want? One where we pretend not to feel this?" He gestured to the charged space between us. "Where you keep fighting what we both know is inevitable?"

"Protection," I said firmly. "Isn't that what this is really about? You outbid everyone else, so now what - I'm supposed to fall at your feet grateful that the mighty Zaven claimed me?"

Something dangerous flickered in his eyes - not anger, but something darker, more possessive. "You think that why I choose you? For your gratitude?" He moved closer, until barely inches separated us. "Think I spend all this time wanting you just for simple ownership?"

"I don't know what you want," I said, hating how breathless I sounded. "You talk about protection one minute, then the next you're promising to bend me over the nearest surface. Which is it?"

His lips curved at my bluntness. "Why must be one or other? Why not both?" He reached out, thumb brushing my lower lip. "I protect what's mine. Also fuck what's mine. Simple."

The crude directness of his words sent an unexpected jolt of heat through me. I jerked away from his touch, needing distance to think clearly.

"I won't be owned again," I said, voice low but firm.

The muscle in his jaw ticked, something dangerous flashing in his eyes. "You compare me to him?" His accent grew thicker with anger. "To weak

American boy who need fists to feel strong?"

"I compare situations, not men," I shot back, my hands trembling despite my defiance. "Another powerful man thinking he can buy me, control me—"

"Enough." The word came out as almost a growl. He caught my arm, not roughly but with unmistakable strength, turning me to face him. "You think I same as him? Look at me, Liliya." His other hand came up to grip my chin, forcing me to meet his gaze. "Really look. Am I anything like coward who hurt you?"

I stared into those dark eyes, seeing the controlled violence there— violence not directed at me but at the mere thought of Jack. My racing heart wasn't from fear but from something far more dangerous—desire mixed with the terrifying possibility of trust.

"No," I admitted softly. "You're nothing like him. That's what scares me."

His grip gentled immediately, though he didn't release me. "Why I terrify you?"

"Because you make me want to trust again," I whispered, the truth spilling out before I could stop it. "And last time I trusted a man, I nearly died. Trust isn't just a risk for me anymore—it's a scar that never fully healed."

Understanding darkened his eyes. He released me and stepped back, giving me space I hadn't asked for but desperately needed.

"Sit," he said, gesturing to the chairs. "We talk. Really talk."

The shift in his demeanor—the way he'd sensed my genuine fear beneath the bravado—caught me off guard. I sank into one of the leather armchairs, gathering my composure while he poured two glasses of amber liquid.

"Contract first," I said, needing the structure of business to steady myself. "What exactly are your terms?"

He handed me a glass, our fingers brushing in a way that sent electricity up my arm. His expression was serious now, the predatory seduction temporarily set aside.

"Simple. You become my *Nevesta*. My fiancée," he clarified, seeing my confusion. "Then wife. We present united front to both society and business associates." [Bride-to-be]

"And your expectations of me in this role?" I asked, taking a sip of what turned out to be excellent whiskey.

"You attend events at my side. Learn Russian traditions, the *vor* code." His gaze held mine. "Show everyone that *vor's* woman is elegant, intelligent, strong. In return, you have my complete protection, my resources."

"And my freedom?" I pressed. "My independence? My ability to make my own choices?"

"Within reason," he replied, voice serious. "Not looking for puppet, Liliya. Want partner. Woman who think for herself." His expression darkened slightly. "But must have loyalty. Complete trust. Life I lead too dangerous for anything less."

I leaned forward, meeting his intensity with my own. "The life you lead. The one with rival organizations and men like Kavelin? If I'm going to be your *Supruga*, I need to know what I'm really walking into." [Wife]

His eyebrows lifted slightly at my use of the Russian word. "*Malenky lisa*," he murmured with appreciation. [Little fox] "Little fox. Always listening, always watching. Already learning the shadows we move in."

"Answer the question," I insisted, refusing to be distracted by his approval. "How much will you tell me about your business? The dangerous parts? The illegal parts?"

His expression grew serious. "You understand asking dangerous questions? Knowledge is weapon. Can protect but also make target."

"I lived with a man who kept me in the dark 'for my protection,'" I said, my voice hardening. "It only made me more vulnerable when everything collapsed around me. I won't do that again."

He studied me for a long moment, weighing my words. "Cannot tell everything," he finally said. "Not because I think you weak, but because some information puts you in real danger."

I opened my mouth to argue, but he raised his hand.

"But," he continued, "will never lie. Will share what I can without putting you at risk. You deserve truth, even when truth is ugly."

"And who decides what I should know?" I challenged.

"We decide. Together." He raised his glass slightly. "As partners, not master and servant."

The word 'partners' resonated more than I wanted to admit. "Alright," I conceded. "What about... other aspects?"

His eyes darkened, understanding my meaning immediately. "Physical relationship?"

I nodded, heat creeping up my neck.

"Is simple," he said, his voice dropping lower. "I want you. Have made this clear, *da*? But will not demand or force. Will pursue you with patience." His lips curved into a dangerous smile. "Though warning—even patient man knows how to make woman burn for him."

"And if seduction doesn't work?" I asked boldly, though my heart raced. "If I'm not interested?"

He shrugged, the movement elegant despite his powerful frame. "Then I suffer with cold showers and lonely nights." His eyes held mine, serious despite his light tone. "Force never option, Liliya. Coercion never option. Only willing consent."

His eyes held mine with an intensity that made me shiver. "I have taken many things in this life without permission. But a woman's desire will never be one of them."

Relief mingled with something like disappointment, which was ridiculous. "Thank you," I said quietly. "For respecting that boundary."

"Not about respect," he corrected, leaning forward. "About desire. Want you desperate for me. Wet and begging. Not submitting out of obligation." The crude intensity of his words made heat bloom between my thighs. "When you come to my bed, *malyshka*, will be because you can't stand another night without my cock inside you."

"Jesus," I breathed, shocked by his bluntness and my body's immediate response to it.

He smiled, clearly pleased with my reaction. "Interesting - you blush at crude words but not at thought of begging for me in bed, *da*? American woman with Russian soul, perhaps."

"I'm not..." I started to protest, then caught myself. "Fuck it. You're right.

I'm not some innocent virgin. I just wasn't expecting you to be so... explicit."

His laugh was genuine, rich with appreciation. "There she is. Real Liliya hiding beneath polite hostess." He raised his glass in mock toast. "To honesty between us. First step to true partnership."

Despite myself, I found my lips curving into a smile. There was something liberating about his directness, about the way he seemed to appreciate rather than judge my occasional crudeness.

"So what happens now?" I asked, surprised by the steadiness in my voice.

Zaven set his glass down, his eyes still holding mine. "Now we begin. You sleep in own room at my house. Safe, protected. We learn each other, work together." His accent grew thicker as he added, "Whole time, I be there, tempting you. Until one day, you decide you ready for more."

I bit my lip, weighing my options. The thought of moving into his home tonight made everything suddenly real. This wasn't just an arrangement on paper—this was my life changing completely.

"Now," Zaven said, his voice gentling as he observed my inner struggle, "shall we discuss how to seal this agreement?"

My eyes snapped to his face, surprised by the shift in tone. "What do you mean?"

His lips curved into a slow smile that made my pulse quicken. "Well, *malyshka*, traditionally, agreements like this sealed with handshake or..." he paused meaningfully, "something more intimate. Choice is yours."

My mouth went dry as I realized what he was suggesting. Part of me—the cautious part that remembered Jack's manipulations—screamed to keep my distance. But another part, one that had been awakened by this dangerous man, whispered that this was different.

"I think..." I hesitated, then found my courage, "I think a kiss would be acceptable."

Something flashed in his eyes—hunger, triumph, something more complex I couldn't name. "You sure, Liliya? Because once we do this, agreement binding. No going back."

Was I sure? This man represented everything dangerous about the world I'd entered—power, control, violence barely contained beneath a civilized surface. But also protection, respect, and a desire that saw me as equal, not possession.

"I'm sure," I said, the words coming out steadier than I felt.

Zaven rose from his chair, and I followed, my legs feeling unsteady beneath me. He approached slowly, giving me time to retreat if I changed my mind. When he stood before me, he gently cupped my face in his hands.

"Last chance to back out, *malyshka*," he murmured, his dark eyes searching mine.

Instead of answering, I closed the distance between us, pressing my lips to his.

The kiss began gently, almost tentatively, but as his arms slid around my waist, pulling me against him, it deepened. I tasted expensive whiskey on his tongue as it traced my lower lip, seeking entrance. When I parted my lips, he growled low in his throat—a primal sound of approval that sent heat pooling between my thighs.

My hands, which had been resting on his chest, now clutched at his shirt, feeling the hard planes of muscle beneath. His heartbeat raced beneath my palm, matching my own frantic rhythm. One of his hands tangled in my hair, angling my head to deepen the kiss further, while the other pressed against the small of my back, molding me to him.

Just when I thought I might melt completely into him, he broke the kiss, pulling back slightly. In that moment, I understood the true danger of Zaven Lazarev—not the violence in his hands, but the tenderness they were capable of.

The look in his eyes—dark with desire barely held in check—made me tremble.

"Zaven?" I whispered, confused by the sudden withdrawal.

His eyes dropped to my hands, which were still fisted in his shirt. "For someone who claim not to want me..." his lips curved into that knowing smile, "seem very reluctant to let go."

Heat flooded my face as I realized how eagerly I'd responded to him. I released his shirt, stepping back slightly. "I never said I didn't want you," I admitted, surprising myself with my honesty. "I said I wouldn't be owned.

There's a difference."

Something like approval flashed in his eyes. "Smart woman. And brave." He straightened his tie, visibly working to regain his composure. "Now, we should get going. Need to stop by your apartment, gather necessities before heading to your new home."

"Wait—tonight?" I blinked, caught off guard by the sudden shift. "I'm moving in tonight?"

"*Da.* For your safety." His tone brooked no argument. "Team will collect your necessities tonight. You will have own wing, own space. Everything else you need will be provided."

"But that's—that's so fast," I stammered, struggling to process this sudden development.

"In this life, must move quickly," he said, his expression softening slightly at my obvious discomfort. "Will give you time to adjust, but safety comes first. Always."

Without waiting for further protests, he moved toward the door. "Car waiting. Take moment to gather yourself. We leave in five minutes."

As the door closed behind him, I sank back into the chair, fingers touching my still-tingling lips. What had I gotten myself into? Yet beneath the fear and uncertainty, something else stirred—excitement, perhaps. A new life beginning, one where I wasn't running or hiding.

One where, despite all the danger surrounding the man I'd just agreed to marry, I might finally feel safe enough to stop looking over my shoulder. I was stepping into the lion's den willingly, not because I no longer feared the lion, but because I'd finally found one who saw me as more than just prey.

16

Zaven

I leaned against the wall outside, struggling to regain control. Her taste lingered on my lips—champagne and something uniquely Liliya. Something I already craved more of.

The softness of her body against mine, the way she'd responded to my kiss—it had taken every ounce of willpower to pull away. But this was about building trust, not just satisfying lust. She needed to know I meant what I said about respecting her boundaries, even when every instinct screamed to claim her completely.

"Well, well. Great Zaven Lazarev, lurking outside doors like lovesick teenager."

I straightened immediately, masking any hint of vulnerability. Kavelin stood at the end of the corridor, his lean frame outlined in the dim light, a vicious smile playing on his lips.

"Kavelin," I acknowledged coolly. "Shouldn't you be mourning failed bid somewhere?"

His smile didn't waver, though his eyes hardened. "American girl worth what you paid? Seem steep price for hostess."

My expression remained impassive, though rage bubbled beneath the surface. "Careful, Ivan. Some thoughts better kept private."

He stepped closer, either brave or foolish. "Strange choice for man like you. Heard American damaged goods. Used merchandise."

The muscle in my jaw ticked—only external sign of the violence I was barely containing. "Last warning," I said softly, voice dropping to dangerous register that had made stronger men than him back down. "Choose next words with exceptional care."

Kavelin's eyes narrowed, assessing how far he could push. "Just curious if American knows what she getting. Your... appetites are legendary. Would hate to see such delicate flower... broken."

Before I could respond—before I could wrap my hands around his throat as every instinct demanded—a female voice cut through the tension.

"*Gospodin* Kavelin." Natasha appeared from around the corner, her expression pleasant but eyes cold. "*Barynya* Petrova requests your presence. Something about..." she paused meaningfully, "discrepancies in your financial declaration for bidding."

Kavelin's face tightened with poorly concealed alarm. He looked between us, clearly calculating his options.

"We continue this conversation another time, Lazarev," he finally said, backing away.

"*Net*." My voice left no room for misinterpretation. "We not continue anything. Matter closed. Permanently."

After he disappeared down the corridor, Natasha's professional smile dropped. "*Mudak*," she muttered, then glanced at me. "Sorry for interruption. Was looking for Liliya when I overheard..."

"Thank you," I said simply, acknowledging what she'd done. "Might have complicated evening if conversation continued."

She raised an eyebrow. "By complicated, you mean his blood on expensive carpet?"

Despite my lingering anger, I felt my lips twitch. "Something like that."

"She inside?" Natasha gestured to the door.

"*Da*. Giving her moment to... process."

Understanding flickered across her face. "She agreed then? To arrangement?"

"She did." I studied her, this woman who had brought Liliya into my orbit, however unintentionally. "You care for her."

"She's my friend," Natasha said simply, but her eyes held challenge. "Only friend who never judge me. Never want something from me."

"Good friends rare in our circles," I acknowledged.

"Which is why I tell you now," she stepped closer, dropping her voice, "if you hurt her, I not care who you are or what power you have. I find way to make you pay."

Most would consider her words a death wish, threatening a *vor* directly. But I respected loyalty, even when inconvenient.

"Fair warning," I conceded. "Though unnecessary. Have no intention of hurting her."

"Not all hurt intentional," she replied sharply. Then, seeming to remember who she addressed, added, "Just... be patient with her. What she survived..." She hesitated.

"Know enough," I assured her. "Will give her time. Space she needs."

Relief softened her features. "Good. She—"

Footsteps from around the corner interrupted her. Viktor appeared, his usual impassive expression momentarily slipping when he saw Natasha.

"Everything ready," he said, composure quickly restored though his eyes flickered briefly to Natasha before returning to me. "Car waiting."

I didn't miss the quick glance between them, nor the slight flush that colored Natasha's cheeks.

"Natasha," Viktor acknowledged with stiff nod.

"Viktor," she returned curtly, though something electric passed between them. "Well, I should find Yelena, let her know arrangements finalized."

As she turned to leave, she added over her shoulder, "Take care of my friend, *Gospodin* Lazarev. She stronger than she knows."

Viktor's gaze followed her retreating form, lingering perhaps longer than strictly professional. Interesting.

"Something you wish to share, old friend?" I asked, momentarily distracted from thoughts of Liliya.

Viktor's expression closed immediately. "Car waiting out front," he reported, deflecting. "Team ready to go to her building for collecting her things. Should we increase security parameter given..." he hesitated, "given earlier events at bidding?”

“*Da.*” The memory of others daring to bid on what was mine made anger curl in my gut. “Double watch tonight. No chances.” I glanced in the direction Kavelin had disappeared. “And have Leonid keep eye on Kavelin. Something about his interest in Liliya feels… targeted.”

Viktor nodded, understanding my unspoken concern. In our world, sometimes interest in a woman was simply means to strike at rival. “Will handle personally.”

I started toward front entrance, then paused. “And Viktor? Make sure Irina prepares east wing for Liliya. Her own space, her own rooms.”

Viktor’s eyebrow rose slightly. “Not the family wing?”

“*Net.*” The decision cost me, but it was the right one. “She needs time. Space to adjust.” My jaw clenched. “But still under my protection.”

Something like approval flickered in Viktor’s eyes. He knew what this restraint cost me. “Want me to have Irina stock her rooms with anything specific?”

“Everything she could need.” No detail was too small when it came to her comfort. “And Viktor? Make sure she knows she can lock her door.”

His expression softened marginally. “You do right thing, *Brat.* Building trust first. Most in position wouldn’t bother.”

“She’s different,” I said simply. “Deserves different approach.”

“Speaking of different interactions,” I said, voice deliberately casual as we walked, “noticed how Natasha affects your usually perfect composure.”

Viktor’s expression remained impassive, though his ears reddened slightly. “Professional interaction only,” he insisted.

“Of course,” I agreed, not bothering to hide my amusement. “Just as my interest in Liliya purely business arrangement.”

Viktor cleared his throat, changing subject. “Should take care with Kavelin. His uncle still controls most of northern shipping routes. Making enemy could complicate Georgian expansion.”

“He made himself enemy moment he bid on her,” I said flatly. “Political consequences secondary concern.”

A ghost of a smile touched Viktor’s lips. “Known you long time, *Brat.*

Never seen woman affect you like this."

I didn't bother denying it. "Makes me vulnerable," I admitted. Only to Viktor would I confess such weakness.

"Or stronger," he countered. "Purpose beyond business, beyond territory... could be advantage."

The door opened behind us, and we both turned to see Liliya step into the hallway. Her cheeks still held a flush from our kiss, lips slightly swollen in way that sent heat through my veins all over again. I moved toward her, taking her coat from Viktor who had retrieved it from the cloakroom.

"Ready?" I asked, holding the fur-lined coat open for her.

She nodded, turning to slip her arms into the sleeves. As I settled the coat onto her shoulders, I leaned close, my lips near her ear.

"Suits you," I murmured, voice low enough for only her to hear. "These kiss-swollen lips. Will enjoy seeing them this way often, *malyshka.*"

The blush that spread across her cheeks was immediate and deeply satisfying. She shot me a look that was half embarrassment, half warning - a look that promised interesting times ahead.

"Car waiting," Viktor announced, diplomatically pretending not to notice our exchange.

As we walked toward the exit, my hand rested lightly on the small of Liliya's back - not possessive, but protective. Things were moving quickly now, perhaps too quickly for her comfort. But in our world, hesitation meant vulnerability, and I would not risk her safety for the sake of a more traditional courtship.

Time enough for that once she was secure in my home, under my protection. Time enough to make good on every promise I'd whispered against those soft lips of hers.

17

Liliya

The sleek black car glided through the night-shrouded streets of St. Petersburg, its tinted windows reflecting the blur of streetlights. I sat in the back, hyperaware of Zaven's presence beside me. We weren't touching, but the space between us crackled with an electricity that made my skin tingle.

I couldn't stop my mind from replaying our kiss. The feel of his lips on mine, demanding yet somehow gentle. The way his hands had held me, strong and sure. His scent stuck with me - that expensive cologne mixed with something that was just...him. My body still hummed with the memory of it all.

A car backfired in the street, the sound shattering the quiet night. My body tensed instinctively, a familiar jolt of adrenaline surging through my veins. The world around me began to blur, present merging with past in that disorienting way I'd come to dread.

The slam of the door rattled the pictures on our walls. The sound I'd grown to dread. Jack was home, and the whiskey smell would be on his breath.

"Lily!" His voice boomed through our small apartment, making my stomach twist into knots. "Where the fuck are you?"

I scrambled to my feet, pulse thundering in my ears. "I-I'm here, Jack. In the bedroom." My voice small, already pleading.

His footsteps – heavy, deliberate, coming closer. I could almost feel the vibration through the floor. Could already taste the copper tang of fear in my mouth.

"Liliya?" Zaven's voice seemed to come from far away. My chest constricted, lungs refusing to expand. The leather seat beneath my fingers turned to the rough carpet of that bedroom. My vision tunneled, dark spots dancing at the edges. I pressed myself against the car door, trying to disappear into it.

Weeks. It had been weeks since my last attack. I'd been doing so well, handling the club, the crowds, the negotiations. Building this new, stronger version of myself. Why now? Why here, next to the most powerful man in St. Petersburg? A man who'd just seen me handle a room full of dangerous *vor* without flinching, only to fall apart at a simple car backfire.

Shame burned through me, hot and bitter as bile in my throat. After standing my ground during negotiations, after all the progress I'd made, here I was falling apart at a simple car backfire. And in front of him—the most dangerous man in St. Petersburg. Fuck. What must he think now?

"*Malyshka*, look at me." Zaven's voice cut through the panic, deep and smooth like aged whiskey. "You safe here. No one hurt you now." His hand hovered near my shoulder, not touching, but radiating warmth through the thin silk of my dress. "Just you and me, *da*? Only safe people here."

Slowly, I forced my eyes open. The leather interior of the car came into focus, then Zaven's face. His dark eyes held concern and something fiercer—a protective rage that made the air feel charged with electricity. The muscle in his jaw ticked, but his expression remained carefully controlled, like a predator holding itself in check.

"That's it, *malyshka*. Breathe with me." His voice dropped lower, gentler, wrapping around me like velvet. "In through nose, out through mouth. Like this." He demonstrated, the sound oddly soothing in the confined space. "Good girl."

As my breathing steadied, I became acutely aware of our positions. Zaven had shifted closer, his body angled towards mine, cologne mixing with the rich scent of leather seats. One arm rested on the seat behind me, not touching but creating a protective barrier that made me feel oddly safe. His other hand remained palm up between us, strong fingers relaxed in silent invitation.

Heat radiated from him in waves, and despite the lingering fear from my flashback, I found myself drawn to that warmth like a moth to flame. My body seemed to lean towards him of its own accord, craving his strength and solidity. The same magnetic pull I'd felt during our kiss threatened to overwhelm my better judgment.

"I'm sorry," I whispered, voice raw. "I haven't... this hasn't happened in weeks. I don't know why–"

"*Net*." Zaven shook his head, voice firm as steel. "No apologies for this, *malyshka*."

His voice, low and reassuring, sent a shiver down my spine that had nothing to do with fear. I found myself staring at his lips, remembering how they'd felt against mine barely an hour ago. My own lips tingled with the memory.

Zaven's pupils dilated, the black nearly swallowing the dark brown of his eyes. His breath hitched almost imperceptibly, the sound loud in the quiet car. I watched, fascinated, as the muscle in his jaw ticked again – this time for an entirely different reason.

"Liliya," he murmured, his accent thicker than before. "May touch you?"

The question, so at odds with the forceful man I'd seen during our negotiations, made my heart skip a beat. I nodded, not trusting my voice.

Slowly, telegraphing his movements, Zaven reached out and took my hand. His skin was warm, slightly calloused, and I could feel the strength in his gentle grip. With his other hand, he began to softly massage my palm, working out the crescents my nails had left.

The tender gesture, combined with the lingering adrenaline from my flashback, sent waves of sensation through me. Each stroke of his thumb seemed to ignite nerve endings I didn't know I had. I felt my cheeks flush, heat pooling low in my belly.

"Better?" Zaven asked, his voice a low rumble that I felt more than heard.

I nodded, mesmerized by the sight of his large hand enveloping mine. "Thank you," I managed to whisper.

Zaven's eyes met mine, and the intensity I saw there made my breath catch. For a moment, I thought he might kiss me again. Part of me hoped he would, even as another part warned me about falling too quickly into this attraction. But then the car slowed to a stop, and the spell was broken.

"We here," Zaven said, reluctantly releasing my hand. His eyes hardened as they scanned through the window. "This where you been living?"

I blinked, surprised by his tone. "Yes. How did you know where I live?"

His jaw clenched, eyes continuing their assessment. "*Znaniye vlast, malyshka.*" [Knowledge is power] He gestured vaguely toward the building. "Place like this... not fit for you. Not safe area, especially not for woman alone."

I felt a flicker of defensiveness. "Natasha found this place for me on short notice. She did her best to help when I had nowhere else to go."

"*Net.*" His voice dropped lower, dangerous. "Is worse than you know. Three attacks in this area last month alone. Building barely passes code inspection."

"How would you even know that?" I asked, brows furrowing.

A muscle ticked in his jaw. "Own many properties in St. Petersburg. This district... problematic. Have been purchasing buildings here, one by one."

"Let me guess," I said, realizing the implication. "You own this one too?"

"*Da.*" His expression remained unreadable. "Acquired six months ago. Not place I would choose for you."

His dismissive tone about Natasha's help sparked something in me. "Well, unlike some people, Natasha didn't have an entire criminal empire to help find me somewhere safer. She gave me a job, found me a place to live, helped me survive." I didn't understand why his attitude was making me so angry, but I couldn't seem to stop. "Not everyone has your... resources."

Zaven's eyebrows lifted slightly at my outburst, something flickering in his eyes - surprise? Amusement? "*Malenky lisa* shows her teeth again, *da?*"

The use of that nickname - little fox - only irritated me more. "Don't patronize me. Natasha is my friend. My only friend here. She-"

"*Net*, not patronizing," he cut in, voice gentling though his eyes still held that frustrating glimmer of amusement. "Like that you defend friend. Show loyalty. But fact remains - this place not safe. Even with best intentions, your Natasha put you in danger."

I opened my mouth to argue further, but he reached out, his hand moving toward my cheek. Instinctively, I flinched, my body tensing as I braced for a blow that didn't come. The moment I realized what I'd done, shame washed over me. I looked up to see Zaven's hand frozen in mid-air, his eyes wide with a mix of surprise and something darker... murderous.

"*Chto za der'mo?*" he muttered, his voice low and deadly. [What the hell/shit] Then, louder, "What that *mudak* do to make you flinch like this?"

The sudden shift to Russian, the raw emotion in his voice, made me shrink back slightly. This was a side of Zaven I hadn't seen before - not even during the negotiations. This was the *vor*, the man who commanded fear and respect in the underworld.

"I... it's nothing. I didn't mean to-" I stammered, unable to meet his gaze, hating how quickly I'd gone from fierce defense of Natasha to this trembling mess.

"*Blyad'*," Zaven swore, his fist clenching at his side. For a moment, I saw murder in his eyes, and I knew without a doubt that if Jack were here, Zaven wouldn't hesitate to kill him.

Then, as quickly as it had appeared, the murderous rage vanished, replaced by a gentleness that took my breath away. The contrast was dizzying.

"Don't," he said, his voice softening. "*Net, malyshka.* Never apologize for his actions."

Slowly, telegraphing his movements, he reached out again. This time, I managed to stay still as his hand cupped my cheek. His touch was surprisingly tender, a stark contrast to the anger I had just witnessed.

"Listen close, *malyshka*," he said, his thumb gently stroking my cheek-bone. "I not him. Never raise hand to you in anger. This I swear."

I nodded, fighting past the lump in my throat.

"Need hear you say it," he insisted softly. "Need know you understand."

"I understand," I managed to whisper, though I wasn't sure if I really did. Everything about this man was a contradiction - the gentle way he touched me versus the violence I'd glimpsed in his eyes, how he could infuriate me one moment and make me feel impossibly safe the next.

"Good." His jaw clenched, and I saw another flash of the dangerous man I knew lurked beneath the surface. "Now, tell me what he do to you."

I shook my head, unable to voice the memories that threatened to overwhelm me. "I can't... not yet, I–"

"Is okay," Zaven cut in, his accent thicker with emotion. "When ready, you tell me. Not because I think less of you, but because need know what I protect you from. What I make him pay for."

The cold certainty in his voice should have frightened me. Instead, it sent an unexpected shiver of something else down my spine – something that felt dangerously like security.

"Let's get your things," he said, his hand falling away from my face. His voice was controlled again, but I could see the tension in his shoulders, the barely contained rage simmering just beneath the surface. "Sooner we out of here, better."

As Zaven opened his door, the bitter wind whipped around us. I hadn't noticed before, but his security team had already positioned themselves around the car – dark figures in black coats, their breath visible in the cold night air. Two moved ahead to sweep the building's entrance while another held an umbrella over us as we stepped out.

The hem of my evening gown brushed against the snow as I carefully navigated the icy sidewalk in my heels, grateful for both the fur coat and Zaven's steadying hand at my elbow. Each delicate step felt weighted with significance – this would be the last time I walked this path as just Lily Sinclair, the American hostess. Next time – if there even was a next time – I'd be Zaven Lazarev's fiancée.

One of his men opened the building's heavy door, and the familiar musty warmth of the old stairwell enveloped us. Zaven's hand moved to the small of my back as we climbed the stairs, his touch protective rather than possessive. The sound of multiple footsteps echoing behind us was new – I'd always made this climb alone before, my own footsteps the only company in the dimly lit space.

As we entered my small apartment, I felt a strange mix of embarrassment and defiance. The space was tiny, sparsely furnished with secondhand items, but it had been clean and it had been mine.

Zaven's men spread out with military precision, checking each corner with practiced efficiency. The contrast between their black suits and my shabby apartment was almost comical—like watching special forces raid a college dorm.

"*Chistiye*," one muttered into his radio after checking the bathroom. [Clear]

"*Bezopasno*," replied another from the kitchen. [Safe]

Zaven nodded sharply, then turned those calculating eyes to me. I stood awkwardly in my tiny living room, still in my evening gown and borrowed fur coat, feeling impossibly out of place.

"I need to go change," I murmured, more to myself than to Zaven. My feet ached in the heels, and the weight of the evening's events pressed down on me like a physical thing.

"*Da*," he nodded, still scanning the room with those calculating eyes. "Take time you need." His gaze softened slightly as it returned to me. "Men finish security sweep first."

As I headed to the bedroom, I heard him murmur to one of his men in Russian, "*Kak ya i dumal—deshevo i nebezopasno.*" [Just as I thought—cheap and unsafe]

I closed the bedroom door behind me with trembling fingers. The familiar space felt different now, knowing it was the last time I'd be here. My few personal items seemed to mock me - the secondhand dresser with its wobbly drawer, the narrow bed with its mismatched pillows, even the cracked mirror propped against the wall.

Catching my reflection, I barely recognized myself. The elegant woman in the gown and fur seemed like a stranger, completely at odds with my humble surroundings. Just hours ago, Natasha had been here, helping me get ready, her excitement about *Smotriny* almost contagious. Now everything had changed.

I shrugged off the fur coat, draping it carefully over my bed, before reaching behind my back to unfasten the gown. That's when I remembered

- with a jolt that was equal parts embarrassment and anticipation - that I couldn't reach the clasps. Earlier, Natasha had helped me into the dress, her nimble fingers making quick work of the fastening while she chattered about the evening ahead. Neither of us could have imagined I'd end up here, needing Zaven Lazarev's help to get out of it.

Taking a deep breath, I steeled myself for what I needed to do next. I opened the bedroom door a crack and peered out into the living room. The hinges creaked softly, the sound seeming to echo in my nervous state.

Zaven stood by the window, his back to me, cutting an imposing figure against the dim light. The moonlight silvered the edges of his broad shoulders, casting his face in shadow as he turned slightly. He was speaking to one of his men in low, rapid Russian, his shoulders tense with barely contained authority. The whispered conversation stopped abruptly when the floorboard beneath my foot groaned in protest.

"Zaven?" I called softly, hating how uncertain my voice sounded.

He turned immediately, his eyes finding mine. The dim light from the window caught the amber flecks in his dark gaze, making them glow like embers. "Yes, *malyshka?*"

I felt my cheeks flush with embarrassment, the heat spreading down my neck. "I... I can't reach the clasp. Could you...?" I trailed off, unable to finish the request, my fingers nervously twisting the fabric of my dress.

Understanding darkened his eyes, pupils dilating as they swept over me. With a quick gesture, he dismissed his man, who retreated to the hallway outside my apartment, the door closing with a soft click that seemed to seal my fate.

Zaven approached me slowly, each deliberate step making the old wooden floor creak beneath his weight. "Of course," he said, his voice low and controlled, though I caught the slight roughness at its edges. "May I come in?"

I nodded, stepping back to allow him into the small bedroom. As he entered, his presence seemed to fill the space, making the room feel even smaller than it was. The scent of his cologne - sandalwood and something darker, more primal - mixed with the familiar smells of my cheap laundry detergent and the faint floral notes of my perfume. The combination made my head spin.

He paused just inside the doorway, his gaze taking in the humble space - the narrow bed with its mismatched pillows, the secondhand dresser, the stack of dog-eared paperbacks on the nightstand. A smile touched his lips, softening the hard planes of his face.

"First man in your bedroom here, *da*?" he asked, voice pitched low enough that only I could hear, even though we were alone.

The question caught me off guard. "I... yes," I admitted, the flush on my cheeks deepening.

Something flashed in his eyes - satisfaction, possessiveness, heat. "Good," he murmured. "Like being your first in many things, *malyshka*."

My stomach tightened at his words, at the promise they held. The room suddenly felt warmer, the air between us charged with an electricity that made the fine hairs on my arms stand on end.

"Turn around," he instructed softly.

I complied, my heart racing as I felt him step closer. The heat of his body radiated against my back, a stark contrast to the chill of the room. I could feel his breath, warm and slightly uneven, against the nape of my neck, sending goosebumps across my skin.

"Let me help with this, *malyshka*," he murmured, his accent thicker than before. His voice wrapped around the endearment like dark velvet, making it sound like a caress.

My heart pounded so hard I was sure he must be able to hear it. This man, this dangerous, powerful man was in my bedroom, about to undress me. The thought sent a shiver of both fear and excitement down my spine.

"Thank you," I managed to whisper, my voice embarrassingly breathy.

I felt his fingers brush against my bare skin as he reached for the first clasp, and I had to bite my lip to stifle a gasp. Even that small touch felt electric, sending sparks across my skin like wildfire. Each clasp coming undone seemed impossibly loud in the quiet room, as he slowly, deliberately worked his way down.

"*Bozhe moy*," he whispered, so softly I almost thought I'd imagined it. His fingertips traced the now-exposed line of my spine, a feather-light touch that made me tremble. "*Krasivaya.*" [Beautiful]

When the final clasp came free, Zaven's hands lingered for a moment on my lower back, his thumbs making small, mesmerizing circles just above the lace edge of my underwear. Heat bloomed wherever he touched, spreading through me like warm honey.

"Been thinking about this," he murmured, his voice rough with restraint. "How you look under silk. If skin as soft as seems." His hands slid to my waist, not pulling me closer but simply holding. "Testing my fucking control, *malyshka.*"

I could feel the slight tremor in his hands, the only indication that his composure wasn't as perfect as it appeared. The knowledge that I affected him as strongly as he affected me was intoxicating, empowering.

"There you go," Zaven said, his voice husky as he finally, reluctantly stepped back. "Need anything else?"

The question hung in the air, loaded with implications. His eyes, when I turned to face him, holding the dress to my chest, were dark with desire, but also with something else—patience, respect. The combination was more seductive than any bold advance could have been.

Did I need anything else? God, yes. I needed his hands on me, his lips on mine. I needed to feel alive and wanted and safe in a way I hadn't in years. The temptation to simply let the dress fall, to step into the heat and promise of his arms, was almost overwhelming.

But I also needed to be careful. To protect my heart. To remember that less than twelve hours ago, I'd been just another hostess at his club.

Swallowing hard, I managed to shake my head. "No, thank you. I can manage from here."

I heard him take a step back, and I both mourned and welcomed the increased distance between us. The loss of his warmth made me shiver.

"Will be in living room when ready," he said, his tone controlled again though his accent remained thick. "Don't rush. Take time you need."

As the door closed behind him, I let out a shaky breath. What was I doing? What was I getting myself into?

* * *

I took a deep breath, smoothing down the soft cream sweater I'd pulled on over a simple long-sleeved shirt. The familiar comfort of the layers felt like armor against whatever was coming next. I adjusted my jeans, making sure they were tucked neatly into my winter boots, the practical choice after hours in those killer heels that were now kicked off by the closet.

"You can do this," I whispered to myself, catching my own gaze in the cracked mirror. "It's just a different house. Different rules. You've adapted before."

But this was Zaven Lazarev waiting for me out there. Not just any man. A man who'd kissed me like he wanted to consume me and then stopped when I needed him to. My fingers trembled slightly as I tucked a stray strand of hair behind my ear.

The burgundy gown lay across my bed, impossibly elegant against my threadbare comforter. I picked it up carefully, the silk cool and slippery against my hands. I folded it over my arm along with the borrowed fur coat that still smelled faintly of expensive perfume. My practical wool coat went over both, protection against the bitter night air I knew waited outside.

"One foot in front of the other, Lily," I muttered, an old mantra from the days after I'd first escaped Jack. "Just like before."

I paused with my hand on the doorknob. Was I really doing this? Walking voluntarily into the home of a man I barely knew? A *vor*, a criminal. I could call Natasha, ask to stay with her instead. Or use the money I'd saved to find another place.

But then what? Keep hiding in cheap apartments, looking over my shoulder every day? Waiting for Jack to find me again? The thought made my stomach twist.

No. This was different. I wasn't being dragged along helplessly. I was making a choice. My choice.

I opened the bedroom door and froze. In my tiny living room, Zaven's men were boxing up my stuff. Not packing - boxing. They had actual cardboard boxes, packing tape, bubble wrap. Professional. Like this was a real move and not another desperate escape.

Zaven stood in the middle of it all, saying something in Russian. "*Ostorozhno s etim. Vse dolzhno byt' ideal'no.*" [Be careful with that. Everything must be perfect] He turned when he heard the door, his eyes moving over me in a way that made me forget I was wearing an old sweater and jeans.

"Feel better, *malyshka?*" he asked, his voice softer than before. "Clothes more comfortable, *da?*"

I couldn't answer, just watched as a stranger wrapped my cheap lamp from the local market in newspaper. Another was emptying my kitchen drawer - all four forks, three spoons, and the one decent knife Natasha had given me from her own kitchen.

God, was this really all I had? After everything?

One of the men, older than the others with salt-and-pepper hair at his temples, approached me with unusual deference. "*Devushka* Sinclair?" He held up my copy of "Pride and Prejudice." "Would you like this packed separate? To keep with you?"

My throat tightened. That book. Mom's book. The only thing I'd grabbed from the nightstand when I ran from Jack. I'd stuffed it in my bag along with the photo inside it and whatever cash I could find, my hands shaking so badly I dropped the photo twice.

Every second thinking he might walk through the door. Every sound making me jump.

"Everything alright?" Zaven was suddenly beside me, his warmth palpable even without touching.

"Yes, I just..." I nodded at the book, not trusting my voice.

Something changed in his face - his jaw tightened, eyes going cold in a way that should have scared me but somehow didn't. He understood without me having to explain.

"Pack it all," he ordered in English. "Every item. If *Devushka* Sinclair even glanced at it, I want it packed. With care. Nothing broken, nothing lost."

The men straightened almost imperceptibly, their movements becoming even more precise. "Yes, sir," the older one responded, wrapping my book with the care usually reserved for expensive china.

"*Gospodin* Lazarev," another man appeared from the kitchen with my single mug, the chipped one with faded flowers. "We finish in ten minutes."

Zaven nodded, then his hand touched my back, surprisingly gentle. "Let's get you out of here, Liliya."

I looked around one last time at the bare walls, the empty shelves. Another temporary home. Another exit in darkness.

But this felt different. For the first time, I wasn't fleeing with just what I could carry. For the first time, someone was making sure I didn't leave anything behind.

Zaven leaned close, his breath warm against my ear. "Never have to run like that again, *malyshka*. From now on, you have everything you need. I make sure of this."

I wasn't sure if that was a promise or a threat. Maybe both.

His voice made something twist inside me. Not fear—something else I wasn't ready to name. Maybe it was the certainty in his words, or the way his hand felt so solid against my back. Whatever it was, for once I believed I might actually be safe.

The men moved with practiced efficiency, carrying boxes down to waiting vehicles. Zaven never left my side, his steady presence like an anchor as I took one last look at the tiny apartment that had sheltered me these past weeks.

"Is moment to decide, *malyshka*," he said quietly, watching my face. "Can still change mind. Can find different arrangement if this not what you want."

The offer surprised me. Zaven Lazarev, the *vor* who commanded fear with just his presence, was giving me a choice. But that's what made this different from Jack, wasn't it? Choice. Agency. Even if the options weren't perfect.

"No," I said, finding my voice at last. "I'm ready."

We stepped outside, and the bitter cold hit me like a slap. Snow fell in fat, lazy flakes that caught in my hair and melted against my skin. Zaven's men moved around us like shadows—one with an umbrella, another already opening the car door. The whole thing felt surreal, like I'd somehow stepped into someone else's life.

I looked back at the building one last time. Four weeks. That's all this place had been to me—just another temporary stop. Another place to hide.

As I turned away from my past, Zaven's eyes met mine, a silent question in their depths. Was I truly ready for what came next?

"Yes," I said, surprised to find I meant it. The old Lily would have been terrified, would have seen another man trying to control her life. But I wasn't that woman anymore.

Lily had fled America in panic. Liliya was choosing to walk into something new.

I slid into the warmth of the car, feeling the weight of Zaven settling beside me. Whatever waited for me at his home—whatever came next—I'd face it on my feet. I was done running.

18

Liliya

The car slowed to a stop, tires crunching on what sounded like gravel. I leaned forward, peering through the window as the security team stepped out first, their dark figures moving with practiced efficiency.

"Wait—this is your house?" The words tumbled out before I could stop them, my breath fogging the cold window.

Zaven's low chuckle rumbled beside me. "You expecting something else, *malyshka?*"

I couldn't tear my eyes away from the... palace? Mansion? "House" seemed like calling the ocean a puddle. Moonlight washed over pale stone walls that stretched in both directions, windows glowing with warm light behind what had to be actual honest-to-God balconies. A fountain stood frozen mid-spray in the center of a circular driveway, surrounded by gardens that even in winter looked expensive.

"I just thought..." My voice trailed off. What had I expected? A luxury apartment? A penthouse? Definitely not this sprawling estate that looked like it had been plucked from a history book about Russian aristocracy.

The door opened beside me, cold air rushing in.

"Time to go inside, Liliya." Zaven's voice had an edge of amusement to it.

I stepped out, my boots crunching on the gravel. The air smelled of pine and something floral that seemed impossible in the winter cold. Maybe it was coming from the greenhouse I could just make out at the edge of the property.

"You live here alone?" I asked, still stunned, my neck craning to take in the full height of the building.

"Not alone," Zaven said, suddenly behind me. His hands settled on my shoulders, warm and heavy through my coat. He leaned down, his breath stirring the hair by my ear. "Staff. Security. And now you."

I swallowed hard, suddenly aware of how small I felt. My entire apartment could have fit in what was probably just his entryway.

"Welcome home, *malyshka*," he said, guiding me forward.

Home. The word felt strange, foreign and frightening and somehow thrilling all at once. This wasn't a home—it was a fortress. A kingdom. And somehow, I was supposed to belong here.

I tugged at my sweater sleeve, suddenly aware of how ridiculous I must look - jeans and boots standing in front of whatever the Russian word for "mansion" was. Behind us, car doors slammed as Zaven's men unloaded my stuff. One box and a single suitcase. Not even enough to fill a corner of this place.

Zaven's hand pressed gently against my back, urging me forward. Each step up those entrance stairs felt like climbing a mountain. The front door was massive - dark wood with carvings so detailed they seemed to move in the shadows. Flowers, vines, birds - all dusted with snow that glittered under the lights.

My stomach knotted. What the hell was I doing here?

Zaven leaned close, his breath warm on my cold ear. "Is alright, Liliya. You safe here."

Before I could answer, the door swung open. A woman with perfectly styled gray hair stood in the doorway, her back straight as a ruler.

"Welcome home, *Gospodin* Lazarev," she said, her voice warm but formal. Her eyes moved to me, curious but kind. "And you must be *Devushka* Sinclair. I'm Irina Petrovna, the housekeeper."

"It's nice to meet you," I mumbled, hating how small my voice sounded.

We stepped through the doorway and into the foyer. I stopped dead in my tracks.

"Holy shit," I whispered, then immediately clapped my hand over my mouth, mortified.

Zaven's laugh was unexpected - deep and genuine. It echoed off the marble floor and soaring ceiling.

"Sorry," I said, but found myself giggling nervously too. "I just... wow."

The space was enormous. A chandelier hung overhead, bigger than my entire bathroom, throwing rainbow light everywhere. The paintings on the walls belonged in museums, not someone's house. And that staircase - it curved upward like something from a movie, all gleaming wood and plush carpet.

I couldn't stop staring. This wasn't a home. This was a palace. And somehow, I was supposed to live here.

I stuck out like a neon sign in a library. My second hand clothes against all this... everything. Four hours ago I was a hostess. Now I was standing in a literal palace.

"Know is late," Zaven said, breaking into my thoughts. "Save full tour for tomorrow. For now, get you settled in room." He studied my face, noticing what I was trying to hide. "Must be exhausted, *da*?"

"Yeah," I admitted, relief washing through me. After everything—the bidding, that kiss, the negotiations, packing up my life—my body felt like lead. But every time Zaven looked at me, with that heat in his eyes, exhaustion wasn't the only thing I felt.

Irina led us upstairs, her sensible shoes silent on the plush carpet. Each step up that massive staircase felt symbolic somehow. Behind me, I could feel Zaven watching—the weight of his gaze almost physical.

The upstairs hallway was lined with mirrors in ornate gold frames. I caught fragments of myself as we walked—pale face, wide eyes, messy hair. In one reflection, I saw Zaven behind me, his dark eyes fixed on the curve where my neck met my shoulder. When he caught me noticing, his lips curved into that knowing half-smile that made my stomach flip.

We stopped at a set of double doors. Actual double doors, like in a hotel suite. Irina unlocked them with a small brass key.

"Your room, *Devushka* Sinclair," she announced, pushing them open.

I stepped inside and froze, my mind struggling to process what I was seeing.

"Holy fuck," I whispered, catching myself this time but not quite managing to censor the expletive.

Moonlight poured through windows taller than my entire apartment. The bed could have fit four people comfortably—all draped in cream-colored silk that probably cost more than my car back home. A fireplace big enough to roast a pig. A sitting area with plush chairs. Built-in bookshelves that reached the ceiling.

"I..." I turned in a slow circle, overwhelmed. "This is for me?"

Zaven stepped in behind me, close enough that I could feel his warmth at my back. "Of course, *malyshka.*" His voice had dropped lower, intimate. "Hope is comfortable for you."

I almost laughed. Comfortable? This place made five-star hotels look shabby.

My fingers touched the back of a nearby chair—velvet, soft as butter. This couldn't be real. Any minute I'd wake up in my creaky bed with the sounds of my neighbor's TV coming through the wall.

The door clicked shut as Irina left. Suddenly the enormous room felt very small with just Zaven and me. The day crashed down on me all at once— everything I'd agreed to, everything that had changed. My legs felt shaky, like they might give out.

"You alright, Liliya?" Zaven moved closer, his voice dropping with concern.

I tried to nod, then shook my head instead. "I... I don't know," I admitted, my voice small in the massive room. "It's all so much. This room, this house... you." My hand gestured vaguely before landing on his chest without me really meaning for it to.

His hand covered mine immediately, warm and solid. Even exhausted, my skin tingled where he touched me. "Know is overwhelming," he murmured. "But you safe here. With me."

I looked up, caught in those dark eyes that seemed to see right through me. "Am I?" The question came out barely audible. "Safe with you?"

His other hand cupped my cheek, his thumb brushing my bottom lip in a way that made my stomach drop. "Safer than ever been," he said, voice rough around the edges. "Meant what I say earlier, *malyshka*. Will protect you. From everything. From everyone."

Something in his intensity made my heart race. "Even from you?" I blurted out.

A slow smile spread across his face—that predator's smile that should have scared me but didn't. "Ah, Liliya," he said, leaning closer until I could feel his breath on my lips. "Maybe I one thing you need protection from most. The way I want to spread you open on that bed and fuck you until you scream my name."

I jerked back, putting space between us, my body flushing hot at his crude words even as my mind scrambled for control. This was exactly what I'd promised myself I wouldn't do again—fall for intensity and protection promises. Jack had been all charm and protection talk at first, too.

"Liliya?" Zaven frowned, genuinely confused.

"I can't—" I wrapped my arms around myself, hating how my body responded to him, my nipples hardening against my sweater, heat pooling between my legs. "This is too fast. I've been here before, trusted too quickly, and—"

"Stop." His voice cut through my spiral. "Look at me, *malyshka*."

I hugged myself tighter but met his gaze. The heat there made me want to step back further.

"Already tell you before—I not him. Not weak boy who need fists to feel strong." His jaw clenched tight. "You compare me to him again?"

His accent thickened with anger, which only sparked my own. "How am I supposed to know that? I've known you for what—a few hours? And suddenly I'm in your house, in this room that's bigger than my whole apartment, with you looking at me like—"

"Like what?" He stepped closer, not touching me but I could feel him anyway—like standing near a fire. "Like man who outbid every other *vor* in city to keep you safe? Like man who promise you honesty, who let you make own choices?"

"That's exactly what I mean!" My voice rose, surprising both of us. "You keep talking about keeping me safe, about choices, but Jack said the same fucking things. It always starts with protection, with promises, until suddenly protection becomes control and—"

"Enough!" The word erupted from him like thunder. "You think I same as him? That I need tricks and lies to control woman?" His eyes had darkened dangerously, but I noticed he kept his distance despite his rage. "Had many chances to take what I want, but that not who I am. Not what I want from you."

He paced a few steps away, then turned back, his control visibly returning. "You know how many women throw themselves at men like me? Offer anything for protection, for status?" His eyes locked with mine. "But you— you stand there with fire in eyes, challenging me, fighting what you feel. That what I want, *malyshka*. Not submission from fear. Surrender from desire."

The intensity of his words sent heat coursing through me, my panties embarrassingly damp. He was right. He'd had countless opportunities to use his power over me, yet at every turn, he'd given me a choice. Even now, furious at being compared to Jack, he maintained his distance, letting his words rather than his physical presence make his point.

"Is not about control, Liliya," he continued, his voice dropping lower, more dangerous. "Is about power freely given. You think I not see how body responds when I near? How pulse jump when I touch?" He took a deliberate step closer. "How you want me right now, even while fighting it?"

My cheeks burned, but I lifted my chin defiantly. "That's physical. It doesn't mean—"

"Means everything," he cut in. "Because even now, even with desire making you tremble, you stand there and challenge me. Fight me. You think your *mudak* could handle woman with such fire?" His lips curved into that predatory smile. "But I? I live for it. Makes my cock hard just watching you defy me."

"Stop trying to make this about desire," I snapped, though my voice betrayed me with a slight tremor. "This isn't about sex, Zaven. This is about trust. About power. About—"

"About fear," he finished for me, his expression softening slightly though his eyes remained intense. "You afraid of wanting me because last time you want someone, he hurt you. Break you. But I not him, *malyshka*." He stepped closer again, still not touching me. "When I finally have you beneath me, when I finally push my cock deep inside you, will be because you trust me enough to surrender. Because you beg me for it. Not because I force."

I forced myself to hold my ground despite every nerve ending screaming for me to either run or close that final distance between us. "You don't know what I feel," I challenged, though my voice came out breathier than intended.

His low chuckle sent shivers down my spine. "*Net*? Then why pupils so dark now, *malyshka*? Why breathing shallow?" He leaned in, his breath hot against my ear. "Why pussy already wet for me? Can smell your arousal from here."

The directness should have offended me. Instead, it sent a jolt straight between my legs, making me clench involuntarily. My breath caught as my body betrayed me, swaying slightly toward him.

"Not begging for anything," I managed, though my voice hitched.

"Yet," he purred, satisfaction evident in his tone. "*Blyad*, love this fire in you, Liliya. Way you fight even when body screams to surrender." His hand came up to cup my face, thumb brushing across my lower lip with barely contained hunger. "But for tonight, we stop. You need rest."

The sudden shift left me disoriented, my body almost crying in frustration. "What?"

"When I fuck you – and I will fuck you – it won't be like this," he said, voice rough with promise. Each crude word landed like a physical touch, making my skin flush hot, my inner walls clenching around nothing. "Want you clear-headed, *malyshka*. Want you choosing me with both mind and body." He stepped back, though the heat in his eyes remained. "For now, sleep. Tomorrow is new day."

I stared at him, caught off balance. One moment he'd been all heat and intensity, making my body hum with need, and the next he was stepping away, leaving me frustrated and confused. Part of me wanted to grab his shirt, to pull him back and finish what we'd started. The other part—the part that had survived Jack—knew he was right, even as my body screamed in protest.

This was exactly what made him different, I realized with startling clarity. Where Jack would have pushed, would have taken my desire as permission regardless of the circumstances, Zaven was walking away. Giving me time. Even as his eyes promised sin, his actions offered respect.

"Into bed, *malyshka*," he said softly, but with that undercurrent of authority that made me shiver. "Need rest after long day."

I found myself moving toward the bed, but couldn't resist adding, "I don't need to be tucked in like a child."

A ghost of a smile played at his lips. "*Net?* Then why you follow when I say get in bed?"

Heat crept up my neck, but I lifted my chin. "Maybe I'm just tired."

"Maybe," he agreed, though his knowing smirk said otherwise. "Or maybe you like when I tell you what to do, even while pretending to fight it."

I opened my mouth to argue, then closed it again, surprised by the realization that he was right. This push and pull between us, this tension - it wasn't like fighting with Jack, where every argument had been laden with fear and threat. This felt more like a dance, dangerous but thrilling. Each time I challenged Zaven, he met my fire not with anger, but with appreciation. It was... liberating.

Still, I couldn't let him have the last word. As I sank into the impossibly soft mattress, I muttered, "I don't pretend anything."

His low chuckle sent warmth pooling in my belly. "Keep telling yourself that, *malyshka*." He moved to remove my boots, and I fought the urge to pull my feet away just to be contrary. "Tomorrow, we see how long you keep fighting what we both know you want."

His hand came up to stroke my hair, and I fought the urge to lean into his touch like a cat - though from his knowing smile, he noticed anyway.

"Sleep now, *moye serdtse*," he whispered, leaning down to press a soft kiss to my forehead. [My heart]

"Still not a child," I mumbled, even as my eyes grew heavy. The last thing I heard was his low chuckle, followed by soft words in Russian that I didn't understand but made me feel oddly safe despite my determination to stay guarded.

The soft click of the door closing behind him felt strangely final. Rolling onto my side, I curled into myself, surprised by how different I felt from just hours ago. The woman who'd challenged Zaven, who'd pushed back and found excitement rather than fear in the confrontation - she felt more like the real me than I'd been in a long time.

But with that realization came uncertainty. Was I letting my guard down too quickly? The banter, the heat between us, the way fighting with him made me feel alive instead of afraid - it was intoxicating. Dangerous, maybe, but in a way that made my pulse race with anticipation rather than fear.

No, I decided, pulling the plush comforter tighter around me. Being cautious didn't mean I had to be afraid. Zaven wasn't Jack - he'd proved that tonight in a dozen small ways, from keeping his distance during our argument to walking away when desire burned hottest between us.

Sleep, when it finally came, wasn't the fitful rest I'd expected. Instead, I drifted off with the ghost of a smile on my lips, my last conscious thought a mixture of anticipation and challenge: let's see what tomorrow brings, Zaven Lazarev.

19

Zaven

The door clicked shut behind me. I stood there like a fucking teenager, hand still on doorknob, unable to walk away from her room. My heart hammered against ribs—a weakness I hadn't felt in... hell, couldn't even remember when.

Chto za khren'? Get shit together, Lazarev. [What the hell?]

Each step away felt like walking through concrete. Body fought every movement, wanting to turn back, to kick that door down and finish what we'd started. Cock still hard, painful against confines of pants. Mind filled with how she would feel beneath me, tight and wet around me.

The halls were quiet. Everything looked same—artwork, those antique vases worth more than most people's homes, carpet that swallowed footsteps. But somehow, all felt different. Kept noticing stupid details—how light reminded me of warmth in her eyes, how some fancy vase pattern looked like her.

Blyad. What fuck was happening to me? I was Zaven Lazarev, *vor v zakone,* man who controlled half of St. Petersburg with iron fist. Didn't turn into some lovesick idiot over green eyes and smile. [Thief in law/made man]

I pushed open door to study and made straight for cabinet where kept good vodka. Not shit we served at club—real stuff, from old distillery outside Moscow. Expensive crystal bottle felt solid in hand as grabbed glass and poured generous measure.

The memory of her hit me like punch to gut. Smell of her hair, how warm she felt against me, that look in eyes even as she trembled—it woke something in me. Made me want to protect her, possess her, mark her as mine in every way.

My cock twitched at thought of spreading her legs, tasting her until she begged, then fucking her until she couldn't remember own name. Wanted to hear her scream my name as she came around me.

The vodka burned going down, but didn't help. Couldn't erase Liliya from mind—so fucking fragile but with that steel core that drove me crazy. Way she challenged me, even while fear and desire fought in those eyes.

I nearly crushed glass thinking about that shithole apartment. Rage boiled up. How dare anyone make my woman live like that? How dare they make her afraid?

My free hand clenched into fist. Wanted to hunt down every piece of shit who'd ever hurt her, starting with that boyfriend of hers. Could almost taste how good would feel to break his bones, to watch him realize mistake in ever touching what was mine.

But even while imagining painting walls with his blood, calculating part of brain was making plans. Needed information first. Names, locations, weaknesses. Viktor would know how to get it quietly. And after that...

Blyad. I finished vodka in one gulp. This was dangerous territory. These feelings—they were liability. In my world, caring about someone meant giving enemies target. Had learned that lesson with father's blood.

So why couldn't get her out of fucking head? Why did defiant little smile twist something in chest? Why did want to go back upstairs and show her exactly what she did to me?

I poured another drink and stared at reflection in liquid. For first time in years, didn't recognize self. Same face, but something in eyes had changed. Gone soft. Weak.

Three quick knocks jerked me back. Viktor.

"Enter," I said, straightening up.

Viktor walked in, face blank as always, but knew him too well. That eyebrow quirk said he knew exactly what—or who—had me drinking alone in dark.

"All settled with *Devushka* Sinclair?" he asked, glancing at bottle before looking back at me. Ghost of smile touched his lips.

Smug bastard. He'd been at *Smotriny*, had seen me outbid everyone in room for her. Had watched me break twenty-year tradition of never participating.

"She here now," I said, unable to keep satisfaction from voice. "That all that matters."

"Ah." Viktor's lips twitched as he studied my disheveled appearance—loosened tie, hair probably mess from running hands through it. "So this why great *Vor v Zakone* hide in dark with bottle? Because girl 'here now'?"

I glared at him. "Careful, Viktor."

"Must be special girl," he continued, ignoring me, "to have you prowling halls like lovesick tiger. Never see you like this before. Not even with Sofia."

Mention of woman from past made jaw clench. "You want test how much patience I have tonight?" I growled, without any real heat. Twenty years of friendship bought him some leeway. Some.

His face turned serious, though amusement still lingered in eyes. "Need you focused, Zaven. We have situation."

His tone told me everything. This was bad.

"Dmitri?" I asked, already knowing.

Viktor's face hardened. "He make moves on north side. Two warehouses hit last night."

This should have been all I could think about. Direct challenge, gauntlet thrown at feet. Before tonight, would already be planning retaliation, running through strategies in head.

But now? All could think was whether Liliya was safe upstairs, if Dmitri knew about her. Had I painted target on her back by claiming her so publicly?

"Zaven?" Viktor's voice cut through. Could see alarm in his eyes. Been quiet too long.

I straightened, pushing thoughts of Liliya back. Was still *vor*. Had empire to protect, men who counted on me. Couldn't let woman—even one with those bewitching eyes—distract from what needed doing.

"Tell me everything," I said, voice cold as winter. "Then call meeting. Time to remind Dmitri why he fear dark."

Viktor turned all business. "Attacks were coordinated, precise. They knew exactly where to hit, when to strike. Not just random hit—was surgical."

"Inside information?" My jaw clenched.

"*Da.* Security systems disabled without single alarm. They take everything—weapons from Kiev, pharmaceutical supplies. Even documents we hold for Councillor Volkov."

Blyad. Weapons could be replaced, drugs meant nothing, but those documents... "*Mudak* makes play for our political connections."

"Not all," Viktor's face grew grimmer. "Dmitri meet with *Solntsevskaya Bratva*. From Moscow." [Solntsevo Brotherhood]

The implications hit hard. *Solntsevskaya* weren't amateurs. If Dmitri had their backing, this wasn't just local—this was opening move in much bigger game. Moscow *bratva* didn't get involved unless they smelled blood in water. Unless they thought I was weak. [Brotherhood/gang]

"Terms?" I demanded.

Viktor shook his head. "Nothing concrete. But more problems. Police commissioner reach out through usual channels. Getting pressure from above for 'crackdown' on organized crime."

"How fucking convenient," I spat, pouring another drink. "Timing perfect, *da*? Right when take Liliya as *nevesta*. Right when everyone at *Smotriny* see how much pay for her."

"*Da.* And someone dig into shell companies. Looking for weak points, Zaven. Deep search, professional. Like someone build case."

I could feel walls closing in. Dmitri wasn't just grabbing territory—*mudak* was trying to dismantle entire operation. And had help. Powerful help. The kind that only comes when they think you vulnerable.

I stood up, needing to move. "Call everyone. Top lieutenants, best strategists. Want options for hitting back at Dmitri."

Viktor nodded, reaching for phone, but I wasn't done.

"One more thing," I said, stopping pacing. "Any word on Liliya's ex? Find anything?"

Viktor's expression shifted, and something in it made blood run cold. "*Da.* Found him. Jack Thompson. Former college athlete, now personal trainer in Chicago." He paused. "He been asking questions, Zaven. About Russia. About St. Petersburg."

"*Blyad,*" I snarled, fury rising hot and fast, blood pounding in ears. "He looking for her?"

"Seems so. Made calls to travel agencies, researching visas. Not subtle about it." Viktor's eyes met mine. "Want me handle it?"

The offer tempted me. Viktor could make problems disappear quietly. But no—this *mudak* was mine.

"*Net.* Keep watching him. Want to know moment he even think about boarding plane." My fingers tightened on glass until it creaked. "If he stupid enough to come here, want personal greeting ready."

Viktor nodded, understanding perfectly. "Need be careful, Zaven. Dmitri look for any weakness to exploit. And Liliya..."

"I know," I cut him off, not needing reminder of danger I'd put her in. American would have to wait. "Focus on Dmitri."

"*Da.*" Viktor turned to leave, then paused, looking back with rare expression of concern. "Zaven, never see you like this over woman before. This could be used against you. Against us."

"Your point?" I growled, though knew he was right.

"Just be careful, *Brat.* You can have woman without giving her your heart. Heart is weakness in our world."

I snorted. "You think not know this? Am not lovesick boy."

Viktor's eyes held mine for long moment. "Good. Because man like you cannot afford such luxury." He nodded once. "What you want done about warehouses?"

Good question. Part of me wanted immediate payback. Show of force to remind everyone why they fear *Vor v Zakone.* But with Moscow dogs now in game, needed to be smarter.

"Double security on remaining holdings. Quiet like. Don't want tip hand that we know about Moscow connection." I moved back to window, looking out at my city. "And Viktor? Find out who sold us out. Someone let them past security."

"Consider it done."

Alone again, I pressed forehead against cool glass. City stretched out before me, beautiful and treacherous. Somewhere out there, Dmitri plotted next move. Somewhere, that American piece of shit made plans he'd live to regret.

And few floors above, my Liliya slept, unaware of storm gathering around us all.

Sleep would have to wait. Had empire to defend, enemies to crush. And most importantly, had woman to protect—whether she thought she needed it or not.

Would give her space. Let her adjust to new surroundings over next few days. Not push too fast, despite how body ached for her. Liliya needed time to feel safe here, to understand this world she'd entered. Could control self that long. Then, when she ready, would show her exactly what it meant to be mine.

20

Zaven

I surveyed the gathering around the long table in my private conference room. Three days had passed since bringing Liliya to my home—three days of giving her space to adjust while I focused on the growing threat from Dmitri. The faces before me were hard as granite, eyes sharp despite the early hour—my most trusted lieutenants. Brotherhood. Steel spine of empire.

Viktor stood at my right, posture rigid as a statue, gaze calculating as he finished laying out the latest developments. The room stank of tension and cigarette smoke, the gravity of Dmitri's continued moves evident in tight jaws and clenched fists.

"*Blyad,*" Sergei muttered, scarred knuckles white against polished wood. "*Mudak* thinks he can fuck with us like this?"

"*Brat'ya,*" I cut through tension, voice cold as Siberian winter. "We at war now. Dmitri made move. Time to show him why people fear *Vor v Zakone.*" [Brothers]

My gaze swept across room, meeting each pair of eyes in turn. Some knew me since I was *malchik* at father's knee, watching him rule this same empire. All waited for my lead, for plan that would crush our enemies. [Boy]

But as I opened mouth to speak, unbidden image flashed through mind: Liliya, sleeping peacefully above us, unaware of monsters plotting in darkness below.

Blyad. Pushed thought aside. Time for that later. Now needed to be *Vor* they expected.

"This *mudak* thinks he can take what's ours," I continued, voice deadly quiet. "Let's show him how wrong he is."

Sergei leaned forward, battle-scarred face twisted in eager grin. "Could hit back hard, Zaven. Take out main operations. Leave message written in blood."

I shook head. "Too obvious. Dmitri expect retaliation. Need be smarter than street thugs."

Nikolai, former FSB now handling intelligence, cleared throat. "What about political connections? Documents from Volkov give leverage. Could squeeze his support, *da*?"

Viktor nodded, expression thoughtful. "Subtle approach. Take time, but break foundation before he know what happen."

Savage smile tugged at lips. This why these particular men sat in this room. Not just muscle—had brains behind brutality. "*Da.* Nikolai, analyze documents. Find every weakness, every crack we can split open."

Yuri, youngest lieutenant but most vicious strategist, shifted forward. "While working political angle, need secure assets. Move valuable cargo, increase security." His eyes gleamed with bloodlust. "Maybe set some traps, *da*?"

"Explain," I prompted, already liking where headed.

"Feed false information. Let him think he find soft target." Yuri's grin turned feral. "When *mudak* comes to bite…"

"We waiting with teeth," I finished, nodding approval. "Good. Viktor, work with Yuri. Make bait irresistible."

"What about port operations?" Sergei cut in, lighting cigarette. "Dmitri's people seen near docks more often lately. Testing our control there."

Nikolai snorted. "Not just docks. Customs officials suddenly very interested in shipping manifests. Too much attention, too coordinated."

"Because not coincidence," I growled. "Dmitri working multiple angles. Trying squeeze us from all sides."

"Could eliminate problem at source," Sergei suggested, face eager for violence. "Few customs officials have tragic accidents, others fall in line quick enough."

"*Net.*" Cut him off sharp. "Too obvious. Draw attention we don't need." Turned to Nikolai. "What dirt we have on port authority?"

His smile was cold as winter. "Chief Inspector's gambling debts growing by day. Harbor Master's daughter just got accepted to expensive British university. Could be... helpful with tuition."

"Good. Use that." Looked to Yuri. "Meanwhile, Kalashnikovs from Ukraine need moving. And Barrett shipment from Turkey."

"The fifty-cals?" Yuri raised eyebrow. "Those promised to Chechens next week. High-value."

"*Da,*" I nodded. "Too valuable to lose. Move them tonight. Use old meat-packing trucks."

"What about Dragunov parts?" Sergei asked. "Still waiting for assembly at warehouse."

"Schedule legitimate shipments," I ordered. "Let them search clean cargo while we move snipers through other channels."

"Construction companies make good cover," Viktor added. "Still have contracts for marina development. Easy to hide rifle parts in building supplies. Steel beams look same on X-ray as barrel assemblies."

"Use Chinese night vision equipment as diversion," I decided. "Let small shipment get 'discovered' – cheap enough to lose, but looks important enough to satisfy them."

Each lieutenant brought different strengths to table—Sergei's muscle, Nikolai's intelligence network, Yuri's creative ruthlessness. Working together, making organization stronger than sum of parts.

"Speaking of equipment," Ivan spoke up from end of table. Finance man had been quiet until now, calculating costs in shrewd mind. "Recent movements of funds for Makarov purchase looking suspicious to certain banking friends. Might need clean new channels."

"Use renovation of nightclub in Nevsky District," I decided. "Already have permits, politicians in pocket. Perfect cover for moving funds."

"*Da,* but speaking of nightlife..." Yuri leaned forward, eyes gleaming.

"Dmitri's new underground poker room near Vasilyevsky Island? Would be shame if authorities discovered drugs on premises."

Sergei barked laugh. "Or if protection money suddenly stop reaching right pockets."

"Both," I said, feeling plan take shape. "Hit him legal side and illegal side. Make him fight two-front war." Turned to Nikolai. "Get people inside his operation. Want to know everything—who he pay, who he fuck, what he eat for breakfast."

After two hours of plotting Dmitri's downfall, solid strategy emerged. Start quiet—political pressure, false leads, moving pieces on board. Then, when *mudak* least expected it, strike with force that would remind all of St. Petersburg why they fear name Lazarev.

As lieutenants filed out, Viktor stayed behind, expression serious.

"Zaven," he started, voice low. "Need discuss other matter."

I straightened spine, exhaustion giving way to irritation. "What now, Viktor?"

His eyes met mine, unflinching. "About *Devushka* Sinclair. Dmitri might try use her against you."

Jaw clenched tight at mention of her name in same breath as enemy. "Already considered. Security doubled around house, guards assigned to her protection."

"*Da*, but not just physical danger," Viktor said, choosing words carefully like man walking through minefield. "She... distract you at critical time."

Patience wearing thin as cheap vodka. "Know how to separate business from personal, Viktor. Head still clear."

"After display at *Smotriny*, everyone know she important," Viktor didn't back down. "Makes her target, makes you vulnerable where never been before."

He wasn't wrong. The thought of Liliya in danger made blood run cold in way no business threat ever had.

"Value your counsel," I said, letting steel leave voice slightly. "But have plans in place. No one touches what's mine."

Viktor accepted this, if reluctantly. As he turned to leave, reached for phone. "Almost forget—Irina ask about breakfast arrangements for *Devushka* Sinclair."

Blyad. In all planning and strategy, nearly forgotten simplest things. My *malyshka* would wake soon to strange house, new life.

"Tell her serve in solarium,this morning" I ordered, mind shifting from war to softer concerns. Morning light would be good there, peaceful. Place to ease her into this world, not overwhelm her. After giving her these past days, time to welcome her properly. "Make sure everything perfect. Russian breakfast, but add some American things too. She might want familiar food."

Viktor's lips twitched, noting shift from war council to domestic concerns, but smart enough not to comment. "*Da.* Will inform Irina."

Alone again, I turned to window. Sun fully up now, painting city in morning light. Despite exhaustion pulling at bones after sleepless night, couldn't rest yet. Had empire to protect, war to plan.

But first, needed shower, fresh clothes. Would not greet her looking like man who spent night plotting violence. Three days of keeping distance enough. Wanted her to see man she could trust, not just *vor.* Strange how much that mattered now—what she thought of me. How she looked at me.

Took one last look at St. Petersburg spread before me. Somewhere out there, Dmitri moved against me. But here, in this house, something new beginning. Something that, against all logic, felt more important than empire itself.

21

Liliya

I'd been up for hours, watching St. Petersburg wake up through these ridiculous floor-to-ceiling windows. My third morning here, and I was still adjusting to the reality of this place. Steam rose from the industrial district, mixing with fog over the Neva River. Nothing like Chicago's skyline, that's for sure.

My forehead pressed against the cold glass, grounding me. Without thinking, my breath fogged up a patch of window, and my finger rose to draw a simple smile—a stupid habit from my days with Jack. Back then, it was my way of reminding myself to keep pretending everything was fine. This morning, though, I realized the smile wasn't completely fake.

That first night felt surreal, still vivid in my memory despite the days that had passed. The way I'd pushed back at Zaven, and how instead of getting angry, he'd looked at me like... fuck, even thinking about it made my pulse jump. Since then, he'd kept his distance, giving me space to adjust to this new world. Well, until now.

"Think I need force my way into your bed, *malyshka?*" His words from that night echoed in my head, sending shivers down my spine. "*Net.* Much more satisfying when you come to me willingly."

My eyes caught the envelope on the nightstand, my name in fancy handwriting. I'd been avoiding it since I woke up, like maybe not reading it would somehow postpone having to face Zaven in daylight.

I traced one last smile on the window—a real one this time, not the fake ones I'd drawn so many times before. Each morning I'd been here, the smiles had become less forced. Maybe that meant something. Or maybe I was being ridiculous, analyzing window drawings like some teenager with a crush.

Finally, I grabbed the envelope I'd been dancing around all morning. Whatever game Zaven and I had started that night, there was no pausing it now.

Malyshka, Join me for breakfast in solarium when ready. Irina will help you prepare. - Z

Short. Bossy. Typical. I couldn't help smiling, thinking about his attempt at control after the other night, when he'd discovered that my challenging him just turned him on more.

"*Devushka* Liliya?" A knock, followed by Irina's voice. "*Gospodin* Lazarev asked me to help you prepare for day. May I come in?"

I looked one last time at the city below, at my fading smile on the glass. Somewhere out there, this new life waited. And for the first time since running from Chicago, I felt something besides fear. Something that felt weirdly like excitement.

"Come in," I called, turning from the window.

Irina entered, those sharp eyes missing nothing—my spot by the window, the letter in my hand, probably even caught the smile on the glass. Nothing got past her.

"Good morning, *Devushka* Liliya." Irina entered, those sharp eyes missing nothing—my spot by the window, the letter in my hand, probably even caught the smile on the glass.

"Morning," I replied, fidgeting slightly under her assessing gaze.

Irina's lips twitched. "Ah, now I see why *Gospodin* likes you." She moved toward what I thought was a closet door. "Come. Let's prepare for solarium."

Even after several days here, I still couldn't quite believe the closet was mine to use. The racks of clothes that stretched seemingly forever, like Zaven had anticipated my every possible need before I'd even arrived.

"What should I wear today?" I asked, running my fingers over fabrics that probably cost more than I'd made in a year at the club.

"*Da. Gospodin* Lazarev was very specific about these selections." Irina moved through the space with purpose, selecting a burgundy sweater dress. "All chosen for St. Petersburg weather, appropriate for *vor's* woman."

'*Vor's* woman.' Just days ago I was managing VIPs at the club. Now I was... what exactly?

"I'll shower first," I said, heading toward the marble bathroom that still felt more like a luxury hotel than something I had access to every day.

The shower, with its array of settings I was still figuring out, had quickly become my favorite part of this new daily routine. After some familiar adjustments to the temperature controls, I stepped in, letting the hot water wash over me.

But then the steam brought back memories—another shower, another morning. Jack pounding on the door, screaming about hot water. My hands shaking as I rushed to finish, knowing what would happen if I made him wait too long.

"Fuck," I gasped, snapping my eyes open, automatically drawing that stupid smile in the steam. This wasn't then. This wasn't him. Zaven might be dangerous, but not like that. Not...

The shampoo I'd come to love over the past few days—jasmine and sandalwood—helped ground me in the present. I focused on that familiar scent, on the hot water, on now. On how Zaven had looked at me that first night, meeting my attitude with heat instead of anger.

I took my time, following what had become my morning ritual. When I finally turned off the water, my skin was pink and my muscles felt relaxed.

The robe—softer than anything I'd owned before—was waiting on its hook. I wrapped myself in it and wiped a spot clear on the mirror, studying my reflection—bright eyes, flushed cheeks, something different in my face that hadn't been there when I'd first arrived. Something that looked almost like confidence.

Irina had laid out the burgundy sweater dress while I showered, somehow more intimidating than that evening gown from *Smotriny.*

"Was favorite of *Gospodin's* mother," Irina said, watching me examine it. Her tone made me look closer. Not just a dress then—some kind of armor for this new world.

"Come," she gestured to the vanity. "Let's make you ready."

While she worked on my hair, I gathered my nerve. "Irina, after these few days here, I'm curious—how long have you worked for *Gospodin* Lazarev?"

Her eyes met mine in the mirror. "Many years. Was here when *Gospodin* Zaven was just boy."

"What..." I hesitated. "What kind of man is he? Really?"

Her hands paused, face going careful. "*Gospodin* Lazarev complex man, *Devushka* Liliya. Fair to loyal ones, dangerous to those who not." She paused. "But not my place to say more. You see for self soon enough."

I thought about that while she finished my hair, trying to match it with the man who'd been both scary and gentle the other night. "What exactly am I supposed to do here?"

"That, *Devushka* Liliya, for you and *Gospodin* discuss." Her voice dropped lower. "But remember—in this house, woman in your position have great power. Your choice how to use it."

I turned to face her. "Irina... would you call me just Liliya? All this '*Devushka*' stuff feels..."

Something softened in her eyes, though she stayed proper as ever. "Not right, in front of others. But..." her lips curved slightly, "when just us, *da*, can call you Liliya."

The burgundy dress fit perfectly—of course it did. Irina helped me with the delicate pearl buttons down the back, her fingers quick and efficient. The fabric felt rich against my skin, warming to my body temperature. His mother's dress. The weight of that settled over me as Irina made final adjustments.

"There," she said, stepping back to survey her work.

I caught my reflection in the mirror and barely recognized myself. The dress hugged my curves without being tight, the color making my skin glow and my eyes look greener. Irina had swept my hair into some kind of elegant twist, letting a few pieces fall loose around my face. I looked...

expensive. Polished. Like I belonged in this world of marble floors and crystal chandeliers.

Irina nodded with satisfaction. "The solarium is this way."

The hallway seemed to stretch forever, our footsteps echoing off the high ceilings. Every surface gleamed—the floors, the mirrors, the brass fixtures. Even the air smelled expensive, like furniture polish and fresh flowers.

The grand staircase curved down to the main floor, each step wide enough for three people. I gripped the polished banister, grateful for its solid support. My new heels clicked against the marble, the sound somehow making this all feel more real.

We passed through what had to be the most elegant greenhouse I'd ever seen. Plants I couldn't name filled ornate stands, their leaves glossy in the morning light. The glass ceiling soared overhead, letting in the pale winter sun.

My heart started beating faster as we neared a set of French doors. Light poured through them, bright enough to make me squint. Somewhere beyond those doors, Zaven waited. The man who'd kissed me like he wanted to consume me, then walked away to let me rest. The man who'd given me his mother's dress to wear.

Irina paused at the doors, her hand on the handle. With a simple nod, she opened them, and I stepped into the light.

The solarium air hit me first—warm and alive, smelling of earth and green things that shouldn't exist in deep winter. Somewhere, Tchaikovsky played softly, making everything feel even more surreal.

I stepped inside and stopped dead. Full-grown trees reached up to a glass ceiling, their winter branches making patterns in the morning light. The floor was covered in moss and ferns, like someone had stolen a piece of Russian forest and trapped it in here. In the middle of it all stood a table that looked like it had grown straight up from the ground, the wood grain swirling like water. Even the chairs had fur throws draped over them, because apparently that's just how things worked in this house.

I wandered deeper into the forest-that-wasn't-a-forest, totally mesmerized. A tiny stream trickled somewhere, and actual birds—where did they even come from?—flitted between the branches. Everything felt magical, like I'd stumbled through some portal into summer. Well, a really expensive, carefully managed version of summer.

Something moved in the corner of my eye. Probably another bird. I turned to look and—

"*Dobroye utro, malyshka.*" [Good morning, little one]

"Jesus fucking Christ!" I practically levitated, spinning around so fast I almost fell over. My heart tried to escape through my throat as I grabbed onto a nearby tree branch to steady myself. "Don't you make noise when you walk?"

Zaven stood there looking way too pleased with himself, fighting back a smile. Even the exhaustion in his eyes couldn't hide his amusement at watching me nearly jump out of my skin. He was dressed perfectly—crisp white shirt, dark slacks—but something was definitely off. His shoulders carried some invisible weight that hadn't been there that first night, and dark circles shadowed his eyes.

"Did not mean to startle you." His lips twitched. "Much."

"Bullshit," I muttered, still clutching my chest like my heart might make a break for it. "Three days of barely seeing you and now you sneak up on me? Do they teach a class in sneaking up on people at *vor* school or something?"

That got an actual laugh out of him, rough and genuine. His whole face changed when he laughed—younger, lighter. It made my breath catch for reasons that had nothing to do with being startled.

"I was just..." I waved vaguely at everything around us, hoping he'd think my flushed cheeks and racing pulse were from the scare and not from how that laugh had affected me. "This place is incredible."

His expression softened as he looked around, pride and something else mixing in his gaze. "Place has that effect. Even after all these years."

"Shall we have breakfast?" He gestured toward that fairy-tale table, and my stomach chose that moment to growl embarrassingly loud.

His lips twitched. "Take that as yes?"

I felt my face heat.

Something darkened in his eyes at that admission, but he just guided me to the table, his hand finding its usual spot on my lower back. Even that light touch sent heat rushing through me, my nipples tightening under the dress. The man definitely knew what he was doing.

A server appeared like he'd been conjured, setting down plates that belonged in a food magazine. The spread was intimidating—*blini* with caviar, smoked salmon, fresh fruit, pastries that looked too perfect to be real. I didn't even know where to start.

"Hope you slept well," Zaven said, watching me eye the food like it might bite me. "These past days... have been okay?"

"Yes, thank you." I fiddled with my napkin, trying to figure out the protocol here. After days of giving me space, what exactly was the etiquette for breakfast with the man who'd promised to make you beg for his cock that first night? Pretty sure that wasn't covered in any manners book.

His lips curved slightly, like he knew exactly what I was thinking, but the smile didn't reach his tired eyes. "If there anything you need, just ask."

The silence stretched between us as we started eating. I couldn't help stealing glances at him between bites. Even exhausted, everything he did was graceful—the way he handled the delicate china, how he moved without seeming to think about it. The memory of those hands on me last night made heat pool between my legs.

"Something wrong with food?" he asked, catching me staring.

"No! No, it's amazing. I just..." I gestured vaguely at everything. "This is all a lot to take in."

He nodded, studying me with those intense eyes. "Will take time to adjust. But hope you feel at home here." He paused, and something shifted in his expression. "Tell me what you thinking, *malyshka.*"

I took a deep breath. Might as well dive in. "What exactly am I supposed to do here? What do you want from me?"

Zaven set down his fork, giving me his full attention. The weight of his gaze made my heart kick up a notch.

"What I want," he said slowly, voice dropping lower, "is for you to be safe. To be comfortable." His eyes held mine. "And in time, to be true partner to me in all things."

I swallowed hard. "A partner? What does that mean in your world?"

He leaned forward slightly, and I caught a glimpse of the *vor* beneath his controlled exterior. "In my world, Liliya, woman in your position holds significant influence. Will be expected to attend certain functions, help maintain important... relationships." He paused, something darker flickering in his gaze. "But more than that, want someone I can trust. Someone who not afraid to challenge me, like you did the other night."

"I don't know if I'm cut out for this," I admitted softly.

Zaven reached across the table, his hand covering mine. Electricity shot up my arm at his touch. But suddenly, his expression changed, his brow furrowing as his thumb brushed over my skin.

"Liliya," he said, his voice low and tight, "what are these?"

My heart stopped when I realized what his thumb was brushing over—the cluster of small, circular scars on the back of my hand. The ones I usually kept hidden with bracelets or sleeves. The ones I tried so hard to forget existed.

Panic hit like a wave. My pulse roared in my ears as I tried to pull my hand back, but Zaven held on—not tight, but firm enough I couldn't hide.

When I finally made myself look at him, what I saw scared me more than any rage would have. His face had gone cold, deadly calm, as he studied the marks. A muscle ticked in his jaw, and something dark moved behind his eyes. But there was something else too—pain, like seeing my scars physically hurt him.

"These look like cigarette burns," he said, voice so quiet it was barely there. That control in his voice was scarier than any shouting.

I couldn't breathe. The walls of the beautiful solarium seemed to close in. Shame and panic twisted in my gut as memories flooded back—Jack's face twisted with rage, the smell of smoke, pain that made me scream until his hand covered my mouth.

"Liliya? Liliya, look at me." Zaven's voice cut through the fog. "Look at me, *malyshka*."

I forced my eyes open, not even realizing I'd squeezed them shut. The concern in his face was almost worse than the anger. Part of me wanted to lean into that concern, to let him make it better. But the part of me that still woke up screaming said to run.

"Is okay," he said softly, his thumb now moving in gentle circles on my hand. "You safe now. Not have to talk if not ready."

His words were gentle, but I could see him fighting for control. His other hand gripped his coffee cup so hard I thought it might shatter. The muscle in his jaw kept jumping, and his eyes—god, his eyes were terrifying. Not at me, but at whoever had hurt me.

I had to say something. Had to make words work. "It... it was a long time ago." My voice came out small, shaky. "I don't... I can't..."

"Shh," Zaven's grip stayed gentle even though I could feel rage vibrating through him. "Just breathe with me, *malyshka*. In and out. Like this."

I tried to match his breathing, and slowly the panic started to fade. The flashbacks eased back, leaving me feeling hollow and drained.

"I'm sorry," I whispered, hating how weak I sounded.

"Enough." His voice was soft but had steel under it. Something shifted in his face—that predator I'd seen last night, but gentler somehow. "No more apologies for what he did. You survive. You fight. Even now, you challenge me when others would cower." A hint of a smile touched his lips. "My *malenky lisa*, still showing her teeth even when afraid."

He traced the scars again, so gently it made my throat tight. "Saw your strength in many ways. How you adapt to completely new country, new language. How you rebuild life from nothing." He lifted my hand and—oh god—pressed his lips to the scars. "This shows true courage."

"I don't feel very strong," I admitted.

"Then trust what I see," he said, voice rough. "Woman who survive this, who still fight, still challenge me like you did those nights ago—she stronger than she know."

His words hit something in my chest. The way he looked at me—like I was precious and fierce at the same time—was overwhelming. Different from Jack's promises of protection that always meant control. Zaven's eyes held admiration, not possession.

But then his expression changed. A shadow crossed his face, and his grip tightened just slightly on my hand.

"This man," he said, voice dropping to something cold and lethal, "he still in Chicago?"

The shift in his tone made me shiver. This wasn't the man who'd just kissed my scars—this was the *vor*, the one other men feared. "Yes, I think so. I try not to... I don't want to know anything about where he is."

Something flickered in his eyes—knowledge?—but vanished before I could be sure.

"Need you understand something, Liliya." His accent was thicker now, emotion bleeding through. "You safe here. Not just empty words, not just promise. Mean something different in my world."

I swallowed hard. "I know you're... powerful. That you can protect me. But Jack, he—"

"*Net.*" His interruption was quiet but final. "Man who do this?" His thumb brushed my scars one last time. "He nothing. Less than nothing. Just matter of time."

The rage I saw building in him was terrifying—not because I thought he'd hurt me, but because I recognized that cold fury. It was the look of someone planning exactly how they'd make someone else suffer.

His hand was shaking slightly against mine. Just that small tell, but on a man like Zaven, it spoke volumes. He pulled away suddenly, running his hands through his hair as he stood. "*Blyad.* Need move. Need—" He drew in a sharp breath. "Come. Need air. Show you grounds."

The change in his voice startled me—his accent thicker, control slipping. This wasn't the smooth *vor* from before. This was raw, dangerous Zaven, struggling to contain whatever darkness my scars had woken in him.

He helped me up from the table, his touch gentler than I expected given how tightly wound he was. His hand settled on my lower back like always, but there was something different in it now—like he needed the contact to ground himself as much as to guide me.

We wound through the house in silence, passing artwork and antiques I might have gaped at any other time. But right now, all I could focus on was Zaven's barely contained energy, the way his jaw kept clenching, how his other hand had curled into a tight fist at his side.

At a set of heavy wooden doors, he suddenly stopped. "Wait." Something flickered across his face—the first hint of normalcy since seeing my scars. He moved to a coat rack, pulling down what had to be the most expensive fur I'd ever seen. "Cannot have you freeze, *malyshka*."

The coat felt like something out of a dream, impossibly soft as he helped me into it. His hands lingered on my shoulders longer than necessary, and I felt him draw in a deep breath, like he was trying to pull himself together.

Winter hit us like a slap when he opened the doors. The air was sharp, clean—cutting through the heavy atmosphere that had built up in the solarium. Fresh snow covered everything, transforming the grounds into the kind of view you'd see on a Christmas card. If Christmas cards came with armed guards stationed discreetly in the distance.

"Garden beautiful in spring," Zaven said, his voice steadier now that we were moving. "But winter has own charm, *da?*"

He wasn't wrong. Formal gardens stretched out forever, all perfect lines under fresh snow. Stone paths wound between frozen fountains that probably ran in warmer weather. In the distance, I could make out what looked like a maze made of hedges, every branch crystallized with frost.

The cold bit straight through the fur, making me drift closer to Zaven's warmth without really meaning to. Whether it was for heat or something else... well, I wasn't ready to think too hard about that.

"Tell me about the gardens," I said, hoping to keep him in this calmer moment, away from thoughts of Jack and scars and revenge.

"Been in family for generations," he said, guiding me down a cleared path. His voice softened a bit, like these memories helped push back the darkness from earlier. "Great-grandmother design original layout. Each generation add something new." He nodded toward an elaborate gazebo covered in climbing vines, frozen solid in the winter air. "That was mother's contribution. Used to practice ballet there as girl."

Something about imagining a young Zaven watching his mother dance made my chest tight. It was the second time he'd mentioned her today—first her dress, now this. I wanted to ask more, but before I could—

A sharp crack echoed through the garden.

Before I could even process what was happening, Zaven moved. In one fluid motion, he spun us around, pinning me between his body and the stone wall of the gazebo. His arms caged me in, his whole frame tense and alert as his eyes scanned for threats.

Another crack, and I realized what it was—ice breaking off tree branches. But Zaven didn't immediately move away. I could feel the heat radiating between us despite the winter layers, his proximity doing things to my pulse I didn't want to admit. Under my palm, where I'd instinctively pressed my hand against his chest, his heart raced just as fast as mine. That small revelation made me dizzy with possibility.

"Just ice," I said softly, trying to ignore how my voice shook. Not from fear—definitely not from fear.

His eyes dropped to mine, and something shifted in them. The predatory alertness melted into a different kind of heat as he seemed to really notice our position. "*Da*," he murmured, voice rough. "But position not so bad, *da?*"

I felt my cheeks flush hot despite the cold. "You did that on purpose."

"Protecting you, *malyshka.*" But his lips curved into that dangerous smile that made my stomach flip. "That position come as... what you say? Happy accident."

One of his hands moved to my face, his thumb brushing over my cold-flushed cheek. The touch was gentle but sent electricity shooting through me. His other hand stayed braced against the wall, keeping me caged in his warmth.

"Should move," he murmured, but instead his thumb traced down to my bottom lip. "Cold out here."

"Then move," I whispered, but my hands betrayed me, gripping his coat to keep him close.

"Trying," he said roughly. But he leaned in closer, his breath warm against my lips. "You not helping, *malyshka.*"

I tilted my face up to his, everything in me aching for his kiss. His lips barely brushed mine, feather-light, teasing. When I made a frustrated sound, I felt him smile.

"So impatient," he murmured against my mouth. Then he kissed me properly, and my brain short-circuited. His lips were warm despite the cold, demanding but somehow still gentle. My hands slid up to his neck, pulling him closer as the kiss deepened.

He pulled back suddenly, and I actually swayed forward, trying to follow his lips. His low chuckle made my eyes snap open.

That satisfied smirk on his face should have annoyed me, but my brain wasn't working well enough for irritation. He stepped back, looking entirely too pleased with himself as he took in my flushed face and dazed expression.

"Rest of grounds this way, *malyshka*," he said casually, like he hadn't just turned my world upside down. But his voice was still rough around the edges, and his eyes... god, his eyes promised this wasn't over.

I had to take a moment to steady myself before following him down the path. Bastard didn't even have the decency to look as affected as I felt.

I had to concentrate on not tripping over my own feet as we continued down the path. My lips still tingled, and every time Zaven glanced at me with that knowing look, my brain short-circuited all over again.

"Through here," he said, leading me past what looked like a small forest of snow-covered evergreens. His hand stayed on my lower back, warm and steady. "Great-grandmother bring trees from Siberia. Say remind her of home."

"You talk about her a lot," I said, partly to distract myself from how good he felt next to me. "Your great-grandmother."

"*Da*. Strong woman. Build much of what family have now." Pride mixed with something darker in his voice. "Would have liked you, I think. She also had... what you call it? Backbone."

"Is that why you chose me?" The question slipped out before I could stop it. "Because I have backbone?"

He stopped walking, turning to face me. That intense look was back, the one that made my knees weak. "Choose you because first time see you handle drunk client at club, you not cower. Not flutter lashes, not play games." His lips curved. "You tell him fuck off, but so polite he actually apologize."

I remembered that night. "He was getting handsy with one of the waitresses."

"*Da.* You protect her without even thinking. Like with Natasha." He reached up, brushing a snowflake from my cheek. "Strength look good on you, *malyshka.*"

The compliment made me flush. "Even when I use it against you?"

"Especially then." His voice dropped lower, making heat pool between my thighs. "Told you before—like when you show teeth."

My lips still tingled from our kiss, and something about the way he looked at me now—like my defiance was a gift rather than a threat—made me wonder if maybe, just maybe, I'd finally found someone who didn't want to break my spirit, but set it free.

22

Liliya

"Tell me you not always this stubborn," Zaven said, amusement warming his voice as we crunched through the snow.

I shot him a sideways glance, fighting my own smile. "Only when it matters. Besides," I pulled the fur coat tighter, "I grew up in Minnesota. This is practically summer weather."

His low chuckle sent warmth through me that had nothing to do with the coat. "Ah, now truth comes out. Finally understand why little American girl not afraid of Russian winter."

The easy moment between us felt... good. Natural. Like maybe I wasn't completely crazy for choosing to stay outside, to face this new world head-on.

"Estate grounds extensive," he said, gesturing to the pristine expanse before us. "Many buildings, each with purpose." The set of his shoulders changed slightly - this was Zaven in his domain, the *vor* showing his territory.

Our footsteps crunched in the snow as he guided me toward a large garage-like structure where several men worked on what had to be millions of dollars worth of cars. I couldn't help but whistle softly at the collection.

"Like what you see?" Zaven asked, that hint of amusement still in his voice.

"I know exactly nothing about cars," I admitted, "but even I can tell these are impressive."

"Igor," Zaven called. A muscular man in his forties looked up, immediately setting down his tools. "Head of transportation and logistics. Meet my *nevesta*."

Igor wiped his hands before shaking mine, his grip firm but careful. His eyes were sharp, observant, taking in every detail. "Welcome, Devushka Liliya," he said, accent thicker than Zaven's. "Any transport needs, just ask."

As we continued our tour, I noticed how everyone deferred to Zaven. It wasn't just respect - there was an undercurrent of something more, a mix of awe and perhaps a touch of fear. But I also saw how he acknowledged each person, knew their names, their roles.

"Over there," Zaven gestured to where a group of men were clearing snow from what looked like training grounds, "security facilities. And there," he pointed to a smaller building with smoke curling from its chimney, "kitchens. Best *borscht* in St. Petersburg, or so staff claim."

"Are you actually admitting something of yours isn't the best?" I teased, the words slipping out before I could stop them.

Instead of offense, his eyes gleamed with that dangerous amusement I was starting to recognize. "Only because you never tried my cooking, *malyshka*. Perhaps show you sometime."

"You cook?" I couldn't hide my skepticism. "Like, actual food that people can eat without dying from food poisoning?"

He actually looked offended, though his eyes still glinted with humor. "Of course. Specialty is beef stroganoff. Mother insist all her children learn. Say even *vor* need know how feed self."

"Now that I have to see." I grinned, trying to picture him in an apron. "The great Zaven Lazarev, terror of St. Petersburg, wearing oven mitts."

"Careful, *malyshka*," he murmured, leaning closer until I could feel his breath on my ear. "Might take as challenge."

The mental image of Zaven in a frilly apron was too much. I burst out laughing—a real laugh that I couldn't hold back. His eyes widened slightly, like he was seeing something rare and precious.

"What this sound?" he asked, looking genuinely pleased. "Liliya actually laughing?"

That only made me laugh harder. I tried to compose myself, but every time I pictured him delicately stirring a pot with those dangerous hands, another wave hit me.

"Your face when I said oven mitts," I managed between giggles. "Like I'd questioned your manhood or something."

His smile was different now—softer, more genuine. He watched me laugh with a look that made my stomach flip in a way that had nothing to do with humor.

"Is good sound," he said quietly. "Should laugh more."

I was about to respond when a group of men in dark suits approached. My laughter died immediately at their serious expressions. These guys were different from the staff we'd met—they moved like predators, alert and dangerous.

"Ah, perfect timing," Zaven said, his posture straightening almost imperceptibly. "*Muzhiki*, meet my *nevesta*, Liliya." [Men]

I recognized Viktor immediately from *Smotriny,* his familiar composed expression revealing nothing as our eyes met. Beside him stood three other men who shared that same dangerous aura.

Zaven introduced them one by one: Viktor, his second-in-command, who gave me a slight nod of recognition; Nikolai, head of intelligence, shorter but with a wiry strength and quick, darting eyes that missed nothing; Sergei, built like a bear with hands that looked like they could crush stone; and Yuri, the youngest, with a boyish face that belied the cunning in his green eyes.

Each man nodded politely, but I could feel them assessing me, as if trying to determine if I was a threat or an asset. It was unnerving, and I found myself stepping closer to Zaven instinctively.

"Something amusing?" Viktor asked, his expression so composed it bordered on severe.

"Ah, Liliya just learning about my hidden talents in kitchen," Zaven replied, still looking slightly amused.

Viktor's eyebrow ticked up slightly. "The stroganoff?" he asked, deadpan.

"Da," Zaven nodded, looking almost proud. "Was telling her about mother's recipes."

I glanced between them, surprised by this revelation. "So it's true? He actually cooks?"

"Once per year," Viktor confirmed, his severe expression cracking just slightly. "For his birthday. Makes whole kitchen staff take day off so no one interfere."

"Only time security on high alert inside house instead of outside," added Nikolai with the ghost of a smile.

Zaven shot them all a look that might have terrified anyone else. "Perhaps you prefer next time I let you all starve, da?"

The brief moment of levity faded as the men exchanged meaningful glances. There was an unspoken understanding that passed between them - these men had clearly worked together for years, communicating in ways that went beyond words.

"Come," Zaven said after they departed, his hand finding its spot on my back. "Show you something more interesting than my grumpy lieutenants."

I couldn't help but smile at his attempt to lighten the mood. "Are they always so... intense?"

"Only on good days," he said, that dark humor back in his voice. "On bad days, much worse."

He led me toward a smaller building set apart from the others. It looked older than the rest—not modern like the garage or utilitarian like the training grounds. This one had intricate woodwork around the windows and door, like something from another time.

"My father's private training room," Zaven explained as we stepped inside.

The warmth was welcome after the cold, but I barely noticed it as I took in my surroundings. One wall was lined with weapons—everything from ancient-looking swords to modern firearms. Another held floor-to-ceiling mirrors. The center of the room had training mats and what looked like a boxing ring.

"This is where you learned to fight?" I asked, drawn to a display of ornate knives.

"Among other things." His voice got that distant quality it seemed to have whenever he mentioned his father. "Spent many hours here as boy. Still do."

I turned to find him watching me with an intensity that made my breath catch. "Show me something?" The request surprised us both.

"Sure you want that, *malyshka*?"

I nodded, curiosity winning out over caution. Zaven moved to the wall of weapons with that predator's grace, selecting what looked like an ornate dagger. The blade was beautiful—swirled damascus steel with patterns that seemed to move in the light. The handle looked like ivory.

"Father gave me this on thirteenth birthday," he said, testing its weight in his hand.

Then the blade began to move.

I caught my breath as the dagger danced between his fingers, spinning and weaving in patterns that made it look alive. Each movement was precise, controlled—years of practice made visible. The blade caught the light as it moved, becoming a deadly blur that somehow never seemed threatening despite being obviously lethal.

"First lesson," he said, his voice taking on a rhythmic quality that matched his movements, "knife not just weapon. Is extension of self."

I couldn't look away. This wasn't just skill—it was art. Dangerous and beautiful, like the man himself. His face had taken on an almost meditative quality, and I realized I was seeing something intimate. The boy he'd been, learning these deadly dances in this very room.

The contradiction fascinated me—this man who could handle a blade like it was part of him, but had touched my scars with such tenderness this morning. Who commanded fear and respect, yet looked at me with such heat.

"Zaven," I said softly as he returned the knife to its display, "I know your business is dangerous - you told me that. But what exactly does it mean to be a *vor*? What does that world involve beyond just *Zolotoy Vek*?"

He turned to me, something shifting in his expression. The warrior I'd just watched transformed back into the controlled vor, though now I understood better how thin that line was.

"Smart questions," he said, a hint of pride in his voice. "Not many outsiders brave enough to ask directly." He studied me for a moment, like he was making a decision.

Without warning, he flipped the dagger in his hand and sent it spinning through the air. My heart stopped as the blade whirled across the room, only to embed itself perfectly in the center of a wooden target I hadn't even noticed on the far wall.

"Holy shit," I breathed, my heart racing. "Show off."

His low chuckle sent heat through me that had nothing to do with fear. "Come. Better discuss this somewhere more comfortable."

As we left his father's training room, I couldn't stop thinking about what I'd just seen—not just the deadly accuracy, but how casually he'd done it, like throwing knives was as natural as breathing. It should have terrified me. Instead, I found myself more intrigued than ever.

* * *

We walked back toward the main house, the snow crunching beneath our boots. There was something different in Zaven's demeanor now—a slight tension, as if my question had shifted something between us.

He led me through the maze of corridors, finally stopping at a heavy wooden door with intricate carvings. "My study," he said, pushing it open. "Where I handle more... legitimate business matters."

The room fit him perfectly—all dark wood and leather, with a massive desk by the windows and a fireplace with deep leather chairs on either side. Books lined the walls, their spines catching the firelight. What really caught my eye, though, was the portrait above the fireplace—a man and woman who had to be his parents. They had that same commanding presence, that same regal bearing I was starting to recognize in Zaven.

"They were formidable people, my parents," Zaven said, noticing where my attention had gone.

"They look intense," I said, still studying the portrait. "I can see where you get it from."

"*Da.*" A hint of pride mixed with something more complex crossed his face. He gestured toward one of the leather chairs. "This your home now too. Free to look, to ask questions."

I sank into the chair, practically melting into butter-soft leather. Zaven took the seat across from me, and for a minute we just sat there in comfortable silence with the fire crackling between us.

"You want know about my business," he said finally, his voice thoughtful. "About what I do."

I nodded, gathering my courage after that knife display. "Yes. I know *Zolotoy Vek* is just part of it."

"*Da.* My business interests... diverse. Some legitimate, some less so." His eyes met mine, dark and serious. "Is complex world, Liliya. Not always safe one."

"So you're a criminal." I said it directly, not as an accusation but wanting clarity. "I mean, beyond just breaking restaurant health codes with your cooking."

His lips twitched at my attempt at humor, but his eyes remained serious. "*Da.* Would be disrespectful to lie to you about this."

The way he said it—not a threat, just a statement of fact—made me sit up straighter. What surprised me most was my own reaction. I should have been horrified, or at least concerned. Instead, I felt... relief? Relief at his honesty, maybe. Or something deeper I wasn't ready to examine.

"Is that why everyone around here treats you with such... respect? Fear?"

A hint of a smile touched his lips. "Respect earned through actions, through loyalty. Through upholding code."

"Code?"

"*Vorovskoy zakon*—thieves' code." His fingers absently traced what looked like a tattoo peeking out from his cuff. "Governs everything we do."

My eyes were drawn to the movement, to those intricate designs I could just see peeking out from his cuff. Without really thinking, I reached out, my fingers lightly touching the edge of what looked like a tattoo on his wrist.

"Can you tell me about them?" I asked, my voice coming out softer than I intended.

A slow smile spread across his face. He unbuttoned his cuff and deliberately rolled up his sleeve, revealing intricate artwork that covered much of his forearm. "Every mark tells story. Some symbols of rank, others of time served. Each has meaning in our world." He paused, watching my face carefully. "Some earned in prison."

"Prison?" The word slipped out before I could stop it.

His eyes held mine, gauging my reaction. "Spent three years there. Is part of becoming *vor*. Part of code."

I should have been scared by this admission. Instead, I found myself more curious. "What other marks did you earn there?"

Something flickered in his expression—surprise maybe, or approval. He pointed to more designs on his arms. "These show status. Respect. *Mir*—my world—knows what they mean."

I felt my face heat up at his tone. I bit my lip, then took a risk. "Do you... do you have more? In other places, I mean?"

Zaven's eyes darkened, that dangerous amusement back. "I do," he said, voice dropping to a rough whisper. "But those, *dorogaya*, are for another time. When you ready to see all of me."

My breath caught at the raw promise in his words. I fought to regain some composure. "And the code you mentioned? What does it involve?"

"*Vorovskoy zakon* governs everything," he said, still holding my hand. "True *vor* must refuse legal work. Not cooperate with authorities." A slight smile. "Not supposed to marry either, though that rule... more flexible these days, at least in my circle. Traditional *vory*, they would frown upon it."

I raised an eyebrow. "Flexible? Is that why you can have a *nevesta*?"

"Partly." His eyes moved over my face, lingering on my lips in a way that made my stomach flip. "Many women enter our world through *Smotriny*. But as my *nevesta*, my chosen, you have protection of *vor* code. All who respect me will respect you." His voice dropped lower. "And many respect me."

"And those who don't respect you?" I asked before I could stop myself.

Something dangerous flashed in his expression, his grip on my hand tightening slightly. "They not people you need worry about. Will always protect you, Liliya." He paused. "My business interests, my resources—they not just for me. They for all who are part of my *mir*, my world. We rise together."

His words hung in the air between us. I stared into the fire, turning them over in my mind. The promises of protection, of belonging, of safety. They were beautiful words. Familiar words.

"What is it?" Zaven asked softly, his thumb tracing circles on my palm. "See shadow cross your face just now."

I hadn't realized my expression had changed. His perception was unnerving sometimes, how he could read the smallest shifts in my mood.

"It's just..." I hesitated, not sure I wanted to go there. Not now, when things felt almost... good. But his eyes held mine, patient, waiting.

His expression shifted, but he didn't speak. Just waited, his thumb still tracing gentle circles on my palm. That small, steady touch somehow gave me courage to continue.

"I've heard beautiful promises before," I said, staring into the fire rather than meeting his eyes. "Jack was all protection and security in the beginning too. He made me feel... chosen." My voice hardened. "Then came the control. The tracking app on my phone. The 'surprise visits' to make sure I wasn't lying about where I was. The anger if I wore something he thought was too revealing."

I could feel Zaven's hand tighten around mine, but when I looked up, his face was carefully controlled. Like he was trying not to scare me with his reaction. His eyes encouraged me to continue.

"When it turned physical, I told myself it was just because he loved me so much, that his jealousy was a sign he cared." A bitter laugh escaped me. "God, looking back, I can't believe the bullshit I convinced myself was normal."

I traced the circular scars on my hand with my finger. "The violence got worse over time. More frequent. More... creative." I took a shaking breath.

"These cigarette burns? That was his response when a male classmate called about a group project. Said he needed to mark me, to remind me who I belonged to."

Zaven's jaw clenched so hard I could see a muscle tick in his cheek, but he still didn't interrupt.

"I stayed after that. Stupid, right?" A bitter laugh escaped me. "Kept thinking it couldn't get worse." I stared into the fire, finding it easier than looking at Zaven. "But then one night, he'd been drinking. I said... I don't even remember what I said. But the look in his eyes..." I shuddered at the memory. "He threw a heavy crystal decanter at my head. It shattered against the wall so hard pieces embedded in the fucking drywall. Then he came at me with one of the broken pieces, screaming that he'd cut my face so no one else would look at me." My hand trembled at the memory. "That's when I knew—next time he wouldn't miss."

Tears were falling now, but I couldn't stop them. "I ran that night. Packed what I could carry while he was passed out. Came to Russia because it was the furthest place I could think of where he wouldn't find me."

The silence that followed felt heavy, broken only by the soft crackle of the fire. Zaven's thumb had stopped moving on my hand, and when I finally made myself look at his face, what I saw made my breath catch. His expression was carefully blank, but his eyes... his eyes held a cold fury I'd never seen before. Not even when he was protecting me from the sound in the garden.

"Liliya," he finally said, voice low and controlled despite the murder in his eyes, "what happened to you... is unforgivable. Understand why trust difficult. Want you know—I not him. Never hurt you like that."

He leaned forward, taking both my hands in his. "This man, this Jack— when find him, will fucking kill him. Not threat, is promise." He said it so matter-of-factly, like commenting on the weather. "He touch you, mark you, try to break you. For this alone, deserves death." His thumbs brushed over my scars gently. "But also understand trust takes time to build. Will earn yours, day by day, for as long as needed."

I looked into his eyes, seeing the sincerity there beneath the rage. His promise to kill Jack should have horrified me. I'd known Zaven for less than a week, and here he was calmly promising murder for my sake. It was extreme, violent, completely outside normal boundaries.

And yet... a strange calm washed over me instead of fear, like a weight lifting that I hadn't known I was carrying. Something about the cold certainty in his voice made me believe him completely. This wasn't an empty threat or a macho display—it was a foregone conclusion in his mind. The realization sent a confusing mix of emotions through me: relief, gratitude, and something darker I wasn't ready to examine. A part of me—a part I hadn't known existed before Jack—wanted Zaven to keep that promise.

"I should be shocked that you just casually promised murder," I said softly, surprised by my own reaction. "But instead, I feel... safer." I shook my head, not fully understanding it myself. "What does that say about me?"

"Says you understand difference between violence that protects and violence that destroys," he replied, his thumb tracing my scars again. "Not same thing."

"Thank you," I whispered. "For listening, for understanding. I want to trust you, Zaven. I think... I think I'm starting to."

As we sat there, the fire crackling between us, I realized this moment had changed something. It wasn't trust, not completely, not yet. But it was a step I hadn't taken with anyone since fleeing Chicago.

A sharp knock at the door broke the moment. A man in a crisp suit entered, his expression serious.

"*Gospodin* Lazarev," he said, tone respectful but urgent. "Apologize for interruption, but there is call waiting in your office."

I felt Zaven tense beside me, his gentle demeanor replaced by the commanding presence I'd glimpsed throughout the day. He stood, his hand lingering on mine for a moment longer than necessary.

"Thank you, Anton." He turned to me, his expression softening slightly. "Sorry, Liliya. Business matter needs attention. House yours to explore. Anton can assist if you need anything."

With a gentle squeeze of my hand, he strode out of the room, his authority filling the space even after he'd gone. As I watched him leave, I couldn't help wondering about all the different sides of this man I was just beginning to know.

And what kind of call could transform him so quickly from the gentle listener to the powerful *vor*? The cryptic nature of Anton's message only added to the mystery surrounding Zaven's world—a world I was now part of, for better or worse.

23

Liliya

After Zaven left, I sat there for a while, trying to process everything. It had been three days since I'd arrived, and today he'd finally opened up to me. He'd been to prison for three years. Had tattoos that told his whole life story. Lived in a world I barely understood. And somehow, I'd just told him things about Jack I'd never told anyone.

I should've been freaked out. A guy with prison tattoos who casually promised murder should have sent me running for the hills. Instead, I found myself... curious? The way he'd rolled up his sleeve, shown me those marks, explained what they meant—it felt strangely intimate. Made my heart beat faster just thinking about it.

My mind drifted to those other tattoos he'd mentioned, the ones hidden under his clothes. What did they look like? Where exactly were they? Before I could stop myself, I was imagining dark ink across his chest, down his back...

Okay, dangerous territory. Despite having been here for days now, I still barely knew this man, and here I was fantasizing about his tattoos like they were some kind of treasure map. After everything with Jack, I shouldn't be thinking about any guy this way. I needed to distract myself.

The study suddenly felt too quiet. He'd said I could explore the house, so why not take a proper look around? Despite having been here for three days, I'd mostly kept to my room and the areas Irina had shown me. There was still so much of this place I hadn't seen yet. At least exploring would keep my mind off... other things.

I stepped into the hallway, my footsteps swallowed by thick carpet. This place was huge—corridors branching in every direction. I tried to remember my path as I wandered, but there was too much to take in.

A partially open door revealed what looked like a war room—maps and screens covering the walls, monitors showing different parts of the estate. I noticed security cameras tucked into corners, windows that were definitely bulletproof despite looking normal. Even those fancy vases seemed placed to slow down an intruder.

All this security made Zaven's talk about "enemies" feel a lot more real.

Turning a corner, I almost crashed into someone coming out of a room. He was young, maybe early thirties, with perfectly styled dark hair and green eyes that reminded me of a cat—beautiful but definitely predatory. His suit probably cost more than my car back in Chicago.

"Oh!" I stepped back. "Sorry, I wasn't watching where I was going."

His surprise quickly turned into a calculated smile. "No harm done," he said, his accent different from Zaven's. "You must be Liliya. I'm Andrei."

"Nice to meet you," I said, noticing how his eyes moved over me with too much interest. "I've been here a few days now but don't think I've seen you before. Do you work for Zaven?"

His smile widened, but something about it made my skin crawl. "You could say that. We're... associates. Zaven and I go way back."

The way he said Zaven's name set off warning bells. Not the controlled danger I felt with Zaven, but something unpredictable.

"I see," I said, keeping my expression neutral. Years with Jack had taught me not to show when someone made me uncomfortable. "Zaven's been giving me a tour of the estate today. It's impressive."

Andrei's eyes gleamed in a way that reminded me of guys at the club who thought the VIP section meant VIP access to the hostesses. "Is that so? Well, I'd be happy to... continue that tour sometime. There's much about our world that Zaven might not show you."

Before I could respond, he glanced at his watch. "Unfortunately, duty calls." His smile sharpened. "But I look forward to seeing more of you, Liliya." He brushed past me, his shoulder touching mine in a way that felt deliberate.

I watched him go, my heart racing—and not in the good way it did around Zaven. There was something about Andrei that set off every alarm Jack had inadvertently taught me to recognize. Mental note: ask Zaven about this guy ASAP.

Further down the hall, I heard voices from another half-open door. I recognized Viktor's deep tone.

"...Dmitri's getting bolder," he was saying, voice tense. "Attack on shipment just beginning. Need to be prepared for—"

The voice cut off as a door slammed somewhere nearby. I moved away quickly, my pulse pounding. Dmitri—Zaven had mentioned that name earlier with cold fury. So this was what had pulled him away, what had him so tense this morning. The abstract danger he'd talked about was suddenly very real and immediate.

I'd known what kind of business he was in—he'd been honest about that much. But hearing Viktor discuss an actual attack, knowing someone was actively moving against Zaven... that made everything more concrete. This wasn't just some vague criminal enterprise—this was a war, with real enemies making real moves.

Part of me wanted to find Zaven immediately, to ask him what was happening. But the more practical side knew this wasn't my place, not yet. I'd been in his world for less than a day. I couldn't expect to be brought into confidential business matters already, especially ones that sounded this dangerous.

Lost in thought, I almost didn't notice Irina approaching. "Ah, *Devushka* Liliya," she called, with a look that made me wonder if she'd seen me eavesdropping. "Perhaps time for lunch? I've prepared your usual spot in the small dining room."

Realizing I was actually starving, I nodded gratefully. Though "small" was definitely relative in this house.

By now I knew my way to the dining room - a space bigger than my entire apartment back home, with windows looking out over snowy gardens. As Irina poured tea from the ornate *samovar*, I found myself staring at a small chocolate pastry on my plate that looked exactly like the ones Natasha and I used to split at that café near the club.

"You remembered," I said, genuinely touched. I'd mentioned these pastries to Irina just yesterday. "They look just like the ones from Café Nevsky. Natasha and I would get one to share after our shifts."

Mentioning Natasha made me realize I hadn't spoken to her since before *Smotriny*. Which made me suddenly aware of something else.

"Irina," I asked, warming my hands on the delicate teacup, "do you know what happened to my cell phone? Last time I had it was in my purse at *Smotriny*."

She nodded in recognition. "Ah, yes. When leaving last night, security collected your belongings. Viktor has your purse with phone."

"Oh." That made sense—I didn't remember having it with me when we'd left. "Could I get it back? I'd really like to call Natasha."

Irina hesitated slightly. "*Gospodin* Viktor said he was adding important contacts first. Emergency numbers, house security." She must have seen my expression change, because she quickly added, "Standard procedure for household, *Devushka* Liliya. All staff have same contacts."

That didn't sound too invasive, though I wasn't exactly thrilled about people handling my phone without asking. But I'd left in such a rush from *Smotriny*, it's not like I'd had time to collect my things.

"So it's just... adding phone numbers?" I asked, wanting to be sure.

Irina nodded. "*Da*. And perhaps removing old number from before. For security." Her eyes met mine with surprising directness. "Some contacts not safe to keep in this house."

Jack. She had to be talking about Jack. I hadn't even thought about the fact that his number was still in my phone—I'd been too afraid to delete it in case he noticed when checking my phone. Now the thought of having any connection to him made my skin crawl.

"That's... probably for the best," I admitted. "Could you check if it's ready? I really would like to call Natasha today."

"Of course. Eat your lunch, I will check with Viktor."

Irina disappeared, leaving me alone with my thoughts and an array of dishes that put any restaurant to shame. I tried a bite of the *pelmeni*—delicate dumplings filled with seasoned meat and topped with fresh dill and *smetana*. The flavors brought me back to my first weeks in Russia, when everything had been overwhelming and strange, and Natasha had insisted I try "real Russian food, not tourist garbage."

Now here I was, sitting in the private dining room of the most feared *vor* in St. Petersburg, worrying about my cell phone. Four days in this house, and I was still adjusting to all of it. Just this morning, I'd seen Zaven's tattoos, learned about his prison time, told him things about Jack I'd never told another soul.

And the weirdest part? I wasn't freaking out. Not completely, anyway. Maybe it was the days I'd had to settle in. Or maybe it was the way Zaven had reacted to my story—with that cold fury directed at Jack, not at me. No victim-blaming, no "why did you stay?" Just understanding and that deadly promise that had somehow made me feel safer rather than scared.

Even this house, as overwhelming as it was with its security systems and armed guards, had begun to feel more like protection than a prison. When Jack had monitored my every move, it had been about control. This— whatever this was—felt different.

I was mid-bite when Irina returned, my phone in hand.

"Found it. All ready for you."

The phone looked exactly the same. I waited until Irina left before hitting Natasha's number, curling up in the chair and tucking my feet underneath me—a habit Natasha always teased me about.

"Liliya?!" Natasha's voice exploded through the speaker. "*Bozhe moy*! Where you disappear to? Been calling for days!"

"Sorry," I said, already grinning at her familiar accent. "Just got my phone back. It's been a crazy few days."

"Ha! Can imagine. Whole club still talking about it. Markov—you know, big security guy with scar?—he say never see Zaven Lazarev bid at *Smotriny* before. Is big deal, *Lilichka*."

I cringed at her nickname for me from our high school days when she'd been the exotic exchange student who somehow decided the quiet girl in the back row needed a Russian best friend. "Please tell me they're not all talking about it."

"Of course they talking! You think *vor* like Zaven claims American girl and no one notice? Pfft." I could practically see her dismissive hand wave. "Now tell me everything. His house—big like palace, *da*?"

"Bigger," I admitted. "I've been here several days now and I still get lost sometimes."

"And I bet breakfast was not sad American cereal, hm?"

"God, no. There's enough food for twenty people every morning. Pretty sure the coffee cups cost more than my entire apartment."

"Good. Now maybe you put some meat on bones." Natasha had been trying to fatten me up since day one. "But forget house—what about him? In bedroom, is he good as rumors say? Those hands look like know what they doing, *da*?" Her voice dropped to a theatrical whisper. "You try his... how you Americans say... equipment yet?"

"Natasha!" I hissed, nearly choking on my water.

"What? Is normal question between friends! Need to know if big, scary *vor* lives up to reputation in all areas."

Her concern warmed me. For all her teasing, she had always looked out for me.

"He's been surprisingly... respectful? He's given me space these past days to adjust. Not what I expected." I traced the pattern on the tablecloth. "He showed me his tattoos this morning."

There was a moment of stunned silence, then: "*Eto pizdets*! Prison tattoos? The real ones, not fake ones tourists get?" [That's fucked up]

"Oh, only arms?" She sounded almost disappointed. "So no... other places yet, hm?"

"Natasha!"

"What? Don't play innocent with me, *Lilichka*. Saw how you look at him at club. Like starving person seeing meal."

"I did not—"

"Did too. Is fine, he very…" She switched to Russian for a word I didn't know, but her tone made the meaning clear enough.

"We just talked, okay?" I insisted, though I could feel my face heating up. "Actually… I told him about Jack."

Her playfulness vanished instantly. "*Vsyo?* All of it?" Her voice dropped lower. "The bad things too?"

"Yeah. All of it."

"*Chto on skazal?*" she asked, then quickly translated. "What he say?"

"He…" I dropped my voice even though I was alone. "He said he's going to kill Jack."

"Good," Natasha said firmly, without hesitation. "Is what such *svoloch* deserves."

"You don't seem surprised."

"Pff. Of course not. Is *vor*. They have code. Man who hurts woman like that? Dead man. Simple."

Coming from anyone else, this conversation would have seemed insane. But this was Natasha, who had literally held my hand through panic attacks in the club bathroom when memories of Jack hit too hard.

"I miss you," I said suddenly.

"Miss you too, *dura*." The insult was affectionate, our usual way. "Club not same without you making those funny faces at rude customers."

"I didn't make faces!"

"Did. Like this." I could imagine her scrunching her nose exactly the way she always claimed I did.

"When things calm down a bit… coffee? Like before?" I asked.

"*Da*, of course. Need to hear everything. Even boring parts." She paused. "He good to you, yes? Not just saying things, but actually good?"

"Yeah," I said softly. "He is."

"Then am happy for you. But tell him Natasha will find way to hurt him if he hurts you, *vor* or no *vor*."

I laughed. "I'm pretty sure he'd be terrified."

"Should be. Know people who know people." It was her standard threat, delivered with complete seriousness despite us both knowing her 'people' were mostly club bouncers and bartenders.

After we hung up, I sat staring at the phone with a stupid grin on my face. Talking to Natasha was like a dose of reality—her particular blend of bluntness, protectiveness, and humor making even this surreal situation feel somehow manageable.

I'd just picked up my fork to try the now-cooling *pelmeni* when Anton appeared in the doorway.

"*Devushka* Liliya? *Gospodin* Lazarev is nearly finished with his business. He asks if he might join you shortly. Says he has something to discuss about dinner tomorrow evening."

The polite request rather than a demand made me smile. With Jack, I would have been expected to drop everything and run to wherever he wanted me. This felt like being treated as an equal.

"Of course," I told Anton. "I'll be right here."

I took another bite of my lunch, no longer feeling any need to rush. Another small difference that felt significant.

24

Zaven

Mind still spinning from Liliya's revelation, I headed down the corridor toward the office. The cigarette burns, the cruelty she'd endured at the hands of that piece of shit... and yet, she trusted me enough to share her pain. To bare her scars.

Viktor fell into step beside me, his face an inscrutable mask. But the curiosity in his eyes was unmistakable.

"She told me about him," I said quietly. "About what he did to her."

Understanding darkened Viktor's expression. We both knew the type of man capable of leaving such marks. Before he could respond, his phone buzzed. "Moscow is waiting," he reminded.

Da. Business always came first. Even when my thoughts were consumed by a pair of haunted green eyes and the trust it took to reveal those scars.

"*Gospodin* Lazarev," Mikhail greeted as I entered office, face grim. "Conference call is set up. *Gospodin* Kozlov and others waiting."

I nodded, rolling up sleeves. "What we know?"

He hesitated, which put me on edge immediately. "There been... incident at port. One of our shipments intercepted."

Cold fury settled in chest. "Details. Now."

"Was shipment from Odessa—specialty electronics." His euphemism for high-tech weapons unnecessary but appreciated. "Our men ambushed during offload. Three injured, one critical. Entire shipment gone."

"Dmitri?" I asked, though already knew.

"Appears so. Attackers used his tactics. Reports of his lieutenant, Lev, seen in area just before."

I clenched jaw, forcing self to stay calm. Dmitri getting bolder, pushing boundaries of our uneasy truce. Loss of weapons bad enough, but attacking my men? That personal.

"And our man inside port authority?" I asked, already dreading answer.

"No word since last night. Fear he may be compromised."

Blyad [damn/fuck]. If Dmitri had turned our inside man, who knew what other parts of operation at risk?

"Very well," I moved toward desk. "Leave us. Ensure no interruptions."

As Mikhail left, took deep breath, centering self. Man who just shared moment with Liliya gone. Now needed to be *vor*, leader my men expected, strategist who could outmaneuver Dmitri.

I pressed button to connect call, large screen flickering to life. Faces of most trusted advisors appeared, expressions grim as mine.

"*Zdravstvuyte, gospoda,*" [Hello, gentlemen] I greeted, keeping voice steady and controlled. "Understand we have situation."

Kozlov, key associate in Moscow, leaned forward, craggy face filling more of screen. "Zaven, *eto ne prosto situatsiya* [this is not just a situation]. This declaration of war."

"*Soglasen.*" [I agree] I nodded. "But need be smart about this. Dmitri expecting retaliation. Will be prepared for direct assault."

"*K chertu ostorozhnost'*!" [To hell with caution] Ivan, fiery lieutenant from Odessa, slammed fist on table. "He attacked our men, Zaven. Need hit back hard, now!"

"And play right into his hands?" My voice cut sharp through screen. "*Net.* We stick to plan. Make him think we weak, then strike when least expects it."

Silence fell as they considered words. Could see struggle on faces—desire for immediate vengeance warring with knowledge that patience would yield better results.

Finally, Kozlov spoke. "*Zaven prav.* [Zaven is right] Dmitri expecting us to lash out. Is what he would do. We need be smarter."

"But cannot let this go unanswered," Sergei interjected. "Our people will think we weak if not respond."

I leaned back, strategy already forming in mind. "*My ne ostavim eto bez otveta.* [We will not leave this unanswered] But response must be calculated, precise. Need hurt Dmitri where really counts—his reputation, his alliances."

"Speaking of alliances," Yuri cut in, "Hermitage Winter Gala coming up in few weeks. Dmitri will be there, no doubt trying shore up support, make new connections."

I nodded, plan crystallizing. "*Da.* My family attended for years. Perfect opportunity."

Kozlov leaned forward, interest piqued. "What you thinking, Zaven?"

"Use gala as distraction," I said, leaning in. "While Dmitri busy schmoozing with St. Petersburg elite, we strike at his business operations."

Slow smile spread across Ivan's face. "*Umno*, [Clever] very clever. He won't see coming."

"Exactly. I be at gala—perfect alibi. Dmitri will watch me, expect some kind of move. Meanwhile, our men hit his most valuable assets."

"And your new *nevesta*?" [bride/fiancée] Kozlov asked carefully. "She ready for such game?"

Image of Liliya's strength as she shared past flashed through mind. "She stronger than any of you know. But for now, she stay protected, out of this. Will tell her only what necessary."

"*Verno*," [True/Correct] I agreed, pushing thoughts of Liliya aside for moment. "Yuri, want everything you can get on Dmitri's business holdings. Weak points, security details, everything. Sergei, coordinate strike teams. Ivan, you be my eyes and ears at gala."

Men nodded, energy palpable even through screen. This why they followed me—not just for name or father's legacy, but for moments like this, when could see strategy coming together.

"One more thing," I added. "Need go to Moscow in two days. Handle situation with buyers personally."

Kozlov's brow furrowed. "Zaven, *ty uveren?* [are you sure] Sure about going now? With all this in motion..."

"*Eto neobkhodimo,*" [It is necessary] I cut him off. "Cannot afford lose buyers' trust. Besides, my absence might make Dmitri lower guard. Can use to advantage."

After call ended and screen went dark, found thoughts returning to Liliya. After what she shared today, leaving her so soon... but business couldn't wait. Would need make most of time before Moscow.

I reached for phone. "Anton. Tell *Devushka* Liliya am nearly finished with business. Will join her shortly in dining room. Have something to discuss."

* * *

As waited for response from Anton, found self growing restless, checking watch more often than *vor* should need to. Should have heard back by now.

"Anton," called through intercom. "Where is *Devushka* Liliya?"

Silence stretched too long before response. "Have not seen her, *Gospodin.* Last known location was dining room with Irina."

Something tightened in chest—instinct honed by years in this life. Shouldn't worry. House secure, guards everywhere. And yet... After three days of keeping distance, now that finally reconnecting, didn't want to lose momentum.

Pushed away from desk, already moving. "Find her. Now."

Made way through mansion, footsteps echoing in grand hallways. Each empty room increased tension in chest until heard soft murmur of voices from kitchen—one recognized as Irina's, other, lighter and tinged with uncertainty, unmistakably Liliya's.

Pausing at doorway, took moment to observe scene before me. Liliya stood with Irina, notepad in hand, brow furrowed in concentration as housekeeper explained something about kitchen operations. Sight of her so engaged, trying to learn this new world, made something warm stir in chest.

"And *samovar* only for morning tea?" Liliya was asking, making careful notes.

"*Da*, *Devushka* Liliya. Is tradition in household."

Chose that moment to make presence known, clearing throat softly. Both women turned, Irina straightening respectfully while Liliya's eyes widened slightly.

"Found you," I said, unable to keep relief from voice entirely. After revelations in study, had been... concerned when she didn't come.

"Zaven," Liliya said, hint of uncertainty in voice. "I... Irina was just showing me around. Should I have come to your office? Anton said no rush..."

"*Net*, is fine." Found self wanting to ease that uncertainty in her eyes. "Good to learn household. But have something to discuss with you, if moment free?"

Irina took hint immediately. "Will continue tour later, *Devushka* Liliya. Much still to show you."

Once Irina's footsteps faded, atmosphere in kitchen shifted. Liliya still clutched notepad, looking unsure what to do with herself now that we alone. Decided time to remind her of what started in garden, what promised her when she arrived.

Moved toward her with deliberate steps, enjoying way her eyes widened slightly, how she took half-step back until kitchen island stopped her retreat.

"Think this conversation be more comfortable if you not standing whole time," I said, voice low as closed distance between us. Before she could respond, placed hands on her waist, lifting her easily onto countertop.

"Zaven!" Surprise in her voice, but no fear. Notepad clutched to chest like shield, cheeks flushing deliciously. "What are you doing?"

"Making you comfortable. And," ran hands slowly down her thighs over soft wool of dress, feeling her shiver under touch, "reminding you of something."

As lifted her to counter, dress inched up, revealing glimpse of pale skin above knees. Couldn't help but notice, couldn't help but pause, thumbs unconsciously tracing small circles just above her knees on newly exposed skin. Felt her tense slightly, then relax under touch.

Her breath caught, pupils dilating. "Reminding me of what?"

Stepped between her knees, causing dress to rise higher. Dark fabric against fair skin - contrast mesmerizing. Control slipping slightly, moved hands to rest on counter instead of where wanted them. Effectively caged her, but also restrained self. Leaned in close, let her feel heat of my body, breathed in scent of her skin. "Of what said that first night. That will make you want me. That will make you beg for my touch."

Pulse jumped visibly at base of throat. "I remember."

"Good." Let one hand trail up her arm, along shoulder, until reached her face. Traced shape of her lips with thumb. "Because am man of word, *malyshka*. [little one/baby - term of endearment] Have patience to make you crave me."

Her lips parted slightly under my touch, breath coming faster now. Desire clear in way she unconsciously leaned toward me, in darkening of those green eyes. But also saw wariness there - caution born from painful past. Would respect that, use it to build trust even while stoking fire between us.

"Actually came to ask you something," said, not moving away, continuing to trace patterns on her skin. "Would like show you bit of my St. Petersburg tomorrow. Proper lunch, maybe. If feel ready for such thing."

She blinked, clearly trying to focus on words rather than closeness of our bodies. "Your St. Petersburg?"

"*Da*. Not tourist places. Real city." Leaned closer, letting lips brush against her ear as spoke. "Places only I know. Only I can show you." Pulled back just enough to see her face, enjoying slight daze in her expression. "Also need discuss Moscow trip. Will be leaving next week."

Flash of something—concern?—crossed her face. "Moscow?"

Let hand drift to back of her neck, fingers tangling in auburn hair. "Only few days. Business that needs personal attention." Studied her reaction carefully, other hand now tracing circles on her knee. "But before go, want spend some time with you. Show you don't need fear this world. Or me."

She bit lip, that gesture learning meant she processing something. Made it difficult not to claim those lips right there, taste her again like in garden.

But this game required patience. Building anticipation until she couldn't stand it anymore.

"I'd like that," she said finally, voice soft but slightly breathless. "To see your St. Petersburg."

"Good." Leaned forward, let lips hover just millimeters from hers, close enough to feel her breath catching. "Will send car in morning. Dress warm—want you comfortable, not freezing while show you city."

Could feel her practically trembling with anticipation, waiting for kiss that deliberately withheld. "What time should I be ready?" she asked, voice husky now.

"Eleven." Moved hands to her waist again, enjoying how easily could lift her, how small she felt in my grasp. "Will give you time to finish tour with Irina."

"And... will I see you later today?" Vulnerability in question made something tighten in chest. "It's just... it's still early and..."

Set her back on her feet, but kept her caged between counter and my body. "Actually, having informal dinner tonight. Few of my men joining us." Ran fingers through her hair, arranging it how liked. "Want them know you properly, not just as *vor*'s [thief/criminal leader] *nevesta*. No pressure, just good food, good company."

Surprise flickered across features, followed by hint of nervousness. "Your men? Like... Viktor?"

"*Da*. And few others. But nothing formal." Traced spine with single finger, feeling her arch slightly into touch. "Just dinner, Liliya. They need see real you, like I do."

"Okay," she said softly, voice definitely breathier now. She squared shoulders slightly in way that made pride surge in chest. "What time?"

Smiled, couldn't help it. This woman with her courage, her fire, even when clearly affected by my touch. Made me want her even more. "Will send for you at seven."

Stepped back then, breaking contact completely, enjoying flash of confusion that crossed her face at sudden loss of proximity. "Until then, *malyshka*."

Turned and walked away without looking back, though could feel her eyes on me. Each step away physical pain—cock hard, blood burning with need to return, press her against counter, rip that dress from her body and watch her eyes darken as I claim her. Mark her in ways that erase memory of that *mudak* [asshole/jerk] who dared hurt her.

Had to bite inside of cheek to keep moving forward. Had seen arousal in her eyes, felt heat of her skin, heard change in breathing. Would be so easy to give in, to take what growing more certain she wanted to give. But needed to be earned, not taken. Especially from woman with her scars.

By time reached door, heard soft, frustrated exhale behind me. Had to suppress groan of my own. Felt mixture of triumph and torture—she affected as I was. But this sweet torment necessary. When she finally came to my bed, would be because she couldn't stand another moment without my touch. Because she chose it freely, with whole heart and body.

And then, *blyad*, would make sure she never forgot who she belonged to. Would erase every memory of pain with pleasure so intense she'd scream my name until voice gave out.

But for now—patience. Most delicious hunts required time. And this particular prey worth every agonizing second of wait.

25

Liliya

I tugged at my cream sweater, my stomach in knots as I headed downstairs. After the intensity of the day - breakfast with Zaven, the tour of the grounds, that heated moment in the kitchen - I was now about to have dinner with his top men. Just the thought of them had my pulse racing. I'd met them briefly in the gardens, and every single one had seemed scary as hell.

What the hell was I doing, thinking I could handle dinner with them? Zaven had said to dress comfortably, but I still felt like I was marching into a lion's den wearing a neon sign that screamed "I don't belong here!"

I forced myself to take a deep breath. "You can do this, Liliya," I muttered under my breath. "It's just dinner. Food, conversation... how hard can it be?" But even as the words left my mouth, I knew I was kidding myself. These men, they weren't just anyone. They were Zaven's inner circle. His closest confidants.

All those thoughts vanished when I spotted Zaven waiting at the bottom of the stairs. I nearly missed a step.

I'd never seen him dressed casually before. The impeccable suits were gone, replaced by a dark fitted sweater that clung to his broad shoulders and tailored black pants. He should have looked more approachable this way, but somehow the casual clothes only emphasized how powerful he really was. My eyes caught on his neck, where the sweater's collar dipped just low enough to reveal a hint of the tattoos I'd traced this morning. The memory sent heat rushing through me. Fuck, the man could make a paper bag look dangerous.

"Liliya," he said, voice low and warm. "You look beautiful."

I felt my face flush. "Thank you. You look... different." My eyes lingered on the way his sweater clung to his shoulders. "Good different," I added with a smile.

He chuckled, the sound sending a shiver down my spine. "Time you see more relaxed side, *da*? Not always suit and tie."

"I like it," I admitted, surprising myself with my boldness. After our kitchen encounter just hours ago, something had shifted between us. The push and pull was still there, but I found myself pushing back more.

His eyes darkened slightly at my words, and his hand found the small of my back, warmth seeping through my sweater. "Men waiting in private dining room. Viktor ask three times already when you coming down."

"Really?" That surprised me. After our brief encounter in the garden and seeing them around the house, I'd started to form an impression of these dangerous men who somehow made me feel more welcome than afraid.

"*Da*. Sergei bring special vodka just for occasion." Zaven's thumb traced a small circle against my back. "Not often they get chance to embarrass me in front of beautiful woman."

I laughed at that. "So I should expect stories about you?"

"Unfortunately, yes." He looked more amused than concerned. "Ready to hear all terrible tales about younger Zaven?"

As we approached the dining room, I heard men's voices—a mix of Russian and English drifting through the doorway, punctuated by deep laughter. The sound was strangely comforting, reminding me of the camaraderie I'd glimpsed earlier.

"Ready," I said, straightening my shoulders. "Let's see what they've got."

The private dining room surprised me. It wasn't the formal space I'd expected, but smaller and warmer, with a round table that felt more intimate than imposing.

Five men looked up when we entered—Viktor, Nikolai, Sergei, Yuri, and

Ivan. They were all dressed casually like Zaven, which made the setting feel more like a family dinner than a meeting of criminal elite.

"Ah, our *Devushka* arrives!" Ivan called out, raising his glass. "Come, come. Tell us how you like our little home."

"Don't overwhelm girl," Viktor chided, though his eyes held amusement. "Still adjusting to our ways."

Zaven guided me to a seat between him and Viktor. "First get her drink," he said. "Then questions."

A crystal tumbler appeared before me, filled with clear liquid that could only be vodka.

"Best vodka in Russia," Sergei proclaimed proudly. "Only kind worth drinking."

"To family," Yuri raised his glass, eyes twinkling. "Old and new."

"To family," everyone echoed, glasses clinking.

The vodka burned smooth down my throat, warming me from the inside. I'd expected to feel like an outsider, but the way they looked at me—curious but welcoming—eased some of my anxiety.

"So, tell us," Nikolai leaned forward, "what you think of our little operation here?"

"Let girl eat first," Zaven interjected as servers brought out plates of steaming *blini* [thin pancakes] topped with caviar.

"*Net*, is okay," I ventured, surprising myself with the Russian. "Everything's been... overwhelming but fascinating."

The meal unfolded in a feast of shared dishes, the table quickly filling with platters and bowls. After the *blini* with caviar, Sergei reached for a large ceramic pot in the center.

"You must try this," he insisted, ladling generous portions of steaming *shchi* [cabbage soup] onto my plate—cabbage, tender chunks of beef, and aromatic herbs in a rich broth. "My grandmother's recipe, best in St. Petersburg."

Ivan passed a platter of golden *pirozhki* [stuffed buns], the plump pastries bursting with mushrooms and dill. "Take two," he urged when I hesitated. "Small ones barely count."

Wooden boards of pickled vegetables appeared—bright purple cabbage, cucumber spears, and marinated tomatoes that Yuri insisted were "necessary for proper vodka drinking." Our crystal glasses were never empty, with vodka flowing as freely as the conversation.

Nikolai silently placed a dish of *pelmeni* near me—delicate dumplings glistening with melted butter and topped with sour cream and fresh herbs. His quiet nod told me these were special, and the first bite confirmed it— the tender dough giving way to savory meat filling perfectly seasoned with garlic and pepper.

"Family meal always like this," Zaven explained, serving me a portion of roasted potatoes with *smetana* before I could protest. "Everyone contributes favorite dish. Shows respect."

I couldn't help but smile at how these dangerous men transformed into enthusiastic hosts, each seemingly determined I should taste their particular contribution.

"Must eat," he declared, eyeing me critically. "Too skinny, American girl."

"*Da, da,*" Ivan agreed, passing warm black bread. "Need strength for Russian winter. And for keeping up with *vor*."

I caught Zaven hiding a smile behind his glass as the men laughed. It struck me how natural this felt—like a real family dinner, albeit one where the family happened to be some of the most dangerous men in St. Petersburg. And here I was, drinking vodka with them like I belonged. What the hell was my life becoming?

As plates were cleared and more vodka appeared, Viktor leaned back in his chair, a gleam in his eye. "Speaking of young ones learning our ways... should tell story about when Zaven first starting in family business."

Zaven's hand found my knee under the table. "Viktor..."

"*Net, net,*" Ivan cut in, already grinning. "Let him tell story. Girl should know what kind of man she dealing with."

The vodka had warmed me enough to feel bold. "Please?" I turned to Zaven. "I'd like to hear."

"It was winter," Viktor began, dropping his voice conspiratorially.

"Colder than witch's tits. And this one," he nodded toward Zaven, "just *patsanenok* [young boy/kid], barely eighteen."

"But already had fire in eyes," Sergei added, nodding vigorously. "Even then."

"*Da, da,*" Viktor continued. "Job was simple. Deliver package to buyer in Kupchino. Easy, *da*?" He paused for effect. "But nothing ever simple in this business."

I leaned forward despite myself, caught up in the story. Glancing at Zaven, I expected to see annoyance, but instead caught a hint of a smile playing at his lips.

"So there's our Zaven," Viktor continued, hands gesturing dramatically, "trudging through snow with package. But he smart, even then. Takes back alleys, keeps to shadows. Knows he being watched."

"Tell her about knife part," Ivan interrupted eagerly, already reaching to refill everyone's glasses.

"Getting there, getting there," Viktor waved him off. "Then—BAM!" He slapped the table, making me jump. "Three men, big as bears, jump out with knives."

I found myself holding my breath, the vodka making the story feel more vivid. Under the table, Zaven's hand squeezed my knee gently.

"But our boy," Viktor's eyes gleamed with pride, "he quick. Grabs broken vodka bottle from ground. First *mudak* comes at him—"

Without thinking, I placed my hand over Zaven's where it rested on my knee. The warmth of his skin, the strength in those fingers that had once wielded a broken bottle, sent a shiver through me. His hand turned under mine, threading our fingers together.

"Slashes right across face!" Sergei interrupted excitedly. "Saw scar years later. Nasty thing."

"*Da*, but best part coming," Viktor leaned forward. "Other two still coming. So what he do? Throws package in air!"

The combination of vodka, the intense story, and Zaven's touch had my pulse racing. Every squeeze of his hand seemed to emphasize the dangerous grace these men spoke of with such pride.

"Package goes up," Viktor mimed with his hands, "and while *mudaki* [assholes/jerks, plural] watching it—BAM! Takes out second guy with kick to *yarista* [balls]. Drops like sack of potatoes!"

The table erupted in appreciative laughter. Even Zaven chuckled, the sound rumbling through him where our shoulders touched.

"Third guy," Viktor continued, clearly enjoying his role as storyteller, "he thinks he clever. Grabs package and runs."

"But Zaven smarter, *da?*" Ivan grinned, already knowing the ending.

"*Da.* Lets him go." Viktor paused for effect. "Because real package?" He tapped his temple. "Hidden in coat lining whole time."

I turned to look at Zaven, impressed despite myself. His dark eyes met mine, something heated in his gaze that made my breath catch. His thumb traced small circles on my palm under the table.

"You were already planning three steps ahead even then," I said softly.

"Always, *malyshka*," he murmured, voice low enough for only me to hear.

"Another story!" Ivan called out, reaching for the bottle again. "Remember that time in Moscow with—"

"*Net, net,*" Yuri cut in. "First, let's hear about our American girl. Tell us, where in States you from?"

The question surprised me—casual, friendly. No probing about why I'd fled to Russia, no hints about my past. Just genuine curiosity.

"Minnesota," I said, grateful for the easy topic. "Small town, nothing like St. Petersburg."

"Ah, Minnesota!" Sergei's face lit up. "Much snow, like Russia. No wonder you not complain about cold like other Americans."

"Minnesotans don't really feel cold," I said with a small smile. "Below zero is just Tuesday in January."

"This true?" Ivan looked skeptical. "Heard stories of Americans putting on coats when temperature drops to fifteen degrees."

"Those are Californians," I said. "Different species entirely. We keep our shorts on until at least November."

Viktor laughed. "See, Zaven? Told you American girl was tough."

"Had to be," I said, surprising myself with my candor. "You try shoveling three feet of snow just to get your car out of the driveway."

"Is why Russians invented vodka," Sergei nodded sagely, refilling my glass. "Makes shoveling more enjoyable."

"Is why Russians invented everything," Ivan corrected. "Makes life more enjoyable."

I found myself genuinely laughing, the easy camaraderie so different from what I'd expected. Zaven's hand squeezed mine under the table, and when I glanced at him, there was something warm in his eyes that had nothing to do with vodka.

As if on cue, servers appeared with dessert—what looked like miniature honey cakes drizzled with something that smelled of cognac.

"Ah, *medovik*!" [honey cake] Ivan's eyes lit up. "Now this, *devochka* [little girl], is proper dessert. Irina's specialty."

The cake melted on my tongue, layers of honey and cream making me close my eyes in bliss. When I opened them, I caught Zaven watching me, heat in his gaze that made my cheeks flush.

"Should tell her about Zaven's first reward," Viktor suggested, eyes twinkling with mischief. "After big deal in Sochi."

Zaven's hand tightened on mine. "Viktor..." There was warning in his voice.

My curiosity peaked. "What happened in Sochi?" I asked, turning to Zaven. The vodka had made me bolder than usual.

"*Net*, not story for dinner table," Zaven said firmly.

"Oh, but is perfect story!" Ivan grinned wickedly. "Show how our Zaven not always so... controlled."

"Now I definitely want to hear it," I said, leaning forward. The more Zaven tried to stop it, the more interested I became.

Zaven muttered something in Russian that made Sergei snort with laughter.

"Was after first big deal Zaven closed himself," Viktor began, ignoring Zaven's dark look. "Father so proud, arranged special celebration at private club."

"Very exclusive place," Yuri added with a significant look.

"Had special entertainment," Sergei continued, watching Zaven's face carefully. "Beautiful dancers."

"Many beautiful dancers," Ivan emphasized with a grin. "All very... appreciative of handsome young *vor*."

I glanced at Zaven, whose jaw was clenched even as his thumb continued tracing patterns on my palm. The contrast intrigued me.

"And one particular dancer—Anya? Alina?" Viktor looked to Ivan.

"Alina," Ivan confirmed. "Blonde. Legs like—" he made an hourglass shape with his hands.

"Took special interest in Zaven," Viktor continued, clearly enjoying his discomfort. "Pulled him backstage after show."

"Boy gone for three hours!" Sergei laughed. "Come back looking like—"

"Enough," Zaven cut in sharply, though I noticed the tension in his neck, the slight flush on his cheeks. This wasn't anger—it was embarrassment.

"What happened backstage?" I asked him directly, oddly enjoying his discomfort. This powerful man, embarrassed by tales of his youth—it humanized him in a way nothing else had.

Zaven's eyes met mine, something dangerous and heated flickering in them. "Private matters, *malyshka*. Some stories better told... one on one."

The promise in his voice sent heat rushing through me. The men exchanged knowing glances, but I held Zaven's gaze, a silent challenge passing between us.

"Perhaps someday you tell us your version," Viktor said to Zaven, breaking the tension. "When not so..." he glanced between us with a knowing smile, "distracted."

"Perhaps when hell freezes," Zaven muttered, but I felt his thumb resume its circles on my palm.

"Enough embarrassing boss," Viktor raised his glass. "Another toast— to good food, good stories, and beautiful women who make us want to *zanimat'sya seksom!*" [have sex]

The men raised their glasses, vodka glinting in the warm light. As they drank, Nikolai, who had been quietly observing most of the evening, suddenly spoke.

"You know," he said, voice carrying that careful precision of someone who didn't waste words, "is good to see light in this house again." His sharp eyes met mine. "Been long time since these walls hear real laughter. You safe here, *devochka*. With us, with him."

The simple statement, coming from the most reserved of Zaven's men, made my throat tight. Zaven's hand tightened on mine beneath the table.

"Enough serious talk!" Ivan broke the moment, reaching for the bottle again. "More vodka! More stories!"

* * *

As the night wore on, the stories grew more outrageous, the laughter easier. I found myself relaxing into Zaven's solid presence beside me, the warmth of vodka and acceptance making everything feel softer around the edges.

The room started to tilt slightly whenever I moved my head, and I realized the vodka had affected me more than I thought. I reached for my glass, only to miss it completely, my hand landing on the tablecloth. Zaven caught my wrist before I could knock something over.

"Think is time we say goodnight," he announced, his voice cutting through the animated discussion about some heist in Moscow. "Liliya need rest."

"But we just getting to good part!" Ivan protested, waving the bottle. "Night still young!"

"Girl can barely sit straight," Viktor observed with a knowing smile. "American tolerance not same as Russian."

"Can too sit straight," I muttered, then promptly proved myself wrong by swaying in my chair. Zaven's arm immediately wrapped around my waist, steadying me.

"See you tomorrow, brothers," Zaven said firmly, helping me to my feet. "Enjoy rest of evening."

The men rose as we left, a gesture of respect that registered even through my vodka haze. As we exited, I heard Sergei's deep chuckle and Ivan's voice:

"Twenty years, never seen him leave party early for woman."

The hallway seemed longer and more confusing than it had earlier. When I stumbled on the first step of the grand staircase, Zaven's patience apparently ran out.

"This not working," he muttered, and before I could protest, he'd swept me into his arms like I weighed nothing.

"Put me down!" I said, but made no actual effort to escape, instead finding myself fascinated by the strong line of his jaw so close to my face. "I can walk."

"Evidence suggests otherwise," he replied dryly, carrying me up the stairs without any apparent effort. The motion made my head spin—or maybe that was just proximity to him.

"You're really strong," I observed, my hand landing on his chest. I could feel the solid muscle beneath his sweater. "Bet you could bench press me."

His lips twitched. "Probably."

"That's hot," I informed him seriously, my inhibitions completely dissolved by Sergei's vodka. My fingers traced the edge of his collar where his tattoo peeked out. "Everything about you is hot. Intimidating as fuck, but hot."

His jaw tightened, but he kept his eyes fixed ahead as we reached the top of the stairs. "Liliya. Vodka talking now."

"Nope. Vodka just saying what I'm too chicken to say sober." I let my head rest against his shoulder, breathing in his scent. "You smell amazing. Like expensive things and danger."

A rumbling laugh vibrated through his chest. "Danger has smell now?"

"Mmhmm. Like yours." My hand slid up to the back of his neck, fingers tangling in his hair. Without thinking, I pressed my lips to the exposed skin above his collar, right over his tattoo.

Zaven froze mid-step, a sharp intake of breath the only sound in the silent hallway. The muscles in his arms tensed around me, and I felt a tremor run through his body.

"Liliya," he warned, his voice dropping to a dangerous growl. "Not testing control now."

I smiled against his skin, emboldened by the way his pulse jumped beneath my lips. "What if I want to?"

He resumed walking, faster now, his breathing noticeably uneven. "Then wait until not drunk. Want to remember what happens when push me too far."

The promise in those words sent a delicious shiver down my spine. By the time we reached my room, I was placing open-mouthed kisses along his jawline, enjoying the slight roughness of stubble against my lips.

He shouldered the door open and stepped inside, then carefully lowered me until my feet touched the floor. His hands remained at my waist until he was sure I could stand, his eyes dark with controlled heat.

"Stay here," he ordered, his accent thicker than usual. "Don't move."

I watched him stride toward the closet, admiring the powerful lines of his back and shoulders under the fitted sweater. His control was slipping – I could see it in the tension of his movements, hear it in the roughness of his voice. The knowledge gave me a heady sense of power even through the vodka haze.

He disappeared for a moment, returning with my silk nightgown. "Can manage rest yourself, or need help?" His voice was matter-of-fact, but his eyes gave away the heat beneath his control.

Through the vodka haze, I found myself staring at his hands—those powerful hands that had just carried me effortlessly up the stairs. "Your hands are so big," I murmured, my filter completely gone. "Always wondered what they'd feel like on me. All over me."

His jaw tightened visibly, a muscle jumping beneath the skin. "Liliya. *Nochnaya rubashka*," [nightgown] he reminded me, voice strained despite the gentle tone. "Need help with clothes?"

"My sweater," I said, fumbling with the hem. "Too complicated right now. Everything's spinning."

I heard a low chuckle behind me before he stepped closer. "Arms up," he instructed, his voice controlled despite the tension I could feel radiating from him. When I complied, he carefully pulled the cream sweater over my head, his knuckles occasionally brushing my skin, sending shivers down my spine.

"You're good at this," I said, words slurring slightly as I sat there in my camisole. "Bet you've had lots of practice undressing women. Lucky bitches."

"Not discussing this now, *malyshka*." His voice had roughened to a gravelly rumble that I felt more than heard.

I reached for the hem of my camisole, but his hands gently stopped mine. "Let me." With careful movements, he helped me out of it. I heard his sharp intake of breath as it fell away, leaving my upper body bare. The air felt charged between us, heavy with things unsaid.

"*Blyad*," he murmured, almost to himself. "Beautiful."

"You could touch me, you know," I said, alcohol making me bold as I half-turned to look at him over my shoulder. "I want you to. Been wanting it since that first night."

His hands settled on my shoulders, warm and firm. I felt them tighten briefly, his control visibly slipping before he reined himself in. "Not like this, Liliya. Not when vodka speaking." He turned me to face him, keeping his eyes locked with mine, deliberately not looking lower though I could see the effort it cost him. "When I have you, want you remember every moment, every touch. Want you choose with clear mind, not regret in morning."

I swayed toward him, drawn by the intensity in his eyes. "I know what I want. Have known since you carried me out of that club."

"*Da*. But deserve better than drunk first time." He reached around me for the nightgown, his arms creating a cage of heat around me. His breath caught as our bodies briefly pressed together. With visible restraint, he helped slide the silk over my head, guiding my arms through the sleeves with hands that weren't quite steady.

"Jeans next," he said, voice rough with controlled desire.

I tried to unbutton them myself, fumbling with the fastening. "Stupid fucking buttons," I muttered.

His hands gently moved mine aside. "Allow me." With quick, almost clinical movements, he unfastened the button and zipper, though his eyes darkened as his knuckles brushed against my stomach. "Can push down yourself?"

I nodded, then promptly lost my balance trying to push them down. Zaven caught me against his chest, one arm sliding around my waist. I felt the heat of him through his sweater, the solid wall of muscle that made up his torso.

"Christ," he muttered, a rare English curse slipping out. "Maybe sit," he suggested, humor returning to his voice despite the tension in his body as he guided me to the edge of the bed.

Once seated, I managed to wiggle out of my jeans while he held the nightgown down for modesty. The silk settled around my thighs, cool against my heated skin.

"There," he said, voice rougher than gravel. His eyes finally allowed themselves a quick sweep down my body, the silky fabric doing little to hide my curves. "You are... breathtaking, Liliya. Fucking perfect."

"You're not so bad yourself," I said, reaching for the hem of his sweater. "Your turn? Want to see those other tattoos you mentioned."

He caught my hand, bringing it to his lips instead. I felt the heat of his breath against my fingers, the slight scrape of stubble. "Not tonight, *malyshka*. Into bed now."

"Spoilsport," I murmured, but let him guide me under the covers. "At least stay with me?"

"*Da*. Will stay." His expression softened as he looked down at me, the hardness melting into something that made my chest ache. "But just sleep."

"Fine," I sighed, already feeling the vodka pulling me toward unconsciousness. "But you have to actually get in bed. Not just sit and watch like some creepy guardian angel."

That earned a real laugh from him, the sound warming me more than the blankets. "Not angel, *malyshka*. Far from it."

He moved around to the other side of the bed and began to remove his watch, setting it carefully on the nightstand. I watched through heavy eyelids as he pulled off his socks, then after a moment's hesitation, unbuckled his belt and removed it too. The soft hiss of leather sliding through belt loops sent an entirely inappropriate thrill through me.

"You could take off more," I suggested, my voice already thick with approaching sleep. "Wouldn't mind the view."

"Not helping, Liliya," he said, but there was amusement in his voice. "Testing patience even when half-asleep."

The mattress dipped as he slid in beside me, staying carefully on his side of the bed. In my vodka-soaked state, this seemed entirely unacceptable. I rolled toward him, seeking his warmth.

"Too far away," I mumbled, reaching for him. "Need you closer."

I felt rather than heard his sigh as he lifted his arm, allowing me to nestle against his side. The solid warmth of him felt perfect against my cheek.

"Your heart's beating fast," I observed, my ear pressed to his chest.

"Difficult situation," he admitted, his voice rumbling beneath my ear. "Beautiful woman in my arms, asking for things she might regret tomorrow. Testing fucking control."

His arm curved around me, hand settling carefully at my waist over the covers.

"Mmm. I like your tattoos." My fingers found one of the designs visible on his forearm. "What's this one mean?"

"Each mark has meaning, *malyshka*. Some not easy to explain. Better when head clear. Will show you tomorrow."

"Promise?" I asked, tracing the pattern with a sleepy finger.

"Promise." His free hand captured mine, stilling my exploring fingers. "Now sleep."

I wanted to ask more questions, to stay awake and feel the solid reality of him beside me, but the vodka and the comfort of his embrace were pulling me under.

"Zaven?" I murmured, already half-asleep.

"*Da?*"

"Thank you for not being like him." The words slipped out, vodka and exhaustion breaking down barriers I normally kept firmly in place.

His arm tightened around me. "Never like him, Liliya. Never."

"I know," I whispered, surprising myself with how much I meant it. "That's why I trust you."

I felt him press a gentle kiss to the top of my head, his lips lingering in my hair. "Sleep now, *moye serdtse*." [my heart]

The endearment, whatever it meant, followed me into dreams—dreams not of the past for once, but of strong hands, dark eyes, and a heart beating steady beneath my ear. For the first time in longer than I could remember, I slept without fear, protected by the one man who could have taken everything but chose instead to simply hold me through the night.

26

Zaven

The vodka had left a faint trace of its scent on her breath, a reminder of last night's laughter, surprising confessions, tentative trust. Liliya murmured something in her sleep, turning further into the pillow that still held the impression of my head.

Dawn hadn't yet broken, the room still bathed in shadow and whispered secrets. For hours, I'd been awake, watching her – learning her in this unguarded state as thoroughly as I'd studied enemies across negotiating tables. Only this study brought no strategic advantage, only a dangerous, unfamiliar warmth.

Her auburn hair was splayed across the pillow, her face relaxed in sleep, free from the wariness that often clouded her features when awake. In the dim pre-dawn light, she looked impossibly young and vulnerable. A stark contrast to the woman who had held her own at dinner last night, matching wits with some of my most dangerous men.

Finally forcing myself to move, my feet carried me to the window. The sun was just beginning to paint the city in gold and shadow. A breath escaped my lips as something caught my attention - there, appearing like a ghost in the condensation, a small smile someone had drawn earlier.

The simple marking held my gaze for a long moment. Such an innocent gesture, yet it twisted something in my chest. Liliya's handiwork, it had to be. What had prompted her to draw it - happiness? Fear? Hope?

After a final glance at her sleeping form, my footsteps carried me quietly from the room. She stirred slightly, mumbling something before burying her face in the pillow just vacated. Aspirin would be necessary when she woke - a small mercy I could prepare for her.

Back in my own rooms, thoughts kept circling that small smile. Such a simple thing, yet it spoke volumes about the woman who'd drawn it. About the trust beginning to form between us.

I shed my t-shirt and boxers and headed for the shower. Steam filled the bathroom as the water heated. These private moments were rare times when a *vor* could just be a man. No image to maintain, no power plays to consider. The hot water pounded against my shoulders, but did nothing to clear my head of memories - Liliya's laugh at dinner, the way she'd curled into my chest, the trust she'd shown by asking me to stay.

I had to be careful. Keep control. Remember why bringing her into this world was so dangerous, yet find a way to show her the beauty in it too. Not just the darkness she'd glimpsed so far.

After stepping out of the shower, water ran down my skin. I wiped steam from the mirror and found myself thinking again of her smile drawn on the window. A simple gesture that had somehow worked past my carefully constructed walls.

I dressed casual today - dark jeans and a charcoal sweater that wouldn't restrict movement but still showed power beneath. Different from the suits she was used to seeing. I wanted her to see the real man, not just the *vor*'s facade.

Running a hand through my damp hair, I caught my reflection again. I remembered her fingers tracing my tattoos last night, the curiosity in those green eyes. Maybe today I would share some stories behind them - test the waters, see if she was ready for deeper truths.

Downstairs, the house was already coming alive. Morning sun streamed through windows, catching crystal decanters that still held evidence of last night's vodka. Irina was moving through the dining room, arranging things with practiced efficiency.

"Irina, I need—" I began as I entered.

"Breakfast for *Devushka* Liliya and yourself," she finished, something knowing in her eyes. "Already prepared, *Gospodin*." She gestured toward the kitchen. "And headache tablets for her, as well."

"*Spasibo*." [Thank you] I nodded, impressed as always by her anticipation. "We have coffee in solarium. And arrange car for eleven. Not usual one—something less obvious."

"*Konechno*." [Of course] She paused, her expression softening slightly. "*Devushka* Liliya handled herself well last night. Men are impressed."

Before I could respond, Viktor appeared in the doorway. "*Dobroye utro,* [Good morning] Zaven."

"*Zdravstvuy,* [Hello] Viktor. Joining us for breakfast?"

"If invitation open," he said with nod of thanks to Irina, who was already setting another place.

The sound of soft footsteps on the stairs drew my attention. Liliya appeared in the doorway, hair still slightly damp from a shower, cheeks flushed. She wore simple jeans and a deep green sweater, but carried herself differently this morning—more confident after last night, despite the slight shadow of hangover in her eyes.

"Hope I'm not interrupting," she said, gaze flickering between Viktor and me.

"Not at all," I said, watching her carefully. "Coffee?"

"God, yes." The relief in her voice made Viktor chuckle.

We settled in the solarium, sunlight streaming through the glass ceiling, warming the space despite the snow piled on the garden outside. Irina brought steaming coffee and a spread of breakfast foods—*blini* with honey and sour cream, eggs with smoked salmon, dark bread with butter and jam.

I discreetly slid the bottle of aspirin toward Liliya as she accepted her coffee. "Might help."

"My hero," she murmured, then blushed as she realized she'd said it aloud.

Viktor poorly disguised his chuckle as a cough. "Sleep well, *Devushka* Liliya?"

"Very." Her eyes flicked to me before returning to her coffee. "Though I don't actually remember getting to bed."

"You were… somewhat affected by Sergei's vodka," I said carefully.

"Oh God." She covered her face with one hand. "Did I do anything embarrassing?"

Viktor laughed outright now. "Only make Ivan blush with story about midnight swim in college."

Her eyes widened. "I did not."

"Did," I confirmed, lips twitching despite myself. "Something about stealing campus security guard's clothes while skinny dipping in fountain."

"And having to run back to dorm wearing nothing but borrowed jacket," Viktor supplied helpfully. "Very… resourceful."

Liliya groaned and reached for the aspirin. "That's it. No more of Sergei's vodka for me."

"Bold statement in this household," I observed, sliding a plate of *blini* toward her. "Eat. Will help."

As she took a tentative bite, her expression changed to surprise, then pleasure. "This is incredible."

"Irina's recipe," Viktor explained. "Family secret for generations."

"I need to thank her for everything. She's been so kind." Liliya took another bite, then looked up at me. "I'm afraid I haven't been a very good houseguest."

"Nonsense," Viktor said before I could answer. "Household has not been this lively in years." His eyes met mine briefly, meaningful.

I knew what he was thinking—how different the atmosphere had been since her arrival. The house felt more like a home than a fortress for the first time since my mother had been alive.

"Plans for today?" Viktor asked, though I could tell from his expression he already knew.

"Taking Liliya into city after breakfast." I held her gaze as I spoke. "If you feel up to it."

"I'd love that." The smile that lit her face made something in my chest tighten. "Though Irina mentioned finishing the house tour first?"

"*Da.* She eager to show you rest of estate." I glanced at my watch.

"Perhaps hour, then we go? Car will be ready when your all finished."

"Perfect." She turned to Viktor. "Will you be joining us?"

"Ah, no. Too much work before Moscow trip." He took a sip of his coffee. "Besides, some places Zaven wants to show you... personal. Better just two."

The subtle emphasis on "personal" made Liliya blush again, a charming color that spread across her cheekbones. I found myself watching the process with perhaps too much interest.

"Speaking of personal," Viktor continued, watching me closely, "Liliya ask many questions about house last night. About family. About mother's paintings."

I stilled, coffee cup halfway to my lips. The paintings were rarely discussed. I'd moved them from the main halls years ago, unable to walk past them daily after her death.

"The ballet dancer in the east wing?" Liliya asked tentatively. "Irina mentioned she was your mother."

"*Da.*" The word came out more stiffly than intended. "Was prima ballerina with Mariinsky before marriage."

"She was extraordinary," Liliya said softly. "There's so much life in those brushstrokes. So much joy."

"Like someone else we know," Viktor said pointedly, looking between us.

Breakfast continued with lighter conversation. Viktor sharing carefully edited stories from my youth, Liliya laughing at the right moments, asking questions that showed she was paying close attention. She ate well, some color returning to her cheeks as the tablets took effect.

When Irina appeared in the doorway, Liliya stood. "I shouldn't keep you waiting."

"Take time," I assured her. "No rush today."

"I'll be quick," she promised, then surprised me by lightly touching my shoulder as she passed. "Don't leave without me."

As her footsteps faded down the hall with Irina, Viktor's expression became thoughtful. "She reminds me of Anya."

My mother's name hung in the air between us. "How so?"

"Way she looks at things. Really sees." He gestured to where Liliya had been sitting. "And way she looks at you. Not afraid, but respectful. Curious."

"She not afraid when should be," I muttered.

"Perhaps sees things worth risk." Viktor refilled his coffee. "Your mother saw same in your father. Behind *vor*, saw man worth loving."

"Different time, different circumstances." But the comparison had struck something inside me.

"Not so different." Viktor's eyes were serious now. "Girl has old soul. Strong. Adapts quickly. Men already respect her."

"After one dinner?"

"After seeing way she handles you." A smile tugged at the corner of his mouth. "Noticed something interesting about you since she arrived."

I raised an eyebrow. "And what is that?"

"The way you look at her. Same way your father looked at your mother." He met my gaze directly. "Still ruthless *vor* with enemies, still feared by all of St. Petersburg. But with her? Different man entirely."

"You reading too much into things," I said dismissively.

"No? Then why take personal interest in her comfort, her safety? Why show parts of yourself even I rarely see?" Viktor's expression grew more serious. "Moscow trip can wait. Dmitri situation under control for now."

"Business comes first. Always has."

"Some things more important than business," Viktor said quietly. "Some things once gone, cannot get back."

The weight of his words hung between us. Viktor had been my father's closest friend, had watched me grow up. Had seen what the life cost my parents, ultimately.

Before I could respond, Viktor's phone buzzed. He checked it, then rose. "Need to handle this, it's Yuri. Think about what I said."

Left alone, I moved to the window, watching the morning light play across the snow-covered gardens. The conversation with Viktor had stirred thoughts I usually kept buried deep. Minutes stretched into nearly an hour as I stood there, weighing business against personal desires for perhaps the first time in my life.

The sound of approaching footsteps ended my solitary reflection. I turned as Liliya's voice came from the doorway, slightly breathless after what had clearly been an extensive tour.

"Tour was wonderful," she said, cheeks flushed with excitement. "This house is amazing. I had no idea it extended so far back into the gardens."

When I turned, she was standing in a shaft of sunlight, hair glowing copper, eyes bright with excitement. For a moment, I simply looked at her, understanding what Viktor had been trying to tell me.

"*Gotovyy?*" [Ready?] I asked, my voice rougher than intended.

"Absolutely." Her smile was warm, trusting.

"Car waiting out front," Viktor said, returning from his call. "Will leave you to your day." He nodded to Liliya. "Enjoy seeing the city, *devushka.*"

As we prepared to leave, I helped her into the wool coat Irina had laid out—deep burgundy that made her hair flame like fire. My fingers lingered at her collar, adjusting it against the wind. She shivered slightly, though whether from cold or my touch, I couldn't be sure.

"Where are we going?" She looked curious, maybe a little nervous, pulling black leather gloves over delicate fingers.

"Show you my city today. Not tourist places." I guided her toward the front door where the car waited—sleek black Audi instead of my usual Mercedes. "Places that matter."

Her eyes widened slightly at the casual car, casual clothes. Snowflakes caught in her hair, melting against the warmth of her skin. "No guards today?"

"*Net.* Today just us." I opened the door for her, caught the scent of her perfume mixed with crisp winter air as she slipped past. Something floral, delicate but lingering. Like her. "Today about showing you real beauty of city."

As we pulled away from the house, I caught Viktor watching from the window. I knew what he was thinking - a *vor* taking unnecessary risks, being too personal. But watching Liliya sink into the heated leather seat, cheeks pink from cold, I couldn't bring myself to care.

She gazed out the window as the city awakened around us, morning light catching golden on snow-covered domes of churches. I watched her reflection in the glass, the way her eyes widened at each new sight. It made me see familiar streets through a new lens - through her eyes.

After a few minutes of comfortable silence, I reached across the space between us and placed my hand on her thigh. A gesture that crossed boundaries I'd set for myself, but couldn't resist. She didn't flinch or pull away. Instead, she placed her hand over mine, her touch warm even through her gloves.

"The city is beautiful in the snow," she said softly, eyes still on the scenery outside. "Like something from a fairy tale."

"Most tourists only see Summer Garden, Peter and Paul Fortress," I replied, hyperaware of the weight of her hand on mine. "Pretty, but... expected. Will show you places with soul."

"Where are we going first?" Her fingers tightened slightly over mine.

"Place from childhood. Important place." I made a turn down a street lined with buildings from another century. "Almost there."

She leaned forward slightly as we slowed. "These buildings are incredible. So much older than anything in Minnesota."

"*Da.* Some from Catherine the Great time." I reluctantly withdrew my hand to park the car along a narrow side street. "From here, we walk."

Liliya looked around with interest as we stepped onto the snowy sidewalk. "This doesn't look like a tourist area."

"Is not. Locals only." I guided her toward a small courtyard between buildings. "Entrance hidden, like many best things in the city."

"A secret spot?" Her eyes sparkled with curiosity.

"Of sorts." I led her through the courtyard to a narrow passage between buildings that opened to a small square where an unassuming storefront nestled between newer construction. Weathered wood framed windows with books visible behind leaded glass.

"First stop," I said, turning down the narrow street most people never found, "place I used to hide when needed escape. Still go sometimes, when world too heavy."

Her curious expression made something warm settle in my chest. The way she looked at everything - not just seeing surface beauty, but trying to understand deeper meanings. Understanding she'd shown with my tattoos, with my men.

"Will like this place," I said softly, more to myself than her. "Shows different side of things."

"Still open?" she asked, eyeing an aged wooden door almost hidden between modern buildings, its ancient-looking lock somehow both imposing and inviting.

"For right people." I pulled an ornate key from my pocket, the metal gleaming dull gold in winter light. Her eyes lit up at the sight with the same spark of curiosity I'd seen when she'd asked about my tattoos.

"Here." I held the key out to her, watching surprise flicker across her face. "Want to do honors?"

She took the key carefully, like it was something precious. I watched her slip it into the lock, heard the soft click of tumblers falling into place.

Metal groaned as the door swung inward at her touch. I placed my hand on the small of her back, guiding her into warm darkness that smelled of leather, paper, and history. "Welcome to my favorite sanctuary."

27

Liliya

The lock clicked, door groaning open to reveal darkness beyond. I hesitated at threshold, but Zaven's hand settled warm and steady at small of my back, guiding me forward.

Lights flickered to life, and my breath caught. Books. Everywhere. Floor-to-ceiling shelves stretched into shadows, leather bindings gleaming rich and warm. A spiral staircase curved upward, promising more literary treasures above. Reading nooks tucked into corners like secret gardens made of paper and leather.

"This is..." Words failed me as I turned slowly, trying to take it all in. The smell of old paper and leather wrapped around me like a familiar embrace. "How did you find this place?"

"Mother brought me here as boy," Zaven said softly. "When needed reminder that world not just about power and control."

I moved deeper into the space, drawn to a section of Russian classics. My fingers traced familiar names - Dostoyevsky, Tolstoy, Pushkin. "These are first editions," I whispered, recognizing the bindings from my library science courses.

My fingers traced gold lettering on spines, remembering hours spent in the university library's special collections. Before everything changed, before Jack, this had been my world - the quiet safety of books.

"Worked at library through college," I explained, catching Zaven's questioning look. Hesitated before adding, "Before... everything."

Something dark flickered in his eyes at that, but his voice remained gentle. "Come. Show you my favorite corner."

He led me to a hidden nook, window seat piled with worn velvet cushions. Snow fell softly beyond leaded glass, making space feel even more removed from world outside.

"Found peace here sometimes," he said, watching me settle among cushions. "When expectations of being *vor*'s son became too heavy."

The admission surprised me - this glimpse of young Zaven, seeking refuge in books. Made me see him differently, this dangerous man who kept a key to a secret library.

"Used to come here after lessons," Zaven said, settling beside me. "Read stories of adventure, heroes. Different world from one father training me for."

Watching him in this space felt intimate somehow. His usual intensity softened by memories, by morning light filtering through old glass. Dark sweater stretched across broad shoulders as he reached past me, pulling leather-bound book from shelf.

"First book read here," he said, placing it carefully in my lap. The Brothers Karamazov. "Mother insisted start with classics."

"Bit heavy for a boy," I said, opening cover reverently. Paper smelled of age and wisdom.

"Was different kind of boy." Something in his voice made me look up. Found him watching me with expression I couldn't quite read. "Like way you handle books. Shows respect for their stories, their history."

My fingers traced gilt edges. "Always found safety in libraries. In stories." Hesitated before adding, "Even in Russia, first thing I did was find nearest library. Before Zolotoy Vek, before everything else."

I turned toward the window, watching snowflakes drift past the leaded glass. "Libraries were the one place Jack never followed me. Too quiet for him, too..." I trailed off, breath fogging the cold pane. Without thinking, I drew a small smile in the condensation, muscle memory from countless library visits.

"Why you do that?" Zaven's voice came low and close as he settled beside me on the cushioned seat.

"Hmm?" I glanced at him, then back at my simple drawing. "Oh. It's silly, really. Started doing it in college, whenever I'd find a good study spot by a window. Like marking my territory, I guess. My little way of saying 'I was here, I was happy here.'" I traced another curve in the fog. "Even after everything went wrong, I kept doing it. Reminder that I could still find moments of peace."

His hand covered mine where it rested against the glass, warmth seeping into my cold fingers. "Not silly. Is... hopeful." He studied the fading smile. "Like you still believe in finding good moments, even in dark places."

I flattened my palm against the cold glass beside the smile, watching it slowly fade. "In the campus library, I used to imagine all the other students who'd sat in my spot before me. All their hopes and dreams and fears fogging up the same window."

"Used to think same thing," Zaven said, voice warm with memory. "First times here, wondered about others who read these books, left their mark on pages."

"Like this?" I carefully opened The Brothers Karamazov again, pointing to a faint pencil mark in the margin.

"That one mine," his lips curved slightly. "Was difficult child. Always arguing with authors in margins."

"You wrote in a first edition?" I gasped in mock horror, though my fingers traced his young handwriting with something like reverence.

"Only pencil," he defended, then added more softly, "Mother would get so angry. Said books deserve proper respect."

"She sounds wonderful," I said carefully, watching his expression. "The way you talk about her..."

"Strong woman. Gentle, but had fire inside. Like you." His hand found mine again.

"I'm not—"

"You are," he interrupted firmly. "See it when you stand up to my men at dinner. When you face new challenges without fear." His thumb traced my palm. "When you leave small smiles on windows, even after everything."

I felt my cheeks warm at that observation. He'd noticed my window drawings - something so private I hadn't realized anyone would pay attention to it. The fact that he had, that he understood what they meant... it made me feel exposed but also seen in a way I hadn't experienced before.

His mention of facing challenges made me think about his upcoming trip. "Speaking of challenges," I said, glancing at him through my lashes. "About Moscow... is it a long trip?"

"Not about business today," he reminded me, though his expression softened at my question.

"I know, but..." I hesitated, then decided to be honest. "I worry. About what you might face there."

A spark of heat entered his eyes, corner of his mouth lifting. "Worried for me, *malyshka*?"

"Maybe." I tried to sound casual, but my fingers tightened on his unconsciously.

"Like knowing you care," he murmured, bringing our joined hands to his lips. "But no need worry. Know how handle Moscow business long time."

"The kind of business that leaves scars?" I asked quietly, thinking of the stories his men had shared.

His other hand came up to cup my face, thumb tracing my cheekbone. "Focus on today. On this moment. Tomorrow bring what it brings."

"Is that your way of saying yes?"

"Is my way of saying need better things to think about." He leaned closer, breath warm against my ear. "Like way you blush when worried for me."

Heat built between us as we sat close in the window nook, snowflakes drifting beyond the glass. When his lips finally met mine, the kiss was gentle for about half a second before something snapped between us. His mouth turned hungry, demanding, as if he'd been holding back for days. My hands fisted in his sweater, feeling his heart hammering beneath my fingers.

He made a sound deep in his throat—half growl, half groan—that sent liquid heat straight between my thighs. His hand slid to my waist, then lower, gripping my ass and pulling me hard against him. I could feel how much he wanted me, the rigid length of him pressing against my hip.

"Fuck, Liliya," he growled against my lips, his accent thick with desire. His teeth grazed my bottom lip, making me gasp as he deepened the kiss, his tongue sliding against mine in a way that had me imagining it elsewhere on my body.

I moaned into his mouth, shameless and needy, as his hand tangled in my hair, tugging just enough to send shivers racing down my spine. Without thinking, I climbed onto his lap, straddling him in the window seat. The position pressed his erection directly against my core, making us both curse at the contact even through our clothes.

"Want to bend you over right here," he muttered against my neck, nipping at the sensitive skin. "Fuck you until you scream my name. Make you come so hard you forget everything but me."

"Yes," I gasped, grinding down against him, beyond caring that we were in a public place. "Please, Zaven."

His hands gripped my hips, guiding my movements as I rocked against him. One hand slid under my sweater, his palm hot against my bare skin as it moved up toward my breast. I was panting, desperate, my body burning from the inside out.

"*Blyad*," he growled, suddenly stilling my hips with iron hands. His breathing was ragged, pupils blown so wide his eyes looked black. "Need to stop. Now."

I made a sound of protest, trying to move against him again, but his grip was unrelenting.

"Not here," he said, voice rough as gravel. "Not like this. First time I fuck you won't be against dusty bookshelf with old *babushka* [grandmother] who owns place potentially walking in."

His words pierced through the haze of desire, bringing me back to myself with jarring clarity. What was I doing? Three days ago, I'd promised myself I wouldn't rush into anything physical, wouldn't repeat my pattern of letting passion override caution. Yet here I was, grinding against him in a public place.

I slid off his lap, my legs shaky and my body still humming with unfulfilled need. The intensity of my reaction to him frightened me—not because I feared Zaven, but because I feared how easily he made me forget my own boundaries.

"I don't usually…" I started, not even sure how to finish that sentence. Jump men in bookstores? Dry hump virtual strangers? My cheeks burned.

"Know you don't," he said, his voice gentler but still rough with desire. He reached out, brushing my hair back from my flushed face. "Is why stopped."

I let out a shaky breath. "This is embarrassing."

"Why? Because body want what mind still figuring out?" He shook his head. "Nothing embarrassing about desire, Liliya."

"I told myself I wouldn't do this," I admitted, straightening my sweater. "After Jack, I promised I'd be smarter next time. Not rush into anything."

His eyes held mine, searching. "Yet just now, seemed very eager to rush." There was no mockery in his voice, just curiosity. "What different now?"

The question made me pause. What was different?

"You don't make me feel afraid," I said finally, the truth surprising even me. "Even when you're intimidating as hell, even when I know what you are, what you do… I don't feel afraid with you. And that scares me more than anything."

"Because trust own instincts again?" he asked perceptively.

I nodded. "And because the last time I trusted them, I ended up with cigarette burns and broken ribs."

He flinched slightly at that, but didn't look away. "Not same man, Liliya. Never hurt you."

"I know," I said, and realized I meant it. "That's why I'm here, why I'm… reacting like this." I gestured vaguely between us, at the space still charged with our interrupted moment. "But I still need a little time. My body's apparently on board, but my head…"

"Need to catch up," he finished for me, nodding. "Understand."

He stood, discreetly adjusting himself in his jeans before offering his hand. "Come. Show you more of city. Though might need moment to…" he glanced down at the obvious bulge in his pants, "…compose self first."

The frankness made me laugh despite my embarrassment. "Glad I'm not the only one affected here."

"If think that, then truly not paying attention," he said dryly. "Have been hard since day you walked into my club."

"Oh my god," I covered my face with my hands, but couldn't help laughing. "How are we supposed to walk around the city like this? I can barely think straight."

"Cold Russian winter help with that," he said, his smile wry as he adjusted himself again. "Though may need extra minute."

As we headed toward the door, each step reminding me of the throbbing between my legs, I had to ask: "Is it always going to be like this? This... intense?"

His eyes darkened again. "Only gets more intense, *malyshka*. Body only beginning to learn what want."

"Then we're both in trouble," I muttered, stepping into the blast of cold air that did, indeed, help clear my head a little.

"Trouble worth having," he said, his hand settling at the small of my back as we walked. "Best kind."

I couldn't argue with that, even if I'd wanted to.

Through the Audi's tinted windows, St. Petersburg's streets glided past in a blur of snow and golden morning light. Zaven drove with the same quiet confidence he showed in everything, one hand resting casually on the wheel, the other finding mine across the center console.

I was still acutely aware of my body's reaction to him in the library. The cold air had helped, but there was still a lingering heat between us, an awareness that hadn't been there before. Every time our eyes met, I felt the echo of his hands on me, his lips against mine.

"Next place special to me," he said, turning down a narrow street lined with historic buildings. "Not many know about it."

I watched his profile, struck by how different he looked in the casual sweater, winter sun catching the angles of his face. More approachable, yet somehow no less powerful - especially now that I knew the strength of his restraint. "Another childhood spot?"

"*Da*. But different kind." His thumb traced circles on my palm, the simple touch sending unwelcome heat through me all over again. "Place that shaped who became."

The car slowed as we approached what looked like an old gymnasium, its classical architecture standing proud against the modern buildings surrounding it. "What is this place?"

A ghost of a smile touched his lips. "Where learned most important lessons. Not ones father planned."

Zaven parked the car and came around to open my door, the cold air rushing in. As we approached the building, I noticed faded Cyrillic lettering above the entrance.

"Boxing club," he translated, leading me through heavy wooden doors. "But was more than that."

The interior smelled of old wood and leather, worn floorboards creaking beneath our feet. Timeworn photos lined the walls - boxers in vintage poses, serious faces staring out from black and white prints.

"Started training here at twelve," Zaven said, his hand warm against my back as we walked deeper into the building. "Father wanted me learn discipline, control. But old trainer here, Boris Voloshyn, he teach different lessons."

The main room opened before us, sunlight streaming through high windows onto a weathered boxing ring. Punching bags hung in corners, their leather cracked with age and use.

"What kind of lessons?" I asked, watching Zaven's expression soften with memory.

He moved to one of the hanging bags, his hand running over the worn leather before throwing a quick, precise punch that made the heavy bag swing. "That true strength not just in fists. In here." He tapped his temple. "And here." His hand moved to his heart. "Most men who come here, want only to learn how fight. Boris, he teach me why to fight. When not to."

A door creaked, and an elderly man emerged from what looked like an office, his weathered face breaking into a broad smile. "Zaven Nikolaevich! Too long since you visit old man."

Zaven's face lit up in a way I'd never seen before. "Boris Pavlovich," he strode forward, embracing the older man warmly. "Still terrorizing young fighters?"

"Bah, these new ones too soft," Boris's sharp eyes found me. "But who is this? Finally bring woman to meet me?"

"This is Liliya," Zaven said, his voice warm with pride as he kept his hand at the small of my back.

Boris's weathered face crinkled in a knowing smile. "Ah, the American girl who has whole city talking. Come, have tea. Tell me how my best student became *vor*, yet still remembers old trainer."

The small office was lined with vintage boxing photos, including several of a younger Zaven in the ring. Boris busied himself with an ancient kettle while we settled into worn chairs.

"Still have best hook in city?" Boris asked, pouring tea into mismatched cups.

"Only because you beat proper form into me," Zaven replied.

"Ah, took years. Stubborn boy." Boris's eyes twinkled. "Always asking why. Why this stance, why that technique. Not like others who just want to hit things."

"Taught me most important lesson," Zaven said, his hand finding mine. "When to fight. What worth fighting for."

Boris nodded sagely. "Power without purpose is just violence. Remember what told you?"

"Man who fights for self is just brawler," Zaven recited. "Man who fights for others—"

"Is warrior," Boris finished with satisfaction. He turned to me, eyes sharp despite his age. "This one, he come here angry boy, leave as man with discipline. In ring, many opponents think they fight against strength." He tapped his temple. "Never realize real battle up here."

His weathered gaze softened as he looked between us. "Now I see what you fight for, Zaven Nikolaevich. Is good. Purpose makes man stronger than any muscle."

The older man's perceptiveness made me blush. The way he looked at us, as if seeing something we hadn't fully acknowledged ourselves yet.

"Need go," Zaven said, setting down his tea. "Have lunch reservation."

"Of course, of course." Boris nodded. "Bring your Liliya back sometime. Maybe teach her too, eh? Woman should know how protect self."

As we stood to leave, Boris caught Zaven's arm. "Still proud of you, boy. Everything you become. Remember that."

Outside, the cold air hit us as we walked back to the car. I waited until Zaven had opened my door before asking, "How did you end up here? As a kid, I mean."

"Father believed physical training essential," he said as he slid into the driver's seat. "Many *vor* send sons to formal martial arts. My father chose boxing. Said needed to feel what it meant to take hit, get back up."

"And Boris taught you more than just how to throw a punch."

A ghost of a smile touched his lips. "*Da*. Taught control. Purpose. That strength without direction just destruction." He glanced at me. "Ready for lunch? Know place you will like."

As Zaven navigated through the snowy streets, I found myself turning over everything I'd learned about him this morning. The library, his mother's influence, and now this glimpse of his past at the boxing club. Each piece revealed a different side of him - not just the powerful *vor*, but a man shaped by both gentle wisdom and hard lessons.

The careful balance between power and control, strength and restraint seemed to define him. The way Boris had looked at him - with genuine pride - spoke volumes about the man Zaven had become despite the world he operated in.

The car turned onto a broader street lined with restaurants, and I found myself surprisingly eager to discover more pieces of him, one sanctuary at a time.

28

Liliya

The restaurant was tucked away in a historic building, its dark wood and brass details speaking of old-world elegance. As we entered, the maître d' recognized Zaven immediately, bowing slightly.

"Zaven Nikolaevich. Your usual table."

It wasn't a question. He led us through the main dining room, where crystal glasses caught the winter sunlight and conversations in Russian and French blended into a sophisticated hum. Our table was partially secluded, offering both privacy and a view of the snow-dusted street through leaded glass windows.

Zaven held my chair, his hand lingering warm on my shoulder as I sat. The maître d' materialized with menus bound in burgundy leather, but Zaven waved them away.

"Trust me to order?" he asked, settling across from me. "Place known for certain specialties."

I nodded, still taking in the refined atmosphere. "This doesn't seem like somewhere that serves a cheese steak and fries."

His lips curved. "*Net.* But think you find something better."

A waiter arrived with a bottle of wine, presenting it to Zaven for approval. After a nod, he poured two glasses of deep red liquid that caught the light like rubies.

"Used to come here with mother," Zaven said, watching me take in the surroundings. "Every Sunday after church. Was different then - smaller, less..." He gestured at the crystal and silk-covered walls.

"But still special?"

"*Da*. Mother loved French cuisine. Said reminded her of time before..." He paused. "Before everything changed."

The waiter returned, and Zaven ordered in fluid French that made my eyebrows raise. He caught my expression and smiled. "Mother insisted. Said proper gentleman speaks French."

"Any other languages I should know about?"

"Few." He took a sip of wine. "But Russian still best for certain things."

"Like cursing?"

His eyes darkened with heat. "Among others. Some things need... proper accent to feel right." His voice dropped lower, accent thickening deliberately.

Heat bloomed in my cheeks at his tone. "Maybe you'll teach me sometime."

"Careful what ask for, *malyshka*." His thumb traced my wrist. "Russian lessons can be... intense."

I caught my breath at the promise in his words. Before I could respond, he shifted, though his eyes still held that heat. "How you finding day so far?"

I twisted my wine glass, watching the light play through the burgundy liquid. "It's been... eye-opening. Seeing these places that shaped you."

"Good eye-opening?" His fingers remained at my wrist, touch light but distracting.

"Yes. Makes me understand why your men respect you so much. It's not just power, is it? It's how you use it."

Something flickered in his expression. "Power complicated thing, Liliya. Easy to misuse."

"Like what Boris taught you about purpose and control?"

I noticed his jaw tighten slightly. "Boris taught many lessons. Some harder than others." His fingers absently traced what looked like a tattoo peeking from beneath his cuff. "Some lessons marked permanently."

My eyes followed the movement, reminding me of his promise earlier.

"You said you'd tell me about them. Your tattoos."

His expression softened, something like resignation mixing with determination in his eyes. "*Da*, did promise." He deliberately rolled his sleeve higher, exposing more of the intricate artwork I'd glimpsed before. The designs were darker than I expected, more complex - violent imagery mixed with religious symbols in a language of ink I couldn't fully read.

"In our world, every mark tells story," he said, voice dropping lower. "Not just decoration. Is history, rank, beliefs. Entire life written on skin."

I reached across, my fingers drawn to a cluster of stars near his wrist. "These?"

"Prison stars," he said unflinchingly, watching my reaction carefully. "Mark of *vor*. One for each year inside. Authority that cannot be questioned."

He turned his arm slightly, revealing a bladed design. "This—knife with blood drops—means have spilled blood for brotherhood. Not random violence," he clarified, eyes holding mine. "Execution of traitors."

My breath caught, but I didn't pull away. Instead, my fingers traced the pattern, feeling the slight raise of scarred skin beneath. I was touching the physical record of violence, of death, yet I wasn't afraid.

"And these words?" I traced Cyrillic script that wrapped around his forearm like barbed wire.

"Names. Not of victims," he said, reading something in my expression. "Of brothers lost. Dates they fell. Reminder of price paid for this life."

The frankness of his answers should have terrified me. He wasn't softening the brutal reality his tattoos represented. Yet somehow, his honesty made me trust him more.

My eyes were drawn to the dark ink visible above his collar. "What about that one?"

Without hesitation, he reached up to the neckline of his dark sweater and pulled the fabric aside, exposing the full design at his throat - a crucifix with words I couldn't read. His eyes never left mine, gauging my reaction to this intentional intimacy.

I reached out, fingers brushing the tattoo at his throat. His skin was warm, and I felt his pulse jump under my touch. The vulnerability of the location struck me - allowing someone to mark such a vital spot required immense trust.

"First one," he said, voice rough with something deeper than desire. "Mark of commitment. To family, to code. Means 'Death before dishonor' in old Church Slavonic."

"When?" My voice had dropped to match his.

"Sixteen." He caught my hand, pressing my fingers more firmly against the mark, holding them there. "Young, but sure. Father present when done."

The heat in his eyes made me forget we were in a public restaurant. "Must have hurt."

"Pain part of commitment," he murmured. "Every mark earned through blood, suffering. No anesthetic, no modern machines then. Just needle, ink, and will." His accent thickened, voice dropping lower. "Each one story of choice made, price paid. Like way you not afraid to touch them. Most people..." he paused, something vulnerable flickering across his face, "they see only monster in these marks."

"I see you," I said simply, my fingers still against his pulse. "All the choices that made you who you are."

The waiter approached with steaming plates, interrupting whatever he'd been about to say. But the intensity in his gaze remained as we turned our attention to the food, making promises his words hadn't finished.

Steam rose from delicate plates of what looked like seared scallops in a saffron cream sauce. "Traditional French–Russian fusion," Zaven explained, watching my reaction. "Chef here trained in Paris, but adds local touches."

The first bite melted on my tongue - rich and delicate at once, with flavors I couldn't quite name. Watching Zaven eat was its own kind of distraction. The same precise control he showed in everything else was present even here, but softened somehow. More man than *vor*.

I found myself studying his hands as he reached for his wine glass, remembering how they'd felt this morning in the library, last night in my bed. The dangerous grace of his boxing demonstration now translated into something almost elegant.

"Like?" he asked, noticing my contemplation.

"Everything." The word came out more breathless than I'd intended, and I wasn't just talking about the food. This morning had changed something between us. The glimpses of his past, the trust he'd shown in sharing those private spaces – it made the *vor* seem more human. More real.

The way he'd reacted to my touch on his tattoo lingered in my mind. There was still so much to learn about him, so many layers to uncover. But for the first time, I wasn't afraid of what I might find. Each revelation only made me want to know more.

"Tell me about the sauce?" I asked, partly to distract myself from the way his throat moved as he sipped his wine, the tattoo I'd touched earlier disappearing beneath his collar.

"Secret blend," he said, voice warm with amusement at my obvious deflection. "Chef guards recipe like state secret. Even I not allowed know."

As we finished our main course, I found myself mesmerized by every small movement he made. The way his strong fingers handled the delicate silverware with surprising grace. How the muscles in his forearms flexed beneath the sleeves of his sweater as he reached for his wine. The slight shadow of stubble along his jaw that I now knew exactly how it felt against my skin.

After our moment in the library, after seeing his markings and hearing their brutal truth, I couldn't stop my mind from wandering to dangerous places. What would those powerful hands feel like on other parts of my body? How would that controlled strength feel when he finally let go?

"Staring, *malyshka*," he said, his voice a low rumble that sent heat spiraling through me. "Something on mind?"

A flush crept up my neck. "Just thinking."

"About?" The intensity in his eyes told me he knew exactly what I was thinking about.

"You," I admitted, the honesty surprising us both. "You're... fuck, you're probably the most attractive man I've ever seen."

His eyebrows raised slightly, that dangerous smile playing at his lips.

"Even with these?" He gestured to the tattoos, the marks of his violent life now exposed between us.

"Maybe because of them," I replied, then clarified, "Not what they represent, but what they say about you. Your honesty. Your willingness to show me all of you, even the darkest parts."

Something shifted in his expression, softening the dangerous edges. "Beautiful women look at me all time, Liliya. Some see money, some power, some danger. None see me." His hand found mine across the table. "Until you."

The words hit something deep inside me, cutting through every defense I'd built.

The waiter cleared our plates, and Zaven's lips curved slightly. "Room for dessert?"

"After a meal like that?" I protested weakly.

"Trust me," he said, that heat returning to his eyes. "Must try this."

The waiter presented a dark chocolate soufflé, still warm from the oven. "House specialty," Zaven explained. Instead of passing me a spoon, he dipped his own into the warm chocolate, bringing it to my lips. The gesture was startlingly intimate, his eyes intent on my face as I accepted the bite.

A small sound of pleasure escaped before I could stop it. The chocolate was rich and bitter-sweet, with hints of what might have been cognac. His eyes darkened at my reaction, spoon still hovering between us.

"Good?" His voice had dropped lower, that Russian accent thickening again.

"Incredible," I managed, very aware of how he was watching my lips as he offered another bite.

"Like seeing you enjoy simple pleasures," he said softly. "Not afraid to show what you feel."

The comment struck deeper than just dessert. All day, I'd been letting my guard down more and more. Touching his tattoos, asking about his past, showing my curiosity about his world. And instead of pulling away, he'd been drawing me closer, sharing pieces of himself I suspected few people ever saw.

"Found something sweet you like more than American pie?" he asked, but there was something serious beneath the teasing.

I met his gaze. "I'm finding I like a lot of things I never expected to."

His hand found mine across the table, thumb tracing my palm like he had in the library. But this touch felt different - more certain, more possessive. Like the *vor* and the man I'd glimpsed today were finally merging into someone I was starting to understand. And maybe starting to fall for.

Something shifted in the air between us, a tension that had been building all day approaching breaking point. Instead of leaning into it, I abruptly changed direction, asking something that had been on my mind since the boxing club.

"Zaven... would you teach me to fight?"

His hand stilled, eyes sharpening with surprise. "Why asking this now?"

"Watching you at the boxing club, seeing how it shaped you..." I traced the rim of my wine glass, choosing my words carefully. "I don't want to be helpless anymore. Not just because of Jack, but for myself."

"Not helpless now," he said, voice low. "Have my protection."

"I know. And I trust that." I met his gaze steadily. "But I need to trust myself too. To know I can..." I paused, thinking of his words from the boxing club. "To know when to fight, and when not to. Like Boris taught you."

Something shifted in his expression - respect, maybe, or understanding. "You surprise me, Liliya. Most women in your position want jewelry, fancy clothes. You want to learn to fight."

"I've never been like most women," I said, remembering how he'd told me that's what had first caught his attention at the club.

"No, you fucking not," he agreed, his thumb tracing my knuckles, as if imagining them curled into fists. "Is why wanted you from first moment. Why still want you now."

"When do we start?" I asked, unable to keep the eagerness from my voice.

"So impatient," he murmured, his thumb continuing to trace circles on my palm. "Tomorrow evening. Seven o'clock." His eyes darkened as they moved over my face. "Will enjoy teaching you many things, not just fighting."

Heat bloomed in my cheeks at the obvious double meaning. "I might be a quick learner."

"Hope not too quick," he replied, voice dropping to that rough whisper that made my stomach flip. "Some lessons best taught... slowly. With attention to every detail."

I bit my lip, remembering how his hands had felt on me in the library, the strength he'd held in check. "Will it be just us?"

"*Da.*" The single word carried a weight of promise. "Private lessons. More effective that way."

"I might be sore afterward," I said, trying to sound casual despite the heat building between us.

His eyes flashed with heat. "Best kind of sore, *malyshka*. Kind that reminds you exactly who put hands on you." He lifted my fingers to his lips, kissing the knuckles he'd just been examining. "Will be gentle. At first."

The waiter approached with the check, and I realized we'd let the soufflé go cold, forgotten in this moment of understanding between us.

"Ready to head back?" he asked as we stepped into the cold afternoon air, his fingers intertwined with mine.

Our joined hands felt different from his usual guiding touch at my back or arm. More intimate, more intentional. His fingers fit between mine naturally, thumb tracing absent patterns on my skin that made my breath catch.

We'd barely made it ten steps when I saw him - one of the men from *Smotriny.* The one with the cold eyes who'd bid far too high, who'd looked at me like I was something to be broken. He moved toward us with deliberate purpose, alcohol fuming from him even at a distance.

"*Amerikanskaya shlyukha*," [American whore] he spat, eyes fixed on me with undisguised hatred. "Think you too good for real Russian men? Fucking foreign cunt—"

The crack of bone breaking cut off his words, followed by the sickening thud of a body hitting brick. Sergei and Yuri materialized from nowhere - I hadn't even realized they'd been there all day. Nikolai appeared from across the street, moving with deadly purpose. The man who'd approached was on his knees, blood pouring from his shattered nose.

"Inside," Zaven ordered, his voice carrying an edge I'd never heard before. Not angry - something colder, more lethal. The *vor* fully emerged in that moment, all traces of the man who'd fed me chocolate replaced by something that made my blood run cold.

He released my hand, guiding me firmly toward the restaurant door with a gentle push at the small of my back. "Wait there."

I stepped inside, my heart hammering against my ribs as I turned to watch through the window. Zaven approached the kneeling man with the languid, predatory grace of a tiger. His men moved back slightly, creating space for him in a choreography that spoke of years of shared violence.

I couldn't hear what Zaven said, but I saw him crouch down, his face inches from the bloodied man. Whatever words he spoke made the color drain from the man's face. Even through the glass, I could see the pure terror in his eyes as he frantically shook his head, blood spraying from his ruined nose.

Zaven stood slowly, saying something to Nikolai. The usually reserved man nodded once, then seized the man by the hair, yanking his head back at an angle that looked painful. Sergei and Yuri dragged him to his feet, his legs buckling as they half-carried him toward a black car that had appeared silently at the curb.

Blood marked a dark path across the pristine snow as they hauled him away. Zaven watched, his posture rigid, until the car door slammed shut. Only then did he turn back toward the restaurant, his eyes finding mine through the window.

When he stepped inside, his expression shifted, the lethal *vor* receding slightly as he approached me. "Are you all right?"

"Yes," I managed, surprised by how steady my voice sounded. "That was the man from *Smotriny*, wasn't it? The one who kept bidding too high."

"*Da*. Man who not understand when thing not for sale." His jaw tightened as he took my hand again, thumb stroking over my knuckles. "Now he fucking learn."

"He followed us here?"

"Followed you." The words came out like ice. "Think because I show softer side today, mean guard down." A cruel smile touched his lips. "Big fucking mistake."

As we waited for our own car, I processed what I'd just witnessed. All day he'd shown me his sanctuaries, his peaceful places. But this was his world too - swift, brutal violence and constant vigilance. The men I'd shared dinner and vodka with last night, now dealing out potentially lethal consequences without hesitation.

"What will happen to him?" I asked quietly, unable to stop myself.

Zaven's eyes met mine, no attempt to soften the truth in them. "He will be dealt with. Won't be problem anymore."

The deliberate vagueness told me everything I needed to know. I should have been horrified, should have been running in the opposite direction. Instead, I found myself nodding, a strange calm settling over me. The blood staining the pristine snow outside wasn't metaphorical - it was real, dark against the white, steaming slightly in the cold. And I couldn't bring myself to mourn for a man who'd looked at me with such hatred.

"Been watching us whole time?" I asked, changing the subject as I glanced toward where Sergei and Yuri had appeared from seemingly nowhere.

"Always watching, *malyshka*. Part of keeping you safe." His thumb traced over our joined hands, the gesture tender despite the violence moments before. "Need get you back to house now."

The car arrived, sleek and black like everything else in Zaven's world. He guided me inside with a protective hand at my lower back, his body language still coiled with barely contained tension. As we settled into the leather seats, I could feel the aggression still radiating from him, his jaw tight, eyes distant as he stared out the window.

Without thinking, I reached for him, turning his face toward mine. His eyes were still dark with violence, with the *vor* who had emerged outside the restaurant. I pressed my lips to his, not gentle or questioning like our earlier kisses, but firm and demanding.

For a moment he froze, surprised, then responded with a hunger that stole my breath. His hand tangled in my hair, holding me to him as his mouth claimed mine. The kiss wasn't like the others—not teasing or exploratory. This was raw, almost desperate, as if he needed to ground himself in something other than the violence.

When we finally broke apart, both breathing hard, I saw the man returning to his eyes, the dangerous *vor* receding. He pressed his forehead against mine, his breath warm on my lips.

"Thank you," he murmured, the words so quiet I barely caught them.

I didn't ask what for. I didn't need to. As the car pulled away from the curb, taking us back to the safety of his fortress, our hands remained linked between us. The day had started with him showing me his sanctuaries, and ended with a glimpse of the brutality that made those sanctuaries necessary.

Somehow, I was still here. Still holding his hand. Still wanting more.

29

Liliya

I hesitated at the threshold of the gym, nervousness and anticipation warring inside me. After yesterday's incident outside the restaurant, Zaven had disappeared to "handle business"—a phrase I was learning carried darker implications than it might elsewhere. I hadn't seen him all day, though I'd caught glimpses of his men moving through the house with grave expressions.

Sleep had come surprisingly easy despite the day's intensity, but my dreams... My cheeks flushed remembering the vivid images that had filled my night. Zaven's hands on my body, not teaching me to fight but exploring, claiming. In my dream, his tattoos had seemed to move across his skin as he moved above me, his voice rough in my ear as he whispered things that made me burn even in sleep. I'd woken tangled in sheets, body humming with unfulfilled need, feeling both embarrassed and strangely safe—like even my subconscious knew he was someone I could trust.

Now, as seven o'clock arrived, I found myself outside the gym where he'd promised to teach me. The room was larger than I expected, filled with an assortment of equipment I couldn't even name. But it wasn't the unfamiliar machines that made me pause – it was Zaven.

He stood in the center of a large mat, his back to me, wearing nothing but a pair of black gym shorts. Holy fuck. The abstractions he'd described about his tattoos were now gloriously visible, inked across expanses of muscle and skin I'd only imagined until now. Each movement as he stretched caused his powerful muscles to ripple beneath the artwork, and I found myself unable to look away, my mouth going dry.

When Zaven turned, I barely managed to stifle a gasp. His chest was even more impressive than his back—a canvas of intricate tattoos covering sculpted muscle that put every fantasy to shame. The large, ornate cross dominated the center, surrounded by the symbols whose meanings he'd shared with me. A trail of dark hair led from his navel down past the waistband of his shorts, drawing my eyes to the sharp V of his hips. The scars scattered across his skin only made him more magnetic—no longer abstract stories but real proof of survival, of the power his body contained.

Zaven's eyes met mine, dark with appreciation at my reaction. "Like what you see, *malyshka*?"

I stepped fully into the room. "Seeing the tattoos is different from hearing about them," I said, my voice sounding strained even to my own ears. "They're... damn, they're beautiful on you." Zaven chuckled, the sound low and rich, sending heat coursing through me to pool between my thighs.

"What?" he asked, eyes darkening with something more than amusement. "Did you expect me to fight in Armani?"

That broke the spell. I laughed, though the sound came out breathier than intended. "I guess I didn't really think about it," I admitted, stepping fully into the room. "Or maybe I did, and that's why I couldn't focus all day."

Zaven's eyes raked over me, lingering on the way my yoga pants hugged my curves. "Good choice," he said, voice rougher than before. "Need freedom to move."

I nodded, trying not to focus on the fact that he was barefoot, toes curling slightly into the mat. There was something dangerously intimate about seeing him like this, stripped of his usual armor of expensive suits and careful control.

"Let's begin." Zaven asked, his voice taking on a more serious tone, though his eyes still held that heat that made my skin tingle.

I took a deep breath, centering myself. This wasn't about attraction or the electricity crackling between us. This was about learning to protect myself.

"Okay," I said, meeting his gaze with determination. The sight of his raw power, the thought of those strong hands on me, brought a flutter of anxiety despite my attraction to him.

He noticed my hesitation immediately. "Need you understand something, Liliya." His expression grew serious. "If want learn real fighting, not just play, must trust me. Cannot hold back because of your past."

"I do trust you," I said softly. "It's just..."

"Know what he did to you." Zaven's jaw tightened. "But my hands not his hands. My strength not for hurting you. For teaching you be strong." He stepped closer, close enough that I had to tilt my head back to meet his eyes. "Can stop anytime want. But if continue, must be all in. Understanding comes through body, through contact. Cannot teach proper form without touching you."

The intensity in his gaze made my breath catch. This was Zaven offering both warning and promise - he wouldn't coddle me, but he wouldn't break me either.

"I want to learn," I said, stronger this time. "Really learn."

Zaven nodded, gesturing for me to join him on the mat. As I stepped forward, my bare feet sinking into the firm surface, the reality of what I'd asked for settled over me.

"We start with stance," he said, moving behind me. "Most important thing." His hands came to rest lightly on my hips, and despite my earlier nerves, my body responded to his touch with instant heat.

"Feet shoulder-width apart," he murmured, his breath warm against my ear. His hands slid from my hips to my waist, the heat of his skin burning through my thin t-shirt. "Knees slightly bent." Every small adjustment brought his body closer to mine, until I could feel the solid wall of his chest against my back.

"Like this?" I asked, proud of how steady my voice sounded despite the way my pulse raced at his proximity.

"Good," he praised, and I felt the word rumble through his chest. "Now, let's work on your punch. Make fist, but keep thumb outside, across fingers. *Yebat'sya s etim* [fuck with this], and you'll break thumb."

The crude Russian slang startled a laugh from me, easing some of the tension. I followed his instructions, curling my fingers tightly.

"Power not from arm alone," he continued, one hand sliding down my arm to position it correctly. "Is all in hips, in rotation." He demonstrated, his muscles rippling as he threw a punch that whistled through the air. "You twist, putting whole body into it. Like this."

His chest pressed against my back as he guided my arm through the motion. Despite the heat building between us, his touch remained professional, focused. This was the boxer I'd glimpsed in those old photos, the student Boris had trained.

"Keep core tight," he instructed, his free hand pressing lightly against my stomach. "Everything connects here. Strong center means strong punch."

As Zaven began to guide me through the basic stance again, a sudden memory flashed through my mind. Jack, his fingers digging painfully into my arms, forcing me to stand still as he berated me. I flinched involuntarily.

Zaven noticed immediately, his hands withdrawing. "Liliya? What wrong?"

I shook my head, trying to dispel the memory. "Nothing, I'm fine. Let's continue."

His eyes narrowed, but he nodded. As we moved on to basic punches, another memory surfaced - Jack's fist connecting with my cheek, the taste of blood in my mouth. My next punch was weak, hesitant.

"Stop," Zaven said firmly. He moved to stand in front of me, his eyes boring into mine. "You holding back. Why?"

I looked away, shame and fear warring inside me, my arms wrapping around my middle protectively. "I... I can't..."

"Can't or won't?" Zaven's voice turned hard, an edge to it I hadn't heard before. His stance shifted, shoulders squaring, radiating the same dangerous energy I'd witnessed outside the restaurant. Part of me recognized what he was doing, pushing me toward the anger I needed to feel. "Asked me to teach you fight, Liliya. Means facing fears, facing past."

Tears pricked at my eyes, my hands trembling at my sides. "You don't understand-"

"Then make me understand," he challenged, stepping closer, his muscled frame towering over me. Sweat glistened on his chest, making the tattoos seem to shift with each breath. "What you afraid of? Who you seeing when throw those punches?"

The dam broke. "Jack!" I cried out, my voice cracking, fists clenching involuntarily. "I see Jack. I feel his hands on me, his fists..." My whole body shook with the admission, years of suppressed rage and fear finally breaking through.

Zaven's expression softened for a moment, a muscle working in his jaw, then hardened with resolve. "Good. Use that."

"What?" My breath came in short gasps, pulse pounding in my ears.

"Use anger, use fear," he said, stepping closer until I could feel the heat radiating from his body. His scent surrounded me - clean sweat and something distinctly male. "Channel it. He hurt you, made you feel weak. But not weak, *malyshka*. Survivor. Now show me."

He held up his hands, palms out, muscles coiled with controlled power. The scars on his knuckles caught the light, telling their own stories of violence. "Hit me. Want you see Jack. Want you hit him with all anger, all pain he caused."

Taking a deep breath that shuddered through my whole body, I closed my eyes for a moment. When I opened them, I let the memories flood in. Jack's sneering face, his cruel words, his punishing hands. But this time, instead of cowering, I felt something snap inside me. The fear transformed into pure, white-hot rage that coursed through every muscle.

With a cry that was part anguish, part fury, I lashed out. My fist connected solidly with Zaven's palm, the impact jarring up my arm, vibrating through my shoulder. But it felt good. It felt right. Sweat trickled down my spine, my chest heaving with each ragged breath.

"Again," Zaven commanded, his voice rough with pride and something darker. His feet shifted on the mat, adjusting to my movements, muscles rippling as he braced for my next strike.

I obeyed, throwing punch after punch. Each one landed with more force than the last, my body finding its rhythm in the violence. My muscles burned, but I welcomed the pain. It meant I was fighting back. My hair had come loose from its ponytail, strands clinging to my damp neck, vision blurred with sweat and tears.

As I fought, something shifted inside me. The fear and shame that had haunted me began to transform into raw power. Each punch carried years of pent-up rage, of silent tears, of moments I'd been too afraid to fight back. My knuckles stung, skin raw from the impact, but I didn't stop.

Zaven moved with me, his powerful body responding to each of my attacks. His skin glistened with sweat, muscles flexing as he absorbed my punches. The tattoos on his chest seemed to ripple with each movement, like they were coming alive. His breath matched mine, deep and heavy in the charged air between us.

Finally, panting and trembling, I stopped. We stood close enough that I could feel the heat rolling off him, could see the rapid rise and fall of his chest matching my own labored breathing. Something had shifted between us, the air charged with more than just exertion.

"Look at me," Zaven commanded softly. When I raised my eyes to his, I saw fierce pride blazing there. "See now? This strength been inside you whole time. Just needed let it out."

His hand came up to cup my cheek, thumb gently wiping away tears I hadn't realized I'd shed. The tenderness of the gesture contrasted sharply with the violence of moments before. His skin was hot against mine, rough with calluses that spoke of both fighting and luxury.

"You fought like warrior today, *malyshka*," he murmured, voice rough with emotion. "Not just hitting - fighting with purpose, with heart." His other hand found my hip, steadying me as my legs trembled from exertion.

Looking into his eyes, seeing the mix of pride and hunger there, I felt different. Stronger. His belief in me radiated like physical heat between us. I'd taken the first step on a new path - one where I wasn't defined by what had been done to me, but by what I could do.

"Ready for more?" I asked, voice huskier than intended. His hand was still on my hip, thumb tracing small circles there.

"Show me," I managed, acutely aware of every point where our bodies nearly touched, of the way his muscles shifted as he moved back into a fighting stance.

"Next, show you how to block," he said, though his eyes still held that heated pride. "Need know how protect self as much as how to strike."

As he positioned himself in front of me, I knew this was more than just a training session. Each touch, each correction, each proud look when I got something right - we were building something between us. Something that made my skin tingle and my heart race in a way that had nothing to do with exertion.

The lesson continued, but the energy had shifted. Every movement felt charged with new meaning, new possibility. And as Zaven's hands guided me through another block, I couldn't help wondering if he felt it too.

30

Zaven

I watched as Liliya stood before me, chest heaving, new fire burning in her eyes. Gone was hesitant woman who entered my gym hours ago. In her place stood fighter - raw and untrained, but with spirit that made something stir deep in chest.

Transformation started when she finally let anger surface. Each punch she threw carried years of pain, of fear turned to rage. Have seen this before in others trained, but with her... with her different. Way she trusted me to push her, to help find that strength - made keeping professional distance fucking impossible.

Ever since moment in library yesterday, when she climbed onto lap and we nearly lost control, been fighting losing battle. Taste of her lips, feel of her body against mine - haunted me all night. Made focusing on Dmitri's man almost impossible.

"You did well, Liliya," I said, reaching out to tuck stray strand of hair behind her ear. My thumb wiped away tear she probably didn't even realize she'd shed. "But this just beginning."

Her eyes met mine, and saw determination mixed with something else - something that made cock stir despite years of practiced control. She nodded, voice stronger than ever heard before. "What else is there?"

"Now we work on breaking holds," I said, moving behind her. Voice might sound professional, but body had other ideas. Could smell her sweat, feel heat coming off her from training. "Most important skill to learn. Could save life one day."

Saw her shoulders tense as stepped closer, but she not pull away. Good. Progress. Trust building with each lesson.

"Going to grab you from behind," I explained. "Don't worry. Won't hurt you. But need feel what it's like, learn to break free."

As I wrapped my arms around her, one across her chest, other around her waist, I felt her stiffen. For moment, thought old fears might surface. But then she took deep breath, and I felt her relax against me. The feel of her ass pressed against my groin tested every bit of my control.

"*Spo'koino*, [Be calm] Liliya," I said, my lips close to her ear. "You're safe. Now think. How break free?"

Felt her mind working, analyzing situation. Then, with sudden burst of movement, she brought heel down hard on instep. Loosened grip, more from surprise than pain, and she took advantage, driving elbow back toward solar plexus.

Pride surged through me as she spun out of grasp. Triumphant gleam in eye, confidence in stance - this what been waiting to see.

"Excellent," said, heat coursing through me at sight of her - flushed with victory, eyes bright with newfound power. Cock hardened against gym shorts as she spun to face me. Not just about training anymore. About wanting to claim what mine.

She moved back into position, and I bit back groan as I gripped her again. The soft curves of her body pressed against my chest, her ass fitting perfectly against me. Every muscle in my body tensed with need. The *vor* in me, always controlled, always contained, was breaking free.

When she broke my hold this time, her movement brought her face to face with me, close enough I could feel her rapid breathing against my lips. The thin fabric of her workout clothes did nothing to hide her hardened nipples. The scent of her arousal mixed with sweat was driving me crazy.

"Now," I said, my voice rough with need, "show you how take down larger opponent."

My control was cracking. The *vor* in me wanted to claim her. The trainer needed to remain professional. But the man just wanted to fuck her until she screamed my name.

"Come at me," I ordered, my accent thicker with desire. "Try to attack."

She moved forward with newfound confidence, but I could see slight tremor in her hands. In one fluid motion, I had her airborne, years of training taking over despite blood rushing south. We landed on mat with soft thud, my body pinning hers down.

Every point of contact burned. Her softness beneath hardness, chest rising and falling against mine, heat of core pressed against thigh. Tattoos seemed to burn where skin touched them.

"Use opponent's momentum," managed to say. Faces inches apart, lips parted. "Make strength work against them."

"Like this?" she whispered, breath hot against lips. Shifted slightly, testing hold, and friction nearly made me groan.

"Careful, *malyshka*," warned. "Playing dangerous game."

Her eyes darkened at my tone. "Maybe I want to play dangerous."

Should have moved. Should maintain distance, keep teaching. But sight of her beneath, trust and desire in eyes, broke something inside. Not scared girl who fled to Russia. Woman coming into power — my woman.

"Now you try," said, starting to release wrists.

But Liliya surprised. With move that made pride and lust surge equally, she hooked leg around mine, using own technique against me. Suddenly on back, thighs straddling hips, hands pressing wrists into mat.

"Got you," she said, triumph in her breathless voice.

A growl rumbled deep in my chest. "Body leading mind again, Liliya?"

"Good thing my mind's finally caught up," she said, her hips shifting deliberately against mine, drawing sharp breath from both of us. "I know exactly what I want now."

My hands flexed under her grip, every muscle ready to take control. "Last chance," I warned, voice rough with need. "Once I start, not stopping."

She leaned down, her lips barely brushing mine. "Then don't stop," she whispered. "I'm done waiting."

That was it. With snarl, I broke her hold, flipping us over. One hand tangled in her hair while other gripped her hip, holding her in place as I claimed her mouth. This wasn't gentle - this was pure hunger, primal need.

She matched my intensity, her nails digging into my shoulders, scraping over my skin. When she rolled her hips against my cock, I broke kiss with curse.

"Been driving crazy," said against neck, teeth grazing sensitive spot below ear. "Every fucking day, watching, smelling. Cannot think straight anymore."

She gasped as hand found breast through shirt, thumb circling hardened nipple beneath thin fabric. "Then stop thinking," she challenged. "And just take what you want."

Hands slipped under shirt, desperate to feel skin. "Want everything," growled, sliding fabric up. "Want feel you come around cock. Want hear you scream name."

Her breath hitched as my fingers traced up her ribs. "Then do it," she gasped, lifting her arms as I pulled shirt over her head.

"*Blyad*," groaned, unclasping sports bra. Sight of her bare beneath made cock throb painfully. Hands cupped breasts, thumbs circling nipples. "Look what you do. Now you mine."

She arched into touch, hesitation gone. Sight of her like this beneath made something primal take over.

"Mine," growled, lowering head to taste breast. Sound she made when tongue found nipple sent fire through veins. Other hand kneaded neglected breast, feeling her respond to each touch.

"Zaven," she moaned, her fingers threading through my hair. Her hips rolled against mine again, more demanding.

Kissed way back up to neck, teeth grazing skin that would show marks tomorrow. Let them see. Let them know who she belong to. "Tell what want," demanded. "Say it."

"You," she gasped, nails digging into shoulders. "I want you inside me. Now."

Control snapped completely. Everything been holding back since moment in library broke free.

"Need taste you first," said, hands already at waistband of yoga pants. Yanked them down legs along with underwear, too impatient for slow seduction now.

"Spread your legs," I ordered, settling between her thighs.

She obeyed without hesitation, opening herself to me. The sight of her wet and ready made my cock throb painfully against my shorts.

"Been thinking about this for days," I said, lowering my head. "How you'd taste."

My tongue found her center, making her cry out and arch off mat. I gripped her thighs, holding her in place as I explored every inch of her with my mouth.

"Oh god," she gasped, her hands finding my hair. "Don't stop."

I looked up at her, her head thrown back in pleasure. "So fucking responsive," I said against her sensitive flesh, before diving back in.

I slid two fingers inside her as my tongue circled her clit, feeling her body tighten around me. She was close already, her thighs trembling under my hands.

Her orgasm hit her hard and fast. She cried out my name, her body shaking as I kept going, only stopping when she tugged at my hair, too sensitive to continue.

Moved up body, wiping mouth with back of hand. "Could taste for hours," said, cock straining against shorts.

She still catching breath when reached for me. "I want to see you," she said, tugging at waistband. "All of you."

Stood, getting rid of shorts in one quick movement. Eyes widened as she took in, thick and hard and ready for her.

"Jesus," she whispered, reaching out to wrap fingers around.

Feeling of hand on cock nearly made lose it right there. She stroked, watching face as explored. When leaned forward to take in mouth, had to stop her.

"Not now," I said, pushing her back onto mat. "Need to be inside you or I'll lose my mind."

Her eyes met mine, dark with desire. "Then do it," she said. "I need to feel you."

I positioned myself between her legs, head of my cock pressing against her entrance. "Tell me if it's too much," I said, barely hanging onto control.

"Just fuck me already," she demanded, surprising both of us with her directness.

With groan, I pushed forward, filling her in one hard thrust. She cried out, her body stretching around me. The tight heat of her nearly undid me right there.

"*Blyad*, so tight," managed, forcing to hold still for moment.

Nails dug into back. "Move," she begged. "Please."

Pulled back and thrust again, setting hard, demanding pace. Each stroke pushed her further up mat, legs wrapping around waist to take deeper.

"That's it," growled, watching face as pleasure overtook her. "Take all of me."

She met each thrust, body welcoming like made for this, for me. Could feel getting close again, inner muscles tightening around cock.

"Going to come again?" I asked, driving deeper. "Come for me, Liliya. Want to feel it."

"I'm close," she gasped, her movements becoming desperate. "Zaven—"

I bit down on her shoulder as I thrust harder, hitting that spot deep inside her that made her cry out. She shattered around me, her body clenching so tight it triggered my own release.

"Mine," I groaned against her skin as I came. "*Ty moya, navsegda.*" [You are mine, forever]

Collapsed on top of her, both sweaty and breathing hard. After few moments, rolled to side, bringing her with me so sprawled across chest.

She looked dazed, lips swollen from kissing, neck already showing marks from mouth. Never remember feeling this... satisfied.

"So," said, when could speak again. "Still think Russian men too intense?"

She laughed, sound vibrating against chest. "You ruined me for anyone else, you know that?"

"Good," said, not hiding satisfaction. Fingers traced lazy patterns on back. "Was plan."

"Worth wait?" she asked, looking up with green eyes that haunted for weeks.

Tucked strand of hair behind ear. "Worth everything," said simply. "Though next time, maybe try not scream so loud. Viktor never let forget."

Eyes widened in horror. "Oh my god, you think they heard?"

"Thick walls," assured, unable to suppress smirk. "But maybe not that thick."

She buried face against chest with groan. "I'm never leaving this room."

"Fine by me." Tightened arms around her. "Could keep here for days."

When looked up again, expression turned serious. "I've never... it's never been like that before," she admitted quietly.

Something in chest tightened at words. Brushed thumb across lower lip. "Because you mine now," said. "And take care of what mine."

"Yours," she whispered, word sounding right on lips. "And you mine too."

"*Da*," agreed, feeling unusually content. "All yours."

Two broken people who somehow fit together perfectly. World outside room still dangerous, still waiting. But right now, with Liliya heartbeat steady against chest, nothing else matter.

31

Liliya

A sharp knock on the gym door made me jump. Zaven's arms tightened around me protectively, his body tensing with the instinct of a predator disturbed.

"What?" he called out, voice carrying that dangerous edge of authority I was beginning to recognize.

"Dinner in thirty minutes, *Gospodin*," Irina's voice came through the door. "And Viktor needs to speak with you before."

I felt Zaven's low growl of frustration rumble through his chest. "Will be fucking there," he muttered, then louder: "Understood."

Footsteps retreated, and I couldn't help the small laugh that escaped me. "Think she knows?"

"Irina knows everything," he murmured, pressing a kiss to my temple. "Is her job." His hands slid down my bare sides, his rough fingertips making me shiver. "But not ready let you go yet."

"Then don't," I whispered, turning to face him. The heat in his eyes made my breath catch.

"Come." He stood in one fluid motion, pulling me up with him. "My rooms have better shower than yours."

The promise in his voice made heat pool between my thighs. "Just a shower?"

His lips curved into that dangerous smile I was growing to love. "Nothing fucking 'just' about it, *malyshka*."

I grinned as he handed me my discarded clothes, my body still humming from our encounter. Everything felt different now - sharper, more alive. The way I'd finally let go, let myself feel everything I'd been fighting against... it should have scared me. Instead, I felt powerful.

"I think you stretched my sports bra."

"Not sorry," he rumbled, eyes darkening as he watched me dress. His hands caught my hips before I could pull my shirt on. "Like you better without. Fucking beautiful."

"Behave," I whispered, though my body betrayed me by leaning into his touch. "Dinner in thirty minutes."

Once we were somewhat dressed, though my hair was beyond help, we left the gym. Zaven moved through his house with the same confidence he showed in everything, making no attempt to hide the possessive way he touched me, the heated looks he gave me. This was his domain, and he'd claimed me openly. My cheeks flushed at the obvious marks on my neck, but his satisfied smirk only made heat pool in my stomach.

His eyes caught mine, a knowing smirk playing on his lips. "That look on your face. What you thinking about, *malyshka*?"

Heat rushed to my cheeks. "Just remembering how you pinned me to the mat back there," I admitted, my voice dropping lower. "Wasn't expecting my self-defense lesson to end quite like that."

His hand slid down to cup my ass possessively, then delivered a sharp smack that echoed in the hallway. "Best kind of training," he murmured against my ear, his voice rough with renewed desire.

We'd just reached the main staircase when Viktor appeared, his presence commanding attention even in such a casual moment. My body tensed instinctively, too aware of my swollen lips, the marks on my neck, my obviously post-workout - post-fucking - state.

"Been looking for you," Viktor said to Zaven, his tone professional despite the knowing look in his eyes. "Need moment about Moscow preparations."

I felt Zaven's fingers tighten slightly on my hip before he turned me to face him. Without hesitation, he claimed my mouth in a kiss that made my toes curl, clearly not caring that Viktor stood mere feet away. When he pulled back, his eyes were dark with promise.

"Go up to my rooms. Second door on right." His voice carried that natural authority that still made my pulse jump. "Won't be long."

As I turned to leave, his hand connected with my ass in another sharp slap, harder than the one in the hallway. I gasped, feeling the sting even through my clothes. Catching Viktor trying to hide his smirk only added to my conflicted emotions – embarrassment at being so openly claimed in front of his lieutenant, yet undeniable arousal at Zaven's possessive display. My cheeks burned as I hurried up the stairs, but the throbbing between my thighs told a different story. Part of me was starting to crave these moments when he marked me as his, both publicly and privately.

* * *

Alone in the grand hallway, reality started to sink in. I'd just had sex with Zaven Lazarev. The man whose very name made hardened criminals pale. The *vor* whose reputation was built on blood and iron. On his gym floor. After he'd taught me to fight. My hand traced the spot on my neck where I knew he'd left marks. Not just sex - he'd claimed me, marked me as his. And I'd done the same to him.

I found his rooms easily - the double doors at the end of the hall practically screamed authority. For a moment, I hesitated, my hand on the ornate handle. This was Zaven's private domain. No one probably entered without his explicit permission.

The door opened silently into a sitting room that matched him perfectly - powerful, masculine, but with unexpected touches of elegance. The space was dominated by dark leather furniture and rich wood paneling. Floor-to-ceiling windows offered a commanding view of St. Petersburg, the city lights just beginning to twinkle in the gathering dusk.

My bare feet sank into a thick Persian rug as I moved deeper into the space. Everything smelled of him - that intoxicating mix of expensive cologne, leather, and something uniquely Zaven that made my pulse quicken and my body respond in ways I was still getting used to. A half-empty glass of what looked like whiskey sat on a side table beside a worn leather chair, like he'd been interrupted while reading.

"So this is where the big bad *vor* sleeps," I whispered to myself, running my fingers along the back of his leather chair, imagining him sitting there, powerful and in control.

I ventured further into the room, hyper-aware that I was alone in his private space. Bookshelves lined one wall, and I couldn't help but smile at the mix of titles - Russian classics next to modern business texts, well-worn spy novels beside books on military strategy. Several framed photographs caught my eye. A much younger Zaven in boxing gear. A beautiful woman who had to be his mother, her eyes holding that same intensity I'd come to know in her son.

Everything about the space spoke of power and luxury, but there were intimate touches that made my heart flutter - a book left open and face-down, a soft throw blanket carelessly tossed over the arm of the leather couch, a chessboard with a game in progress.

I moved to the chessboard, studying the game in progress. "Someone's in trouble," I murmured to myself, seeing the trap being set. My fingers hovered over a knight before moving it. "There. Good luck getting out of that one."

The partially open doors of his closet drew me next. Inside, suits hung in military precision - blacks, grays, and the occasional deep blue, all obviously custom-made. I ran my fingers along the sleeves. "More fucking suits than any man needs," I whispered, then grinned. "But damn if you don't wear them well."

A drawer left slightly ajar caught my attention. When I pulled it open, my breath caught - a matte black handgun lay nestled in silk. Of course he'd have weapons here. This was still the *vor*'s private space, after all. I closed the drawer quickly, but not before noticing what looked like a knife collection beyond it.

"What other secrets are you hiding in here?" I wondered aloud, continuing my exploration. The bathroom door was open, revealing gleaming marble and chrome. The counter held expensive grooming products, all meticulously arranged. "Even your bathroom is intimidating."

I turned back to the bedroom, taking in the massive bed with its dark sheets. "This is insane," I muttered to myself. "I'm in Zaven Lazarev's bedroom, talking to myself like an idiot."

The sound of the main door opening made my heart jump. I turned to find Zaven watching me from the doorway, his eyes dark with an emotion I couldn't quite read.

I froze, caught between embarrassment at being discovered snooping and lingering desire from earlier. Zaven stood in the doorway, hands casually tucked in the pockets of his gym shorts, but there was nothing casual about the way his eyes moved over me. Without breaking eye contact, his foot shot out, kicking the door shut with a bang that made me jump. His low chuckle at my reaction sent heat coursing through me.

He prowled into the room with that fluid grace that made him look more panther than man, each step deliberate, unhurried.

"Find anything interesting?" His voice was low, amused, but his eyes held heat as they tracked my every movement.

"Just checking if the *vor* keeps his closet as organized as everything else," I managed, aiming for casual despite the way my pulse jumped when he took another slow step forward.

"And?" He continued his measured approach, muscles rippling beneath his skin with each movement. One hand left his pocket to trace along his desk as he passed it, the gesture somehow both lazy and predatory.

"Very impressive. Though I did help your opponent in chess. They were in trouble."

His lips curved into that dangerous smile, head tilting slightly as he considered me. "Helping enemy of *vor*? Serious offense, *malyshka*. Could get you in trouble."

"Going to punish me?" The words slipped out before I could stop them, my voice taking on a sultry edge that surprised even me. His eyes darkened immediately, pupils dilating until only a thin ring of gray remained.

He closed the distance in two long strides, one hand tangling in my hair while the other gripped my hip. "First, shower. Then…" his teeth grazed my ear, his voice dropping to a growl that sent shivers down my spine, "show you exactly what happens to naughty girls who need proper punishment."

My knees weakened at his words. I let him guide me toward the bathroom, his hand possessive at the small of my back. With each step, the anticipation built, my skin tingling where he touched me. He kicked the bathroom door open, spinning me inside with that effortless strength that never failed to make my heart race.

He pressed me against the cool marble wall, his body a furnace against mine as his mouth claimed me. I melted into him, arms winding around his neck as his hands explored with renewed hunger. The bathroom was stunning—gleaming dark tile and multiple shower heads waiting to spring to life.

I pulled back slightly, trying to catch my breath. "We should probably…" I gestured vaguely toward the shower, my voice husky with desire.

"*Da*. Get clean." His eyes darkened with mischief as he tugged at the hem of my shirt. "Then get very, very dirty again."

He undressed me with a practiced efficiency that was somehow still sensual—my shirt over my head, yoga pants down my legs, underwear following quickly after. His eyes devoured every inch of exposed skin, making me feel beautiful rather than vulnerable. I reached for him next, pushing his gym shorts down his powerful thighs, my breath catching as he stood fully naked before me.

He reached behind me to turn on the shower, and water immediately cascaded down, steam rising around us as Zaven pulled me under the spray, our bare skin finally meeting with nothing between us.

For a moment, we simply stood there, his forehead pressed against mine, water sluicing between our bodies. My hands explored the hard planes of his chest, the defined ridges of his abdomen, admiring how the water made his skin glisten.

"Should be thinking about dinner," he murmured, sucking in a sharp breath as my fingers dipped lower. "Irina will have meal ready."

"I'm not hungry." My palm flattened against his stomach, feeling the muscles there contract. "At least, not for food."

His laugh was low and rough, rumbling through his chest. "So bold now, *malyshka*? Where was shy girl I first met, always looking away when I caught her staring?"

"She figured out what she wants." I nipped at his shoulder, tasting the water droplets on his skin, savoring the salt and heat that was all Zaven. "Who she wants."

"And what exactly you want?" His hands settled on my hips, thumbs tracing slow circles that made me shiver despite the heat. "Tell me."

Before I could answer, he turned me suddenly, his strong hands spinning me to face the shower wall. I gasped as he pressed against me from behind, his chest hot against my back, his hard cock evident against my lower back. One hand slid up to cradle my throat while the other pinned my hip, holding me firmly against the cool tile.

He paused then, his lips close to my ear but his grip gentling. "Need know you're okay with this, Liliya," he murmured, his voice rough but sincere. "Not want remind you of him. Not want frighten you."

The care in his words amid such raw desire made my heart clench. I turned my head to meet his eyes, finding concern mingled with the heat there.

"This is nothing like that," I assured him, reaching up to touch his face. "With you, I feel... safe. Even when you're taking control." I pressed back against him deliberately. "Especially then."

Something shifted in his expression – relief, followed by renewed hunger. "You trust me this way?"

"Yes," I whispered, then with growing confidence: "I want you to teach me. Fuck me the way you need to. The way I need you to. Don't hold back."

His expression changed at my words, something hungry and possessive flashing across his features. "*Ty idealna*," he growled, his accent thickening with desire. "Perfect."

A growl rumbled through his chest as his grip tightened once more, his powerful body caging me against the wall. Water cascaded down between us as his lips found my ear.

"You like this, *da?* When I take control?" His teeth grazed my earlobe. "When I make you mine?"

"Yes," I breathed, surprised by how much his dominance affected me, heat pooling between my thighs.

"Need show you," he murmured, his free hand stroking down my side, over the curve of my hip. "What real pleasure feels like. What happens when trust someone completely."

His fingers found their way between my legs, exploring with confident strokes that made my breath catch. "Already so wet," he observed, voice thick with appreciation. "Ready for me. But not yet."

"Zaven," I gasped, trying to press against his hand.

"Patience, *malyshka.*" He withdrew his touch, earning a whimper of protest. "First lesson is learning to wait. To feel everything."

His hand that had been at my throat moved to tangle in my wet hair, tugging just enough to expose my neck to him. The slight sting sent a surprising jolt of pleasure through me.

"Sometimes little pain makes pleasure stronger," he explained, his lips tracing my pulse point. "Like contrast of bitter and sweet. You trust me to know difference?"

"Yes," I whispered, my body responding to his words, his touch, in ways I never expected.

"Good girl." His teeth scraped against the sensitive juncture where my neck met my shoulder, then bit down – not hard enough to truly hurt, but enough to send shockwaves of sensation cascading through me.

I cried out, my body arching involuntarily. His hand returned between my legs, fingers circling, teasing.

"See?" he murmured against my skin. "Pleasure and pain, when done right..." His fingers slid inside me as he sucked at the spot he'd bitten, the dual sensations making me dizzy with need.

"Zaven, please," I gasped, no longer caring how desperate I sounded.

"Please what?" His voice was rough with his own restraint, his hard length pressing insistently against me. "Tell me what you need. Want hear you say it."

"I need you inside me," I managed, turning my head to meet his eyes. "I need to feel all of you."

His control seemed to slip at my words. "Been holding back too long," he admitted, his fingers withdrawing to grip my thigh instead, lifting it to open me to him. "Worried would frighten you with how much want you. How much need to claim every part of you."

"Don't hold back anymore," I urged, reaching behind to grasp his hip, pulling him closer. "Show me everything."

The blunt head of his cock pressed against me, the position making me acutely aware of how large he was, how completely he would fill me.

"Look at me," he commanded, his free hand turning my face toward him. "Want to see your eyes when take you like this."

I met his gaze, finding an intensity that took my breath away – desire, yes, but something deeper too. Something that made my heart race as much as my body ached for him.

With a controlled thrust, he pushed inside, the angle making me gasp at the delicious intrusion. He paused, letting me adjust, his breathing harsh against my ear.

"*Tak khorosho*," [So good] he groaned, the Russian words falling from his lips like a prayer. "So perfect. So tight."

When he began to move, it wasn't with the desperate frenzy of our first time in the gym. This was deliberate, controlled – each thrust calculated to hit exactly where I needed him, to build pleasure with meticulous precision.

Acting on pure instinct, I reached for his hand that was braced against the wall, guiding it to my throat. His rhythm faltered for a moment, surprise evident in his sharp intake of breath.

"Are you sure?" he asked, his voice rough with desire but tinged with concern.

"Please," I whispered, pressing his fingers more firmly against my neck. "I trust you."

A sound that was almost a growl rumbled through his chest as his fingers tightened slightly around my throat, just enough pressure to make my pulse race faster, to make each sensation more intense.

The feeling was nothing like I'd expected – not frightening or suffocating, but strangely freeing. In yielding control to him this way, I found a different kind of power. My senses sharpened, every touch magnified, every nerve ending alive with sensation. This wasn't submission out of fear or coercion; this was freely chosen vulnerability with someone I trusted completely.

"*Takaya khoroshaya devochka.*" [Such a good girl] he praised in his native tongue, making me even wetter. His other hand sliding from my thigh to deliver a sharp smack to my ass that made me gasp. "Taking me so well."

The sting blossomed across my skin, transforming immediately into heat that radiated through me. Nothing like the pain I'd known before – this was pleasure with an edge, intensifying rather than diminishing my desire. I'd never felt so present in my body, so connected to my own needs and desires.

His hips snapped forward with renewed vigor, his grip on my throat carefully controlled as he thrust deeper. Another smack landed on my other cheek, the sound echoing off the shower walls.

"Again," I begged, surprising both of us with my boldness. "Harder."

The words came from someplace deep inside me that had been silent for too long – a part of myself I'd forgotten existed. With Jack, I'd made myself small, accommodating, afraid. With Zaven, I was finding my voice, my power, my ability to ask for exactly what I wanted.

"So fucking perfect," he growled, delivering a harder slap that left a delicious sting. "Love how you take everything I give you."

Each thrust now came with the sharp sting of his hand on my sensitive skin, no hesitation in his movements. His voice was a constant stream of praise against my ear, accent thicker with each passing moment.

"That's it, *malyshka.* Take all of me. Show me how much you need this."

His hand at my throat tightened fractionally as his pace increased, the slight restriction making every sensation more vivid, more intense. I felt simultaneously anchored and set free – held safely in his powerful grip while my mind soared with pleasure I'd never known possible.

"Going to mark you everywhere," he promised, teeth grazing my shoulder. "Inside and out. So everyone knows who you belong to."

His possessiveness didn't feel like a cage but like a shield – not confinement but protection. For the first time, I understood that giving myself to someone could be strengthening rather than diminishing, that trust freely given could open doors to pleasure I'd never imagined.

The pressure of his hand around my throat, the sting of his palm on my skin, the relentless rhythm of his thrusts – everything combined to build a tension inside me that was almost unbearable in its intensity. My body trembled on the edge of release, every muscle taut with anticipation.

"Come for me," he commanded, his voice raw with need. "Want to feel you come apart around my cock."

As if my body was wired to respond to his commands, the tension snapped. My orgasm crashed through me like a tidal wave, more powerful than anything I'd experienced before. I cried out his name, the sound reverberating through the steam-filled shower as my body clenched around him, drawing him deeper.

"That's it," he praised, his rhythm never faltering despite my body's convulsions. "Take your pleasure. Show me how good I make you feel."

"Give it to me," he demanded, his lips against my ear as he pressed me harder against the wall. "Everything. All of you."

My second orgasm hit with such force that tears sprang to my eyes, my entire body clenching around him as wave after wave of pleasure crashed through me. My forehead pressed against the cool tile as I surrendered completely to the sensation.

As the last tremors of my release rippled through me, Zaven moved his hand from my throat, both hands now gripping my hips with bruising intensity. He pulled me hard against him, his thrusts becoming erratic, driven by pure instinct rather than control.

"Liliya," he groaned, his fingers digging into my flesh as he held me exactly where he needed. His chest pressed against my back, his breath hot against my neck as he drove into me one final time.

With a guttural growl, he found his own release, his powerful body shuddering against mine. His grip on my hips never loosened as he pulsed inside me, marking me as his from the inside out just as he'd promised.

For long moments, we stayed locked together, his forehead coming to rest on my shoulder, our ragged breathing filling the steam-filled shower as we both struggled to come back to ourselves.

Slowly, tenderly, he turned me to face him, though his arms remained around me, supporting me when my knees threatened to buckle. The water was growing cooler, but neither of us seemed ready to break contact just yet.

With surprising gentleness, he began to wash me, his strong hands sliding soap across my shoulders, down my back, between my breasts. There was something almost reverent in the way he touched me now, his eyes following his hands as if memorizing every curve, every freckle.

"Water getting cold," he murmured, rinsing away the last of the soap before reaching to turn off the spray. His thumb traced my lower lip, wiping away a drop of water. "But worth it."

"*Ty moya*," [You are mine] he murmured, pressing a soft kiss to my temple. "My Liliya."

I felt the truth of it in my bones – I was his, just as he was mine. Something fundamental had shifted between us in the space of a day, a connection forged through trust and vulnerability, through pleasure freely given and received.

His eyes held that rare softness I was beginning to treasure. "Now," he said with a small smile, reaching for a towel from the nearby rack, "maybe ready for dinner after all." His hand slid down my body, making me shiver as he wrapped the plush fabric around me. "Need strength for rest of night."

"Rest of night?" I raised an eyebrow, still breathless. "You think you can go again after this?"

The smile that spread across his face was pure masculine arrogance. "*Malyshka*," he murmured, securing his own towel around his waist, "we just getting started."

His hands lingered as he dried me off, turning the simple act into something sensual. When he lifted me into his arms, I couldn't help but laugh.

"I can walk, you know."

"Not after what plan to do to you next," he murmured, carrying me to his massive bed. The dark sheets were cool against my skin as he laid me down, his eyes roving over me with heated possession.

"So," I said, stretching deliberately beneath his gaze, "about that dinner…"

"Dinner can fucking wait," he growled, crawling over me like some magnificent predator. "Still hungry for you."

His answering laugh was deep and rich, full of promise. As his lips found mine again, heat immediately rekindled between us. So much for dinner. At this rate, we'd starve to death in the most pleasurable way possible.

I had one crystal-clear thought as he settled against me: if this was what surrendering to Zaven Lazarev felt like, I should have waved the white flag sooner.

32

Liliya

I woke to the sound of Russian, soft and melodic in the darkness. Zaven stood by the window, phone pressed to his ear, his back to me. The glow of St. Petersburg outlined his powerful silhouette, accentuating every sculpted muscle of his back, the broadness of his shoulders, and—I couldn't help but notice—a truly impressive ass that somehow hadn't gotten the proper appreciation it deserved during our earlier activities.

His voice was different when he spoke Russian—richer, more fluid, the words flowing together like dark honey. There was an authority in it that made heat pool low in my stomach despite my exhaustion. The sheets whispered against my skin as I propped myself up on one elbow, openly admiring the view while he remained unaware of my awakening.

Something in his tone shifted—sharper, more commanding. Even without understanding the words, I recognized the voice of the *vor* giving orders, not asking questions. Whoever was on the other end of that call was getting clear instructions, not suggestions.

He must have sensed my gaze—or perhaps heard the sheets rustling—because he turned suddenly, ending the call with a clipped "*Da. Ponimayu. Konechno.*" [Yes. I understand. Of course.] Our eyes met across the darkened room, and I didn't even try to pretend I hadn't been staring.

"You enjoy view?" he asked, a hint of amusement in his voice.

"Can't say I've ever woken up to quite such a... spectacular sight," I replied, not bothering to hide my appreciation.

A smile played at the corner of his mouth as he crossed back to the bed, moving with that predatory grace that still made my breath catch. The mattress dipped under his weight as he slid beneath the sheets beside me. Something was different now—the guards he typically kept in place had lowered. The *vor*'s usual masks were gone, leaving just the man beneath. His skin was warm against mine where our legs tangled beneath the silk sheets, his heartbeat steady under my palm.

The lights of the sleeping city twinkled beyond the glass like stars, but they seemed distant, unimportant. Here in this moment, wrapped in darkness and each other, we existed in our own world. One where he wasn't the feared *vor* and I wasn't the American runaway. Just us, stripped of everything but truth.

His hand caught mine where it rested on his chest, calloused fingers pressing it flat against the solid muscle where I could feel his heart beating. For a long moment, he just looked at me, like he was memorizing every detail. The ambient glow from outside caught the angles of his face, making his eyes appear almost midnight black against his skin.

"Tell me about this one," I whispered, fingers trailing over a raised scar near his collarbone. The skin there was smooth, paler than the rest of his chest.

A shadow crossed his face, his jaw tightening. "From night mother died. Was protecting her from man father trusted. Learned then - trust and loyalty not same thing."

The raw pain in his voice made my heart ache. I traced the scar gently, understanding now why he'd tensed when I'd touched it earlier. His hand covered mine, holding it there as if anchoring himself to the present.

"Can see you thinking," he murmured after a moment, his fingers drawing idle patterns on my bare shoulder, raising goosebumps despite the warmth of his touch. "Not just about scar. What going on in that pretty head?"

I nestled closer, drawing comfort from his warmth, breathing in that uniquely Zaven scent that lingered despite our shower—a hint of his expensive cologne mixed with something distinctly him. "Was thinking about my mom. Her birthday's next week."

His arms tightened around me fractionally. In the quiet darkness, it felt safer to voice the guilt I'd been carrying. "I haven't spoken to her in almost two years. She tried... God, she tried so hard to reach me. But I couldn't bear to tell her about Jack, about what I'd let myself become."

"What he made you become," Zaven corrected, voice soft but firm. "Not same thing at all."

"She used to call every day at first," I whispered into the darkness, watching how the faint illumination played across his skin. "Then once a week. Then holidays. I'd stare at the phone, wanting to answer, but so ashamed..."

"Like my mother," Zaven said quietly, his accent thicker with memory. "Always tried to protect me from darkness in our world. But darkness always find way in."

"What happened? That night?" The question slipped out before I could stop it. His muscles tensed under my touch, but he didn't pull away.

"Man father trusted—Karlov." His voice hardened on the name. "Came to house when father away. Drunk, angry about business deal." His hand tightened on my hip. "Mother tried send me to room, but saw way he looked at her. Knew that look. Was only sixteen, but already knew what it meant."

I pressed closer, offering what comfort I could as he continued.

"She fought him. Was beautiful, my mother, but also strong. When he pulled knife..." His voice roughened. "Threw myself between them. Got this." He touched the scar. "But knife meant for her heart found its mark anyway."

"Zaven," I breathed, my heart breaking for the sixteen-year-old boy who couldn't save his mother.

"Father arrived too late," Zaven continued, his voice low in the darkness. "Found me trying to stop bleeding, trying to save her. Remember way he looked at her body, at me. Was moment *vor* truly born in him."

"What happened to Karlov?" I asked, though part of me already knew.

A cruel smile touched his lips, so different from the one I'd seen earlier. "Father made example. Showed everyone what happens when betray *vor*'s trust. Was first time I saw true power of what we are." His fingers traced up my spine, gentle despite the violence in his words. "But mother's death… changed something in him. In both of us."

I pressed a kiss to the scar, feeling his sharp intake of breath. "And now you're showing me your scars."

"*Da.*" His hand cupped my face, thumb brushing my cheekbone. "Because you understand. Carry own scars, even if can't see them."

"My mom," I whispered, tears pricking my eyes. "She deserves to know I'm okay. That I'm… that I found strength again."

"Then tell her." His voice firm but gentle, a command softened by understanding. "Call her. Let her hear voice of daughter she loves."

"Not sure how that conversation would go," I said with a weak laugh. "'Hi Mom, sorry I disappeared. I'm in Russia with a mafia boss who just taught me how to throw a decent punch.'"

His chest rumbled with unexpected laughter, the vibration of it comforting against my cheek. "Could leave out part about punches." His hand slid possessively down my bare back to grab my ass. "Definitely leave out part about how *vor* made you come so hard you nearly broke headboard."

My jaw dropped. "Zaven!" I smacked his chest, heat rushing to my cheeks even as laughter bubbled up. "That is absolutely not going in any conversation with my mother."

"What?" The smirk on his face was pure wickedness. "Not something to be proud of? Fucking *vor* until he can barely remember own name?"

"Oh my god." I buried my face against his chest, mortified and amused in equal measure. "You're the absolute worst."

"Not what you said few hours ago," he replied, his accent thickening deliberately. "Think exact words were 'fucking incredible' and 'don't stop' and—"

I clapped my hand over his mouth. "I was there, I remember what I said."

He nipped at my palm, eyes dancing with mischief I'd never seen in him before. When I pulled my hand away, his smile was almost boyish, a glimpse of who he might have been in another life.

"You're just saying all this because I managed to land a punch earlier."

"Let you land it," he corrected, though his smirk remained firmly in place. "Was distracted thinking about bending you over desk in study next."

I propped myself up on one elbow, looking down at him. "Let me? Pretty sure that bruise on your ribs says different."

His hand snaked around my waist, pulling me on top of him in one fluid motion that reminded me just how easily he could maneuver me if he wanted to. The playfulness in his eyes shifted to something more predatory. "Careful, *malyshka*. Still need teach lesson about challenging *vor*."

The playfulness faded as I traced the tattoo pattern over his heart. "Speaking of challenges... Moscow?"

His expression sobered immediately, the transition from lover to *vor* happening in the blink of an eye. His hands, however, continued their gentle exploration of my skin, a contrast to the hardness that entered his voice. "Three days. Need handle some business there."

"Dangerous business?" I asked, trying to keep my voice steady despite the cold fear coiling in my stomach. I knew enough about his world now to understand that "business" often meant violence.

"All business dangerous in our world," he said carefully, measuring his words. "But have good men. Strong plans." His thumb traced my lower lip, his eyes following the movement with intensity. "And now, have better reason to come home safe."

The weight of that admission hung between us in the pre-dawn darkness. Outside, the city was beginning to wake, the first shifts in light barely visible through the floor-to-ceiling windows, but neither of us moved to break this intimate bubble we'd created.

"When you're gone..." I started, then hesitated, unsure how to express the sudden anxiety taking root in my chest.

"Viktor stay with you. Sergei, Nikolai too." His voice took on that edge of authority I knew so well, the lover momentarily replaced by the *vor*. "But you stay in house. No club, no city. Not until I return."

The shift in his tone made something rebellious flare within me. "Keeping me locked away?" I meant it as a tease, but when I saw his expression turn serious, I pressed further. "Can I at least see Natasha?"

"*Net*, not safe," his reply was quick, brooking no argument.

I sat up straighter, the sheet pooling around my waist. "No Natasha? But you said I could go places with Viktor or the others. She's my best friend, Zaven. The only reason I even made it to Russia."

His expression hardened, jaw tightening as he sat up too. The intimacy of moments ago seemed suddenly distant. "Is different now."

"How? Because of what happened between us?" Heat crept into my voice, a flash of indignation warming my cheeks. "You said I wasn't a prisoner here."

"Not prisoner." The shadows cast across his muscled chest highlighted the tension in his shoulders. "But things changing in city. Moscow business make waves. Not just about us anymore."

I crossed my arms, unwilling to back down so easily. "Then explain it to me. Help me understand instead of just giving orders. I didn't leave one controlling man just to—"

"Is not same," he cut me off, something dangerous flashing in his eyes. Then, seeing my expression, he softened slightly. His jaw worked for a moment before he spoke again. "Already lost people who matter to me because of trust placed wrong way." His voice dropped lower, rougher. "Not risk you. Not when you become... important."

The weight in that word—"important"—seemed heavier than its simple meaning, carrying something deeper he couldn't quite express. My anger dissolved instantly, replaced by a fluttering sensation in my chest that made it hard to breathe.

The silence stretched between us, heavy with the unspoken. I studied his face in the dim light, seeing the vulnerability he rarely showed, the slight widening of his eyes as if surprised by his own admission.

"Important?" I whispered finally.

His hand came up to cup my face, thumb tracing my cheekbone with surprising tenderness. "*Moya dorogaya*," [My dear] he murmured, the Russian endearment making my heart race. "Scares you? Too much maybe."

"No," I said quickly, covering his hand with mine. "Not scared. Just..." I took a breath. "Overwhelmed. Yesterday I was learning to fight, and now..."

"Now what?" His voice was low, careful, a man testing thin ice.

"Now I'm in bed with the most dangerous man in St. Petersburg, and he's looking at me like..." I couldn't finish the thought, the intensity in his eyes stealing my words. A small laugh escaped me. "My life has become very strange."

The tension in his shoulders eased slightly. "Strange good or strange bad?"

Instead of answering with words, I leaned forward to press my lips to the scar on his collarbone—the one from losing his mother. The gesture said what I couldn't yet voice aloud. "Good strange. Terrifying sometimes, but good."

His breath caught at my touch, and when I looked up, his eyes held an emotion I'd never seen before—something almost vulnerable beneath the usual intensity, like a glimpse of the boy he'd been before loss had hardened him.

"Not good with words like this," he admitted roughly. "Easier to show with actions. With protection." His fingers threaded through my hair, anchoring me to him. "Never thought would feel this way about anyone. *Vor* not supposed to have... weakness."

"Is that what this is? Weakness?" I asked softly.

"*Net.*" He pulled me closer, pressing his forehead to mine. "But makes me vulnerable in ways never been. Makes me want things never wanted. Makes me fear things never feared." His accent thickened with emotion, words coming slower as he searched for the right ones. "Cannot explain why. Just know when look at you, whole world shifts. Everything different now."

I understood what he meant. Everything had shifted—the way I saw myself, the way I saw him, the way the world looked through the lens of whatever this was building between us. I'd come to Russia running from a man who'd tried to own me, only to find myself choosing to belong to another. The difference was everything.

"So no Natasha?" I asked softly, but this time there was understanding in my voice rather than defiance.

"Three days," he promised, pressing his lips to my forehead. "Then we figure out way. But now..." His arms tightened around me possessively, the tension in his body revealing how much this vulnerability cost him. "Need know you safe. Need focus on Moscow without this..." He tapped his chest, searching for the word. "This fear in gut."

The admission—that he feared for me, that it would distract him—told me more about his feelings than any declaration could have. This powerful man, feared throughout the city, was admitting a weakness: me.

His lips found my temple, warm against my skin. "Have ways keep you occupied while gone."

"Oh?" I traced a pattern on his chest, feeling his muscles flex under my touch. "Going to give me homework?"

"*Da*. Viktor show you more about business operations, security protocols." The matter-of-fact way he said it couldn't hide what he was really offering—trust. His fingers traced idle circles on my hip. "Also time learn about household, how everything run. Irina teach you—she manage entire estate, know all secrets."

The responsibility in that statement wasn't lost on me. He wasn't just offering distraction—he was offering integration. A place in his world beyond just warming his bed. This wasn't about keeping me entertained; it was about preparing me for something more permanent.

"And what else?" I asked, trying to lighten the mood.

His expression shifted, that predatory look returning to his eyes as he traced a finger down my sternum. "Will need something to think about while in Moscow."

"Such as?" I asked, my body responding instantly to his touch despite how thoroughly he'd worn me out earlier.

"Such as knowing exactly what you not doing while I'm gone." His voice dropped lower, accent thickening deliberately as his hand splayed possessively across my stomach.

"And what am I not doing?" I asked, warmth spreading through me at his darkening expression.

"Not touching yourself." The command came with a wicked smirk. "That belongs to me now. Want you aching for me when I return." His fingers traced dangerously close to where I was already responding to him. "Three days of thinking about this, wanting this. But not taking."

"That's not fair," I protested, though the idea sent an unexpected thrill through me.

"Never claimed to be fair, *malyshka*." He leaned down to brush his lips against my ear. "Want you desperate for me. Only me."

"And what about you?" I challenged, running my hands down his chest. "Same rules apply?"

The smile that spread across his face was pure sin. "Why think will need to touch myself when memory of you so fresh?" He nipped at my lower lip. "But yes. Same rules."

"For now..." he murmured against my neck, his stubble creating delicious friction against my sensitive skin, "think have better way pass time until sun rise."

"Is that so?" My question came out breathier than intended as his hand slid between my thighs. "You think I'll forget you?" I gasped as his teeth grazed my pulse point.

His eyes met mine, something primal and possessive in their depths that made my heart race. "Plan on making damn sure you don't, *malyshka*," he said with a growl that vibrated through my entire body. "Not for single moment I'm gone. Want you feeling me with every step you take."

As the first rays of morning light began to filter through the windows, Zaven set about ensuring I'd have plenty to remember while he was away— and every mark he left felt like a promise of return.

33

Liliya

"Three crates of farm-raised caviar?" Oleg's outraged voice carried through the kitchen. "*Gospodin* Lazarev would never serve this to his guests!"

Welcome to day two of running a Russian crime lord's household.

I stepped into the chaos of the kitchen where Oleg, Zaven's temperamental chef, was facing off with a nervous delivery man. The scene might have been intimidating a few months ago when I'd first arrived in Russia, but after handling demanding VIPs at Zolotoy Vek, I'd learned how to manage explosive personalities.

"Is there a problem?" I asked, keeping my voice steady despite the weight of responsibility still settling on my shoulders. Two days since Zaven left for Moscow, and already the household was testing my ability to maintain his exacting standards.

"*Devushka* Liliya," Oleg turned to me, his face red with frustration. "This *durak* [fool] has brought us farm-raised caviar instead of wild! It's completely unsuitable for *Gospodin* Lazarev's tastes."

I suppressed a smile. Behind Oleg's outrage, I saw Sergei lean against the doorframe, watching the scene with barely concealed amusement. Even with Zaven gone, his men maintained their constant, if subtle, presence.

"I see," I said calmly. "And how urgently do we need this caviar?"

"*Gospodin* Lazarev always insists on having a stock of the finest caviar for unexpected guests or business meetings," Oleg replied, still glaring at the delivery man.

I nodded, an idea forming. "Alright, Oleg, please accept this delivery for now. I'll make some calls and see if we can source wild caviar immediately. In the meantime, I trust you can prepare some alternative appetizers that meet *Gospodin* Lazarev's standards?"

Oleg's expression softened slightly at the implied compliment. "Of course, *Gospozha* [Madam] Liliya. I have several dishes that I'm sure will suffice."

"Excellent," I turned to the delivery man, channeling a bit of Zaven's quiet authority. "And you, please inform your company that we expect our usual quality in the future. We won't be so accommodating next time."

The delivery man nodded hastily, clearly relieved to escape both Oleg's wrath and the steady gaze of Sergei in the doorway.

After calming Oleg and dismissing the relieved delivery man, I'd barely taken two steps from the kitchen when Irina hurried toward me, clipboard in hand.

"*Devushka* Liliya, new linens arrive for guest rooms. And..." She glanced at Sergei who still followed nearby. "Have small problem with new staff member."

That caught my attention. "What kind of problem?"

"Alexi. Found in west wing. Again." She lowered her voice, her accent thickening with concern. "Say he check windows, but..." She shook her head, "nothing wrong with windows there."

My skin prickled with awareness. After seeing how Zaven's world worked - the threat outside the restaurant still fresh in my memory - even small irregularities felt significant. I remembered how Zaven had mentioned the new staff member during our last night together, expressing mild concern that Viktor had hired him without Zaven having time to personally vet him.

"Show linens first," I decided, noting how Sergei straightened at mention of Alexi. "Then deal with our wandering window checker."

The next hour passed in a blur of Egyptian cotton and thread counts. Once the linen situation was handled and Alexi's suspicious behavior reported to Viktor, I found myself drawn to Zaven's study. The room still held echoes of our last night together - the chess piece I'd moved still exactly where I'd left it, his half-empty glass on the desk.

"All good with linens?" Sergei's voice came from the doorway.

"*Da*," I replied, noticing how naturally the Russian word came now. "Though think Alexi needs watching."

Sergei nodded, his expression darkening slightly. "Viktor already know. We handle."

Once he'd moved back to his post, I ran my fingers over the smooth wood of Zaven's desk, fighting the memory of his body pressing me against it, his lips at my ear whispering exactly what he planned to do when he returned. My phone buzzed, pulling me back to reality.

A text from Zaven: "Missing that spot on your neck that makes you moan. Will be home tomorrow to remind you."

Just seeing his name on my screen sent heat racing through me. Two days without him felt like an eternity, every inch of my body aching for his touch. I traced the fading marks on my neck, evidence of his possessive nature that I'd come to crave.

My phone felt heavy in my pocket as I thought of Natasha. She deserved to know I was okay, that I'd found something real with Zaven. Something that had nothing to do with Jack or the past I'd fled.

Before I could second-guess myself, I dialed her number. She answered on the first ring.

"Finally!" Natasha exclaimed. "Where *blyad* [fuck] you been? Two days with just these cryptic little texts? Been going crazy!"

I couldn't help but smile, missing her crude bluntness. "Sorry, things have been... intense."

"*Yebat*! [Fuck!] You sleep with him, *da*?" She didn't wait for an answer. "Knew it! Way he look at you in club - like want to devour whole. Tell details. Now."

"Natasha!" I laughed, my cheeks burning.

"What? Like am wrong? Way you avoid question say everything." She lowered her voice conspiratorially, "He good as look? Because *bozhe moy*, that man is walking sin."

"Better," I admitted, my body heating with the memory. "Much better."

Her squeal of delight made me hold the phone away from my ear. "*Ya tak i znala*! [I knew it!] You stay at his place now, *da*? Run his household? My little American snag herself *vor*."

"It's more than that," I said, unable to explain exactly how much more it had become in such a short time. How he'd helped me find strength I didn't know I had. How he'd seen parts of me I'd kept hidden from everyone else.

"Of course is more," she said, her tone softening. "Way he look at you... not just want you in bed. Was something else."

"Yeah," I agreed simply, not ready to name what that "something else" might be.

"So when I see you? *Ya skuchayu po tebe*! [I miss you!] Need catch up properly, not over phone."

I sighed. "Zaven doesn't want me leaving the house while he's gone. Security concerns."

"Bullshit!" Natasha exclaimed. "What, he keeps you locked up now? You're not his prisoner."

"It's not like that," I defended, though her words hit uncomfortably close to arguments I'd had with myself. "He's worried. Things in the city are tense, especially with him in Moscow."

"So bring the security!" she countered. "I just want coffee with my friend. The cafe near the club is literally crawling with Zaven's men. It's the safest place in the city."

The idea was tempting. So tempting. Just an hour away from these walls, catching up with Natasha face to face. I pictured Viktor's stern disapproval and winced.

"He'll be back tomorrow," I hedged.

"Come on," she pressed. "One coffee. I miss your face. Plus, I have so much club gossip you wouldn't believe."

That laugh, that familiar teasing – I missed it more than I'd realized. "I'll try to talk to Viktor," I said finally. "But no promises."

"Yes! Tell that sexy mountain of a man I said hi. Still working on getting him to crack a smile."

"Still no luck with that?" I teased.

"Yet! No luck yet. Rome wasn't built in a day, and neither was getting into Viktor's pants."

I laughed again, feeling lighter than I had in days. "I'll call you back after I talk to him."

"You better. And wear something cute - you're Zaven Lazarev's woman now, can't be looking like a slob."

"Goodbye, Natasha," I said, still chuckling as I hung up.

Finding Viktor wasn't difficult - he practically lived in Zaven's office while the *vor* was away. I knocked, steeling myself for the conversation ahead.

"Enter," came his gruff response.

He didn't look up from the security reports spread across the desk as I stepped inside. I waited, knowing better than to interrupt. Finally, he glanced up, eyebrow raised in question.

"I want to meet Natasha for coffee," I said, going straight to the point. "At the cafe near the club. The one under Zaven's protection."

"*Net.*" Viktor didn't even pause to consider. "*Vor* gave clear instructions."

"About not going out alone," I pressed. "You could come with me. It's just coffee with Natasha."

"Answer is *net*." His tone left no room for argument as he returned to his reports.

Anger flared inside me - at his dismissal, at being kept inside these walls, at the echo of control that reminded me too much of Jack. Without thinking, I turned and stormed out, letting the door slam behind me.

I made it halfway down the hall before I heard his heavy footsteps following.

"Liliya." His voice was sharp with warning.

I ignored him, heading for the closet near the entrance where I knew my coat would be. I yanked it off the hanger, shoving my arms through the sleeves with jerky movements.

"What are you doing?" Viktor's tone held genuine surprise. Clearly, he wasn't used to being defied.

"Going to see my friend," I said, not looking at him as I buttoned the coat with trembling fingers. "You can come with me, or I can go alone. Your choice."

"*Vor*'s orders –"

"Are that I be protected, not imprisoned," I cut him off, finally turning to face him. "I didn't leave one controlling asshole just to be controlled by someone else."

Something flashed in his eyes – understanding, maybe, or respect. We stood in tense silence for a long moment, neither willing to back down.

"Fifteen minutes," he said finally, his jaw tight with disapproval. "Get ready. We take two cars."

I exhaled slowly, surprised he'd given in. "That's all I need."

"But," he added, his voice hardening, "we do this my way. Two more men. No arguments."

"Fine." I nodded, relief mingling with lingering frustration.

"Don't thank yet," he said, checking his weapon as he moved toward the door. "Still have to explain to *vor* when he return."

The black SUV pulled away from Zaven's estate, Viktor beside me while Sergei and Yuri followed in a second vehicle. I glimpsed the city through the tinted windows – my first taste of freedom in days.

"Remember rules," Viktor said as we approached the cafe. "One hour. Stay in sight. No wandering."

"I know." Through the window, I spotted Natasha waiting at an outdoor table, looking impossibly chic as always.

Viktor scanned the area before nodding to Sergei, who moved to check the perimeter. The level of security might have seemed excessive for a coffee date, but after seeing how quickly violence could erupt in Zaven's world, I understood better now.

Natasha's face lit up when she saw me, though her smile faltered slightly at the sight of three of Zaven's most dangerous men positioning themselves around the cafe.

"*Bozhe moy*," she whispered as I sat down. "When you say Viktor coming, not expect whole security team. Hello there, handsome," she added, throwing Viktor a wink.

He remained stoic, though I swore a muscle in his jaw twitched.

"Still working on that, huh?" I grinned.

"Challenge accepted," Natasha said with determination. "One day crack that sexy statue. Now, tell everything. Those marks on neck not from training sessions."

Heat rushed to my cheeks. "Natasha! Not so loud."

"What? Viktor already know you fucking his boss. Probably hear through walls."

"Oh my god," I buried my face in my hands. "You're the worst."

"Why you love me," she smirked. "Seriously though, is good as looks? Because way Zaven watch you at club... *blyat*."

The waiter brought our coffees - a simple americano for me, some complicated concoction with extra shots for Natasha. I took a sip to gather my thoughts.

"It's..." I searched for words. "Intense. He's intense. Not just physically, but..." I gestured vaguely, unable to articulate the connection we'd formed.

"But he treat you well," she said, suddenly serious. "Not like that American pig."

"Nothing like Jack," I confirmed, my heart warming at her concern. "With Zaven, I feel... strong. Even when he's being all domineering and protective. It's different."

"Good." She nodded firmly. "Or I have to kill him, *vor* or not."

I laughed at the absurdity of my five-foot-nothing Russian friend threatening one of the most dangerous men in St. Petersburg.

"So, club gossip," she said, leaning forward conspiratorially. "Yelena sleep with bartender - one with tattoos. And Maxim caught stealing from register. Zaven's men take him out back." She made a cutting motion across her throat.

"They didn't kill him," I said with more certainty than I actually felt.

"No, just scare him shitless. Not walking straight for weeks." She took a long gulp of her coffee. "Everyone talk about you, you know. American who catch Zaven's eye. Some girls jealous, but I just say, 'That my best friend, *suki*!'" [bitches]

I smiled, grateful for her loyalty. "I miss it sometimes. The club. The energy."

"Miss you too," she admitted. "Not same without-"

My phone buzzed, interrupting her. I glanced down, expecting Zaven. Instead, an unknown number.

I must have gone pale, because Natasha leaned forward in concern. "What?"

My hands shook as I read the message: 'Miss me, Lily-pad? Coffee looks good.'

My head snapped up, eyes scanning frantically. There - across the street at the rival cafe. Jack sat at an outdoor table, one leg crossed casually over the other like he didn't have a care in the world.

He looked exactly the same - that carefully cultivated charm that had once fooled me. Expensive suit, perfect hair, disarming smile. But now I saw the predator beneath the polished exterior. His eyes met mine across the busy street, and he had the audacity to wink, raising his coffee cup in a mock toast.

"Liliya?" Natasha's voice seemed far away. She reached for my shaking hand. "What wrong?"

I couldn't speak. Couldn't breathe. The busy street sounds faded to a dull roar in my ears. The coffee cup rattled against its saucer as I set it down. All the strength I'd found in Zaven's arms, all the confidence I'd built, evaporated in an instant. I was that scared girl again, trying to make herself small.

Viktor must have noticed because suddenly he was there, his massive frame blocking my view of the street. "What. Happening." Not a question - a demand. His voice carried that same lethal edge I'd heard in Zaven's when dealing with threats.

"Jack," I whispered, the name sticking in my throat like glass. "He's watching us. Sent message." I held out my phone with trembling fingers.

Viktor's hand shot out, snatching the device. His face turned to stone as he read the text. In one fluid motion, he pulled me up from the chair, barking orders in Russian that had Sergei and Yuri moving into position, weapons barely concealed.

"Get in car. Now." His grip on my arm was iron as he scanned the crowd, eyes deadly. "Should have listened about staying in house."

When I risked another glance across the street, Jack's table was empty. Just an abandoned coffee cup and a folded newspaper. Somehow that was worse - not knowing where he'd gone.

"Need get you safe," Viktor growled, already moving me toward the SUV. "Then call *vor*."

The word '*vor*' made my stomach drop. Zaven. What would he do when he found out I'd defied him? That I'd put myself at risk?

Viktor turned to Natasha, his expression hard but with something else flickering beneath the surface. Without a word, he grabbed her arm too, pulling her along with us.

"What-" she started, surprise evident in her face.

"You not safe either," he said gruffly, not meeting her eyes as he guided both of us toward the car. "He saw you with her."

For a brief moment, I caught something pass between them - concern in his eyes, gratitude in hers. Then his professional mask slammed back into place as he shoved us both into the backseat.

In the back seat, I lay curled on my side, my head in Natasha's lap as violent tremors wracked my body. Her fingers stroked through my hair, a gesture meant to soothe, but nothing could calm the storm of fear inside me.

"*Devushka* in car," Viktor spoke into his phone, his voice terse. "*Da. Da.* American was there, watching. Sent message to her phone... *Net*, got her out fast." A pause. "Natasha with us. Coming home now."

Even through my fear-clouded mind, I could hear Zaven's voice on the other end - that dangerous edge that promised violence.

Jack had found me. After everything - running to Russia, finding safety with Zaven, learning to be strong - he'd still found me. And now...

"Shh," Natasha whispered as a sob escaped me. "You safe now. *Vor* will handle."

That only made me shake harder. I could hear Zaven's voice growing louder through Viktor's phone, though I couldn't make out the words. The city blurred past the tinted windows as we raced back to the safety of his compound. But I couldn't shake the feeling that everything had just changed - again.

285

34

Zaven

"Situation unfortunate, Lazarev." His voice oozed false concern. "Very valuable shipment, *da*? Perhaps meet, discuss proper compensation."

The Moscow skyline burned orange in the setting sun, heat rippling off glass and steel. Stood at window of hotel suite, phone pressed to ear, listening to Morozov's thinly veiled threats. Fucking games. Always games with these Moscow *mudaks*.

Swirled vodka in crystal glass, watching ice crack in clear liquid. Three fucking days in this city, playing their games while mind kept drifting back to Petersburg. To her. To way her body fit against mine, sounds she made when came apart beneath me.

"Nothing to discuss, Morozov. Unless ready to tell who leaked information." Kept voice cold, detached. Not let him hear impatience burning beneath surface.

"Careful, young *vor*." His tone hardened. "Maybe meet at warehouse where shipment... disappeared. Talk properly."

Of course. Where deals either got made or got bloody. My kind of meeting. "Fine. One hour."

Ended call, knocked back vodka in one burning swallow. Behind me, Yuri shifted from his position by door. "Boss?"

"Get car ready." Moved to closet, shoulder holster familiar weight as strapped it on. "And call Viktor. Want update on situation at home before handle this *mudak*.”

Memory of her flashed through mind as checked weapon - way she’d looked at me that last night, trust and need in those green eyes. Her body trembling under mine, begging me not to stop, those perfect lips whispering words that made cock harden even now thinking about them. Strange how quickly everything changed. From *vor* she feared to man she let see real self. To man who finally admitted feelings never thought would have.

“Intel says Morozov bringing five men minimum,” Yuri reported. “Want me call in more backup?”

“*Net*. Take six of ours.” Adjusted jacket over holster, caught reflection in window. *Vor*’s mask sliding into place, but underneath... “Just need end this shit. Get back to Petersburg.”

Back to her. To soft curves that fit against my hands like made for them. To wet heat that gripped my cock like heaven. To strength she showed in gym, fire when fought back against own demons. Pride swelled, remembering how she’d transformed that day. My brave, beautiful Liliya.

Phone buzzed. Viktor’s update from home. Something felt off in message, tension between lines that made instincts prickle. Mentioned Alexi again - third time that week found where not supposed to be. Mental note to handle personally when return. Or maybe just own unease at being away these past days when everything still so new, so fucking fragile between us.

“Car ready, Boss.”

Holstered weapon settled against ribs as adjusted jacket one last time. Grabbed phone, wallet. Everything in its place, controlled, like always needed be. Three days in this city, playing their games, while mind kept wandering to Petersburg. To marks left on her skin, claiming her as mine. To taste of her still lingering on tongue.

The click of my shoes on marble floors echoed through hotel’s hallway, each step taking me further from man who’d held Lily that last night, deeper into *vor* these men needed fear. Underground garage smelled of exhaust and damp concrete, familiar scent of business about to turn bloody.

The SUV’s leather creaked as shifted into backseat, metallic taste of anticipation thick on tongue. Moscow’s lights smeared past rain-spotted windows, city's pulse beating different rhythm than Petersburg's. Different from home. From her.

Caught glimpse of own reflection in rain-streaked window - shoulders too tense, jaw too tight. Like young *vor* again, not man who held half of Petersburg in iron grip. Not man who'd found unexpected peace in green eyes and soft thighs wrapped around waist. Need focus. These thoughts of her, of that last night together when made her scream name until voice hoarse, making me weak when need be anything but.

"How many cars you see?" asked Yuri, his fingers drumming calculated pattern on steering wheel.

"Three following since hotel." Watched their headlights weave through traffic behind us. "Getting sloppy. Think we not notice tail?"

"Want handle now?"

"*Net*. Let them think they clever." Same mistake made with Lily at first - underestimating. Thinking pretty face meant weak mind.

The car's heater fought against Moscow's bitter cold, but couldn't touch ice forming in veins. This familiar chill - one that came before blood spilled. Mind betrayed me again, drifting to way Lily had traced scars that night, her touch melting years of frozen walls. The way she'd guided my hand to throat, showing trust that made cock harder than diamond. *Blyad*. Dangerous thoughts. These feelings that made chest tight, made focusing impossible when needed be *vor* these men feared.

Rain turned to sleet, clicking against windows like warning bells. Warehouse district emerged from darkness - graveyard of Soviet ambition, buildings hunched like wounded animals against black sky. Two SUVs waited, their headlights cutting through fog like predator's eyes.

Yuri eased our SUV to stop, gravel crunching under tires. Through windshield, counted Morozov's men emerging from shadows - seven of them. More than agreed. Each one positioned casual but careful, hands too close to weapons.

"Let them make first move," voice low, dangerous. The *vor* in me already calculating angles, exits, weak points. "Want see how far they willing to push."

Steam rose from hood of car, mixing with fog and sleet. Air stank of wet metal and oil, scent of weapons that should have moved through port without issue. Memory of lost shipment made jaw clench. Not about merchandise - about respect. About power.

"Zaven Nikolaevich." Morozov's voice carried false warmth across empty lot. "Good you come. Have much talking need do."

Stepped out into freezing rain, let it soak through expensive suit. Let them see calm on surface while ice spread through veins. Same cold focus always came before violence.

"*Net* more talking," let edge creep into voice, one that usually made smarter men step back. "Only truth now. Who help take shipment from my port?"

Morozov's smile didn't reach eyes. "Careful. Not good make accusations without proof."

"Proof?" Let cold smile touch lips. "Have dead men at port. Have missing shipment worth millions. Have you, playing games in my territory." Took step forward through rain, pulling jacket and shirt aside with deliberate slowness. Finger traced single star inked over heart, earned in blood and respected throughout Russia. "This star not just for show, Morozov. Think I not earn it?"

Watched his eyes track movement, saw flash of unease cross face. My reputation preceded me - youngest *vor* to earn mark in decades.

Morozov's face hardened, fake warmth vanishing. Sleet gathered on his expensive coat, drops rolling off like blood. "Star mean nothing when *vor* forgets traditions. Hear you let American whore into our world. Make *vor* weak, letting cunt control-"

He never finished sentence. Rage exploded through veins, different from usual cold violence. This burned. Personal. Took another step forward, close enough to smell his fear beneath expensive cologne.

"Choose next words careful," cut him off, voice deadly quiet. "Think hard about consequences."

"Touch nerve, *mladshiy vor*?" [younger vor] Morozov sneered, using diminutive deliberately, though he took half step back. "Perhaps rumors true - great Zaven Lazarev gone soft for pretty face. For American pussy-"

Behind me, felt Yuri shift slightly. Ready. Waiting. Through rain, caught glint of metal as one of Morozov's men reached inside coat.

The first punch came from Morozov's man - exactly what been waiting for. Acrid stench of fear mixed with gun oil as he lunged forward, metal glinting dully in rain. Amateur move. Stepped inside his reach, rain-slick concrete solid beneath feet as blade whistled past ear. Crack of his wrist breaking echoed off metal walls, bone giving way beneath grip with sound like wet branches snapping.

His howl of pain cut short as elbow connected with face. Cartilage collapsed with wet crunch, hot blood spraying across knuckles, metallic taste filling air. Familiar dance of violence, but tonight felt different. Personal. Every word about Lily fueling each strike with rage that burned through usual cold precision.

Around me, chaos erupted in warehouse. Sound of flesh meeting flesh, grunts of pain, squeal of boots on wet concrete. Yuri moved like death itself, taking on two men at once. Wet crunch as drove knee up, choked gurgle of man trying to breathe through crushed windpipe. These men might work for Morozov, but weren't true fighters - didn't understand difference between thugs and those born to violence.

Through melee, tracked Morozov backing away, expensive shoes scraping across broken glass as fumbled inside coat. Rain plastered hair to skull, making him look smaller, weaker. "Not so brave now?" Advanced on him, letting him see *vor* he'd been stupid enough to insult. "No more words about American girl?"

His eyes went wide as finally drew weapon, chrome gleaming dully in dim light. But before could aim, was on him. Tendons in wrist strained against grip as forced gun upward. Shot cracked through warehouse, flash briefly illuminating faces twisted in violence. Bullet embedded in rusted metal above, raining rust and debris down on us.

Fear rolled off him in waves now, pulse hammering beneath grip where held throat. This - this was where respect had come from. Not words in conference rooms, but primal understanding that came with true power.

"Please," he choked out, blood from broken nose bubbling with each word. "Was just business–"

"Business?" Tightened grip until eyes bulged. "Insult *vor*'s woman, call that business?" Slammed him against support beam, rust flaking onto expensive suit. "The star on my chest was earned in blood. The woman in my bed is earned in trust. Only a fool disrespects either."

Each word punctuated with another slam, feeling fight drain from body with each impact. Around us, sounds of combat died down, replaced by groans of pain and Yuri's steady breathing.

Fight drained from Morozov's body as slid down beam, leaving wet smear of blood on rusted metal. Expensive suit torn, soaked with rain and worse. Far cry from man who'd sat so smugly across conference tables these past days.

Stepped back, adjusting jacket with careful precision. Ran fingers through rain-soaked hair, neck cracking as rolled shoulders. Familiar calm after violence settled over me, ice returning to replace fire in veins.

"Now," wiped blood from knuckles with silk handkerchief, each movement deliberate. "About shipment. Who you working with? Who gave port information?"

Morozov coughed, spitting blood onto concrete. Eyes darted between me and fallen men, calculating odds that no longer existed.

"Only get to answer question once," voice quiet, lethal. "Make it count."

"Was Dmitri," Morozov choked out, blood still bubbling from nose. "He... he has plans. Big plans for Petersburg. Said if help with shipment..." Voice faltered as my expression darkened.

"What plans?" Moved closer, letting him see death in eyes.

"Gala. Something at Hermitage Gala. Has people inside your organization, people who–"

My phone's sharp ring cut through tension. Viktor's ringtone. Something in gut twisted – he wouldn't call during meeting unless...

"Answer it," ordered Yuri, already moving to secure Morozov. "We handle this *mudak*."

Viktor's voice came through tight with tension. "Boss. Have situation.

American here in Petersburg. Liliya's ex. He found her."

Ice crystallized in veins, different from usual cold focus. This wasn't business anymore. This was personal. This was mine.

"What happened?" Each word carved from frost. Gripped phone so tight plastic creaked.

"She at cafe with Natasha. He sent message. Saw her there." Viktor's voice carried edge rarely heard. "Got her out fast, bringing her home now. She shaking bad, Boss. Never seen her like this."

Blood roared in ears, drowning out Morozov's whimpers. Liliya. My Liliya. Trembling, afraid. After all work to make her feel safe, to help her find strength. After promises made with body pressed to hers that would keep her protected.

And Jack. That *mudak* dared come to my city. Dared threaten what was mine. Vision went red around edges.

"She was at cafe?" Voice dangerously quiet. "Told her stay at house."

Brief hesitation from Viktor. "She... was determined. Said would go with or without protection. Made choice to accompany rather than let her go alone."

"Not your fault." Cut him off, rage building not at Viktor but at American pig who reduced my strong Lily to trembling girl again. "She there now? Safe?"

"*Da.* Brought back to compound. Natasha with her."

"She hurt?"

"*Net.* Just... scared. Very scared."

Hand clenched so tight blood dripped where nails cut into palm. "Find him," voice barely recognizable through rage. "Use every resource. Every man. Want him found before return to Petersburg. Want him alive."

Ended call, turned back to Morozov who flinched at whatever saw in face.

"Tell Yuri everything about Dmitri's plans." Each word carved from ice. "Every detail. Leave anything out..." Let threat hang in air.

"Not know much," he wheezed. "Only that something planned for Gala. Has people inside your organization. Didn't trust me with more."

Grabbed his collar, forcing him to meet eyes. "Better pray that true.

Because if find out lying..."

Left him to Yuri's tender mercies. Needed get back to Petersburg. To her. Someone had helped Jack find her - someone who'd pay dearly for that mistake. And Jack... Jack would learn what happened when touched what belonged to *vor*.

Remembered Lily's face when spoke of him, fear that still lingered beneath surface. Remembered marks seen on her body first night together - not my marks of pleasure, but old scars of cruelty. Time American bastard learned difference between man who controlled through fear and *vor* who protected what was his.

Phone already out, booking earlier flight back to Petersburg. To her. To woman who'd somehow become more important than business, than revenge, than anything.

"Yuri," called over shoulder. "Get everything he knows. Then finish this."

"*Da*, Boss. And Dmitri?"

"Dmitri waits. First, handle American problem." First, reclaim what was mine. First, remind Lily who she belonged to now. Who would never let anyone hurt her again.

Because there were two kinds of men in this world—those who left scars and those who healed them. And I had chosen which kind of man I would be for her.

35

Zaven

The jet's engines hummed, a constant drone that did nothing to calm the storm raging inside me. In the small bathroom mirror, I barely recognized the man looking back - dark streaks of dried blood across my face and knuckles, my white shirt now a canvas of crimson and grime. The metallic taste lingered in my mouth, mixed with Moscow's bitter victory.

"Handle rest here," I'd told Yuri before leaving the warehouse, air still thick with copper and violence. "Get what information can from him. Then make sure message crystal fucking clear about consequences of disrespect."

I splashed water on my face, watching pink-tinged rivulets swirl down the drain. Each movement sent fresh pain through my bruised muscles, but physical discomfort meant nothing compared to the image of Lily trembling, of Jack watching her.

"Thirty minutes from Petersburg," the pilot's voice crackled through the intercom as I made my way back to the cabin.

The leather seat creaked as I sank down, my hands clenching until fresh blood welled from my split knuckles. I checked my phone again—third time in ten minutes. No new messages from Viktor. No updates on Lily's condition. No word on Jack's whereabouts. Nothing but fucking silence.

"*Davai, davai,*" [Come on, come on] I muttered under my breath, willing the plane to move faster through the night sky. I'd never felt this before— this restless burning that made sitting still impossible. Usually patience came easy. I could wait hours for the right moment to strike, for an enemy to make a fatal mistake. But this...this was different. This was her.

I unlocked my phone again, staring at the last photo I'd taken of her—asleep in my bed, hair spread across the pillow, sheets barely covering her perfect curves. I remembered taking it without her knowing, treasuring the rare moment of complete peace on her face. Now I imagined that peace shattered by Jack's presence, by the reminder of pain she'd escaped.

The unfamiliar feeling clawing at my chest had a name I rarely allowed myself to acknowledge: fear. Not for myself—never that—but for her. For what his appearance would do to the strength she'd fought so hard to build.

Power meant controlling everything in my world—every territory, every deal, every enemy. But Liliya taught me a brutal truth: the more you care for something, the less control you truly have. This was real weakness, not the softness Morozov accused me of. And still, I would choose this weakness over strength that came from feeling nothing at all.

Thirty minutes stretched like eternity. I checked my watch. Checked my phone. My fingers drummed a rhythm on the armrest, matching my thundering heartbeat. I ignored the stab of pain from my bruised knuckles, welcomed it even. Physical pain was understood. Controlled. This other feeling—this desperate need to reach her—had no such controls.

Finally, the lights of Petersburg glittered below as we descended, night air heavy with coming rain. Each city light was a reminder of how vast this territory was, how many places Jack could be hiding. But he'd made a fatal mistake coming here. Coming after her.

The wheels touched down with a jolt that sent fresh pain through my bruised ribs. Before we'd even reached a full stop, I was on my feet. The door opened to Petersburg's brutal winter air, the cold biting deeper than Moscow's. Sleet mixed with snow pelted the tarmac where a black Mercedes waited, engine running, exhaust creating clouds in the frozen night.

The city blurred past tinted windows, street lamps casting halos through the winter storm. Each traffic light was an eternity. Streets I normally commanded now felt like obstacles keeping me from her. Ice crusted the edges of the windows, matching the cold focus of thoughts pounding through my head - get to her, protect her, kill him.

The estate's iron gates finally came into view, snow gathering on the ornate metalwork as they opened silently at our approach. Gravel and ice crunched under the tires as we pulled up to the main entrance. Guards stationed at the doors straightened immediately, hands instinctively moving toward weapons—pure reflex at the sight of danger—before recognizing who approached.

I stepped out of the car into the biting cold, my blood-stiffened shirt cracking slightly with movement. I didn't wait for the usual respectful greetings, didn't acknowledge the nods of deference as guards opened the heavy wooden doors. One young guard—a newer recruit—visibly flinched at the sight of me. I understood his reaction. I had seen my own reflection. I knew what he saw: a *vor* returning blood-soaked from Moscow, death walking in human skin.

The main hall stretched before me, chandeliers casting golden light across marble floors. The house felt different, the air charged with tension that hadn't been there before my departure. Security personnel moved with heightened alertness, eyes tracking my progress through the hallways. Word had spread about the American's appearance, about Liliya's fear. About what would happen when I returned.

I strode through familiar territory now made unfamiliar by the violation of her safety. Each step echoed against marble, matching the rhythm of pulse pounding in my temples. The need for information warred with the need to see her first. Information won—I needed to know everything before I faced her.

"Where's Viktor?" My voice came out like broken glass.

The young guard swallowed visibly before answering. "In the study, sir."

I threw open the study door with enough force to make the hinges groan. Viktor looked up from a stack of papers, his usual stoic expression faltering as he took in my blood-stained appearance.

"*Bozhe moy,*" he muttered, rising quickly. "Business in Moscow-"

"*Net.*" I cut him off, advancing on his desk. "Know she went out. Know she was with Natasha. What don't know is how that *yebanyi urod* [fucking monster] found her. How he got close enough to make her afraid again." I slammed my palm against the desk. "Thought made myself crystal fucking clear about level of security needed."

Viktor's jaw clenched, but to his credit, he didn't back down. "Had four men with her, Boss. Two inside cafe, two outside. Still don't know how he found her location-"

"Then should have stopped her!" I slammed my fist on the desk, sending papers scattering. My split knuckles stung, fresh blood spotting the documents. "Could have locked every fucking door in house."

"She's not a prisoner," Viktor said, his voice careful but firm. "And you left her in charge. What was I supposed to do? Defy a direct order from the woman you put in control of the household?"

For a moment, I saw red. I grabbed his collar, yanking him close. "Was supposed to keep her safe," my voice came out deadly quiet. "That was only fucking job."

Viktor didn't flinch, meeting my gaze steadily. "And we did. Got her out fast. She's safe, unharmed. Shaken, but safe."

I released him with a shove, turning to pace the length of the study. The room felt too small, my rage too big to contain. He was right, damn him. Lily was safe. But the fact that Jack got close enough to see her, to send a message that made her tremble...

"Where is she now?" I forced the words through clenched teeth.

"Sleeping. In your rooms." Viktor straightened his collar, his eyes shifting briefly toward the east wing before meeting mine again. "Refused to stay in hers. Said felt safer there." A moment's hesitation. "Natasha refused to leave compound. Put her in guest suite near my quarters—for security." Something in his tone changed subtly when he mentioned her name. "Insisted on checking on Liliya herself every hour."

Something twisted in my chest at that - pride, possession, need to protect all tangled together. Lily in my bed, seeking safety in my space.

"Triple security," I ordered, already moving toward the door. "No one in or out without my direct approval. And Viktor-" I turned back, letting him see the death in my eyes. "Find him. Find that *mudak* before I do, or there won't be enough pieces left for wolves to find."

I made my way through the halls, every footstep echoing with barely contained violence. Staff pressed against walls as I passed, eyes widening at my blood-stained appearance. Let them stare. Let them see what a *vor* does to those who threaten what's his.

I reached my rooms, opening the door quietly. Moonlight spilled through the windows, casting silver shadows across the bed. I stopped dead at the sight before me - Lily curled in the center of the dark sheets, her skin looking pale as snow. She clutched my pillow against her chest, face buried in it like she was seeking comfort from my scent.

The sight of her there, in my space, triggered something primal. Mine. To protect. To keep safe. I had to force myself to step back, to not go to her immediately. I needed to clean up first, wash Moscow's violence from my skin before touching her.

In the bathroom, I stripped off my blood-stained clothes, letting them fall to the marble floor. Hot water hit like physical punishment, exactly what I deserved for not being here. Steam filled the space as I pressed my forehead against the cool tile, letting the water pound my bruised muscles.

When the steam finally cleared from the mirror, I saw it. There in the condensation - a small unhappy face drawn in simple lines. Lily's work, had to be. So different from the smile she'd left before. Evidence of her fear, her pain while I was gone.

Something cracked in my chest at the sight of that unhappy face. I didn't bother with clothes - the need to feel her against me was too strong. I needed to know she was real, was safe.

The sheets whispered as I slid into bed behind her. She still clutched my pillow, but even in sleep, her body recognized mine. She shifted, pressing back against my chest as I wrapped my arm around her waist, pulling her close. Her skin felt like silk against mine, warm and alive.

"Zaven?" Her voice was thick with sleep, but relief was clear in that one word.

She turned in my arms, eyes wide and searching in the moonlight. Her fingers reached up, hesitant, tracing dried blood at the corner of my mouth.

"You're hurt?"

"*Net.*" I caught her hand, pressed my lips to her palm. "Not my blood."

Relief flooded her face, then something else—uncertainty. "Jack—he found me. Sent a message to the cafe. Said he was watching me." The words tumbled out, her voice small. "I didn't listen. I should have stayed home like you said."

I tightened my arm around her waist, pulling her closer. "Shh. Don't. Not now."

"You're not angry?" Surprise flickered across her face, muscles still tense beneath my touch.

"At you? *Net.*" I brushed hair from her face, gentler than most would believe these hands capable of. "At him? *Da.* At myself for not being here? Most of all."

She shook her head, fingertips now tracing my jawline like she was memorizing every angle. "Not your fault. It was mine. I shouldn't have—"

I silenced her with my thumb against her lips. "Enough. You safe now. Only thing matters."

That knot in my chest—the one I'd carried since Viktor's call—finally loosened. I had her in my arms, unharmed. Under my protection again. I could feel the steady beat of her heart against mine, proof of life beneath my fingertips as I stroked down her spine.

"I thought about you," she whispered, pressing closer. "Every minute you were gone. Even before..." She trailed off, not wanting to speak his name. "I drew that unhappy face on the mirror. Stupid."

"I saw it." I pressed my lips to her forehead, inhaling the scent of her— vanilla and sleep-warmth. "Not stupid."

Something shifted in the air between us. Her hands slid up my chest, fingers tracing my collar bone, shoulders, like she was checking I was really there. I felt her shiver, but not from fear. A different trembling altogether.

"I need you," she whispered, surprising me. After today, after Jack's appearance, I expected her to need distance, comfort. Not this. "I need to feel you. Need to forget everything else."

I pulled back slightly, studying her face in the silver moonlight. "Sure, *malyshka?* After today—"

Instead of answering, she pressed her lips against mine. Not a gentle kiss of comfort, but a hungry one of need. Her hands tangled in my hair, pulling me closer with a desperation that matched the storm inside me since receiving Viktor's call.

"Please," she breathed against my mouth. "Make me forget everything but you."

That one word—that plea—broke the last thread of my restraint. I claimed her mouth with bruising intensity, swallowing her gasp as my hands gripped her hips. I pulled her flush against me, letting her feel exactly what she did to me, how much I wanted her.

Her hands roamed across my chest, nails scraping over my nipples, down my stomach, leaving trails of fire on my skin. When her fingers wrapped around my hard length, I hissed through my teeth at the jolt of pleasure so intense it bordered on pain.

"I missed this," she murmured, stroking slowly, her thumb circling the sensitive tip. "Missed you. Thought about your cock every night you were gone."

The crude word on her elegant lips sent my blood rushing south, made me throb in her grip. It was still new, hearing her talk this way. Still fucking intoxicating.

She slid down my body before I could stop her, her mouth replacing her hand. Hot, wet heat engulfed the head, her tongue swirling around the sensitive ridge. I cursed in Russian, my fingers tangling in her hair as I watched her take me deeper. The sight of her—this elegant, refined woman—taking my cock into her mouth with such hunger nearly undid me.

"*Blyad,*" I groaned as she hollowed her cheeks, sucking harder. "Your fucking mouth, Liliya."

Her eyes flicked up, meeting mine as she took me deeper. The connection—watching her pleasure me while she watched my reaction— was the most intimate thing I'd ever experienced. Different from fucking. More vulnerable somehow.

She moaned around my length, the vibrations sending shockwaves of pleasure through my body. Her hand worked what couldn't fit in her mouth, her other hand cupping my balls with gentle pressure that had my muscles tensing, my release building too quickly.

"Stop," my voice was ragged as I tugged her hair gently. She pulled off with an obscene pop, her lips swollen and wet. "Want be inside you. Need feel you come around my cock."

Her eyes darkened at my words, pupils blown wide with arousal. "Yes," she breathed, moving back up my body. "I want you to fuck me. Now."

I flipped our positions, pinning her beneath me. I attacked her neck with teeth and tongue, leaving marks that would bloom purple by morning. Mine. Everyone would see. Know who she belonged to.

Her skin tasted like salt and that unique flavor that was just her. Addictive. I could spend hours just tasting every inch. But patience was gone tonight. Need too urgent.

I moved down her body, taking a nipple into my mouth, biting gently then soothing with my tongue. Her back arched, pushing her breast further into my mouth as her hands clutched the sheets.

"Zaven," she gasped, hips bucking as I pinched her other nipple between my fingers. "More. Please."

"Not yet," I murmured against the soft skin of her stomach, moving lower. "Need taste your pussy first. Need feel how wet you are for me."

I settled between her thighs, spreading them wider. Exposed to my gaze, to my mouth. Pink and swollen and so fucking wet already. I ran my tongue through her slick folds, groaning at the taste of her arousal. Sweet and tangy and addictive as the finest vodka.

Her thighs trembled as I circled her clit with my tongue, teasing around the sensitive bud before sucking gently. The sound she made—half sob, half moan—sent blood rushing to my already painfully hard cock.

"Oh god," she cried, hips grinding against my mouth as I slid a finger inside her tight heat. "Yes, like that."

I added a second finger, crooking them to find the spot that made her see stars. I found it instantly—I had memorized her body like a map of Petersburg. Knew every sensitive spot, every place that made her moan, whimper, scream.

She grew wetter around my fingers, her inner muscles clenching as I built her toward her peak. I could make her come like this—had done so many times in the days before Moscow. But tonight I needed more. Needed the connection only achieved when buried deep inside her.

I withdrew my fingers, ignoring her whimper of protest. I moved back up her body, positioned at her entrance, slick with her arousal.

"Look at me," I demanded, needing to see the truth in her eyes. "Only mine, *da*?"

"*Da*," she echoed, the Russian word sounding like a prayer on her lips. "Only yours. Need your cock inside me. Need you to fuck me, Zaven. Hard."

Her words—crude, desperate, honest—undid the final thread of my control. I thrust forward, burying my full length in one smooth stroke. We both cried out at the sensation—her tight, wet heat gripping me like a velvet fist.

"So fucking tight," I groaned, holding still to let her adjust. "So perfect for me."

Her nails dug into my shoulders, urging movement. "Please. Don't stop."

I set a punishing pace, each thrust a declaration and promise. Mine to protect. Mine to pleasure. Mine to keep safe. Her nails raked down my back, marking my skin, urging faster, harder. I wanted those marks. Needed them. Physical proof that we belonged to each other when words weren't enough.

I lifted her leg higher, changing the angle to hit deeper. Her eyes widened, mouth forming a perfect O of pleasure as I hit the spot that made her see stars.

"Right there," she gasped, inner muscles clenching around my length. "Oh god, Zaven, right there."

"Come for me," I commanded, my voice barely recognizable with need. "Want feel you come on my cock."

I slid my hand between us, my thumb finding her sensitive bundle of nerves, circling with precise pressure. She shattered instantly, her back bowing off the bed, my name torn from her throat like a prayer. Her inner muscles clenched rhythmically, milking my own release.

I buried deep inside her, the hot pulse of my release stronger than anything I remembered feeling before. My vision blacked at the edges, the pleasure so intense it was almost painful. I bit down on the curve where her neck met her shoulder, marking her as I rode out the waves of orgasm.

I collapsed beside her, pulling her against my chest. Both of us were breathing hard, our bodies slick with sweat, hearts thundering against our ribs.

"Missed that," she murmured, pressing a kiss to my chest, right over my heart. "Missed you. Bed felt too empty."

I tightened my arm around her, tucking her closer. "Won't leave you unprotected again."

She tensed slightly, then deliberately relaxed against me. "I know you'll keep me safe."

Simple words, but they hit harder than any bullet. Trust. Complete trust. After everything she'd been through, she trusted me to protect her. To keep my promises.

Some men spent their lives collecting things—money, cars, real estate— thinking possession equaled power. But true power was this: a woman who'd seen your violence choosing to sleep in your arms, believing herself safer there than anywhere else in the world.

I traced patterns on her bare back, feeling tension drain from both our bodies. Tomorrow would bring new battles. Tonight, only this mattered. Her safe in my arms, the ghost of fear banished from her eyes. This connection forged in fire and need.

"Sleep now," I murmured against her hair. "I'm here. Not going anywhere."

She nodded, already drifting, her body relaxed completely against mine. Trusted me enough to sleep. To feel safe. The greatest gift anyone had ever given me.

Outside, the Petersburg storm raged on. Inside, for the first time since the plane touched down, I felt calm return. A different kind of power than what I'd wielded in Moscow tonight. But somehow stronger. More necessary.

Sleep came eventually. Dreamless. Peaceful. Her body curved against mine, where she belonged.

Where I would keep her, no matter what tomorrow brought.

36

Liliya

Morning sun streamed through dining room windows, catching the steam that rose from coffee cups and silver serving trays. Natasha sat across from me, trying too hard to keep conversation light despite the armed guards visible through every doorway.

"These *blini* perfect, *bozhe moy!*" she declared, reaching for more. "Almost make up for fact we basically under house arrest, *da?*"

"Not house arrest," Zaven's voice came from doorway, making us both jump. He moved into room with that lethal grace, suit perfectly tailored but doing nothing to hide the predator beneath. "Is protection."

His hand brushed my shoulder as he sat beside me, the casual touch carrying weight of possession. When he reached for his coffee, I caught sight of his knuckles - raw and split, evidence of what he'd done in Moscow. My stomach twisted, not with revulsion but with the realization that those same hands had held me so gently just hours ago.

"Speaking of leaving house," he said, cup barely hiding fresh bruises. "Need take you shopping. For gala."

My stomach clenched. "Maybe we should skip-"

"*Net.*" His tone softened seeing my fear. "Will be fine. Nothing happen to you again." The promise carried edge of steel. "Need proper dress for first public appearance as *vor*'s woman. Want everyone see who belongs to me now."

"About yesterday," I started, eyes fixed on his injured hands. "I shouldn't have-"

"Already discussed," he cut me off, but gentle edge to his voice softened command. "Eat breakfast. Need strength."

"Yes, eat," Natasha chimed in, determinedly cheerful. "Cannot believe *vor*'s woman so skinny. What will people think?" She winked at Zaven. "Though maybe you like skinny girls, *da*?"

"Natasha," I warned, but caught the slight curve of Zaven's lips.

"Speaking of what *vor* likes," she continued, eyeing Viktor who stood guard at doorway. "Some men appreciate woman with curves. Don't you agree, Viktor?"

Viktor's stoic expression didn't change, but I swore his ears reddened slightly. He shifted his weight almost imperceptibly, his eyes briefly meeting Natasha's before returning to their professional scan of the room.

Zaven's gaze moved between them, something knowing in his expression. "Viktor appreciate many things. Though strange he not mention guest suite had issue with heating last night." He sipped his coffee, watching Viktor over the rim. "Curious why you not sleep when on duty, Viktor. After moving Natasha to more... comfortable quarters."

Viktor's jaw tightened, but he remained impressively expressionless. "Security was maintained at all times, Boss."

"I'm sure it was," Zaven murmured, amusement flickering in his eyes.

Natasha's smile grew more catlike. "Oh yes, Viktor very concerned with my comfort. Checked on me personally. Very thorough in his... protection."

"After breakfast, we go shopping." Zaven stood, movements fluid despite what his knuckles revealed about Moscow. "Going to gym. Need release some... tension."

"Ah, yes. Much tension," Natasha grinned. "Must be why Liliya sleep in your rooms last night, help with tension?"

"Natasha!" But her attempt to lighten mood worked - even Zaven's eyes held hint of amusement beneath the darkness.

"*Da*," he responded, surprising me with his directness. "Very effective method." His eyes met mine briefly, heat flickering in them before being carefully banked.

He leaned down, pressing kiss to top of my head. "Eat," he murmured against my hair. "Then rest. Will find you later."

As he passed Viktor at door, I caught his low words. "Watch out for that one. Like tigress going after prey. Though seems tigress already caught what hunting for, *da*?"

Viktor's face remained stoic, but tips of his ears definitely reddened this time. Something almost like a smile ghosted across his features for a millisecond before disappearing—so quickly I might have imagined it.

Once they'd gone, Natasha leaned forward. "So? Tell everything. How bad was he when returned? Was he all..." She made exaggerated angry face that somehow still managed to look elegant.

"No," I sighed, but couldn't help small smile. Even with everything happening, she could still make me laugh. "But speaking of telling everything... what exactly happened with you and Viktor last night?"

She waved her hand dismissively, but her eyes sparkled. "Guest suite very cold. What kind of host would Viktor be if not help warm me up? Russian hospitality, nothing more."

"Nothing more? Your lipstick is on his collar. I noticed when he shifted."

A satisfied smile curved her lips. "Maybe I leave little mark. To remind him." She leaned in, lowering her voice. "Man like that—all control, all duty—makes most interesting sounds when finally lets go."

"Come on," Natasha urged, pushing more *blini* onto my plate, changing the subject. "Need details. *Vor* rushes back from Moscow covered in blood for you - is very romantic, no? Most women lucky to get flowers. You get *vor* ready to burn city down."

"Romantic isn't exactly the word I'd use." The memory of his bruised knuckles, the barely contained rage in his muscles made me shiver. "He was... I've never seen him like that."

"Of course not. Is *vor*. Man of power. When someone threatens what belongs to him..." She paused, studying my face. "But was gentle with you, *da*?"

I thought of how he'd held me through the night, his touch so careful despite the violence still thrumming through him. "Yes. It's strange – he can be so dangerous, but with me…"

"Not strange," Natasha said, suddenly serious. "Is how should be. Power means nothing if cannot control it. Cannot be tender when matters."

"I just feel stupid," admitted quietly. "For not listening about staying home. For putting everyone in danger."

"*Net, net*," Natasha waved dismissively. "Cannot live in cage, even golden one. Besides," her eyes sparkled with familiar mischief, "way *vor* look at you just now? Way he fuck you with eyes across breakfast table? Worth little danger."

"Speaking of way *vor* looks at me…" I traced rim of coffee cup. "The Gala. It's a big deal, isn't it? First time being seen publicly as… as his."

"Huge deal," Natasha's eyes lit up. "All important families there. Everyone who matters in Petersburg society." She leaned forward conspiratorially. "Is where *vor* shows off his woman. Makes clear to all that you belong to him."

My stomach fluttered with nerves. "That's what I'm afraid of. I don't know how to act, how to be what everyone expects."

"Bah," Natasha scoffed. "Just be woman who caught *vor*'s eye. Who made him rush back from Moscow ready to burn city down for you." She grinned. "Besides, will help you find perfect dress. Make all those society wives choke on their champagne with jealousy."

"But after yesterday… with Jack…" The fear crept back in.

"Think *vor* let anything happen to you at his own event?" Natasha raised perfectly shaped eyebrow. "Will be most protected woman in room. Though," her eyes twinkled, "maybe save one dance for Viktor, *da?*"

"Viktor?" I managed a laugh. "You'd have better luck getting one of the marble statues to dance. He's like Zaven's shadow, but… scarier."

"Ah, but I like challenge." Natasha's smile turned wicked. "Already got him to do much more than blush last night. By Gala, maybe even get public smile."

We both laughed, and for a moment, everything felt normal. Like we were just two friends sharing breakfast, planning for a party.

But as conversation drifted on, I couldn't shake the cold fear lurking beneath the surface. All the strength I'd found in Zaven's gym, all the confidence I'd built... it felt fragile now. Jack was here, in this city. He'd found me, watched me, despite everything.

Natasha's voice faded to background as I stared into my coffee. The woman who'd stood up to Zaven's men at dinner, who'd matched the *vor*'s passion in the gym, who'd finally started feeling worthy of his world - she seemed far away now. In her place sat the same scared girl who'd fled Chicago, jumping at shadows.

But then I remembered Zaven's promise in the darkness, the lethal grace of him this morning. The way his bruised hands had held me so gently, even while promising violence to those who'd hurt me. Maybe I wasn't that scared girl anymore. Maybe I was something new - someone who could be both strong and protected, fierce and cherished.

The thought settled over me as Natasha launched into plans for dress shopping, her voice warm and familiar in the morning sun.

37

Zaven

The punch bag's chain creaked rhythmically with each strike, my knuckles screaming protest despite hand wraps. Didn't care. Pain helped focus rage still burning from Moscow.

"Yuri called," Viktor's voice cut through sound of fists hitting leather. "Says Morozov still breathing. Barely."

Another strike. Harder. "He talk?"

"*Da*. But not much useful. Keeps rambling about traditions, about *vor* getting soft." Viktor paused. "About American woman."

The chain snapped with next punch, bag hitting floor with dull thud. Sweat dripped down chest as turned to face him. "His exact words about her what set me off. Not shipment, not business. Calling her whore who make *vor* weak."

"Know this." Viktor's expression remained carefully neutral. "Question is - can you separate personal from business? Multiple threats now need cold head to handle."

"*Da*," I growled, grabbing water bottle. "But all connect to her. Jack showing up not accident. Someone feeding information."

"*Da*." Viktor leaned against wall, watching as stalked to next bag. "Yuri working on finding rat. But Zaven..." He hesitated. "Taking her dress shopping, being seen in public right now-"

"Need show her safe." First punch landed precise, controlled. "Need her trust *vor* can protect what his. But also need find these *mudaks* who think can touch what belongs to me."

Struck bag again, harder this time. The familiar rhythm of violence clearing head. After several more hits, tension eased enough for mind to shift. Noticed Viktor checking phone, slight change in his usually impassive expression.

"Message from Natasha?" I asked, landing another precise hit. "Or still thinking about last night? Guest quarters must have better beds than thought. Natasha not look like woman who just slept."

Viktor stepped forward, holding bag steady as I struck again. His expression didn't change, but jaw tightened slightly. "Security was maintained at all times."

Landed harder jab, making him brace. "Didn't ask about fucking security." Couldn't help small smile at his discomfort. "Asked about marks on neck. Unless using new technique where enemy attacks with lipstick?"

Viktor actually sighed - rare show of emotion. "Woman like hurricane. Beautiful, but leaves destruction." A pause, almost reluctant admission. "Worth it."

I barked out laugh, genuinely surprised. "*Blyad!* Stone-face Viktor admits weakness for woman?"

"Others whisper," Viktor countered, clearly trying to shift focus back to business. He pushed bag toward me hard, challenging. "Say love make *vor* weak."

Stopped mid-strike. "You think weak?" Let edge creep into voice that would make smarter men step back.

"*Net.*" Corner of his mouth lifted slightly. "Think different. See how she change you. But not weak change. Like mother did for father, before..."

"Tell me something, old friend." Turned to face him fully. "That first dinner, when she challenged me at table. Refused to be intimidated. You saw it then?"

"Saw *vor* finding equal," Viktor straightened. "Woman strong enough to stand beside you, not behind. Like traditions say should be."

Started unwrapping hands, knuckles still raw from Moscow. "Morozov, others like him - they see only Liliya playing at being *vor*'s woman. Don't understand she..." Words failed, remembering how she'd faced her fears in this very gym.

"They will learn." Viktor's voice carried weight of certainty. "At Gala, when you present her properly. But Zaven-" his expression hardened, "first need handle Jack. Need send message about consequences of touching what belongs to *vor*."

"Already have men searching city?"

"*Da*. Every district, every contact. He surface, we find."

Blood hummed with need for violence, remembering Liliya's trembling. "When find him-"

"Will handle personally," Viktor finished. "As should be."

Moved to bench, muscles burning from workout but mind clearer. "Gala plans set?"

"*Da*. Security in place. Dmitri will be there - invitation already accepted." Viktor's lips curved slightly. "Old man too proud to refuse. Too stupid to see trap."

"And others? Families taking sides?"

"Most wait, watch. Want see how power shifts." Viktor handed me towel. "But Zaven... Dmitri desperate now. After losing shipment, losing Morozov's support. Makes him dangerous."

"Good." Wiped sweat from face, remembering Morozov's broken body. "Let him be desperate. Let him make mistakes. Then at Gala, show all families what happens to those who challenge *vor*'s power."

"And Liliya? She part of plan?"

"*Net*." Voice turned sharp. "She there as my woman, nothing more. Keep her away from business side. Safe."

"May not have choice," Viktor said carefully. "She already part of this, whether want or not."

"She distracts without knowing." Stood, muscles coiled with tension. "All eyes on *vor* presenting woman at Gala. Dmitri's men watching her, watching me..."

"While our men hit every warehouse, every operation he has." Viktor nodded. "Perfect cover. No one expect attack during such traditional event."

"But she stay innocent of plan." The memory of her sleeping in my bed, trusting me, made voice harder. "Just need her be herself. Be woman who caught *vor*'s eye. Rest..." Let dangerous smile touch lips. "Rest we handle."

"And after?" Viktor asked. "When Dmitri's empire burns, when Jack dealt with... what then?"

Paused at door, remembering how she'd traced my scars in darkness. How she'd asked to learn fight instead of just seeking protection. "Then show Petersburg what real power looks like. *Vor* with woman strong enough to stand beside him." Couldn't resist adding, "Though perhaps need find you proper woman too. Unless already found in guest suite last night?"

Viktor's face remained impassive, but something like amusement flickered in his eyes. "Perhaps both find what not know were seeking."

Door burst open, Sergei breathing hard. "Zaven. Found rat. Alexi - caught him trying access your private office."

Everything in me went cold, lethal. The *vor* Liliya never fully seen emerging like blade from sheath. "Where?"

"Main hall. On knees waiting."

Didn't bother with shirt, let them see *vor*'s marks, let them see violence written on skin. Each step down marble hallway echoed with promised violence. Servants scattered at sight of approaching storm, disappearing into side rooms, eyes averted. They knew better than to witness what was coming.

Grand staircase stretched before us, morning sun streaming through high windows, catching dust motes like falling snow. Perfect stage for what about to happen. Viktor fell into step beside me, silent but ready. Sergei two steps behind, predator's grace in every movement.

Main hall emptied quickly at our approach, last maid slipping through side door with frightened glance. Could hear Alexi's panicked breathing echo off marble. Blood drops on white marble from his split lip made pattern like modern art.

He knelt between Yuri and Nikolai, their hands heavy on his shoulders. Expensive suit now wrinkled, torn. Had tried dress like *vor*'s men, play at belonging. That just made it worse.

"So." Voice came out like ice. "Boy who thinks can spy in my house. Can put my woman in danger."

His eyes went wide seeing me approach, bare-chested, still sweating from workout. More animal than man in this moment. More *vor* than lover who'd held Liliya hours ago.

"Please," he started, blood bubbling from split lip. "Can explain-"

"*Net.*" Cut him off with single word. "Only thing you explain is what told Dmitri. What told Jack."

Circled him slowly, letting fear build. This was how power maintained - through spectacle, through consequence.

"Thought could play in *vor*'s world?" My hand shot out, gripping his hair, yanking head back. "Thought could betray man who gave you place here?"

"Was just... just messages," he choked out. "About routines, schedules. Didn't know about Jack-"

Crack of my fist meeting his jaw echoed off marble. Not wild punch - controlled, precise. Meant to hurt, not end too quickly.

"*Pizdish, suka!*" [You're lying, bitch!] Voice dropped lower, more dangerous. "Lie to me again, see what happens."

Viktor moved forward, handed me something. Alexi's eyes went wide seeing his own phone. "Found this. Messages to number in America. To Jack."

Another strike, this one driving him fully to marble floor. "Still want claim not know about him? *Yebat!*" [Fuck!]

Blood pooled under his face as he sputtered. "Dmitri... Dmitri said needed inside man. Said big plans for Gala, for Petersburg. Just wanted be player, be somebody-"

Grabbed his throat, lifted him partially off floor. "You nothing. Less than nothing." Slammed him back down. "Now tell everything about Dmitri's plans. Every fucking detail. Or next hour become very unpleasant."

"Dmitri..." he gasped, blood staining perfect white marble. "Has men inside Hermitage already. Service staff, security. Plans to-"

My bare foot drove into his ribs, cutting off words with sharp crack. "Not interested in what planning. Want names. Every person involved."

Started listing them, each name bought with another blow. Each piece of information extracted with precision. This wasn't rage like with Morozov - this was calculation. Cold. Professional.

"And Jack?" Grabbed his hair again, forced him to look up. "What told him about Liliya?"

"Her schedule," blood sprayed as he coughed. "When she leave house. Which guards with her. But didn't know he would-"

Something snapped inside me. Next few moments lost in red haze of violence. When vision cleared, Viktor's hand rested on my shoulder. Warning. Reminder needed him alive for now.

"Please," Alexi wheezed through broken teeth. "Was just business. Just trying to-"

"Business?" Let him see death in eyes. "Let explain business to you, *ty mudak*." [you asshole]

"Zaven?"

Her voice cut through blood-haze like knife. Turned to see Liliya frozen at bottom of stairs, Natasha's hand gripping her arm. Both women's faces pale at scene before them - blood on marble, Alexi's broken form, *vor* standing shirtless and bloody in morning sun.

Something shifted in chest, seeing fear flash across Liliya's face. Not of Alexi, of mess he'd become. Of me. Of what I was capable of doing.

"Take him downstairs," ordered without looking away from her. "Will finish discussion later."

Yuri and Nikolai dragged Alexi's limp form away, leaving trail of red across white floor. Silence hung heavy as marble, thick with violence just witnessed.

"Liliya-" Started toward her but she stepped back, Natasha's grip tightening on her arm.

"I... we were just..." Her voice trembled, eyes fixed on blood pooling on marble.

Viktor moved smoothly between us. "Perhaps better if ladies return upstairs. Staff will bring fresh tea."

But something in her expression shifted, steel entering her spine as she looked at me. Not just fear in those green eyes - understanding. Recognition of what my world truly meant. What I truly was.

"*Net.*" Found myself saying. "Stay. Need understand this part too. Need see all of what chose."

"Zaven," Viktor warned quietly.

"This man," continued, gesturing at blood trail, "betrayed trust. Gave information to enemies. To Jack." Let her see truth of it, harsh as it was. "In our world, betrayal has price."

"He... he told Jack where to find me?" Her voice steady despite pallor.

"*Da.* Watched you, reported movements." Fought urge to go to her, to soften this somehow. But she needed to see, to understand. "This is *vor*'s world, Liliya. Not always beautiful. Not always gentle."

She started to say something else, but her eyes caught on my blood-streaked knuckles. She turned away sharply, one hand pressed to mouth.

"Perhaps tea upstairs better idea," Natasha said softly, arm going around Liliya's shoulders. But she paused, looking back at me with knowing eyes. "She understand, *vor*. Just need time. Is different - knowing about violence, seeing it with own eyes."

As Natasha guided Liliya up the stairs, she caught Viktor's gaze, something passing between them that spoke of their night together. The way his posture softened slightly at her silent communication betrayed more than any words could.

"Your tigress has good instincts," I murmured to Viktor as we watched them climb the stairs. "Knows when to retreat, when to advance."

"*Da,*" he responded, voice low. "More than just beauty and fire. Has wisdom too."

Watched them climb stairs, every muscle screaming to follow, to explain. But sometimes understanding came with distance. With time to process what it meant to be *vor*'s woman.

Found them in solarium, winter sun casting warmth through glass dome above. Liliya sat curled in window seat, Natasha beside her speaking soft Russian. Both looked up as entered, now cleaned and dressed properly.

Met Natasha's eyes, gave slight nod. She squeezed Liliya's hand before rising gracefully. "Will be in library if need me, *devochka*."

As she passed, heard her murmur to Viktor who waited by door, "Perhaps check on me later, *da*? Have much to discuss about... security arrangements."

His face remained professional, but incline of head more personal than usual. "Will find you."

Silence stretched after door closed. Liliya's eyes followed snow falling beyond glass, wouldn't quite look at me.

"Think can hide you from this?" Voice came out harder than intended, anger at situation bleeding through. "From what *vor* must do? Man betrayed us. Put you in danger. Told Jack-"

Cut off, pacing length of solarium. "This is my world, Liliya. Violence, power, consequences. Cannot pretend otherwise."

She remained quiet, fingers tracing patterns on glass like drawing those little faces she left everywhere. Let me work through rage still simmering.

"Protect what mine. Always. By whatever means necessary. If that makes you fear me-"

"Not frightened of you," she finally spoke, voice soft but firm. "Understand why... what had to be done. But not in our home. Not where we sleep, where we eat. Not here."

Our home. Words hit like physical force. Pride mixed with something deeper - she claimed this place, claimed right to have say in it.

Moved toward her, hand reaching out. The slight flinch stopped me cold.

"Still see blood," she whispered, wrapping arms around herself. "Know you're clean now, but..."

Dropped hand back to side. "Cannot always keep business separate from home. Nature of what I am-"

"You're *vor* everywhere," she said, finally meeting my eyes. "Know this. Accept this. But this house... what we're building here..." She took shaky breath. "Need one place that's just ours. Where violence doesn't touch."

Understanding dawned. Not asking me to be different man. Asking for sanctuary.

"Some men build empires of fear, others of money," I said, voice low. "True power lies in creating a space where even the most feared man in Petersburg can remove his armor. Only a woman of real strength can offer that gift."

She looked up at me then, surprise in her eyes at my words.

"Can try," I continued carefully. "But Liliya, when threats come-"

"Then handle them. But not in great hall. Not where I have breakfast with Natasha, where staff brings tea, where..." Her voice caught. "Where we sleep."

Studied her for long moment. Still wouldn't let me touch her, but steel returning to spine. My brave, complicated woman - wanting both safety of *vor*'s protection and peace within these walls.

"Will renovate basement," decided. "Proper place for dealing with problems. Away from main house."

Something in her shoulders relaxed slightly. "Thank you."

"But Liliya," moved closer, needing her understand. "Gala different story. Will be dangerous. Enemies watching, waiting. Need you prepared."

"Because of Dmitri?" Finally looked up at me fully.

"*Da*. Will be there, other families too. All watching, measuring worth of *vor*'s woman." Left out darker parts of plans, need to keep her innocent of that. "Must stay close to me, to Viktor. Follow every instruction without question."

"Like being locked in house now?" Hint of challenge in voice that made pride swell despite situation.

"*Net*. Like trusting *vor* knows best way keep you safe." Risked reaching for her again. This time, she didn't flinch from my touch. "Cannot lose you, Liliya. Not to Jack, not to Dmitri, not to anyone."

Let my fingers trace her jaw, relief flooding through me when she leaned into touch. "Will do better about keeping business separate," promised softly. "But need you understand - at Gala, cannot hide ugliness of this world. Will be there, just beneath surface."

"I know." Her hand came up to cover mine. "Just... need time. To reconcile the different sides of you." She swallowed hard. "And you need to make this up to me."

Tension eased slightly at unexpected words. "Make up to you?"

A small smile touched her lips, surprising both of us. "*Da*. By letting me choose whatever dress I want for Gala. No matter how much costs."

Despite everything, felt corner of mouth lift. "Expensive apology."

"Blood on marble floors deserves expensive apology," she countered, spark returning to eyes. "Diamond earrings too, perhaps?"

"Already negotiating like true *vor*'s woman," I murmured, relief flooding through me at this glimpse of her resilience.

She rose on tiptoes, pressed soft kiss to corner of my mouth. "I know who you are, Zaven. All of you. And I'm yours. *Vor* and man."

But as held her close, knew darker truth. Gala would test everything – her trust, my control, our world. Enemies waited in shadows, thinking *vor* weak for loving her.

Would show them exactly opposite. Love made *vor* more dangerous. More lethal. More willing to burn world to keep her safe.

38

Liliya

The car's interior wrapped us in leather-scented quiet, city lights bleeding past tinted windows as we made our way to the Hermitage. My emerald silk gown whispered against the seats, diamonds at my throat catching the intermittent glow from passing streetlights. Zaven's hand found mine in the darkness, his thumb tracing familiar patterns on my skin.

Three days since blood stained the marble floors of our home. Three days of tense preparation for tonight. Three days of trying to reconcile the gentle man who held me at night with the *vor* who'd extracted information with brutal efficiency.

"Stop fidgeting," Natasha scolded from across the limo. "Will wrinkle silk. Though *vor* probably not mind - way he look at you lately, could wear sack and still make him crazy."

I couldn't help but smile at her, grateful for her presence tonight. In her midnight blue gown and expertly applied makeup, she looked every bit the sophisticated Russian beauty. But I knew the slight bulge in her small purse was the weapon Viktor had insisted she carry. My own clutch felt heavier with similar protection.

"You ready for this?" Natasha asked, more serious now. "First time being presented as *vor*'s woman. Many eyes watching tonight."

"Not just watching," I said softly, remembering Zaven's warnings. "Waiting. Looking for weakness."

"Bah," Natasha waved dismissively, but I caught the tension in her shoulders. "Let them look. You survived Jack, survived seeing *vor*'s darker side. Tonight?" She grinned wickedly. "Tonight we show them what American girls made of."

"So, Viktor," she continued, shifting her attention across the seat. "Tell truth - you practice that scary face in mirror every morning, or just natural talent?"

I bit back a smile as Viktor's stoic expression flickered slightly.

"Maybe smile just once tonight?" she pressed, undeterred. "For me? Promise won't tell anyone, ruin reputation."

"Natasha," Viktor's voice carried warning, but something else too. Something that made Zaven's lips twitch beside me.

"Fine, fine," she sighed dramatically. "Keep mysterious brooding look. But know this - by end of night, will make you dance."

The quiet laugh that escaped me earned a squeeze of Zaven's hand. When I looked up, I caught flash of tenderness beneath *vor*'s mask. Reminder that despite dangers ahead, despite everything we'd seen and learned about each other this week, something deeper had grown between us.

"Remember," he said softly, voice carrying edge of authority now. "Stay close. Always in sight of me or Viktor."

"Or me," Natasha added, suddenly serious. "Though probably safer with Viktor. Man built like tank."

That earned actual snort from Viktor, making Natasha's eyes light up triumphantly. "Ah! Almost got sound of amusement. Night still young."

But levity faded as our convoy slowed. Through windows, I could see flash of cameras, crowd of Petersburg's elite flowing up marble steps. Zaven's thumb traced my knuckles one last time before *vor*'s mask fully settled.

"Ready?" he asked, though we both knew wasn't really question.

I nodded, squaring shoulders. Tonight wasn't just about being seen. Was about showing strength. Proving *vor*'s woman could handle this world - beauty and violence both.

As we emerged from car's warmth into biting winter air, cameras flashed like lightning. Zaven's hand settled possessively at my waist, guiding me up marble steps. I could feel weight of watching eyes - some curious, some calculating, some hostile.

The Hermitage's grand entrance opened before us, golden light spilling onto snow. Inside, warmth and music wrapped around us as attendants moved to take our coats. Zaven's fingers brushed my neck as he helped with my fur, touch lingering just long enough to send shiver down spine.

"*Bozhe moy*," Natasha breathed beside me, taking in opulent scene. "Now this is party." She cast sideways glance at Viktor. "Perfect for dancing, don't you think?"

But any response was cut off by approach of first well-wishers - Petersburg's elite coming to pay respects to *vor*. I watched how they moved around Zaven, like moons orbiting dangerous star. Each interaction carried weight of politics, of power plays I was only beginning to understand.

"Zaven Alexeyevich," a man's voice cut through crowd, making Zaven's posture shift subtly. I turned to see older man approaching, smile not reaching cold eyes. "And this must be American girl everyone talks about."

"Mikhail Petrovich," Zaven's voice carried carefully measured respect. "Good see you well."

Those cold eyes assessed me like buyer studying horse at market. "So this is one who make *vor* break tradition. Must be... special."

I felt Zaven tense beside me, but kept smile fixed on face. Remembered his warnings about tonight, about showing any weakness.

"Traditions change," I said, voice steadier than expected. "Like Russia herself, *da*?"

Surprise flickered across old man's face before he laughed - harsh sound that drew attention from nearby guests. "She has spirit, this one. Maybe understand better now, Zaven Alexeyevich."

"Oh, you have no idea," Natasha chimed in, champagne appearing magically in her hand. "Should see her handle *vor*'s household. Even Irina impressed."

Strategic mention of respected housekeeper seemed to carry weight. Man's expression shifted slightly.

"Perhaps dance later?" he asked, but looking at Zaven not me. Still treating me as *vor*'s possession, not partner.

"Perhaps," Zaven replied smoothly. "But first, must greet other guests."

Zaven guided me through crowd, each step carefully orchestrated. I noticed how his men had spread through room - Sergei near bar, Yuri by main entrance, others positioned strategically. Even in this glittering setting, danger lurked.

The grand ballroom took my breath away - crystal chandeliers casting rainbow light across marble floors, gilt mirrors multiplying candlelight into infinity. But beneath beauty, I caught undercurrents. The way certain groups clustered together, whispering. How conversations stopped as we passed.

"Your Russian better," Zaven murmured as we moved between clusters of guests. "Sound more natural now."

"Good teacher," I squeezed his arm lightly. Though wasn't just him - living in house, hearing language daily, had helped. I even caught myself thinking in Russian sometimes.

Natasha kept close behind with Viktor, her constant commentary about guests' fashion choices making his lip twitch occasionally. Her presence helped ease tension, reminded me not everything here was threat or power play.

But then I caught sight of man across room - tall, distinguished, radiating authority that reminded me of Zaven. The way crowd parted for him... "That's him, isn't it?" I whispered. "Dmitri?"

Zaven's fingers flexed slightly at my waist. "*Da*. Remember what told you - do not engage if approaches. Let me handle."

I studied the man who'd caused such tension in house lately. Who'd worked with Jack somehow. Despite silver at temples, he carried himself like fighter. His eyes met mine across room - calculating, cold. He lifted his glass in mock salute that made Zaven's jaw tighten.

"Ah, look," Natasha's voice cut through tension deliberately. "String quartet setting up. Perfect time for dance, no?" She turned hopeful eyes to Viktor.

"Need watch room," he replied, but something softened in his expression.

"Can watch while dancing," she insisted. "Better view from floor, *da?*"

Before Viktor could protest again, Zaven pulled me closer. "Dance with me," he murmured, leading me onto floor. Message clear to watching crowd - *vor* choosing his woman first, politics could wait.

His hand settled warm at my waist, other clasping mine as we moved to music. Despite dangers lurking, despite Dmitri's cold eyes following us, I felt safe in his arms.

"Doing well tonight," he said softly, just for me. "Proud way you handle yourself."

"Starting to understand," I leaned closer, breathing in his familiar scent. "This world of yours. Though still scared sometimes."

"Good." His thumb traced patterns on my back. "Fear keep you alert. Keep you alive. But you stronger than think."

I caught movement that made me smile - Natasha had finally worn Viktor down. More surprising was actual grin on his face as she said something in his ear.

"Look," I nodded toward them. "She finally did it."

Zaven's chest rumbled with quiet laugh. "Poor man never stood chance."

As music faded, Zaven guided me toward bar, his hand never leaving my waist. The brief peace of our dance dissolved as reality of night settled back in. I caught Dmitri watching our approach, timing his own movement to intercept.

"Think I need champagne," announced Natasha, appearing beside us with still-smiling Viktor. Her attempt to lighten mood cut short as Dmitri reached us.

"Zaven," his voice carried false warmth. "Been too long."

"Not long enough," Zaven replied coolly, fingers tightening slightly at my waist.

Dmitri's gaze shifted to me, assessment in his eyes making my skin crawl. "Ah, Liliya Nikolaevna. Finally meet *vor*'s chosen woman properly."

"Beautiful night for Gala," Zaven replied smoothly, though I felt tension in his body. "Museum outdid itself this year."

"*Da*, very beautiful." Dmitri's smile didn't reach his eyes. "Though hear interesting rumors about recent... business developments. Perhaps moment to discuss?”

The shift was subtle but immediate. I felt temperature around us drop several degrees as Zaven's public mask hardened into something more dangerous.

Before either could continue, rustle of silk and expensive perfume surrounded us. Group of women approached, diamonds glittering like armor, smiles sharp as knives.

Zaven's fingers pressed gently at my waist - silent instruction we'd discussed. I caught Natasha's slight nod as she moved closer to my side.

“Go,” he murmured, eyes now fixed on Dmitri. “Will find you after handle this.”

“Liliya, darling,” one of the women cooed, voice dripping honey-sweet venom. “We've been dying to meet you properly.”

I stepped away with Natasha at my side, feeling weight of Zaven's gaze follow us. Through crowd, I caught glimpse of his face - all trace of warmth replaced by *vor*'s cold mask as he turned back to Dmitri.

“Liliya, darling,” the blonde in red silk repeated, drawing my attention back. “I'm Anastasia. We simply must chat. Been so curious about *vor*'s American...”

“Woman,” Natasha cut in smoothly. “*Vor*'s woman. Though suppose hard keep up with changes when spend so much time chasing rich husbands, *da*?”

Anastasia's perfect smile faltered. Others shifted like sharks scenting blood.

“Only meant,” another stepped forward, diamonds catching light as she moved, “must be quite adjustment. Our world so... different from what used to.”

Their circle tightened subtly, predatory grace in every movement. But I remembered Zaven's training, his faith in me. I straightened my spine, met their eyes directly.

“Different, yes,” I kept my voice steady. “But I've found exactly where I belong.”

"Have you?" Anastasia's eyes glinted. "Must say, quite bold choice - emerald. Though perhaps trying bit too hard to fit Russian tastes?"

"Speaking of trying hard," another stepped closer, voice honey-sweet poison. "Your Russian improving. Still charming little accent though. Zaven always did have soft spot for... exotic things."

"Tell us," green silk rustled as third woman moved in, "how does American girl end up catching *vor*'s eye? Must have special... talents."

My heart thumped but I kept my face neutral, remembered way Zaven handled verbal attacks. Let them see only what I wanted them to see.

"Careful," Natasha's voice carried edge of warning. "Some questions better left unasked in our world."

"Only being friendly," Anastasia's smile sharpened. "After all, we've known Zaven so long. Just want make sure he's... properly taken care of."

"Properly taken care of?" I let a smile touch my lips, one learned from watching the *vor*. "Sweet of you to worry. Though it seems Zaven made his choice clear enough."

"Choices can change," Anastasia leaned closer, perfume cloying. "Men like Zaven... they enjoy new things for a time. Then remember where they truly belong."

"With proper Russian family," green silk added. "Traditional values. You understand, of course."

"Oh, she understands plenty," Natasha cut in, champagne glass appearing in hand. "Understands exactly what Zaven needs. Why else think he chose her over... what was it, Anastasia? Three times you threw yourself at him?"

Color flooded Anastasia's cheeks. Others shifted, sensing change in power dynamic.

"But then," I said softly, holding her gaze, "I suppose it's hard to keep track of rejections when you spend so much time chasing the *vor*'s attention."

Something flashed in Anastasia's eyes – recognition that I wasn't just decoration on Zaven's arm. That the *vor* had chosen a woman with teeth and claws of her own.

"Come," Natasha linked her arm through mine, turning us away before they could respond. "Need freshen makeup anyway."

The walk to ladies' room felt endless, silk skirts whispering against marble floors. Only once the door closed behind us did my hands start shaking. I gripped the cool marble counter, staring at my reflection.

"That was…" my breath came shaky.

"That was brilliant," Natasha grinned, checking her lipstick. "Did you see their faces? Especially Anastasia - looked like swallowed lemon."

But triumph of standing up to them mixed with something else. Understanding of what it really meant to be *vor*'s woman. Wasn't just about beautiful dresses and grand parties. Was about navigating these shark-infested waters, about being strong enough to handle both violence and venom.

"Hey," Natasha's hand squeezed my shoulder. "You did good. Showed them exactly who you are - woman worthy of *vor*."

"Still feel like shaking," I admitted quietly.

"Good. Means you human. Now fix lipstick, hold head high, and-"

I leaned toward the mirror, red lipstick in hand. The bathroom's warm lighting softened my reflection as I steadied my still-trembling fingers. The door behind us opened with deliberate slowness, the sound making my gaze flick upward.

In the mirror's reflection, I saw a face I'd prayed never to see again.

Jack filled the door frame , his familiar shape sending ice through my veins. Our eyes met in the mirror before I could turn. His face – once loved, then feared – looked exactly the same, right down to that small scar above his eyebrow. Behind him, shadows moved - more men.

"Hello, Lily-pad."

That nickname froze me in place, lipstick clutched forgotten in my fingers. In the mirror, I watched his smile spread – the same one that had once meant pain would follow.

That nickname, once sweet, now twisted my stomach. Bile rose in my throat as memories flooded back - his hands, his rage, his control.

"How-" Natasha started forward, but stopped as metal glinted in low light.

"Ah ah," Jack's smile hadn't changed. Still held that edge of cruelty I'd tried so hard to forget. "Let's keep this civil. Just need have chat with my girl."

"Not yours." My voice came stronger than I felt, even as my heart hammered against my ribs. "Not anymore."

His laugh, short and sharp, echoed off marble. "Still think that's your choice?" He stepped into room, others following. "Dmitri sends regards. Says *vor*'s woman worth quite price."

The door closed with heavy click behind them. Four men total, including Jack. One moved toward Natasha as she reached for her purse, his boots scraping marble floor. Her perfume mixed with their sweat and gun oil, making my stomach turn.

"Careful," he warned in thick accent, meaty hand grabbing her arm. She fought like tiger, heel connecting with his shin, elbow driving back until second man caught her from behind. The crack of his fist meeting her face echoed off tile.

"Feisty friends you've made," Jack's eyes never left mine, that familiar gleam making my blood run cold. "New life treating you well? Playing mob princess in stolen diamonds?"

"Leave her alone," my voice shook watching blood trickle from Natasha's split lip. "Your problem with me."

"See, that's where you're wrong." He moved closer, cologne I used to love now making bile rise. "This is about a much bigger game. Though," his hand shot out, fingers bruising my jaw, "getting you back is just a bonus. Maybe I'll teach you a lesson about running first."

Behind him, Natasha's Russian curses cut off as cloth pressed over her face. Her designer heels scraped marble as her struggles weakened.

"Remember this?" Jack's grip tightened, other hand tracing the emerald silk at my waist. "How easily you bruise? How pretty you look when you're scared?"

I tried to pull away but my back hit cold marble wall. His body pressed closer, trapping me like he'd done countless times before. But something different stirred beneath terror now - rage. I remembered Zaven's lessons in the gym, his faith in my strength.

"Won't get far," I managed through clenched teeth. "Zaven will-"

His laugh cut sharp. "Your *vor* is a bit occupied at the moment. Dmitri is making sure of that." His fingers twisted in my hair, yanking my head back. "Now, it's time to go home, Lily-pad. Unless you want your friend here to suffer more."

Natasha lay too still on the floor now, blood marring blue silk. One man lifted her limp form while another produced cloth reeking of chemicals.

"Last time I'm doing this the nice way," Jack's breath hot against my ear. "I always did like when you made things difficult."

The chemical-soaked cloth moved toward my face. In that moment, time slowed - I saw Natasha's unconscious form already being carried toward the door, saw Jack's cruel smile, saw all the progress I'd made about to shatter.

I thought of Zaven - his strength, his faith in me. Thought of watching him handle betrayal in the main hall. Thought of the diamond necklace that felt like armor.

"*Net*," the word came out stronger than I ever had with Jack. I started to bring my knee up like Zaven taught, but the cloth pressed hard over my nose and mouth. Sweetness filled my lungs as the room began to spin.

The last thing I saw was Jack's triumphant grin as darkness crept in. My last thought before the world went black wasn't of fear - it was of Zaven, and how the city would burn when he discovered we were gone.

39

Zaven

Watched Dmitri's retreating back, tension coiling in muscles. Every instinct screamed to end him here, but business required patience. Politics required restraint. Turned to scan crowd for flash of emerald silk, for Liliya's auburn hair.

Nothing.

Unease crept up spine as eyes swept ballroom again. No sign of midnight blue either - Natasha's presence usually impossible to miss.

"Viktor," voice came out sharp. Second-in-command materialized at shoulder.

"How long since saw them with group of women?"

Viktor's expression shifted slightly. "Twenty minutes, maybe more. Thought returned to you."

Ice formed in veins. Too long. Even with Natasha's social nature, too long to be just chatting.

"Find them. Now."

"Checking with security teams now," Viktor already had phone to ear. "Yuri positioned near ladies' room, Sergei at main entrance."

Kept outward appearance calm as moved through crowd. Years of practice made it easy to maintain *vor's* mask while every instinct screamed danger. Something felt wrong. Terribly wrong.

Nikolai pushed through crowd, face tight with concern. "Boss. Those women - Anastasia's group. Say Liliya and Natasha left them nearly half hour ago. Headed to powder room."

Too long. Far too long.

Viktor returned, expression grim. "Zaven." Just my name - not 'Boss' - telling me already what he'd found. His hand extended, holding something that made blood freeze. Liliya's diamond necklace - clasp broken, few drops of red staining delicate stones.

Something primal ruptured inside chest. Room tilted for fraction of second before control slammed back. But not before Viktor saw it - the flash of raw terror that hadn't touched me since boyhood.

"*Yebat*!" The curse escaped through clenched teeth, barely audible but carrying weight of avalanche. "Lock down venue. Every fucking exit. No one leaves. Want every camera, every corner searched. Now."

Turned back to crowd, scanning faces with new purpose. Caught sight of Dmitri near bar, that same smug smile playing at lips. He lifted glass in mocking salute.

Red filled vision. Not hot rage - something colder, deadlier. The kind of fury that didn't cloud judgment but sharpened it to knife's edge. Every muscle vibrated with need to cross room, to wrap hands around Dmitri's throat until that smug smile disappeared forever.

Heart slammed against ribs, not from fear but from primal need for violence. For blood. For vengeance. These people took what was mine. Took my Liliya. Would make them beg for death before this night ended.

But *vor's* control won out. Couldn't give him satisfaction of public scene. Not yet. Not when Liliya and Natasha's safety hung in balance.

"Viktor." Name came out like command. "Get team to ladies' room. Want every detail. Every scent, every mark. Need know exactly what happened."

"Already called in more men," Viktor's voice equally controlled, but saw muscle jumping in jaw. His own rage barely contained. Natasha meant something to him too. Personal now for both of us. "Sergei securing exits. Yuri checking security footage."

Moved through crowd with deadly grace, guests instinctively stepping aside. Could feel Dmitri watching, waiting for reaction. Playing his game.

"And Viktor?" Paused, letting ice fill voice. "When find who responsible… want them alive. Need have conversation about consequences of touching what mine."

The ladies' room screamed wealth - marble and crystal mocking signs of violence beneath. Broken heel from Natasha's designer shoe. Smudge of red against white tile that matched shade of Liliya's lipstick. Air still held trace of chemicals that made jaw clench.

Fingers traced red smear on wall. Her lipstick. Her blood. Both sacred. Both desecrated by these *mudaks*. Chest tightened until breathing became conscious effort.

"Found this," Yuri approached, holding delicate purse. Natasha's - clasp broken, contents scattered. "Security feed shows gap. Someone professional."

Crouched to examine marks on floor. Scuff from expensive shoes - men's size. Multiple sets. Not just random attack - coordinated team.

Every mark on marble told story that made blood simmer. Drag marks where Natasha fought. Splash of water where Liliya must have thrown something at attackers. The faint smell of chloroform lingering in air.

"Four, maybe five men," noted patterns of struggle. Pride mixed with rage seeing evidence they'd fought back. "Professionals, but needed numbers. Means not expect easy grab."

The evidence painted clear picture. Professional job. Planned. My women hadn't gone easy - pride mixed with rage at signs of their struggle.

Straightened slowly, every muscle coiled with lethal purpose. "Find out how they got in, got out." Voice barely recognizable through ice forming in chest. "Want every detail."

Started for door but Viktor's hand caught arm. His own control slipping - saw it in whitened knuckles, in tremor of fingers against sleeve.

"Will find them," his voice dropped low, accent thicker with emotion rarely shown. "Will make these *svolochi* pay. But need be smart now. For them."

Our eyes locked in shared understanding. For first time in years, saw naked emotion in Viktor's gaze - same murderous rage burning in own chest. Natasha had become more than security assignment to him. Much more.

He nodded once, composure returning but eyes still hard as diamonds. "*Da*. Family." Single word holding weight of all left unsaid between us.

Returned to ballroom with deadlier purpose. Crowds sensed danger, shifted away like prey from predator. Found Dmitri still at bar, playing at casual indifference while my world burned.

"Where are they?" Voice came out deadly quiet.

"Ah, Zaven." Dmitri turned, false warmth not reaching eyes. "Something wrong? You seem... tense."

Had to physically stop hand from reaching for his throat. Thought of Liliya, of Natasha, kept voice controlled. Barely.

"No games." Stepped closer, invading space. "Where are they?"

"They?" Eyebrows raised in mock confusion. "Afraid don't know what–"

Grip on his arm cut off words. Around us, conversation died. Music faltered. Could feel eyes of Petersburg's elite watching drama unfold.

"Boss," Viktor's warning came low. "Ladies present. Need keep calm."

"Return them." Each word carved from ice. "Now. Or will rain hell down on everything you hold dear."

Dmitri's mask slipped, hint of smirk playing at lips. "Such accusations, Zaven. And in front of all these witnesses. What would *gubernator* think?"

Felt muscle in jaw twitch. "Think I care about appearances?" Let hint of violence show through *vor's* mask. "Will burn this entire city to find them."

"Zaven, please," Viktor's grip tightened on shoulder. Warning. Reminder of where we were. Who watched.

But Dmitri's eyes held something that made blood run cold. Satisfaction. Like piece in game just moved exactly where wanted.

"Perhaps," he said softly, adjusting sleeve where my grip had wrinkled fabric, "you should check with security team. Sure your... women just stepped out for air."

Something in his tone - the way he said "women" - made vision darken at edges. Leaned close, let death show in smile.

"Have until midnight. After that..." Let threat hang between us. "Will take apart everything you built. Piece by bloody piece."

His answering smile made rage crystallize into something darker. "Careful, *mladshiy vor*," voice dropped so only I could hear. "Threats dangerous when don't hold all cards. Especially when cards so... delicate."

Caught his wrist in grip that made bones grind. "There are two kinds of men in this world, Dmitri," voice dropped to whisper only he could hear. "Those who know when game lost, and those who die still holding cards. Tonight—you decide which you are."

Every muscle screamed to end him here. Instead, pulled back slowly. "Midnight," let promise of violence fill word. "Then find out exactly how much willing lose."

Viktor's hand steadied at shoulder as turned away. Couldn't afford scene here. Not with Liliya and Natasha's safety at stake. Time for that would come.

Private room at *Zolotoy Vek* hummed with lethal energy. Had shed formal wear - jacket, tie gone, sleeves rolled to show *vor's* marks. No more playing at society games.

"Status," barked at assembled men. Yuri's team watching Dmitri's properties. Sergei's men combing recent acquisitions. Others tracking every vehicle left Hermitage.

For brief moment, alone with my thoughts, mask slipped. Ran fingers over Liliya's broken necklace, still stained with her blood. Memory of her face, her smile, her body pressed against mine hit like physical blow. Had promised to protect her. Had failed.

The fear that gripped chest wasn't *vor's* strategic concern - was man's terror for woman he couldn't bear to lose. Not after finding her. Not after she'd seen darkness and chosen to stay anyway.

Door burst open. Two guards dragged in Alexi - face already mess of bruises from earlier questioning. Threw him to floor at my feet. Mask snapped back in place, but something had changed. Something darker, more primal now driving actions.

"Time finish our talk," crouched to his level, let him see death in eyes. "Tell everything know about Dmitri's plans. Every detail. Or make what did to you before seem gentle."

Viktor moved forward with black bag, contents clinking with familiar promise. Alexi's good eye darted between us, sweat beading despite room's chill.

"Already told everything," words slurred through split lips. "Swear on mother's-"

Backhand cut off words, fresh blood spraying marble. "Don't speak of family," voice came deadly quiet. "Not after betrayal."

Opened bag slowly, let him see tools laid out. Each one chosen carefully. Each one promising different kind of pain. Different path to truth.

"Now," selected pliers that gleamed in harsh light. "Tell about Dmitri's plan for Gala. Every detail missed first time. Starting with who helped take my women."

Alexi's eye widened at sight of metal. "Please... I don't-"

Grabbed his hand, positioned pliers under fingernail. "Wrong answer."

His scream echoed off walls as first nail came free. Let him feel pain, let it sink in that this just beginning. But this wasn't *vor's* calculated violence now - this was man's rage, barely controlled, seeking outlet.

"Think careful about next words," wiped blood from pliers on Alexi's expensive suit jacket. "Have nine more chances to start telling truth."

"I swear," he sobbed, cradling mangled hand. "Only knew about distracting you. About keeping eyes away from certain exits. Didn't know they would take-"

Second nail cut off words with fresh howl. "Lying," studied his face through pain. "Know more. See it in eyes."

Viktor moved closer, voice carrying edge rarely heard. "Tell him. Or next hour become very unpleasant."

"There's... there's warehouse," words tumbled out between gasps. "Near old port. Where kept missing shipment. Heard Dmitri mention safe room there. Built special for... for holding someone."

Exchanged look with Viktor. Information clicked into place - warehouse, safe room, missing shipment. Pieces of puzzle suddenly aligned.

"Address."

"Please," Alexi begged as finished listing details - security rotations, guard numbers, access points. "Told everything now. Will disappear, never show face in Petersburg again. Spare me?"

Drew pistol from holster, movement smooth as silk. "*Net.*"

Single shot echoed through room. Didn't watch body fall - already turning to Viktor. "Get teams in position. Want eyes on warehouse within hour."

"*Da.*" Viktor already on phone. "Sergei's men can approach from water side. Yuri has blueprints of building from city records."

Spread map across table, still spotted with Alexi's blood. "Here," pointed to service entrance. "Dmitri's men expect front assault. Will be watching main gate. But if come through old loading dock..."

"Boss," Nikolai stepped forward. "What about other properties? Could be diversion."

"*Net.*" Certainty filled voice. "Know Dmitri. He want this personal. Want me know exactly where they are but be unable to reach." Let cold smile touch lips. "His mistake."

Studied map while men discussed approach. But beneath strategic planning, beneath *vor's* calculated violence, could only think of Liliya. Of her face in firelight that first night. Of green eyes meeting mine across dinner table. Of soft curves pressed against chest in darkness.

Picked up diamond necklace again, thumb tracing over bloodstain. Men around table fell silent, watching.

"In old days, when *vor* took another's woman, retribution was absolute," voice came low but carried to every corner. "Not just death - but erasure. Complete. Final. His name forgotten, his legacy dust, his blood washed from streets like common filth."

Closed fist around necklace, feeling diamonds cut into palm.

"Tonight, we honor tradition. Tonight, we remind Petersburg why *vor* is feared. Why I am feared." Looked up, meeting each man's eyes. "Not because hold territory or move product. Because when someone takes what belongs to us, what we protect... we become death itself."

Around table, saw same lethal focus mirror in men's eyes. These women weren't just *vor's* possessions - they were family. And in our world, family meant everything.

"Two hours until midnight," Viktor's voice cut through thoughts. "Need move soon."

"Then move now." Straightened, let men see *vor* ready for war. "Want every asset in place. When hit, hit hard. No mercy."

"For Liliya," Viktor said, voice steady but eyes burning. "For Natasha."

"For family," I answered, the word carrying weight beyond blood ties. "Time remind Dmitri exactly why people fear *vor*."

40

Liliya

Pain was the first thing I registered - a dull throb at the base of my skull pulsing in time with my heartbeat. The concrete floor pressed cold and rough against my cheek, gritty with dirt and what smelled like old blood. Somewhere, water dripped steadily in the darkness, each drop echoing off bare walls.

"Liliya?" Natasha's voice came weak through the shadows. "You here, *devochka?*"

I forced my heavy eyes open, immediately regretting it as harsh fluorescent light stabbed my vision. Through the spinning room, I made out Natasha's form slumped against the wall. Her midnight blue silk was torn and stained dark in places, perfect hair matted with blood at her temple.

"I'm here," I managed through my cotton-dry throat. "Are you okay?"

"Been better." Her attempt at lightness couldn't hide the pain. "Think ruined dress though. Now Viktor definitely not dance with me."

Even in this nightmare, her gallows humor made my lips twitch. But the moment shattered as the heavy metal door creaked open, bringing a blast of cold air and footsteps.

"Well, well. Look who's finally awake."

That voice. Jack's voice. Every muscle in my body locked with the memory of pain.

"Rise and shine, Lily-pad." Jack's shoes clicked against the concrete as he approached, each step making my heart hammer harder against my ribs. Behind him, two men dragged Natasha to her feet.

"Such pretty guests we have," one man sneered in thick Russian accent, fisting his hand in Natasha's hair. "Boss say we have fun while wait, da?"

"*Net*," Natasha spat blood at his feet. "Touch me, lose fingers, *mudak*."

Jack's laugh bounced off the bare walls. "You found yourself a little Russian fighter, Lily. Not like those weak little bitches you used to hang around with." His hand shot out, gripping my jaw hard enough to bruise. "Though she'll learn. Just like you will."

"Get your fucking hands off her," Natasha struggled against her captors. "When *vor* finds you–"

"Your precious Zaven isn't here," Jack's fingers dug deeper into my face. "It's just us now. Just like old times."

"Take that bitch," he nodded toward Natasha. "Show her what happens to mouthy Russian whores."

"Liliya!" Natasha fought as they dragged her toward the door. "Stay strong! Remember who you are now! Don't let this *pizdyuk* break you–"

The door slammed shut, cutting off her words. But I could still hear her cursing in Russian, the sounds of her struggle echoing down the hall.

"Now then," Jack turned back, and I recognized that cruel gleam in his eyes. The one that had always preceded the worst nights. "Just us. Like it should be."

I tried channeling the strength I'd found in Zaven's gym, but the ropes bit deep into my wrists with every movement. The emerald silk of my gown hung in tatters around me, leaving my skin exposed to the dank cold of the room.

"Nothing to say?" His fingers dug into my jaw. "You used to never shut up. Always crying about how I hurt you, how I controlled you." He leaned closer, his breath hot and sour against my face. "Now look at you. Some mobster's little whore."

Natasha's scream pierced through the walls. I flinched, and Jack's smile widened.

"Hear that? That's what happens when people don't learn their place."

His hand wrapped around my throat. "Ready to learn yours again?"

"Go fuck yourself." The words came out stronger than I felt.

The backhand was explosive, snapping my head sideways. Blood filled my mouth as fresh screams echoed from down the hall.

"Still got that smart mouth." His voice turned eerily calm - that tone that had always meant the worst was coming. "Good. I'm going to enjoy breaking you all over again."

His fist connected with my ribs, driving the air from my lungs. Before I could catch my breath, his fingers twisted in my hair, yanking my head back until my scalp burned.

"Look at me when I talk to you," he snarled, his face inches from mine. "I want to see those pretty eyes when you realize the truth - your Russian thug won't want you when I'm done. When he sees what I've done to his precious American..."

Natasha's voice carried through the walls - defiant Russian curses turning to pain-filled screams. Each sound twisted in my gut like a knife.

"Poor Natasha," Jack's mock sympathy dripped with venom. "Suffering because you couldn't just behave. Because you had to play at being strong." Another blow split my lip. "Her blood's on your hands, Lily-pad. Just like always - hurting everyone around you."

"That's bullshit," I spat blood onto his shoes, crimson spatter marking his polished leather.

His eyes went cold - that familiar glacial stare that meant someone was about to end up in the hospital. His hand closed around my throat, squeezing until black spots danced in my vision.

"Is it? Let's see how many people have to suffer before you learn." His grip loosened just enough to let me gasp for air. "Starting with your friend down the hall."

He began untying the ropes with deliberate slowness, each movement a threat. "But first, let's remind you exactly what you are. What you've always been."

The moment the last rope fell away, his polished dress shoe connected with my ribs. Pain exploded through my chest as I hit the concrete hard, trying desperately to crawl away.

"Dmitri found me," his weight pinned me down before I could move, hand fisting in my hair to slam my head back against concrete. "Told me about the American girl who'd caught Zaven's attention. Imagine my fucking surprise when it was my Lily-pad."

Through the halls, Natasha's defiant cursing turned to muffled screams.

"Missed this," Jack's hands tore at the remains of my gown, his expression turning predatory. "Missed your body. Missed showing you your place."

I twisted beneath him, fighting with everything I had despite the searing pain in my ribs. "Get off me!"

"Still pretending to fight?" His hand covered my mouth as I tried to scream. "Know what I've been thinking about since Chicago? Taking what's mine back." His free hand fumbled with his belt. "Going to remind you who you really belong to."

I bit down on his palm until I tasted blood. He jerked back with a howl, giving me the chance to drive my knee up between his legs. Not hard enough to connect fully, but enough to make him shift his weight.

"You fucking bitch!" He backhanded me across the face, splitting my lip open.

"What's wrong, Jack?" I laughed through the blood, the sound unhinged even to my own ears. "Can't get it up unless she's unconscious? Zaven never has that problem."

His face contorted with rage. "Shut your fucking mouth about him."

"Why? Jealous?" I could feel my own blood trickling down my chin but kept pushing. "Jealous he knows how to make me scream his name? That I come so hard for him I see stars?"

Jack's eyes went dark with rage. "You think that Russian piece of shit is better than me?" His hand found my throat. "After everything I did for you?"

"He's twice the man you'll ever be," I gasped through his grip. "In every way that matters."

His fist connected with my ribs again, the crack of bone audible even over my strangled cry. I curled in on myself, trying to protect my already broken ribs, but he yanked me back by my hair.

"Should have seen him at the Gala," Jack hissed, his face inches from mine. "The look on his face when his precious Li-li-ya," he drew out my name mockingly, "was gone. Dmitri said he'd never seen the great Zaven Lazarev lose control like that." His eyes darkened with cruel pleasure. "Going to make him lose control again when he sees what I've done to his little Russian whore."

Something about hearing Zaven's name in Jack's mouth ignited something in me. Through the pain of cracked ribs and split lips, through the terror that had ruled my life with Jack, something deeper took hold. Not just anger - a fierce, burning need to protect what Zaven and I had built. The realization hit hard - I loved him. Truly loved him. Not the weak, desperate love I'd thought I had for Jack, but something powerful enough to burn away fear.

"You're a fucking dead man," laughter bubbled up, surprising us both. "You think you know about violence? About control?" My lips curled into a bloody smile. "You're fucking nothing compared to him."

Jack's face contorted with rage. His hand cracked across my face, but even as fresh blood filled my mouth, I kept going.

"You're just Dmitri's little bitch," I spat red at him. "Following orders, thinking you have power. But when Zaven finds us..." I let my smile widen, felt blood stream down my chin. "He'll tear you apart piece by fucking piece."

His hands wrapped around my throat, squeezing hard enough to make black spots dance in my vision. But even as I gasped for air, I saw the flicker of doubt in his eyes. This wasn't the same girl he'd terrorized in Chicago. Every bruise, every drop of blood only proved how pathetic his violence was compared to Zaven's controlled power.

"Shut your fucking mouth!" His grip tightened, but the fear in his voice only made me want to push harder.

"What's wrong, Jack?" I choked out. "Scared? You should be. When Zaven-"

The beating that followed was brutal. Each blow meant to break not just my body, but my spirit. But with every strike, every kick, I thought of Zaven. Of the strength he saw in me. Of the love I finally understood I felt for him. Even as ribs cracked and blood ran, something inside me grew stronger.

Something in my defiance must have terrified him, because suddenly he stepped back, chest heaving. That look crossed his face - the one that meant he was about to do something unforgivable.

"Bring her in," his voice turned deadly calm. The sound of chains and locks clanking made my heart stop.

The door crashed open. They threw Natasha into the room like a broken doll. My stomach lurched at the sight of her. Her midnight blue silk hung in tatters, the skin beneath mottled purple and crimson. Blonde hair matted with blood, one eye swollen completely shut. But even through split and bleeding lips, she managed a defiant smile.

"Liliya," she crawled toward me, each movement a testament to her pain. Her bloody fingers found mine. "*Net* your fault, *devochka*. None of this your fault."

"How touching," Jack's voice dripped with mockery. He nodded to his men who ripped us apart, dragging us to our knees. His fist tangled in my hair, forcing my head back, making me watch as they yanked Natasha's head back by her matted hair.

"You think I'm weak?" His voice carried an edge I'd never heard before. Something unhinged. "Think I'm nothing?" The sound of his gun being cocked echoed through the concrete room. "Let's see how fucking strong you are now."

"Liliya, *net*-" Natasha's words cut off as they wrenched her head harder.

"You did this," Jack pressed the gun against her temple. "Your defiance. Your pride. Always consequences for disobedience, remember?"

"Jack, please," my voice broke watching the gun press against Natasha's temple. "Don't do this. I'll do anything-"

"*Net*, Liliya," Natasha's voice cut through like steel despite the blood trickling down her face. "Don't give this *mudak* what he wants." Her one good eye blazed with fury. "Be strong, like true Russian woman. Like Zaven's woman."

"Shut your fucking mouth," Jack pressed the gun harder against her skin.

"You think you scare me?" Natasha's laugh held no fear, only contempt. "You're nothing. Pathetic little man playing with real power. When *vor* finds-"

The gunshot cracked through room like thunder.

41

Zaven

The acrid scent of gunpowder and steel filled the war room as I checked my Glock for the fourth time in as many minutes. My hands, always steady when dealing death, betrayed me now with the slightest tremor. Every tick of the ornate clock on the wall echoed like a gunshot - each sound another second they suffered. Both my Liliya and Natasha - taken because I'd failed to protect what was mine.

Behind me, the wall of surveillance feeds cast blue shadows across marble floors where Alexi's blood had dried hours ago. His screams still echoed in my mind, each secret torn from him bringing us closer to this moment. But not close enough. Not fast enough.

"Zaven." Viktor's voice carried an edge I'd rarely heard in fifteen years of violence together. His usual stoic mask cracked with something I recognized - not just worry for the mission, but raw fear for Natasha. "Yuri has something."

My intelligence officer hunched over the feeds, his face ghostly in the electronic glow. Dark circles beneath his eyes betrayed sleepless hours since the Gala. Since everything went wrong. Since I'd watched Dmitri's smug smile while my world burned.

"Found thermal signatures," Yuri reported, his accent thicker with exhaustion. "North warehouse showing activity, but pattern strange." His fingers traced the screen. "Like they want us to see it. Too obvious."

"Trap," Viktor said what we all knew, his hand unconsciously checking his weapon. "Dmitri expecting us."

"Good." Ice formed in my veins - familiar cold of *vor* preparing for war. Let my hand settle on the grip of my Glock, finding comfort in its weight. "Then let's not disappoint the *mudak*." I turned to the assembled men, each face set with lethal purpose. "Move out. Ten minutes."

The next few minutes passed in practiced efficiency - tactical gear donned, weapons checked, comms tested. No words needed between men who'd fought together for years. Only the quiet sounds of preparation for war.

Three black SUVs waited in the underground garage, engines already purring with deadly promise. I watched my men load in, each movement precise despite the urgency thrumming through us all. Through tinted windows, familiar landmarks blurred past - now twisted into something darker by circumstance. No sirens, no lights - just purpose.

In the back seat, I checked my weapon one final time, the familiar weight doing nothing to calm the storm inside. The tactical gear felt too constrictive against my chest, each breath carrying the phantom scent of Liliya's perfume from the Gala. The diamonds from her broken necklace still sat in my pocket, edges sharp enough to draw blood - a reminder of promises broken.

"Five minutes," Viktor's voice came from the front seat. His knuckles white on the steering wheel betrayed what his face wouldn't show - fear for Natasha. The man who'd stood emotionless through countless battles now radiating tension that filled the vehicle's cabin.

The warehouse district rose before us, a skeleton of Soviet industry perfect against the night sky. Viktor killed the headlights two blocks out, vehicles rolling silent through shadows. We left the SUVs in a darkened alley, moving on foot through the industrial maze. The first drops of rain hit as we approached our target - sharp and cold against exposed skin, drumming against tactical gear. Perfect cover for the hunt.

"Ready," Viktor's voice barely a whisper as we took our positions at the north entrance. The rain fell harder now, drops snaking down my neck beneath the tactical gear. Each cold trail a reminder of time slipping away.

Through my scope, I spotted two guards ahead. Their cigarettes glowed in the darkness like beacons, smoke curling up into the rain. Amateur move. They weren't Dmitri's best men - probably expendable scouts meant to draw us in. My hand signaled to Sergei on my left. Three. Two. One.

We moved in perfect sync, years of violence choreographed like deadly ballet. My knife found the first guard's throat before his cigarette hit the puddle at his feet. Viktor's hand clamped over the second guard's mouth as his blade slid between ribs. We lowered the bodies silently to the wet concrete, the rain already washing away spreading crimson.

The warehouse door loomed before us, and my heart stuttered at the sight of a dark smear of blood on the handle catching the dim light. Fresh blood. Copper scent cut through the rain. Every muscle in my body screamed to rush in, to tear through walls until I found her. But the *vor*'s control won out. Had to be smart. Had to be cold.

The air inside hit like a wall - mold and copper scent of blood mixing with something else. Something chemical. Something wrong. Our boots moved silent on concrete as we cleared the first room. Flashlight beams caught empty chairs, restraints hanging loose, fresh blood spatter on the floor telling its own story of violence.

Movement ahead snapped us all to attention. Two shadows crossing the hallway. Viktor and I moved as one - his knife taking the guard from behind while I snapped the second one's neck. No time for noise. No time for mercy. Not tonight.

We moved deeper into the darkness, each room cleared methodically despite the rage burning in my chest. Down the long corridor, past empty offices filled with nothing but dust and broken dreams of Soviet industry. Until sound of voices ahead stopped us cold. Three guards, relaxed, laughing - the sound echoing obscenely through concrete halls.

Their last mistake.

Sergei took one, Viktor another. I drove my knife up under the third guard's jaw, the familiar twist cutting off his scream before it started. His body slumped, still warm, but I felt nothing. These men meant nothing. Just obstacles between me and what was mine.

"Zaven." Viktor's whisper drew me left. His flashlight beam caught something through a doorway - a flash of midnight blue silk against grey concrete. My blood turned to ice.

The metal door creaked open, sound echoing off bare walls like some horror film sound effect. And there she was. Natasha. Her body crumpled like a discarded doll, but her face... even in death, her face still held that defiance that had made her uniquely her. The silk of her Gala dress hung in tatters, dark stains telling story of her final fight.

Viktor's sharp intake of breath beside me - the first time in fifteen years I'd ever heard him show shock. He moved forward, his legs giving out as he knelt beside her. His hand, always so steady with blade or gun, trembled as it hovered over her cheek. A single word escaped him, so soft I almost missed it: "*Solnyshko moyo...*"

"*Vor,*" Yuri's voice cut through darkness from behind us. "Here."

His light illuminated the wall beside Natasha's body. There, in half-dried blood - the curved line I'd seen a hundred times before. The beginning of one of those little faces Liliya drew everywhere. But this one wasn't playful. This one was a message. A breadcrumb left in blood.

She was alive. She was fighting. And she was leaving me a trail to follow.

Something snapped inside me. The cold, calculating *vor* I'd always been gave way to something rawer, more primal. Without a word to the others, I moved forward, following the direction the mark pointed. No more methodical clearing. No more patience. Just the hunt.

"Zaven!" Sergei's voice echoed behind me, but I was already moving deeper into the warehouse, driven by rage and desperation. The bloody mark pointed toward a narrow hallway, past empty offices with broken windows and rusted filing cabinets.

I barely registered the sound of boots behind me until Viktor's hand caught my shoulder, spinning me around.

"Are you trying to get yourself killed?" His voice was low, controlled, but his eyes blazed with the same grief that was driving me forward. "Running ahead alone? Is that how you honor what Natasha died for?"

His words cut through the rage. The *vor* in me knew he was right, but the man... the man just wanted to burn the world down.

"Sent others to check east side," Viktor continued, his grip on my shoulder loosening slightly. "Sergei taking west corridor with team. We stick together. Find her smarter, not just faster."

I nodded once, the control I'd prided myself on for decades slowly reasserting itself. Viktor was right. Getting myself killed wouldn't save Liliya.

We moved forward together in the direction Liliya's mark had indicated. Signs of struggle appeared as we continued - overturned chair, bloody handprint on the wall. Liliya had fought here. The pride that surged through me was almost painful in its intensity.

"Look." Viktor pointed to a smeared trail of blood leading to a stairwell. The trail descended into darkness.

"Basement level not on blueprints," I said, studying the pattern. Only Liliya would have left such a clear sign. She wasn't just running - she was deliberately marking her path, knowing I would follow.

"Trap waiting below," Viktor stated flatly. "But choice already made, *da?*"

"*Da.*" I checked my weapon again, familiar ritual focusing rage into sharp point. "Choice made moment they took what's mine."

The stairs descended into pitch darkness, our boots silent on concrete despite urgency burning through veins. Air grew thicker - mix of damp and copper scent of blood stronger here. Each breath tasted like death.

At the bottom of stairs, we found evidence of Liliya's passage - small drops of blood leading toward a corridor of doors.

"Four heat signatures ahead," Viktor whispered, checking the thermal scanner. "Maybe more behind walls."

Row of doors lined the concrete corridor - old storage rooms converted to something darker. Each one told a story of suffering - chains bolted to walls, dark stains on floor. Dmitri had planned this. Built this place for one purpose.

Fresh blood trail led to a door at the end of the corridor. The smears were more erratic here, as if Liliya had been struggling or running.

"No more obvious signs," Viktor said quietly, tension in his voice. "Not good."

I nodded, the absence of her message more chilling than any warning could have been. "Stay sharp. Whatever's behind that door..." I didn't finish the thought. Didn't need to.

Viktor positioned himself at the opposite side of the door, checking his weapon one last time. For Liliya. For Natasha. For family.

"Three," grip tightened on my gun. "Two." Every muscle coiled for violence. "One."

The door exploded inward under my boot, wood splintering as we moved in perfect formation. But the room was empty. No guards. No Liliya. Just an old office with a metal door on the far side.

"Something's wrong," Viktor hissed, scanning the corners. "Where are the guards she marked?"

Before I could answer, a flash of movement caught my eye - a figure lunging from behind a filing cabinet. I pivoted, raising my gun, but too late. The impact sent me crashing into the wall, weapon clattering away. Two more figures materialized from shadows, converging on Viktor.

They'd been waiting. Not where Liliya had marked.

I broke free from my attacker with a savage elbow strike, reaching for the knife at my belt. But more men poured through the metal door - six, maybe eight. Too many, too fast. A blow to my knee sent me down, another to my head leaving stars bursting across my vision.

Through the chaos, I glimpsed Viktor fighting like a demon - two men already down, a third reeling back with a slashed face. But even he couldn't hold against these numbers.

Something hard cracked against the back of my skull, driving me to the floor. Rough hands seized my arms, wrenching them behind my back, fingers digging painfully into my muscles. Two men pinned me down, knees pressing into my spine and shoulders. Beside me, Viktor finally went down under the weight of three men, blood streaming from a gash above his eye.

"The mighty Zaven Lazarev," a voice drawled from the doorway. Dmitri stepped into the room, immaculate in his tailored suit despite the squalor around him. "How disappointing. I expected more of a challenge."

I spat blood onto the concrete, eyes promising death. "Where is she?"

"Ah, the American girl." Dmitri's smile grew colder. "She's been... entertaining us." He gestured to the men holding me. "Bring them. Jack is waiting for his reunion."

They dragged us through the metal door into a larger space - old loading dock converted to something like a torture chamber. Industrial lights cast harsh shadows, making blood on concrete look almost black. And there, in the center of it all - my Liliya.

Jack's arm wrapped around her throat, pulling her against him like a shield. Her emerald silk hung in tatters, skin beneath painted with bruises and blood. But her eyes - those green eyes met mine with fierce determination despite her split lip, despite darkening marks around her throat.

"Welcome to the party." Jack's voice carried that American arrogance, but I caught the edge of fear beneath. His gun pressed against Liliya's temple. "Your girl and I were just catching up on old times."

They forced me to my knees in front of them, Viktor beside me. Blood trickled into my eye from a wound on my forehead, but I never broke my gaze from Liliya's.

Dmitri circled us slowly, savoring his moment of triumph. "You know, I almost can't believe it was this easy. The great Zaven Lazarev, brought down by a woman." He chuckled. "Just like your father."

I kept my face expressionless, but inside, calculations were running. Two men holding me. One on Viktor. Jack with Liliya. Dmitri. At least four more guards around the perimeter. Terrible odds.

"You should thank me for American dog," Dmitri continued, gesturing to Jack. "Was surprisingly easy to find him. All it took was mention of pretty American girl with green eyes in St. Petersburg."

"He didn't need much convincing," Jack added, his free hand trailing down Liliya's arm in a way that made murderous rage burn through my veins. "Chance to get my property back and hurt the man who took her? Win-win."

"Property?" Viktor's voice was a dangerous growl beside me.

"Oh yes," Jack smiled, tightening his grip on Liliya's throat. "She's always been mine. Just needed reminding who she belongs to."

Dmitri laughed, circling behind me. "You see, Zaven, this is poetry. You take my shipments, I take your woman. You kill my men, I break yours." He leaned closer, his voice dropping. "And when I'm done with you, I'll take your territory, your properties, everything that was meant to be mine when your father promised alliance."

In that moment, I caught a flicker of movement in Liliya's eyes - a glance toward the far wall. Following her gaze, I noticed the almost imperceptible shadow movement near a broken window. My men. They'd found us.

I needed to buy time.

"My father never promised you anything," I said, loud enough to draw attention. "You weren't worthy then. Still aren't."

The backhand across my face was expected, welcomed even. Blood filled my mouth, but I smiled through it, eyes never leaving Dmitri's.

"Not worthy?" Dmitri's face contorted with rage. "Look around you! I planned this for years! Every fucking detail perfect!" He gestured wildly. "I found the American. I broke your security. I took everything you care about!"

"And yet," I said softly, "you still need audience to feel powerful. Still need to explain brilliance of plan instead of just killing me." I looked up at him with contempt. "Always the same with you. All spectacle, no substance."

His kick caught me in the ribs, pain exploding through my chest. Definitely cracked, possibly broken. I wheezed through it, buying seconds with each taunt.

"You talk too much," I continued, voice raspy but defiant. "Always problem with you, Dmitri. All big words, no action."

Dmitri's face purpled with rage. "No action?" He grabbed a fistful of my hair, wrenching my head back. "I killed your men. I took your woman. I have you on your fucking knees!"

A muffled thump from somewhere in the warehouse froze everyone for a split second. Dmitri's head snapped up.

"Check it," he barked to two of his men, who immediately moved toward the door.

The distraction was all I needed. Liliya's eyes met mine, a silent question. I gave her the barest nod.

In one fluid motion, I twisted against the man holding me, using the momentum to slide the small blade from my boot cuff into my palm. Before he could react, I drove it deep into his thigh. His scream provided perfect cover as chaos erupted.

Liliya drove her elbow back into Jack's solar plexus - the move I'd taught her in the gym just weeks ago. His grip loosened, but not enough. I watched in horror as he dragged her backward, his gun now pressed against her temple. Our eyes locked for a split second before he yanked her behind a stack of crates.

Viktor was already moving, despite his injuries. He slammed his head back into his captor's face, the sickening crunch of breaking bone barely audible over the sudden gunfire.

My men breached the warehouse from multiple entry points, their precision fire cutting through Dmitri's guards. I seized a fallen weapon, desperate to reach Liliya, but Dmitri's men closed in, blocking my path to where Jack had dragged her.

A scream of rage and pain rang out from behind the crates - Jack's voice. I fought with renewed fury, knowing Liliya was fighting back, but not knowing if she was winning.

The warehouse exploded into complete violence.

42

Liliya

The warehouse exploded into violence.

Gunfire, breaking glass, shouts in Russian punctuated by screams of pain. The moment chaos erupted, Jack's grip tightened painfully around my throat, his panic making him erratic.

"You set me up, you bitch," he hissed in my ear, dragging me backward toward a side door.

I clawed at his arm, fighting for air. My vision spotted with black dots as his forearm crushed my windpipe. Through the chaos, I caught Zaven's eyes for a split second before Jack yanked me behind a stack of crates.

"I'll kill you before I let him have you," Jack growled, gun now pressed against my temple. The cold metal bit into my skin as bullets ricocheted off concrete around us.

A body fell nearby—one of Dmitri's men, blood pooling beneath him. Jack's attention flickered to the dead man, his grip loosening just enough. I drove my elbow back with every ounce of strength I had left, catching him in the exact spot Zaven had taught me during our training sessions.

The sweet taste of air filled my lungs as Jack's arm fell away. I stumbled forward, but his hand caught my torn dress, yanking me backward. I fell hard, my already-injured ribs screaming in protest as I hit the concrete. Jack stood over me, his face contorted with rage and fear, gun aimed at my chest.

"If I can't have you, no one—"

The shot rang out, deafening in the enclosed space. I flinched, waiting for pain that never came. Instead, Jack staggered backward, blood blooming across his leg. He fired wildly in response, bullets embedding in the wall inches from my head.

Survival instinct took over. I scrambled away on hands and knees, glass and debris cutting into my palms. The cabinet nearby offered the only shelter. I dove behind it as another explosion rocked the warehouse, sending dust and concrete fragments raining down.

That's when I curled into myself, hands over my ears, and tried to become invisible as the battle raged around me. The world shrank to the deafening sound of gunfire and men shouting. I pressed my hands over my ears, squeezing my eyes shut, trying to block out the violence erupting around me. My entire body trembled, each breath catching on silent sobs.

This couldn't be happening. Not after everything. Not after Natasha.

I don't know how long I stayed there, huddled against the cold concrete, time measured only in gunshots and screams. When hands grabbed my shoulders, I lashed out blindly, a wounded animal fighting for survival.

"Liliya! *Eto ya.* It's me."

That voice - deep, accented, familiar. I kept struggling, fear overriding recognition.

"*Ya lyublyu tebya. Moye serdtse.* Look at me." Fingers gently but firmly tilted my face up. "I love you. Come back to me."

The Russian words penetrated my panic first, their meaning taking a moment to register. Then the English words followed, shocking me into stillness. My eyes focused slowly. Zaven's face, bloodied but alive, swam into view. His dark eyes held mine, grounding me as the world spun.

"Zaven?" My voice cracked, barely recognizable. "You... you love me?"

"*Da, malyshka.* Always." His thumb brushed tears from my cheek. "It's over. You safe now."

As the ringing in my ears subsided, I became aware of the sudden, eerie quiet. The gunfire had stopped. Around us, Zaven's men moved with practiced efficiency, securing the area, tending to the wounded. Through the doorway, I could see Dmitri on his knees, hands zip-tied behind him, blood seeping from a shoulder wound as two of Zaven's men stood guard.

And there, just a few feet away, lay Jack. He was still alive, blood pooling beneath him from a wound in his leg. His eyes found mine - those same eyes that had watched impassively as he burned me with cigarettes, as he broke me piece by piece in Chicago. But there was no power in them now. Only fear.

"Can you stand?" Zaven asked, his arm supporting me as I wavered to my feet.

My legs felt unsteady, but I nodded. Something pulled me toward Jack, something stronger than fear. I moved away from Zaven's protective embrace, each step painful but deliberate.

Jack's eyes tracked me as I approached, widening slightly. "Lily," he croaked, a pathetic attempt at the manipulative tone that had once controlled me. "Help me. Please. You know I always loved you."

I stared down at him, this man who had haunted my nightmares for so long. In Chicago, he'd seemed so powerful, so in control. Now he was just a wounded, desperate man bleeding on a dirty warehouse floor.

"You never loved me," I said, my voice steadier than I'd expected. "You just wanted to own me."

From the corner of my eye, I saw Viktor approach, a gun in his hand. He stopped beside me, offering it to me handle first, his face expressionless save for the cold fury in his eyes.

"Your choice," he said simply.

I looked at the weapon, then back at Jack. My hand reached out, fingers closing around the grip. It felt heavy, foreign in my grasp. Jack's eyes tracked the movement, realization dawning in them.

"You're not going to—" he started, voice rising with panic. "You can't—"

"I can," I interrupted, surprised by my own calm. "You taught me that, Jack. You taught me exactly what people are capable of doing to each other."

The gun felt surprisingly steady in my hand as I raised it. Behind me, I sensed Zaven watching, not interfering. This moment was mine.

"Lily, please—" Jack's voice broke, eyes darting between my face and the gun. "I'm sorry. I'll never—"

"I told you," I said quietly, "I don't belong to you. I never did."

The gunshot echoed through the warehouse, startlingly loud in the aftermath of the battle. Jack's body jerked once, then went still, a perfect hole between his eyes. I lowered the gun, a strange emptiness filling me where I'd expected to feel... something. Triumph. Relief. Regret. Instead, there was just a cold certainty - like clicking the final piece of a puzzle into place.

Zaven's hand gently took the weapon from my fingers. I turned to find him watching me with an expression I couldn't quite read - somewhere between pride and sorrow.

"It's done," he said softly.

As the adrenaline ebbed, pain and exhaustion crashed over me in waves. My legs began to give way, but Zaven caught me, his arms strong despite his own injuries.

Across the room, a commotion drew my attention. Viktor had disappeared through a side door, returning moments later with a bundle wrapped in his coat. With a jolt, I realized what he carried - Natasha's body, carefully cradled in his arms.

"Wait," I said to Zaven, pulling away slightly. He understood, supporting me as I made my way to Viktor.

The big man's face was carved from stone, but his eyes... his eyes told a different story as he looked down at Natasha's still form. He had arranged her gently, covering the worst of her injuries, smoothing her hair back from her face.

"I'm sorry," I whispered, tears blurring my vision. "She was so brave. She tried to protect me."

"*Da.*" Viktor's voice was rough, barely audible. "Always brave. Always... stubborn." The way he held her, with such unexpected tenderness, told me everything I needed to know about feelings he'd never voiced.

"She cared for you," I said, reaching out to touch his arm. "She never said it, but I could tell."

Viktor's eyes met mine, a world of unspoken grief in them. "Not your fault, *devushka*. None of this."

In that moment, some understanding passed between us - a shared loss, a shared resolve. He nodded once, a gesture between equals rather than vor's second and vor's woman.

"Time to go," Zaven said gently, his arm around my waist taking more of my weight as my strength continued to fade.

Viktor led the way out, Natasha's body in his arms. Zaven helped me follow, past Dmitri's kneeling form, past Jack's sightless eyes, past the carnage of the night's violence. Each step was agony, but each step took us farther from the nightmare.

Outside, the rain had stopped. First light of dawn broke over the warehouse district, painting everything in shades of gold and shadow. Three black SUVs waited, engines running. Zaven helped me into the middle one, wrapping his jacket around my shoulders despite his body's obvious protest at the movement.

As we drove away, my head rested against his shoulder, exhaustion finally claiming me. Through half-closed eyes, I watched the warehouse shrink in the side mirror, knowing Viktor would ensure nothing remained of what had happened there. No evidence. No bodies. Nothing but ghosts.

My fingers found Zaven's hand, curling into his palm. "You said you love me," I whispered, the words barely audible even to myself.

His fingers tightened around mine. "*Da*," he replied, pressing his lips to my temple. "Since moment you drew smile on bathroom mirror."

A different kind of warmth spread through me, stronger than pain, than grief, than exhaustion. He was damaged, wounded - but alive. We both were. And in that moment, it was enough.

This was Zaven's world - our world now. A world of violence and consequences, of power and protection. And as consciousness began to slip away, I realized I finally understood what it meant to be a vor's woman.

It meant being strong enough to fight your own battles, but never having to fight alone.

* * *

The weak winter sun streamed through the glass panels of the solarium, creating a pocket of warmth that defied the snow-covered landscape outside. I curled deeper into the plush armchair, wincing slightly as my still-healing ribs protested the movement. The steaming mug of tea in my hands helped ease the lingering ache - both physical and something deeper.

The solarium had been Natasha's favorite room. Sometimes I still expected to hear her teasing voice, to see her trying to make Viktor smile. Her absence was its own kind of wound, one that wouldn't heal as easily as the physical ones.

We'd held her service during my second week of recovery, as soon as I was strong enough to attend. Just family - because that's what she'd become. Viktor had stood like a statue throughout, but I'd seen his hands trembling when he placed white roses on her grave. Zaven had whispered the traditional prayers in Russian, his voice carrying both power and grief. She'd died protecting me, died with that same defiant spirit that had made her uniquely Natasha. Now she rested in the Lazarev family plot, honored as vor's family. As my sister.

Telling her family had been one of the hardest things. Her mother's quiet grief over the phone, speaking softly in Russian as I explained what I could - not the whole truth, but enough. They lived in a small village outside Moscow, too elderly to travel, but Zaven had arranged for everything they needed. Had made sure they would be taken care of, the way Natasha would have wanted. The way family does.

It had been three weeks since that nightmarish evening at the warehouse, but the memories still felt raw, etched into my mind with brutal clarity. The physical reminders were fading; angry purple bruises had mellowed to sickly yellow, and the cuts were slowly knitting into scars. But the real changes went deeper, less visible but far more profound.

My fingers traced a small heart on the cold glass, so different from the little faces I used to draw. Those had been about finding joy in small moments. This felt like something else - marking a change, honoring what was lost, acknowledging what was gained.

And true to his word, Zaven had been merciless in his dealings with

Dmitri. Over the past weeks, I'd watched - not with horror, but with fierce satisfaction - as he systematically dismantled everything Dmitri had built. Businesses seized, allies turned, secrets exposed. Dmitri himself had disappeared from public view, but the whispers in Zaven's world spoke of a man broken in every way possible. The old Lily would have been horrified by such ruthlessness. But I wasn't that Lily anymore, I was Liliya now. This was justice in Zaven's world – in our world. Because that's what it had become, undeniably. Our world.

The soft click of the solarium door pulled me from my thoughts. I turned to see Zaven entering, his imposing frame softened by the gentle smile he reserved only for me. My heart sketched on the glass caught the winter light between us.

"Deep thoughts, *moye serdtse?*" he asked, crossing the room to stand behind my chair. His hands came to rest on my shoulders, thumbs gently working at knots of tension I hadn't realized were there. Through the glass, I could see his reflection studying my face, looking for signs of nightmares that still sometimes came.

I leaned back into his touch, a contented sigh escaping my lips. "Just reflecting," I said, tilting my head to look up at him. The heart I'd drawn cast a faint shadow across his features. "Everything changed so much."

"*Da,*" he murmured, leaning down to press a kiss to my forehead. His fingers traced along the healing cut at my temple with familiar gentleness. "Tell truth - any regrets, *lyubimaya?*"

The question carried weight - about Natasha, about Jack, about choosing this life with all its darkness and complexity. I reached up, cupping his cheek in my hand. "*Net.* Not one."

His smile was like sun breaking through Petersburg winter clouds. "Good," he said, reaching into his pocket. "Have something to show you, *detka.*"

He produced a sleek tablet, pulling up what looked like floor plans. "Time start planning proper Russian wedding, *da?* Want you see venue options."

My heart skipped a beat. We'd talked about marriage, of course, but seeing these plans made it suddenly, thrillingly real. As I scrolled through images, taking in the opulent ballroom and state-of-the-art security features, I realized something. This was my life now. The danger, the luxury, the complex morality of Zaven's world – I had chosen all of it.

"What you think?" His fingers gently kneaded my shoulders as I studied the layouts. "Must be perfect. *Vor*'s wedding big event in Petersburg."

I zoomed in on the security layout, noting multiple escape routes and panic rooms. "It's beautiful," I said, "and impressively fortified. Is this level of security really necessary for a wedding?"

Zaven's hands stilled for a moment. "In our world, *moye serdtse*, always necessary." His voice gentle but firm. "After what happened..." He paused, jaw tightening. "*Net.* Will not take chances with your safety. Never again."

I reached up, covering one of his hands with mine. "I understand," I said softly. And I did. This was part of loving Zaven, of being part of his world. Our world.

Zaven moved around the chair, kneeling beside me so we were eye to eye. "But will not all be bulletproof glass and armed guards," he said, hint of smile playing at his lips. "Tell me, what you want for wedding? Anything yours."

I set the tablet aside, taking both his hands in mine. "Honestly? I don't need anything extravagant. Just you, me, and the people we care about." I paused, considering. "Although... wouldn't say no to a spectacular dress."

His laugh was rich and warm, a sound I never tired of hearing. "*Da*, know perfect designer." Then his expression shifted to something more serious. "But first..." He reached into his jacket pocket, producing a small velvet box. "Have waited too long for this."

Inside nestled a ring that took my breath away - platinum and diamonds arranged like winter frost, with a deep blue sapphire at the center that reminded me of Petersburg nights.

"Belonged to my mother," he said softly, his accent thicker with emotion. "She tell me, give only to woman strong enough to stand beside *vor*. Woman worthy of legacy." His eyes met mine. "Know now - was always meant for you, *moye serdtse*."

As he slipped the ring onto my finger, I thought of everything that had led us here. The scared girl who'd fled Chicago, the faces I'd drawn on windows, the strength I'd found in Zaven's world. Thought of Natasha, who'd believed in me from the start, who'd died protecting the woman I was becoming. The sapphire caught winter light from the solarium windows, casting blue shadows like secrets across both our faces.

"Perfect fit," Zaven murmured, pressing a kiss to my knuckles. "Like was waiting for you."

"Like everything was," I replied softly, understanding flowing through me like winter sunlight. This was where I belonged - not as victim or *vor*'s possession, but as equal. As partner. As keeper of a legacy written in blood and love.

Zaven pulled me close, his heartbeat steady against my cheek. Outside, snow began falling over Petersburg again, white as Natasha's roses, pure as new beginnings. But inside, in this moment between what was and what would be, I was exactly where I needed to be.

I was home.

43

Epilogue

My heart pounded as I pressed my back against the wall, straining my ears for any sound of approach. Zaven crouched beside me, his body a familiar heat at my side. My yoga pants and thin sweater did little to block the warmth radiating from him, making my skin tingle where we touched.

"Do you think they've found us?" I whispered, barely audible.

His eyes, dark with both playful tension and something more intimate, scanned the ornate hallway. "*Net* yet, *moye serdtse*, but won't be long." His hand slid to my hip, fingers playing with the strip of bare skin where my sweater had ridden up. "Need move quick, *da*? Unless want be caught..."

The suggestive tone in his voice made my breath catch. Two years of marriage hadn't dimmed the electricity between us - if anything, the danger in our lives only heightened it. I slipped off my socks for stealth, catching how his gaze traced up my legs as I did.

"Careful, *Vor*," I teased in a whisper, "getting distracted during mission could be dangerous."

His low chuckle sent heat through me. "Always dangerous with you, *lyubimaya*. Is why love this game so much."

A floorboard creaked nearby and we both froze. His body pressed closer to mine, protective yet provocative.

"*Ty slyshal eto?*" A voice called out in Russian, alarmingly close. "Did you hear that?"

"*Blyad'*," Zaven muttered, his breath hot against my ear. "Run!"

We sprinted down the hallway, his hand never leaving my waist, ducking into the study. I immediately moved to the secret panel behind the bookcase – an escape route he'd shown me long ago, one we'd used more than once when real danger threatened our home. His body caged mine as I reached for the mechanism, his lips finding that sensitive spot below my ear.

But before I could activate the panel, the door burst open. Viktor stood there, his usual stoic expression replaced by determination. Despite being family now, his timing was still terrible as ever.

"Found you," he said, a rare smile tugging at his lips.

Suddenly, a tiny whirlwind of energy burst past Viktor's legs. "*Nashla!* Found!" came the triumphant cry in a mix of Russian and English.

Our daughter, Zoya, barely eighteen months old, toddled towards us with the determined waddle of a child still mastering the art of walking. She had Zaven's intensity when focused on a task, the same calculating look in her green eyes - my eyes - when planning her next move. Her dark curls bounced with each step, and that little smirk on her face was pure Zaven.

Zaven scooped her up, the heat in his eyes transforming instantly to pure adoration. It never ceased to amaze me how this man, who could strike fear into hardened criminals with a single look, could melt so completely with our daughter in his arms.

"You getting too good at this, *malyshka*," Zaven said, his voice losing its commanding edge, taking on the warmth reserved only for these private family moments. "Has *Dyadya* Viktor been teaching you his tricks?"

Zoya's tiny hand reached up, patting Zaven's stubbled cheek. "*Da! Dyadya* Vitya!" she exclaimed, her limited vocabulary not hampering her enthusiasm. Her little fingers curled into his t-shirt - so different from the suits he wore for business, but just as appealing to me.

I couldn't help but smile, the last vestiges of our playacted "mission" tension melting away at the sight of my little family. "That she will," I said, stepping closer to run a hand over Zoya's curls. "Imagine, the big, bad *Vor* and his wife, outmaneuvered by a toddler who's barely walking."

She had Zaven's intensity when focused, that same calculating look in her eyes when planning her next move. Her dark curls and determined spirit were all him, but her laugh, the way she drew little faces on every surface she could reach, that was purely me.

Zaven's free arm wrapped around my waist, pulling me into their embrace. I could still feel the lingering heat from our earlier chase, but it transformed into something deeper, warmer as we held our daughter between us.

"Little boss learn too quick," Viktor said, shaking his head. "Soon be running operations before can tie shoes, *da*?"

"*Da*," Zaven chuckled, pressing a kiss to Zoya's curls. "Takes after mother - too clever for own good sometimes."

"*Net*, takes after *vor*," Viktor countered with a rare smile. "Same look in eyes when planning something."

As if on cue, my parents' voices carried from the doorway. I turned to see them standing there, both beaming at the scene before them. The sight still amazed me sometimes - how seamlessly they'd adapted to our world once they knew the truth.

"*Babushka! Dedushka!*" Zoya called out, squirming in Zaven's arms with excitement.

"Ah, perfect timing," Zaven said, smile warming his voice. "Think someone ready for *babushka* and *dedushka*, *da*?"

My father stepped forward, arms already reaching for his granddaughter. "Come here, my little *zaychik*," he said, the Russian term for 'bunny' still sounding charmingly awkward on his American tongue.

"Thomas getting better with Russian," Viktor noted with approval. "Soon speak like local."

"*Net*," Zaven scoffed, keeping one arm around my waist as he passed Zoya to my father. "Still too American. Like wife first day in Petersburg."

I elbowed him playfully, remembering those early days. "If I recall, you liked my American accent."

"Still do, *moye serdtse*," he murmured in my ear, voice dropping to that intimate tone that made my skin tingle.

My mother was already crossing the room, Christmas tree lights catching the silver in her hair. "Now, now," she said, reaching for Zoya. "Less flirting, more family time. Someone needs to help *dedushka* with the presents."

"Presents!" Zoya echoed, clapping her tiny hands. "*Podarki!*"

The room filled with warmth as my mother and father took turns bouncing Zoya between them. The twinkling lights of our Christmas tree caught my eye, reminding me how far we'd come. Two years ago, I couldn't have imagined this - my parents here, completely at ease in our world, our daughter switching effortlessly between Russian and English as Viktor slipped her another candy when he thought no one was looking.

"*Dyadya* Vitya," Zaven's voice carried authority despite the playfulness beneath. "Spoiling her again?"

"*Net,*" Viktor replied, face perfectly straight despite the chocolate evidence on Zoya's cheeks. "Little boss very persuasive. Like mother."

I'd finally told my parents everything just a few months ago - about Jack, the real reason for my sudden move to Russia, and the truth about Zaven's business. I'd been terrified, certain the whole truth would send them running back to America, never to return.

"Remember faces when told truth?" Zaven murmured against my ear, his arms tightening around me as if reading my thoughts. "Father went so pale, thought would pass out right there."

But I'd underestimated them. They'd listened, tears in their eyes, as I recounted everything. And when I'd finished, my mother had hugged me tighter than ever before.

"Look now," Zaven continued softly. "Father teaching our daughter Russian curses when think we not listening."

Sure enough, my father was whispering something to Zoya that made Viktor cough to hide his laugh.

"Thomas," my mother scolded, but her eyes sparkled with amusement. "No teaching her those words until she's at least five."

As the evening wore on, filled with laughter and the warmth of family, I couldn't help but marvel at how naturally our worlds had merged. We'd faced real threats over the past two years - assassination attempts, rival organizations, even a tense standoff with a corrupt government official. But here, watching my father attempt Russian Christmas carols while Viktor corrected his pronunciation, those dangers felt distant.

"*Net*, Thomas," Viktor said for perhaps the tenth time. "Like this - *Ded Moroz...*"

"Ded Mo-what now?" my father stumbled, making Zoya giggle.

"Hopeless," Zaven muttered against my neck, his arms still wrapped around me from behind. "Like teaching fish to climb tree."

Later, after we'd tucked an exhausted Zoya into her bed - a fantasy of pink and gold fit for the princess she was in our eyes - Zaven pulled me close in the hallway.

"Happy?" he asked softly, that heat from our earlier chase returning to his eyes.

I thought about the empire we'd built, the dangers we still faced, the love that had grown between us, and this beautiful, brilliant child we'd created. I thought about Natasha, whose picture sat prominently in Zoya's room – the aunt she would know through our stories. I thought about the journey from the scared girl who fled Chicago to the woman who now stood confidently beside one of the most powerful men in Russia.

"Absolutely," I replied, rising on tiptoes to kiss him.

His hands slid down to my hips, then lower, gripping with that possessive intensity that still made my breath catch. "Know what thinking?" he murmured, teeth grazing my lower lip in that way he knew drove me wild.

"Mmm?" My body was already responding to his touch, muscle memory of countless nights together.

He pressed me against the wall, his body hard against mine. "Time give Zoya little brother or sister, *da*?" His voice dropped to that dangerous register that always preceded our most intense nights. "What say, *moye serdtse*? Ready for me to fuck you until forget every language but my name?"

Heat pooled low in my belly at his words. Even after two years, the raw possession in his voice still had the power to make me weak at the knees. I slid my hands beneath his shirt, nails dragging lightly down his muscled back.

"Bring it on, *Vor*," I whispered against his lips, deliberately using the title I knew would ignite that primal side of him. "Show me exactly why I married the most dangerous man in Petersburg."

As we headed to our bedroom, I felt that familiar thrill of excitement for what the future held. Our life might not be conventional, but it was ours, filled with love, danger, and endless possibilities.

And I wouldn't change a single thing about it.

Sneak Peak

Turn the page for an exclusive first look at:

Roses in Ruin
Book 2 in Thieves in Law Series
Coming Soon!

Roses in Ruin

Chapter 1 - Katya

The blood on my hands is still warm when they find us.

I sit on the floor of Studio Three, back against the cold mirror, watching red droplets fall from my split knuckles onto the pale wooden floor. The studio smells like sweat and rosin and now something metallic—copper pennies and salt. Each drop makes a small, perfect circle, soaking into the wood grain. The overhead fluorescent buzz softly, casting everything in harsh white light that makes the blood look almost black.

Pavel Petrov lies three meters away, his famous face no longer quite so symmetrical. The left side is... different now. Swollen. Wrong. His breathing sounds wet, labored through what might have been his nose before I introduced it to my elbow. The sound echoes off the mirrors, multiplying his pain into a chorus.

Deputy Minister Petrov's precious son. The golden boy who thought his father's position in the government meant he could touch whatever he wanted.

"*Bozhe moy*," whispers Anya from the doorway. [my God] My understudy, always dramatic. Her pointe shoes squeak against the floor as she shifts her weight. The hallway behind her smells like old wood and the cleaning solution they use to mop the floors after evening performances.

I look at her with eyes that feel strangely calm. My left shoulder throbs where it connected with the mirror during our... conversation. "He put hands where they not belong."

The others crowd behind her—dancers, instructors, even old Madame Volkov with her ancient, disapproving face. They stare at me like I am some wild animal that has wandered into their civilized world. The air conditioning unit kicks on with a mechanical wheeze, pushing stale air through the vents.

"Someone call ambulance," Madame Volkov commands, but her voice shakes. She has never seen a principal dancer sitting in a pool of blood before. Neither have I, until tonight. "And... and someone must call theater administration. This is son of Deputy Minister."

"Already is called," says Alexei Romanov, one of the corps dancers. He holds his phone with trembling fingers. "Police coming too. Many police."

Police. Yes, they will come. Especially for him. Especially for the untouchable son of Deputy Minister Petrov, who sits on the Culture Committee that funds our theater. They will ask questions. They will want to know why Pavel Petrov, principal dancer and choreographer extraordinaire, lies unconscious in a puddle of his own blood while Ekaterina Morozov sits calmly beside him like a statue.

I could tell them the truth. Could explain how his hands found their way under my costume during partnered rehearsals. How his whispered comments about my body became bolder, filthier, more insistent. How he cornered me after tonight's performance, pressed me against this very mirror, and informed me that my career advancement depended on how... accommodating... I chose to be.

"My father owns this theater," he had said, breath stinking of cognac and entitlement. "One word from him and you'll never dance in Russia again. But be nice to me, Katya, and I'll make sure you get every role you want."

But they would not believe me. Or worse—they would believe me and do nothing. Because Pavel Petrov was important. Pavel Petrov's father controls funding. Pavel Petrov's uncle is dangerous man in St. Petersburg underworld.

Was. His importance was past tense now.

"Katya." Anya approaches slowly, like I might bite. "You need wash hands. Before police—"

"*Net.*" [no] The word comes out flat, final. "Let them see."

Let them see what happens when someone tries to break me. Let them understand that Ekaterina Morozov is not a delicate flower to be plucked by an entitled boy who thinks his papa's position makes him a god.

The irony tastes bitter in my mouth. For weeks, I endured his touches, his words, his assumptions about what I would accept for the sake of my art. I swallowed my rage, kept my violence locked away in the prison of my ribs. I performed the role of perfect ballerina—graceful, compliant, beautiful.

Until tonight, when he pushed too far. When he mentioned how his father could destroy Papa's business with one phone call. How his uncle's files could expose every secret, every questionable deal, every connection Papa tried to keep hidden.

"Your papa not so clean either," he had whispered against my ear, hands already pulling at my costume. "Uncle Mikhail has files on everyone in this city. Banking records, phone transcripts, photographs... So you be good girl for me, *da*? [yes] Or maybe everyone learns exactly how diamonds really flow through St. Petersburg."

That's when something inside me snapped. Not broke—snapped. Like a rubber band pulled too tight, releasing all its stored energy at once.

"Ekaterina Morozova?" The voice comes from doorway. Police have arrived—not just two officers, but six. All male, all looking at scene with mixture of shock and something else. Calculation. They know who is bleeding on the floor.

I stand slowly, my reflection multiplying in the mirrored walls. There are dozens of me—some covered in blood, some clean, all wearing the same expression of cold satisfaction.

"*Da*. I am Ekaterina."

"You did this?" The older officer—graying hair, tired face—steps closer. But carefully. Like he knows I'm dangerous.

"*Da*."

"To son of Deputy Minister Petrov?"

"To man who thought he owns me."

They exchange glances. Someone is already on phone, probably calling their superiors, asking how to handle this delicate situation. A beat cop didn't arrest the Deputy Minister's son's attacker without clearance.

"*Grazhdanka* Morozova," the older officer says carefully, "you must come with us. For questioning." [citizen - formal address]

"I understand." I collect my dance bag, my street clothes, moving with the same fluid grace that has made me principal dancer. The blood on my hands has begun to dry, darkening to rust color. It will stain.

Good. Let it stain.

As they lead me toward the door, I hear whispers following in my wake. The other dancers, the staff, the witnesses to my transformation. They speak in hushed, frightened tones about what they have seen. About the girl who dared to touch the untouchable.

"Always so quiet," someone murmurs. "So controlled."

"Son of Deputy Minister... *Bozhe moy*, her career is finished."

"Her father's business too. They destroy them both for this."

I almost smile. They speak as if my violence is something new, something that appeared tonight like sudden storm. They do not understand that violence has lived in me for years, patient and careful, waiting for the right moment to show itself.

Tonight was that moment. When Pavel Petrov, protected by his father's position and his uncle's connections, learned that some things cannot be bought or threatened into submission.

In the hallway, my phone buzzes. Text message from Papa: "*Dochka*, coming home soon?" [daughter]

I stare at the words, knowing this will reach him within hours. Not just the scandal, the arrest, but the political nightmare of his daughter putting Deputy Minister's son in hospital. The threats that will come. The pressure from above and below.

He will be terrified. Not just heartbroken, but genuinely afraid of what the Petrovs can do to us.

But he will also, finally, understand what I am capable of.

The police car waits outside, engine running, exhaust creating small clouds in the October cold. St. Petersburg air bites at my exposed skin— arms, neck, the places where my costume leaves me vulnerable. But as they help me into the backseat, I catch sight of myself in the window reflection.

My hair has come loose from its performance bun, dark strands framing my face. My makeup is smeared but my eyes are bright, alive in a way they have not been for months.

I look dangerous. I look free.

Even if that freedom comes with a price I cannot yet calculate.

The younger officer slides into the driver's seat, adjusting the mirror to watch me. "You not seem upset," he observes.

"About what?"

"About... this. What you did. Who you did it to." He pauses. "You understand who is Pavel Petrov's father?"

"*Da.* I understand perfectly."

"And his uncle? Mikhail Petrov? You know this name too?"

The information broker. The one who knows everyone's secrets in St. Petersburg. The one who can destroy lives with a single file.

"I know who they are."

"Then you know what kind of trouble you in."

I meet his eyes in the mirror. "They should teach their boy to keep hands to himself."

The car pulls away from the theater, carrying me toward whatever comes next. Through the window, I watch the building disappear into the darkness. The Mariinsky Theatre, where I have spent eight years of my life perfecting the art of controlled movement, disciplined beauty, restrained power.

Tonight, I stopped restraining.

My hands rest calmly in my lap, dried blood under my fingernails like dark polish. These hands that have created art, that have conveyed emotion through gesture, that have tonight shown their true purpose.

These hands that have finally, finally, refused to be a victim to anyone—no matter how powerful their father.

Roses in Ruin

Chapter 2 - Boris

The call comes at 2:47 AM.

I know before I answer. The ringtone—specific to theater administration—cuts through my study like a blade through silk. The grandfather clock in the corner ticks its judgment, each second echoing off mahogany panels that have absorbed thirty years of cigarette smoke and whispered deals.

"Boris Mikhailovich?" The voice trembles. Probably some junior administrator who drew the short straw. Behind him, I hear muffled voices, the static of police radios. "This is regarding your daughter, Ekaterina Borisovna..."

I listen to the stammered explanation while staring at the photograph on my desk. Katya at sixteen, still soft around the edges, accepting flowers after her first starring role. The silver frame is tarnished at the corners where my fingers have worried the metal during difficult phone calls. Before grief carved her into something harder. Before I failed to protect what mattered most.

"Intensive care," the voice continues. "Deputy Minister Petrov's son... the family is... they are asking questions. Many questions."

I hang up.

My hands do not shake as I pour three fingers of vodka. Good vodka, not the poison I sell to tourists. The crystal decanter catches lamplight, throwing prisms across papers that detail shipments, certificates, carefully constructed lies. The burn down my throat is familiar, almost comforting. Like an old friend who never lies to you.

The leather chair creaks as I lean back, springs protesting after too many late nights in this exact position. Outside, October wind rattles the windows, carrying the smell of coming snow and the distant sound of sirens. Always sirens in St. Petersburg at night.

Pavel Petrov. I know the name, know the boy. Soft hands and soft life, playing at being an artist while his father's position ensures every door opens for him. The kind of boy who takes what he wants because no one has ever told him no.

Until tonight. Until my Katya told him no with her fists.

Bozhe moy, what has she done? [my God]

But the deeper question, one that tastes like ashes: What did he do to make her finally snap? My quiet daughter who learned to swallow her rage, to hide it behind perfect fouettés. Who danced through her mother's funeral without shedding a tear. Who smiles for patrons while something sharp and dangerous lives behind her amber eyes.

The vodka bottle sweats condensation onto the desk, leaving rings that will stain the wood. Elena used to scold me for not using coasters. The memory stings worse than alcohol.

I know what comes next. Have lived in St. Petersburg long enough to understand how these things work. Deputy Minister's son in hospital means phone calls. Investigations. Pressure from above and below. And worse— the uncle. Mikhail Petrov, who trades in different currency than his brother. Information instead of influence. Secrets instead of power.

My study suddenly feels too small, walls pressing in with the weight of every questionable decision that built this life. The air tastes of stale smoke and fear-sweat. Through the window, the city sprawls in darkness, windows lit like eyes of predators waiting to strike.

My business survives on careful balance. Legitimate enough to pass inspection, profitable enough to matter. But there are always questions about shipments from Antwerp. Always gaps between what arrives and what gets certified. Always hands that need greasing to keep wheels turning.

The Petrovs will not let this pass. Cannot let their boy be humiliated without response. They will come for us—not with violence, but with paperwork. With investigations. With careful exposure of every corner

I've cut, every rule I've bent.

I pour another vodka. Then another. The bottle grows lighter as my thoughts grow heavier.

My daughter, my fierce *dochka* who carries her mother's face and her mother's rage. [daughter] Who dances like an angel and fights like a demon. Who just destroyed a boy who probably deserved destroying but whose family can destroy us in return.

She needs protection I cannot provide. The kind that understands both violence and politics. The kind that can stand between her and the storm that's coming.

My hands shake now—not from fear but from the decision that cannot be unmade.

I reach for the phone. Scroll to a number I saved three years ago but never used. A number given to me by a mutual friend who said: "If you ever need someone who solves problems permanently, call this number. But be certain. His solutions cannot be undone."

My finger hovers over the screen. The study's silence presses against my eardrums, broken only by the clock's relentless ticking and my own ragged breathing. Once I make this call, there is no going back. But what choice do I have?

The phone feels cold against my ear, like pressing a gun to my head.

The line rings twice. Each ring echoes like a funeral bell.

"*Da?*" [yes]

The voice is like gravel soaked in motor oil, carries the weight of a man who has never needed to raise it to be obeyed. I know this voice, though we have spoken only a handful of times at careful distances.

"Is Boris Mikhailovich. Need favor. Big one."

"Boris Mikhailovich." A pause. The sound of exhaled smoke. Even at three in the morning, he sounds fully awake, alert. "Is late for social call."

"Is not social. Is about my daughter."

"The ballerina? I heard she had... incident tonight."

Of course he heard. He hears everything that matters in St. Petersburg. I imagine him in his office, surrounded by his own carefully balanced empire, deciding whether my problem is worth his attention.

"She put Deputy Minister's son in hospital. Beat him badly. His family..." I pause, choose my words carefully. The weight of each syllable could determine Katya's fate. "They will not let this pass quietly."

"The Petrovs." Not a question. A statement. Another exhale, and I can almost smell the expensive cigarettes through the phone. "Mikhail is dangerous man to have as enemy."

"*Da*. My business, my daughter's career, everything we built—they can destroy it all with few phone calls."

"What you need from me?"

"Protection for Katya. Someone who can..." How to say this? The words stick in my throat like broken glass. "Someone who can handle her. She is... difficult."

"Difficult how?"

The leather chair protests as I shift, trying to find words that explain without condemning. How to explain? That she breaks men who try to control her? That she seduces them or manipulates them or simply ignores them until they quit? That seven bodyguards in three years have failed because they see a pretty dancer, not the wolf underneath?

"She is like her mother was," I say finally. The words taste of grief and gunpowder. "Beautiful and terrible. Full of rage she cannot always contain."

"Ah." Just that. Like he understands everything from those few words. Background noise of pages turning, perhaps files being consulted. "I have man. But Boris... is not conventional choice."

"Do not need conventional. Need effective."

"Is that. Perhaps too effective." Another pause. Ice clinks in a glass— even crime lords need their comfort at three AM. "Former *spetsnaz*. [special forces] Now he... solves problems for me. Permanently."

Executioner. The word hangs unspoken between us, heavy as a body bag.

"Need him to protect, not eliminate entire Petrov family," I say carefully.

"He follows orders. When motivated properly." The voice pauses. "But Boris... is not same man he was. Lost someone three years ago. Since then has become something else. Something darker."

Perfect. Someone as damaged as my daughter. Someone who speaks the same language of controlled violence.

But still I hesitate. This is my little girl we're discussing. The child who used to dance in my study, spinning until she fell down laughing. Now I'm hiring an executioner to...what? Cage her? Control her?

"Boris?" The voice cuts through my thoughts. "You want to think about this? Call me back?"

"*Net.*" [no] The word comes out harsh. I cannot afford to think. Cannot afford to remember her as a child when she is now a woman who puts men in hospital. "Send him."

"You are certain? Once I assign, he does not leave until job is complete. His way or no way."

Through the window, the first hint of dawn touches the sky—pale gray like old bones. Soon Katya will be released. Soon she will come home expecting comfort, not a cage.

"Send him tomorrow. Early."

"*Khorosho.* [good/well] One more thing, Boris. Your daughter must not know full situation. If she understands how bad things are, she tries to handle herself."

"*Da,* I understand. What I tell her?"

"Tell truth. Just not all of it. That she needs protection after tonight. That you hired professional to keep safe." A pause. "Let him handle rest. He is good at making people accept things they do not want to accept."

"*Spasibo,* Zaven." [thank you]

The name hangs in the air like confession, like damnation. Zaven. I have just put my daughter's life in the hands of St. Petersburg's most dangerous *vor.* [thief in law]

"*Spokoynoy nochi,* Boris. [good night] Try to sleep. Tomorrow, your daughter meets her match."

The line goes dead with the soft click of finality. I stare at the phone, its screen dark as my thoughts, wondering what I have just done. What kind of man I have summoned to contain my wild daughter.

The vodka bottle is empty now, but I barely feel its warmth. The study smells of sweat and desperation, of choices made in darkness that must be lived with in light.

I stand on unsteady legs, joints protesting after hours in the same position. The floorboards creak under my weight—this whole building settling into its bones, keeping its secrets. I pause at Elena's portrait on the wall—my wife, my love, my greatest failure. Oil paint has captured her beauty but not her fire, her grace but not the fury that lives now in our daughter.

"Could not protect you," I tell her image. My reflection in the glass looks back—older, grayer, defeated. "But I will protect her. Even if she hates me for it."

The first buses rumble past on the street below, bringing a new day whether I'm ready or not. In a few hours, the sun will rise properly. Katya will come home from jail, expecting comfort, expecting her papa to make everything better like when she was small.

Instead, she will find Zaven's executioner waiting.

And then we will see who is stronger: my daughter's rage or his will.

Gospodi. [Lord] What choice did I have?

About the Author

A. Jayne is a debut novelist who has been a voracious reader since the moment she first learned to decode words on a page. After years of devouring every genre imaginable, she found herself completely captivated by the dark romance world when she discovered J.T. Geissinger's *Beautifully Cruel*. That book opened the door to an obsession with mafia romance that would eventually inspire her to craft her own story.

Drawing inspiration from favorite authors like Zoe Blake, J.T. Geissinger, and Jane Henry. A. Jayne spent nearly a year developing the intricate story line for *Lilies in Winter*. Music became her creative muse throughout the writing process, with Grace VanderWaal's "What's Left of Me" and Marshmello's "Silence" providing the emotional soundtrack that shaped this novel's heart.

When she's not writing during late-night sessions fueled by vodka and mafia movie marathons, A. Jayne is navigating the beautiful chaos of life in central Pennsylvania with her husband and four children. She believes the best stories are the ones that make your heart race, and she hopes to give readers the same thrilling escape that her favorite authors have given her.

Connect with A. Jayne on TikTok @plain_jayne89 or Instagram @a_jayne_author for behind-the-scenes glimpses into her writing journey and updates on future releases.